Marianne Bly

Deborah Rowland

First published in Great Britain by Deborah Rowland, 2021

Copyright © Deborah Rowland

Deborah Rowland has asserted her right under the Copyright,
Design and Patents Act 1988 to be identified as the
author of this work.

A CIP catalogue record for this book is available from
the British Library

ISBN 978-1-9163788-2-7

Printed and bound by KDP
Typesetting and cover design by Linda Storey

www.deborahrowlandauthor.com

For Mal,

and all the earth's healers

CAST LIST

Marianne Bly: former teacher's assistant
Freddie Bly: Marianne and Warren Silk's son; social worker
Warren Silk: Marianne's ex-partner; Gil and Spencer Armstrong's
    former business partner
Mike and Evelyn Bly: Claire and Marianne's parents
Gil Armstrong: owner of Armstrong Security
Bonnie Armstrong: Gil's deceased sister
Imogen Armstrong: Gil's wife, Owner of Urbane Event
    Management
Zak Armstrong: Gil and Imogen's son
Rudy: Zak's Border Terrier
Nik and Cilla Marsalis: Imogen's parents
Lena Armstrong: Gil's mother
Jimmy Knox: Lena's deceased ex-husband; Gil's father,
Spencer Armstrong: Gil's cousin, joint owner of Armstrong Security
Nicole Armstrong: Spencer's wife, manager of the Lee Morrell
    Charity Shop
Esme and Georgia: Spencer and Nicole's daughters
Jean Armstrong: Spencer's mother
Lionel Armstrong: Jean's deceased husband
Della Carthy: Marianne's friend, nanny, former co-worker
    at Wanstead Hall
Terence Carthy: Della's brother; former valet-butler at
    Wanstead Hall
Peter Lewellyn: diplomat, formerly of Wanstead Hall
Malika Lionnet: ex-wife of Peter Lewellyn; business woman
Shane Bennett: gardener for the Armstrongs
Joel Midwinter: wildlife ranger for The Rose Foundation
Kurt Van Lynden: wildlife cameraman; Joel's best friend
Anya Maclean: Kurt's partner
Blair Maclean: Anya's brother
Professor Sir Clifford and Dorothea Rose: founders of the
    Rose Foundation

Meg, Larry, Lori, Gareth, Mitch: wildlife rangers for the Rose Foundation
Travis: Larry's teenage son
Irene and Dudley Midwinter: Joel's grandparents
Annette Desai: Imogen's business partner at Urbane Events Management
Sabrina Cohen-Rockley: Joel's consultant
Oscar Goodchild: Gil and Imogen's neighbour
Andie Lawton: Joel's friend
Nina Kossi: Epping Bugspotter; Zak's friend
Dino Scuderi: Gil's former boss; family friend
Clive Osgood: project manager, Armstrong Securities
Niall Osgood: Clive's son; works for Armstrong Securities
Ashley: Niall's partner
Rachel: Freddie's partner
Sadie: Marianne's aunt
Bill Brett: Gil's former employer, Brett's Alarms
Darren Turner: business associate
Julie Brooking: cleaner for the Armstrongs
Olivia Donohue: counsellor
Marcus Frobisher: counsellor
Mrs Werner: Zak's biology teacher
Hilda Paxton: one of Marianne's house-sitting clients
Jane Gregory: Jane Gregory, singer/songwriter

Hal and Pippa Hopkins: Owners of Sundown Apartments and Harlequin Gallery
Beattie Hopkins: Hal's mother, Sundown's housekeeper
Arnie Wilkes: Hal's sailing friend
Vera Winiata: artist
Toni and Daryl Roebuck: owners of The Bootwash Café
Hugh Ridley: jeweller and Armstrong Security client
Roger and Shirly Ridley: Gil's business acquaintances

PART ONE

MARIANNE

WAS THERE anything more luxurious than relaxing in the garden under benevolent sunrays, having savoured a rich *rigatoni* and sparkling Rosé celebratory lunch (courtesy of your best friend), while said friend, unable to sit still for more than thirty seconds, unpegs and expertly folds your freshly blown washing? In terms of satisfaction, you might think that this particular bar was set exceptionally low, but not so for Marianne Bly, whose expectations were unfashionably undemanding. In any case, these were her observations on that glorious Friday afternoon in July, and may well have continued, but a whisper of guilt brought the contented wallow to an end. As Della placed the last item, a pair of pale blue linen trousers, in the washing basket, Marianne moved the peg box from the bench. 'Come and sit down, Della. This is your day off. I'd have done it later.'

'You'd be cutting it fine, Marianne. It's almost four o'clock, and we've choir practise tonight. That doesn't leave much time to pack.'

'I'm not leaving until midday. The trousers and tops are the last things to go in.'

Della stroked the nicely tailored slacks. 'Did these come from Lee Morrell's?'

'Four years ago, or thereabouts.'

'That charity shop must be the most profitable in the county. The designer clothes fly out the door quicker than

9

an eyelid can bat.' Della's nose crinkled at the creases. 'Will I run the iron over these?'

'I wasn't going to bother, but thanks anyway.'

'Don't tell me you're wearing the linens for decorating in?'

'My working gear is packed. These are for the evening,' Marianne replied firmly, hoping for an end to the inquisition but suspecting it had only just begun.

'When we worked at Wanstead Hall, you used to love ironing, and keeping everything ship-shape, including the children and the staff.' Della sighed pleasurably at the long-distance memory before returning to her previous line of concerned enquiry. 'Living alone *and* unemployment – it's a slippery slope, Marianne. Now you've chucked in your job at the school, there'll be no routine. How long before you're dodging soap and wearing the same egg-stained jumper for weeks on end? What's the forecast for Norfolk?'

Marianne smiled. Only Della Carthy could predict the worst-case scenario and swiftly change the subject in a single, continuous breath. 'The weather is improving. There are only three rooms to paint, all in the same colour. Nothing to it.'

'Anyone with a posh holiday home with a name like 'The Tower' can afford to pay the going rate. Gil Armstrong must have heard about your redundancy and has made you an offer you can't refuse. Is that why you've agreed to go back to Norfolk, after all this time?'

'Della, the roof is leaking, the car just about scraped through the MOT, and the washing machine is on its last legs. If only good things came in threes.'

'You didn't answer my question, Marianne.'

No, she didn't answer the question because as yet, she hadn't the wherewithal to work anything out. After twenty years at Hazelwood Primary, Marianne was still digesting the fact that her full-time employment as teaching assistant, dinner lady, and general dogsbody was over. During those final days, she had steeled herself for the emotional waters to break, but they had held firm throughout the children's rendition of 'The Goodbye Song', and the presentation, when tearful colleagues and parents filled her arms with parcels and flowers. Despite several attempts to change her mind, Marianne simply could not see herself in the new school. She'd become accustomed to the draughty, brick-painted, high-ceilinged Victorian building, the *Alice in Wonderland* furniture, and the convenience of living a ten-minute walk away. Moving school would not only mean a daily drive through the increasingly busy Epping traffic, but there was no garden, or animals, and the head teacher had a formidable reputation. When her son Freddie left Hazelwood Primary all those years ago, she considered trying her hand at something else, but then Zak Armstrong arrived, wide-eyed and cheery, followed by his cousin Esme, and she decided to stay. Now, it was time to move on.

Marianne had given herself a single week's grace before beginning the first in a long line of summer jobs which included a spell of house and dog-sitting, a splash of decorating, and short bursts of holiday cover at Carthy's Chickadees, Della's childcare business. There was just enough redundancy to clear the mortgage and top up the rainy-day pot. Long school holidays were never the extravagance they were generally believed to be as Marianne worked through the summer, and occasionally took in overseas students, but holidays? When was the last time she'd gone to another county, let alone another country? She was determined to rectify this, or at the very least, create opportunities in which to discover that there was more to life than what she had experienced during her forty-four years on the planet.

The generous shade bestowed from her large straw hat did little to stop the afternoon's heat from seeping through her long-sleeved cotton blouse and into her tired bones. The compact and lovingly planted garden was a hive of activity. Various species of bee trampolined between dazzling Cranesbill geraniums and leggy English lavender bushes, while two Orange-tip butterflies and a single Small Tortoiseshell flitted to and fro. The tiny pond's trickle harmonised with the wooden chimes suspended from her neighbour's plum tree, the boughs creaking under the weight of ripe purple fruit, some of which landed in her garden, and made a tasty crumble or jam. A heavenly scent settled over the women as they sipped highballs of mint and raspberry cordial.

'Would you look at this! What I wouldn't give for your green digits, Marianne. The wee garden looks grand. What's that box up there? I hope it's not a home for retired wasps.' She sipped the cool, refreshing drink. 'Is Freddie coming down any time soon?'

'It's a bee hotel. No, he's on a weekend shift. Did I tell you it was Zak who invited Freddie and me to Norfolk?'

'I'm surprised Zak and Freddie keep in touch. There's a ten-year age gap between Gil's lad and yours, not to mention two hundred miles. Why did Zak invite you, out of the blue like that?'

'I'm not sure. Freddie likes to keep an eye on him, especially now he's at the tricky teenage stage. Zak must have heard about Hazelwood Primary's closure, and you know how fond he was of the school. He's always been sensitive about these things.'

'Zak's invitation was prompted by either initiative or desperation. When all's said and done, he needs his parents.' Della's bony chest inflated indignantly. 'Gil and Imogen's careers are more important than their only child's welfare. They'll live to regret it.'

'You make it sound as if they neglect Zak. What have you got against the Armstrongs?'

'Marianne, some people don't have a choice and have to work all the hours. Gil and Imogen have pots of gold, but they are ambitious and self-serving. At least they've that in common. The best young years of Zak's life are over. Soon, he'll be past wanting his mum and dad to pay attention as he'll find it elsewhere. Anyway, if you're feeling broody, there's work galore at my place. We've a nine-month-old coming, and I could use the extra help.'

'I thought you weren't taking any more babies.'

'It's for a friend. Just two days a week, until she gets on her feet.'

Marianne spied the sheepish look and grinned. Beneath the armour-plate, Della Carthy's heart was as big as a crop circle. At Wanstead Hall, she had been a terrific nanny to the Llewellyn children. No one could have loved and cared for them more, particularly while their diplomat father and mother were abroad. As housekeeper, Marianne's duties were light, so much of her time was spent with Della and the children in what were the most carefree days of her life. When the Llewellyns left the country, it was no surprise that Della set up her own nursery. Carthy's Chickadees' gold standard reputation came with a long waiting list and lived up to the chickadee symbolism of truth, happiness, curiosity, and good luck.

'That's good of you, Della. Can I let you know?' A long yawn suddenly made a bid for freedom. Maybe she'd treat herself to a nap before choir. 'Gil's having a barbeque on Saturday night, hence the trousers and blouse. My contribution is a mushroom tart and a summer fruit pudding. Thankfully, he hasn't booked a gastropub. I'm spared the embarrassment of choosing the cheapest meal on the menu as the prices make your eyes smart.'

Della returned her empty glass to the tray and picked up her bag. 'Gil and Spencer Armstrong can afford to shout you a fish platter on their expense account, Marianne. The Tower must be worth a fortune. The cousins will have made sure it was renovated to a high standard, and North Norfolk is *the* place to have a holiday home.'

'I'm fed up with feeling grateful, Della. This is a fair exchange. I can manage one evening with the family before opening my paint pots.'

'Ah well, I wish you luck. I'm glad you're coming to choir practise tonight, although fair play to you if you cried off. Why can't Carol Norbury's breath be half as sweet as your roses? What a honk! D'you think Lewis will let me sing *contralto*.'

The friends chuckled. Several attempts to cajole their baby-faced choirmaster to address the issue of oral hygiene had failed, and Della had threatened to take matters into her own hands. Marianne passed her a peg from the basket. 'Here, put this in your pocket, just in case.'

It was ten o'clock. Marianne lay propped up in bed reading one of her leaving presents, *Inspirational Thoughts*. Carol Norbury hadn't showed up for choir after all. Her husband had been taken to the A&E department with a suspected fractured hip, and he did all the driving. Carol's timely absence prompted an unusually robust performance from Della during *Don't Stop Me Now*, and significant praise from Lewis who invited her to take the solo at the forthcoming Guildhall concert. This had sparked a feverish gabble throughout the entire journey home. Now all was quiet, and Marianne was hopeful for a restful night.

Number 7's present occupant worked shifts at Stansted Airport. He appeared to be in the dark as to what constituted neighbourliness, neither was he remotely concerned that the Sycamore Crescent Residents Group had threatened to call in the council's noise abatement team, in the desperate hope of curbing his regular all-hour music fests. Theirs was a fairly sedate mix of owner-occupiers and tenants whose houses, built by Epping Forest District Council in the nineteen-sixties, comprised twenty robust 'cottage-style' terraced dwellings, the odd numbers appearing opposite the evens (much like eyelashes around a lid) with a communal green in between. The residents shared its upkeep and were eager to do their bit. Their latest hedgehog corridor project was a success, as was the community nature reserve, whereby each householder set aside three-square yards for wildlife. Marianne's previous neighbours had been enthusiastic participants, but not so the new incumbent. When asked to continue to support the hedgehog runway, his Anglo-Saxon reply swiftly ended the conversation. The residents had passed the point of no return.

During an emergency committee meeting, it was suggested the matter be raised with the landlords, who happened to be Gil and Spencer Armstrong. Alongside their security business, the cousins had acquired several properties in the Hazelwood area, Marianne's cottage included, (although she had bought the freehold to Number 5 many years before). As she was on friendly terms, perhaps a personal approach was appropriate, as surely the letting was their responsibility. Feeling pressured to act, Marianne contacted Gil. Their connection may have stretched back many years, but they had never been especially close. His prompt arrival with the warning letter in hand had taken her by surprise, as a personal visit was neither necessary nor expected. Gil was, as usual, immaculately turned out, but that day he had looked frayed, and seemed grateful to be offered tea. He had learned about the redundancy from Spencer's infamously indiscreet wife, Nicole, whose mischievous fingers were in all the social network pies. Before he left that day, Gil offered Marianne the decorating job at The Tower, along with an invitation to join the family's last-night barbeque, and so it was arranged.

The wood pigeon's *cooing* call filtered through the swirl of her night-time recollections and back to practical matters. The house was clean; plant watering was arranged; everything was packed, including her sketch book and pencils. Closing the book, Marianne mulled over the inspirational quote. Wouldn't that be something – to start each day afresh, and not carry past hurts and disappointments over like ledgers, waiting to be balanced. Knowing that there were people living on this earth who were committed to a peaceful, loving life was a comforting thought on which to drift into sleep. Marianne turned off the lamp and snuggled under the duvet. This time tomorrow she'd breathe fresh salty sea air, hear new sounds, and feel new feelings. Perhaps it was time to put the past behind her, and after all, a job was a job.

🌑 GIL 🌑

GIL STACKED the breakfast crockery in the dishwasher. By sheer force of habit, he and Spencer were up early and had shared bacon rolls and coffee. Zak, having once again left a spoonful of cereal floating in half a bowl of milk, was now intently focused on messaging his school friends. The overnight rain had evaporated, helped along by a brisk Norfolk breeze which was forecast to weaken as the day passed. The previous week's sullen weather had cast a blue mood over the household, and far from being the usual exciting start to the summer holidays, much of it had been spent dodging the rain, and each other. Apart from kitesurfing, there was only so much eating out, gallery browsing, and screen-watching two families could do together before tension broke out. The unspoken agreement of 'holiday means holiday' had lapsed by the second day as Gil, Spencer, and Imogen scrolled through their respective work messages, hoping the others hadn't noticed. By day five, no one cared enough to comment.

Imogen floated into the kitchen, dressed for shopping. The short choppy bob suited her ash black hair, as did the floral long sleeve T shirt and trouser jeans. Gil couldn't recall ever seeing his wife in scruffs. Maintaining a certain image had been something to share during the early days of their marriage. Imogen had succeeded in substituting his Ben Sherman button downs for Ralph Lauren slim fits, but he resisted her attempts to fill his wardrobe with anything other than a dozen working outfits. Nothing would persuade him to give up his attachment to all things Mod: in Gil's eyes, its timeless style transcended trend: it endured, as did his love of West Ham F.C. However, if his wife and her business partner updated their collections every season, it was none of his concern. For Urbane Event Management, presentation was everything. He knew the line by heart: *Annette and I are the shop window, Gil.*

Nicole and Esme were the last to join the family. It was hard to tell just how alike mother and daughter were, such was the amount of make-up plastered on Nicole's face. Gil poured her a strong, black coffee and was rewarded with a lopsided smile, revealing two pink-lipsticked front teeth. He didn't bother to point it out. Esme wore just enough of something or other to give her the feeling of being grown-up, but no more. Spencer was laid back about most things, but he had strong objections to western culture's trend to sexualise the young, especially his beloved thirteen-year-old daughter. Imogen agreed. There was no need whatsoever for her niece to cover her gorgeous skin in foundation, but a touch of lip gloss surely could do no harm. Nicole couldn't see what all the fuss was about.

The mingled scent of Marc Jacobs and Miss Dior hung in the air like thick Dickensian smog. Gil opened the kitchen doors onto the balcony, where several seagulls bickered over breakfast. He smiled ironically. The girls had planned a shopping spree in Norwich, which meant a peaceful morning for him, at least.

Imogen took a last look at her phone before sliding it into her bag. 'What time are we expecting *Fanny Price?*'

Nicole sniggered into her coffee. Zak shot his aunt a scornful look. 'You haven't a clue who she's talking about, Nicole.'

'Imogen is referring to a novel called *Mansfield Park* in which the heroine, (in her opinion), in some way resembles Marianne,' said Spencer, who was currently immersed in a biography of Alan Turing. For reasons he could not compute, whenever Marianne or Freddie Bly's names were mentioned, Nicole's reactions were frosty to say the least. His wife appeared to have forgotten that their first-born Georgia had grown up, and was good friends, with Freddie.

'Marianne can hardly be considered the poor relation of this family. She's *real* and she listens, which is more than can be said for a lot of people I know.'

'I'm so pleased you are paying attention at school, Zak. I wasn't aware Jane Austen was on your reading list.'

'Try *paying attention*, Mum.'

Imogen's attempt to ruffle her son's thick, dark hair was brushed off with an annoyed shrug. Marianne's arrival at The Tower was of little consequence to her as they were hardly friends, and as the building was exclusively owned by Gil and Spencer, they could invite whosoever they wished without asking her permission. Marianne's friendship was, however, clearly important to Zak, and his happiness was paramount.

Gil sensed another argument brewing as had Rudy, his son's nervous Border Terrier. It was customary for the dog to take cover at the slightest hint of tension, and who could blame him? No one had the faintest idea how to successfully parent an adolescent boy. If Gil had spoken to his mother that way, she'd have cuffed him for it. 'Marianne is due after lunch. What time will you be back? We need to know when to start the barbeque.'

'Four o'clock-ish. Apart from putting together the salad, surely there can't be much more to do.'

Imogen took an apple from the fruit bowl and was immediately mirrored by Esme, who thoughtfully passed one to her lifelong weight watcher mother. Esme was a studious, slightly awkward girl, totally in awe of her aunt Imogen's sophistication. Their affection was mutual. No one was more excited about this relationship than Nicole. When Gil first introduced Imogen to the family, Nicole quickly overcame her inclination to jealousy and was smitten by the oh-so-sleek daughter of a grocery millionaire, and spent the subsequent years sloughing off the rougher parts of her Cockney accent in a bid to jump the class divide. Not quite the best friend status Nicole had hoped for, she was nevertheless content to bask in Esme's reflected glory and accompanied Imogen on shopping trips or spa jaunts whenever invited.

If it weren't so comical, it would be painful to watch. Gil's mind wandered back to the Bethnal Green days, when an over-ripe, pubescent Nicole Smith had relentlessly tailed him and Spencer, and eventually settled for his older cousin's kindly, bespectacled gawp. After university, Spencer was determined to focus on building the technical side of the business, rather than be side-tracked into Nicole's idea of domestic bliss, but as Gil had reminded him, they already lived together with baby Georgia, so what difference would marriage make. Nicole finally got the wedding she had so impatiently waited for, after which Spencer poured his considerable intellect into cementing the re-branded Armstrong Solution's position in the growing security market. He had neither wanted nor expected to father another child, but when Imogen gave birth to Zak, Nicole announced she was pregnant. Spencer's frustrations evaporated when Esme arrived. He was besotted and settled in comfortably for the long haul.

There was a rustle of jackets and handbags. Imogen tapped her French-polished fingernails impatiently on her bag strap, watching him.

'Did I miss something?'

'I said, we don't *have* to have a barbeque, Gil. There are several fabulous restaurants on this coastline.'

'And we've eaten in most of them this week, Imogen. Spencer and I fancy a home-cooked meal. What's the problem with that?' The last thing he wanted was to embarrass Marianne by hauling her along to an expensive restaurant. Did he have to spell it out?

'I apologise if my resumé doesn't run to five-star suppers. Oh, I've a brilliant idea for my fortieth birthday present. Why don't you sign me up for a cookery course at Auguste Escoffier?'

'Here we go. Do you really want to argue over which one of us works the hardest?' As soon he said it, Gil wished he hadn't, but he could no longer batten down his rising frustration. Why couldn't they sod off shopping and leave him in peace.

Zak's slow handclap ended the spat. 'Spencer and me are going to Brancaster, to check on the kite repairs. Are you coming, Dad?'

'Sorry, son. I've got things to do before we leave

22

tomorrow. I'll take Rudy with me when I close up the beach hut.'

Rudy's tail twirled as he trotted over to his hand-stitched tartan bed for a power nap. Zak was his number one, but right now, Gil needed him more, and a scramble on their favourite beach would clear the air.

Gil poured himself another coffee and sat by the huge picture windows, grateful for the silence. Spencer's idea to buy the rundown chandlery warehouse in Ropemaker's Yard was inspired. Not only had an important building been saved from demolition, but it had provided the entire Armstrong clan with a fine holiday home for two decades. The cousins had drawn up a limited company in which The Tower, along with the chalet, and the beach hut were listed as assets, should either of them divorce. It was important to protect their children's inheritance. The three-storey wooden-clad tower stood proud amongst Wells' colourful collection of terraces and holiday cottages. Its half-moon balcony wrapped snugly around the second storey, affording breath-taking views across the harbour and beyond. Of the six bedrooms, (two on each floor), the top two, his and Spencer's, were the most impressive, and were separated by a galleried space from which Scolt Head Island and The Albatross's rigging could clearly be seen through binoculars. The walled and patioed garden afforded privacy, and the large basement functioned as storage area for all manner of holiday paraphernalia, keeping the main building free of clutter – just how Gil liked it.

Several boats bobbed and weaved, while a number of holidaymakers walked the beach mile. Summer was officially here. Although Wells-next-the-Sea attracted thousands of annual visitors, the beach was large enough to swallow everyone up. Gil couldn't recall ever having to wrestle for space, unlike the previous week spent inside. Reflecting on the unfortunate exchange with Imogen earlier, he was frustrated at his lapse of control. Urbane Event Management were about to host their most important function to date, this time in Singapore. Gil had experienced first-hand just how much a deadline raised the stress levels, and while Imogen was extremely capable, the pressure was showing. Short bursts of tension had sprung up between them like hot air spouts, and the moody Norfolk sky had draped its heavy overcoat over them, the weight of which could not be shifted. It wasn't unusual for Imogen to spend time away, but Gil rarely stayed anywhere overnight, preferring the reassuring atmosphere of the Spitalfields' office, and the reasonable working hours. It was from here that the tight-knit team kept things in order, where the engineers picked up their job rotas, or stopped for tea and chitchat in the mess. Spencer relished the growing number of European site visits, which kept things nicely balanced between them.

Although Gil and Imogen had always supported each other's business endeavours, he was increasingly uneasy about Urbane's latest commission. The Singapore trips had kept her from home for at least a week each time, and she had missed Zak's end of year presentation, the first ever. It was difficult to know if their son was annoyed or upset by his mother's absence that day, as when Gil raised the matter, Zak changed the subject. His stoicism was rewarded by an evening with his grandmothers, Lena and Jean, who lived nearby. They made his favourite meal, played cards, and watched *The Italian Job*. Imogen assuaged her guilt by presenting Zak with a backstage pass to an Ed Sheeran gig, although the family were accustomed to having their dreams come true through her extensive networks and contacts. When Gil finally found a way to tell her that there were only so many idols you wanted to meet in person, as wasn't part of the fun dreaming about them, Imogen accused him of ingratitude, and the 'surprises' came to an abrupt end. After the school presentation incident, they had taken better care to co-ordinate diaries, but it wasn't easy. Gil would be relieved when the Singapore event was over but for Imogen, without an exciting stimulus to focus on, he suspected their unresolved issues would resurface.

The phone pinged.

Hello Gil. I aim to arrive at 2pm. Do I need to bring rollers and dust sheets? Marianne

Gil smiled at the formality of the text. The days of red telephone boxes, hand-scrawled notes, and faithful pledges to meet outside bingo halls or by specific park benches seemed quaint by today's standards. Although the world had acclimatised to technology, he couldn't help but feel that something had been lost.

No need, Marianne. Parking bay number three reserved outside The Tower. Gil

As the sun shouldered its way from behind a bulbous cloud, a droplet of light spread through Gil's chest. The change in weather was guaranteed to lift everyone's mood, and they might even manage an evening without bickering. It was now eleven-fifteen: time to stop thinking and get cracking. He picked up the hut keys, clipped on Rudy's lead, and headed out in the direction of the beach.

JOEL

THE MITSUBISHI Outlander took a left turn towards North Creake Road in the direction of Coltsfoot Wood. The windows were wound down, and the two occupants upbeat. 'That went well, didn't it Joel?'

'Yeah, a great job. The group were made up to see so many butterflies. Before I forget, Meg, when you write up the report, make sure you mention the fence repairs by the heath's western boundary. We'll have to add that to next week's list.'

'Sure. Looks like the hot stuff's on its way. We can kiss goodbye to quiet clean beaches and salt marshes until October. The country code is worse than useless. How difficult is it to close a gate behind you? And why people don't clear up after themselves, or their dogs, is beyond me.'

'Come on Meg, let's not spoil a top morning. We earthlings have achieved so much, and there's a lot more to come, now that the momentum is with us. How about the Dogger Bank boulder drop? That will prevent industrial trawlers from destroying our precious marine habitats – way to go, Greenpeace! Don't forget the truck load of countrywide initiatives going on, like WildEast's mission to restore East Anglia's natural ecosystems. And may I point out young lady, that 'B Corps', 'circular economy' and 'plant-power' are no longer buzzwords for eco-nuts like us. We've gone mainstream, Meg!'

Meg pulled over to let a lorry rattle past. 'You're right, Joel. I must focus on what I can change and rejoice in the good things. Just keep reminding me. Why don't you put your sounds on? There's nothing like a dose of stadium rock to flush out my mental garbage.'

'Really? Okay then, just a short blast as I don't want to do your head in before tonight.' Joel selected a couple of tracks from his playlist and sat back, reflecting on what Meg had said. Of course there were lows, and the planet was already undergoing unprecedented challenges. Even climate sceptics could no longer ignore or deny the scale of unpredictable weather patterns and worldwide natural disasters occurring at alarming rates. Warning shots by way of SARS and MERS had done nothing to stop cross-species contamination, with bigger waves predicted to arrive, and no amount of personal wealth could prevent forests and properties from burning or flooding. But Joel was an optimist. Like his fellow wildlife rangers who worked for the Rose Foundation, and many of his friends, his life was dedicated to the protection and preservation of the natural world. The general consensus amongst them was that as the adult human species were doing a great job at wiping themselves out, best to focus their efforts on Mother Nature. Joel turned the music down. 'What time are you coming to the pub? There's a surprise in store.'

'Let me guess: Kurt's back from Cuba.'

'Norfolk is on red alert! Kurt flew in last week, and is coming over for tea before we hit the pub. Do you want to join us? Gran won't mind. She'll have made enough to feed an army.'

'Aw, I'd love to, but Gareth is making dinner, a once-in-a-lifetime event. We'll see you after that. Wouldn't miss it for the world.'

'Kurt said the project went better than expected, after an initial hiccup with the equipment. Did you see his footage of the bee hummingbird? Just think, Meg, eighty wing beats per second and weighing under two grammes – two thirds less than a Goldcrest! How can that not perk you up. The film will be released next year. It's the first time Kurt has spoken from behind the camera, apart from those three-minute *Springwatch* jobs.'

'It has to be more rewarding for the camera crew, and cheaper for the programme makers, eh?'

'I reckon. Kurt's got a few weeks to play with, so be prepared for his appearance at The Kedge. He'll be hitching a ride on our jobs. I get the feeling he wants to shift his focus on projects closer to home.'

Meg drove into the Foundation car park and switched off the engine. 'It's a difficult one, isn't it, Joel. Filming wildlife to educate the public is essential and yet, the accumulated carbon footprint of those involved is colossal, not to mention the networks' entertainment agendas. I dread to think what mileage Kurt has clocked up during his career.'

'That's why he's having a rethink. Anyway, we'll find out more tonight – that is, if Mr Van Lynden, wildlife rock star, isn't waylaid by the green groupies.'

Meg's eyes twinkled. 'You cannot mean me, Joel Midwinter. I only have eyes for you.'

Joel unloaded the gear from the boot, pondering Meg's remark. Some years before, his steadfast promise not to get personal was temporarily suspended when he asked Meg for a drink. As soon as he mentioned a childhood 'heart defect', her concerned expression and subsequent interrogation signalled the end of what might have been a lasting relationship. It had happened before, and fortunately this time, Joel hadn't crossed any lines, but Meg took it upon herself to monitor his every move as if he were an invalid, even after she and fellow ranger Gareth Parry moved into together. Joel had to find a way to tackle her. 'Meg, you've only got eyes for Nan's sweetcorn and chilli scones. She packed extra for lunch today.'

'Where would we be without Irene Midwinter's tasty bakes. Looks like Gareth and Lori are back. Bet you another scone they can't match our morning's haul.'

The Rose Foundation's headquarters, known as The Kedge, was situated between Creake and Stanhope, on the outskirts of Coltsfoot Wood. The owners, Professor Sir Clifford and Dorothea Rose lived in the farmhouse which was tucked away in the heart of Coltsfoot's broadleaf and conifer wood, the majority of which had been donated to the Norfolk Wildlife Trust. The remaining four acres were returned to orchard and wildflower meadow. Amongst the various outbuildings and housed in what appeared to be a tumbledown scout hut, was a twenty-five-metre oxygenated, rain-water swimming pool, (designed and built by the professor) which provided essential relief for Dorothy Rose's painful arthritic joints, fun for the grandchildren, and exercise for good friends. The delightfully gregarious professor was a naturalist by profession, and counted amongst his skills inventor, storyteller, and banjo player, although not as talented as his professional violinist wife. Since their retirement, the couple were often on the road, sharing a lifetime of stories with small groups of interested souls and ending each gathering with knee-slapping renditions of *Dueling Banjos*.

The Kedge functioned exactly as its dictionary definition stated: a light anchor for all comers. It consisted of two converted barns housing a staff accommodation block, office, meeting space, and a rest area containing a kitchen and showers. The principle role of the rangers was to support existing wildlife trusts and conservation groups through educational projects, guided walks and talks, maintaining footpaths and fences, and monitoring wildlife. There were no appraisals or hierarchy: every ranger earned the same, regardless of qualifications, the salary increased yearly in line with inflation, and accommodation was free. A passion for the job was essential. Requests for assistance were collated by two job-share employees before being passed to the six-strong rangers team who met every morning at 8.30am. Oftentimes, specific requests were sent directly to the rangers, and where possible, attended to in an ad hoc manner.

The Foundation's beating heart philosophy was 'to reawaken our innate relationship with nature, regardless of background or education'. Mitch, Gareth, and Lori were post-graduates while Meg, Larry, and Joel had no environmental, wildlife management or conservation qualifications. Everyone increased their knowledge on the job. Joel's particular expertise lay in communication. He had formulated a remarkable series of talks and interactive educational workshops which were so popular, most of his week was allocated to them. While he would have liked to do more of the adventurous activities, Joel accepted the importance of this work. Several independent groups and organisations were booked in at The Kedge during the summer and numbers were limited, unlike the school events whose classes were often sizeable and could be as far away as seventy miles. Although rewarding, it made for a long, tiring day.

Joel dropped his rucksack in the rest room, washed his hands, and pulled up a chair at the large Formica table where Lori was filling four large mugs with tea. She and Gareth had been fixing up owl and bird boxes and would need an energy boost. The daily pooling of scones, sandwiches, pasties, salad, veg, and cake never lasted long.

'I'm loving the chilli flakes, Joel. Be sure to thank your gran,' said Meg, who had smothered her scone with vegan spread.

Lori cut through the thick fruit cake. 'Midge and Larry finished up early at Titchwell Reserve. They'll see us at The Windlass at eight o'clock tonight. Did your group find their butterflies, Joel?'

'Did they! The scrub clearance has paid dividends. They recorded six Silver Studded Blues, and a Large Blue which has already been posted on the website. I'm not sure how much they noticed the landscape, though. Gosling Heath is stunning first thing, but this lot were more interested in the numbers.'

Gareth finished his last mouthful of pasty before swiping Meg's uneaten scone with a magician's sleight of hand. 'It just goes to show we don't all see the big picture.

Me and Lori secured twenty new boxes, across two sites. A low-flying magpie all but knocked her off the ladder.'

'Yeah, and Gareth found it so hilarious, I almost dropped a box on his head, but then I remembered it's his turn to buy the first round of drinks tonight.'

'I've got twenty quid left in the whip from last time, and Kurt always buys a round. He'll be buzzing from his Cuban adventures.'

'That'll come in handy, Joel. I'm still waiting for my grant to arrive. Is Kurt coming in next week?'

Lori's cheeks flushed. Such an innocuous question by anyone else wouldn't have raised an eyebrow. For the environmental biologist however, no matter how brilliant and fearless she was in the field, when it came to the human male, she was uniquely shy.

'We've a new project, and Kurt wants to film one or two of the rangers. It's called 'A Day in the Wild Life'. We thought it'd be a great idea to delve into the background of someone like you, Lori: what brought you to the work, your hopes for the future, that sort of thing.'

'Kurt wants to film me?'

'Only if you want to.'

A pause. 'Okay, I'll do it.'

Everyone cheered. Gareth stretched.

'Right, let's make tracks, Meg. I'm banking on a rest before we go to the pub.'

'Is that before or after you cook the anniversary feast?'

Gareth's expression was blank.

'Meg says you're cooking tonight.'

'Yeah – 'course I am Joel, but what I really need is a minder to keep her from tidying up every two minutes.'

Amongst the good-natured banter and a building excitement for the evening, it was time to head home. No one was on call as such, but if a request came through for emergency assistance, or a special event was on the horizon, the team made themselves available. It was more than a job: it was a lifestyle, and you were never really off duty. There was always a report of a rare bird spotting, a wildflower, or some other phenomenon, and not uncommon for Joel and his colleagues to take off mid-meal to witness the spectacle. The Rose Rangers were the professional and personal equivalent of a murmuration. As the foursome filed out of the door, a symphony of electronic pings had them instinctively reaching for their phones. The Seal Rescue had put out a call for extra assistance. A pup had beached over at Wells, but they were currently dealing with two other situations, and needed someone to standby. Joel lived just ten minutes away. He was about to reply when Meg stopped him.

'Me and Gareth will go.'

'It's not three o'clock yet Meg, and there's plenty of time before tea. I want to feel the sun on my back.'

'I'll come with you.'

As the others drove away, Joel climbed in the driver's seat and waited for Meg to buckle her seatbelt. 'You should have gone back with Gareth. It's your anniversary ...'

Meg cut him off. 'So, we'll celebrate tonight. As you said, it'll be nice to feel the sun on our backs.' Sensing Joel's frustration, she switched on the music system and changed tack. 'Right then, ranger: Bryan Adams is on speaker and I'm playing it loud, so put the pedal to the metal and take me to Wells beach.'

 ZAK

IN A RARE act of subversion, Zak pulled a corner from his cheese sandwich and passed it under the table to Rudy, whose head was resting, in anticipation, on his right knee. Imogen was laid back about many things, but she disapproved of feeding the dog at the table. His dad usually agreed but had been known to turn a blind eye, just as he did right then, and had winked at him. Zak was elated. He and Spencer had returned from a fab morning at Brancaster beach just in time for lunch. Gil had filled the warm *ciabatta* bread with a thick wedge of Binham Blue, (Zak's favourite Norfolk cheese), and remembered to spread the pickle on the non-cheese side of the sandwich. Three glasses of ginger beer had stood at the ready, although it wasn't really beer at all, but it was as close as this fourteen-year-old was going to get. Zak swigged the last of the sweet, fizzy liquid and burped under his napkin. Although hormonally disjointed, good manners were kite marked. 'Oops, sorry. Thanks, Dad. That really hit the spot.'

'Did you have a good session?'

'Spencer was going like the clappers and at one point, I thought he'd come flying off, but you hung on, didn't you, Spence?'

Spencer grinned. He was relieved not to have come a cropper, but the kite's overhaul, and wheel adjustment had made a difference. 'I didn't think we'd get the chance to beach-test the kites before going home, so that was a

34

bonus. We blew off a bit of steam, didn't we, Zak. By the way, your balance has improved by a mile.' He turned to Gil. 'The boy did good.'

Zak beamed. It was exhilarating, especially when he got into a head-to-head with another kite boarder and outran her by several metres. He loved his uncle's company, and this week had been fun despite the rain. Spencer reminded him of a huge, friendly, and super-brainy bear who had oodles of time for him. He insisted on regular school updates, particularly on science and technology, and was only too willing to help with the incomprehensible mound of homework. It wasn't that his dad didn't ask, but Spencer knew all sorts of things, probably because he'd been to university, whereas Gil was self-taught. Zak felt as if he had two fathers, as they were together all the time, either at work, or the health club, or at Stratford, watching West Ham play football. When their team got a result, it was priceless to see his dad's generally dour expression break into a grin. Lately though, he was preoccupied with something or other, and there was tension at home. Spencer's house was in the next road, while his grandmothers' bungalow was a five-minute bike ride away. Marianne lived at Hazelwood, which was just a mile from his house, so there were escape routes. Zak hadn't seen her or Freddie since Easter. It was a shame Freddie couldn't make it, but Marianne was coming, and she was really nice.

Without being asked, Zak slid out of the chair and cleared the plates and glasses, grateful that the tense morning atmosphere had blown away. His mother's *Fanny Price* comment had infuriated him, as had Nicole's ignorant snort. It was baffling to think that Esme was her daughter. He didn't see much of his cousin at Noke House as she was in the year below, but as Esme was better at science and Spanish, he'd occasionally let her help him out. In fact, while the rain kept them indoors, they had finished their holiday homework which was a massive bonus. She was going through a phase just like he was, but it wasn't something he could or would talk to her about.

It was almost two o'clock. Zak suddenly felt nervous. When his dad told him about Hazelwood Primary's closure and Marianne's redundancy, his alarm bells started clanging. Not only had his beloved school gone forever, but he was worried for Marianne. How would she manage without a full-time job? At least she'd agreed to stay on to decorate the living rooms which meant extra cash. If she needed cheering up, that was no problem. The door chime triggered Rudy's ferocious bark, which was comical as he was as soft as chocolate spread and would lick her to death. Zak ran down the stairs, two at a time, to greet Marianne. The one thing his mum and Grandma Lena agreed on was that he was a 'fine young man with a charming personality'. It was time to prove them right.

MARIANNE

THE WARM breeze flapped at Marianne's linen trousers as she ambled along the vast unspoilt beach. Zak's repeated attempts to get Rudy to retrieve the ball from the water had mixed results. There were too many distractions for the excitable dog, but he never strayed far. It was shaping up to be a fine afternoon, and by all accounts a good week of weather was to come. Seeing Zak so content was hugely gratifying, and soon she would see Esme.

Marianne sighed. She was so glad to be out of The Tower after the awkward greeting. Just one hour ago, she had stood beside Gil like strangers waiting for a bus when Spencer bounded up the stairs, apologising for not being there to welcome her. Unsure whether to hug, or shake hands, the adults did neither. If Gil had told her he was holidaying with Spencer and Nicole, she wouldn't have come. Marianne's heart sank at the prospect of an evening wedged between Imogen's cool indifference and Nicole's inane hot gossip. The women were out shopping, so the prospect of another uncertain reception was at least postponed until late afternoon.

Before Zak had the chance to whisk her off for a tour, Gil suggested she catch her breath over a cup of tea, during which they made small talk: the M11 was light, and she had a good journey; Freddie was well, and enjoying work; she wasn't sorry to have left Hazelwood Primary. The contents of her cool bag prompted an enthusiastic response from

Spencer as these were the first dishes they'd eaten which hadn't come from the deli. He looked just the same as when they last saw each other (was it at Lena's seventieth party, two years before?) although his mossy hair had retreated a few millimetres, like the tide going out. Gil had arranged Sunday lunch in Burnham Market from where they would drive home. Marianne smiled politely at the invitation to join them and left it at that. After tea, she and Gil discussed the job, and he passed her a sealed envelope. They'd already agreed on a fee but recalling Della's words about a bumper pay-day, Marianne tucked it into her bag, grateful he had walked away to spare any potential blushes.

The air, distilled and refreshing, had the marvellous effect of revitalising her tired mind. Marianne formulated a strategy: after the barbeque she would retreat to the guest bedroom for an early-ish night with her new book. The following morning, she'd visit Staithe Street's art centre as soon as it opened. It would keep her out of The Tower until the family left. Gil hadn't asked her opinion of the building but what could she say that he didn't already know? The local architect had waved a wand of shiny curves, clean lines, and spacious octagonal reception rooms, big enough for four families to co-exist. Her bedroom – comfortable, minimal, and bright – was on the ground floor, with a shared bathroom. With one flight between her and the children, and another between her and the adults, Marianne was confident of a good night's sleep.

Zak came towards her, the wet ball dangling from his hand.

'I was really sorry to hear about Hazelwood Primary.'

'It was an exceptional school, wasn't it? The donkeys and chickens have been rehomed, and the garden will remain as part of the conversion into flats. I could have moved to the new school, but sometimes change is a good thing, Zak.'

'Yeah, I guess so, as long as you're okay.'

Marianne stopped walking and faced the boy-man. A faint hairline bordered his upper lip, and his voice had a fine timbre. Zak's caramel eyes almost reached hers. Soon he'd tower over everyone, just like his parents. 'There's no need to worry, Zak. I've lots of work lined up, and Della wants me at the nursery. It's good of you to ask, though.'

Zak put his gangly arms about her, almost dislodging her hat, before sprinting after Rudy. Marianne wiped her eyes, feeling suddenly bereft. Freddie's last visit was at Easter when Zak and Esme had joined them for tea. They had played games, and Freddie talked about Liverpool, his adopted home, *where the real people live*. How much longer the tradition would continue was anyone's guess. With Rachel now on the scene, he'd want to spend the holidays with her family. Oh, well, there was no point in speculation. Adjusting to self-employment was enough to be getting on with.

Up ahead, a group had gathered behind a cordon. As they approached, Marianne called to Zak. 'Why don't you clip on Rudy's lead and we'll walk up along the dunes to avoid the crowd.'

Zak intercepted Rudy, who was mid-scramble with another terrier, both edging closer to the gathering. The other owner had the same idea in mind and instantly ended the chase. By the time the dog was safely back on the lead, they had reached the barrier. 'Hey, Marianne, look! It's a seal – I think it's a pup.'

Marianne paused, relieved that Rudy was secure but deeply uncomfortable to see the helpless pup under such scrutiny. She was about walk away when Zak pulled out his phone. Her hand reached for his arm. 'Before you do that Zak, take a moment to think about it.'

'What d'you mean?'

'That has to be the pup's mother out there. If I'm distressed just looking at them, how do you think they feel, separated as they are?'

Before Zak could answer, a nimble, fresh-faced man wearing a camo-coloured bush hat approached from the inside of the cordon. His official-looking shirt contrasted with his beaming smile.

'You're so right about that. They are distressed, and I wouldn't fancy people taking pictures of me with my mum waiting around – talk about embarrassing. Hi, I'm Joel Midwinter, and that's my colleague over there, Meg Swayne. We work as wildlife rangers for the Rose Foundation.' He offered a freckly hand to Zak, who hastily put his phone away to shake it, and then to Marianne, after which he bent down to stroke the wet dog. 'And who is this fine-looking young man?'

'This is Rudy.'

'Have you stopped your messing around, Ru-deee?'

Zak laughed at The Specials musical reference and was mesmerised by the ranger who held Rudy's face gently in his hands (his dog didn't like that sort of thing) before ruffling his damp coat. 'Is the pup really in danger?'

'That depends, Zak.' The ranger stood. 'We've checked

him over and there are no obvious injuries. If he's approached by a dog or a human, his mother could leave him behind.'

'Oh, how awful! Come on, Zak, let's go back.'

'No, you're alright. I wish other people were as understanding. The likelihood is that he's washed up with the tide, and Mum is waiting for him to wash back in. The Seal Rescue are on their way. We'll keep him safe until then.'

Zak was suddenly extremely interested in the man who agreed with Marianne and had hypnotised his dog. 'What does a ranger do? I haven't seen you before, and we've a house here.'

As the crowd drifted away, Marianne and Zak found themselves engaged in a fascinating conversation with the charismatic ranger, covering a raft of subjects so wide, it would be hard to recall the details later. What was impossible to forget were his eyes, so alive and sparkling, a fervour she only ever saw in young children. His colleague must have felt the same way as she was equally as enthusiastic, but clearly needed to be somewhere else.

'Come on, Joel, I've got to get back.'

'Sorry, Meg, didn't realise the time.' Joel turned to Zak. 'A group of us are meeting tonight at The Windlass as my best mate is a wildlife cameraman and is back from filming in Cuba. Why don't you join us? He'll tell you all about his adventures, which are substantially more exciting than mine.'

Marianne was so taken aback by the request that before she could articulate a polite refusal, Zak accepted it spontaneously in the way that young people do.

'Wow! Sounds fab. What's your friend's name?'

'Kurt Van Lynden. Look him up online. He's filmed in all four corners of the planet and is what you might call a wildlife legend.'

'Awesome! Count us in.'

'Hadn't we best check with your dad first?'

'I s'pose, but he won't mind.' Zak pulled out his phone. 'What's the name of the place again?'

'The Windlass. It's our local pub, just off The Buttlands. Fun starts at eight. Sorry, gotta go. See you there!'

The stupefied pair watched the rangers disappear along the beach as the rescue squad took over. Only a scattering of people remained as the crowd had long since departed for their cottages and chalets to prepare for an evening of coastal fun. Marianne attributed the ranger's invitation to his unambiguous friendliness, and in all likelihood, he had invited other onlookers too. They made their way back to The Tower, chatting about the incredible conversation.

'Joel and Meg were super cool. Do you think my dad will agree?'

'Do you really want to go, Zak? Wasn't Joel just being polite.'

'Nah – I can't imagine he'd invite anyone to the pub. Besides, he's the most interesting person I've met in ages, and as for his cameraman friend …'

'Kurt Van Lynden.'

They laughed, and in the next moment, Zak ran off after Rudy.

'For the last time Zak, we're not going to a pub we don't know, to meet a bunch of strangers who could turn out to be nutters. Now, do you want another piece of chicken or not?'

'No – *thank you.*' In desperation, Zak turned to his mother who was playing chess with her tomatoes and cucumber. 'Look, Mum, this is Kurt Van Lynden's website. He's made lots of wildlife films and has won zillions of awards. It'll be so cool to meet him, won't it?'

Zak plonked his laptop onto Imogen's lap in the hope of winning her consent. She seemed genuinely pleased he was being attentive and obligingly scanned the screen. 'Hmm, he definitely has the air of a rock star. Hey, Nicole, Kurt Van Lynden is hotter than the barbeque.'

Snatching the laptop away, Zak retreated to his chair to prevent Nicole from sticking her nose in, although he allowed Esme to get a better look. 'I don't know why I'm asking either of you as the invitation was for Marianne and me.'

Silence descended on the group and all eyes turned towards her. Marianne groaned inwardly at the inevitability of it. Any hope of a tension free evening was dashed as soon as they returned from the beach. Not only were they late (Spencer had begun cooking), but Nicole's welcome scarcely registered on the general civility scale, most likely a reaction to Esme's affectionate hug. Imogen was, for all of three seconds, super-friendly. She thanked her for the delicious tart and pudding, which really was unnecessary, and it was spectacularly generous of her to remain behind to freshen up the house. As Zak's relentless campaign continued apace, Gil's sour mood dampened the warm evening air. The fate of the pub visit appeared to lay in Marianne's hands.

Maybe the invitation wasn't as empty a gesture as the others believed. It was impossible to gage a person's sincerity in so short a time span, but Joel Midwinter didn't appear to be insincere. There was no denying his impassioned and engaging manner as it had shone over the crowd, particularly on the young ones, who had rapid-fired questions at him and his colleague, and each time the rangers patiently answered each one. It was extraordinary. Just as Marianne was about to speak, Spencer put down the tongs and turned to his cousin.

'Gil, if it's okay with you, I'll take Zak to the pub.'

'Why don't we all go? We've almost finished here, and it will be good for Zak to meet new people,' said Imogen, who was inexplicably now fully on board with the idea. She unfolded her long legs and stretched languidly. With the exception of Gil, enthusiasm swept through the Armstrongs like a summer cold. No wonder his jaw had tightened, being caught on the ropes like that. Marianne felt genuinely sorry for him.

'Okay, but don't overdo it with your glad-rags. The Windlass isn't a trendy, uptown venue. In fact, let's go as we are.'

'No bloody chance, Gil. I can't remember the last time we went out for an *actual* drink, in a *proper* pub, like we used to, when even you knew how to enjoy yourself. So, I'm going up to change. C'mon, Esme, you can wear your new skinny jeans,' said Nicole, sizzling with anticipation of a fun night out.

'Esme looks nice as she is. If you take too long Nicole, you'll have to meet us there,' said Zak firmly to his aunt's back, as she gathered her bag and shoes.

Esme blushed at her cousin's unexpected compliment, while Nicole, now as perky as a spring lamb, trotted behind Imogen's slender figure as they disappeared upstairs to do who-knew-what to their impeccably dressed bodies. Marianne scraped the half-eaten food onto an empty plate. Perhaps a gin and tonic would get her through the evening. It was impossible to back out, but did she really want to? She was so unaccustomed to spontaneity, but something inside her was making waves, and the sensations were far from unpleasant. Gil took the plates and scuttled into the house, his expression apologetic. Did he make the comment about outfits on her behalf? How did he know she hadn't brought anything suitable to change into? Marianne glanced at her trousers. The linens weren't too crumpled, and she'd changed into a fresh cotton blouse before dinner. In all likelihood, the pub would be too dark and too busy for outfits to be weighed and measured. It was good to see Zak and Esme excited, though. Marianne made her way downstairs to brush her teeth and fetch her bag. It had been a lovely afternoon, so one more hour couldn't hurt.

JOEL

Kurt Van Lynden stretched out his long denim-clad legs and patted his washboard stomach, all killer smile and flashing eyes. 'Cuban cuisine is as tasty as anything I've eaten, but you can't beat Irene's homecooked grub, washed down with a glass of Dudley's cider.'

'It's great to see you, Kurt. I've missed your gorgeous mug. Are you glad to be back?'

'Yeah, although the flat is just somewhere to hang my hat, unlike this ultra-cosy rig. I'll be glad to get started on our 'Day in the Wild Life project', if you're still up for it.'

'You bet your sweet butt I am. Lori has agreed to be the first guinea pig. Why don't you talk to Larry tonight? He'll be a good counter-weight: different background, education, and suchlike.'

'Will do. So, Joel, how are you?'

'Flourishing, much like the Foundation, as you'll see next week at The Kedge. We've so many great things in the pipeline. If you stick around, I'll help you build a den of your own.'

Kurt thoughts jumped back to the cabin's construction, when an enthusiastic group of friends sawed, banged, drilled, sang, ate, and drank their way through Irene's inexhaustible pantry. Professor Rose had insisted on joining the build, which was fortunate, as his expertise proved invaluable. While the group discussed the pros and cons of a sedum roof and solar panels over yet another brew, the professor drew the design on a scrap of paper showing exactly how to fit the panels, where to put the compost loo, and how to wire in the water heater. The thick sheep's wool insulation and green electricity created a sustainable living space at a minimum cost, and they had great fun in the process. A decade on, and the cabin was as solid as ever. Kurt could still smell the fresh pine cladding under the packed bookshelves, files, photos, cards, and maps pinned to the walls. Joel was obsessively tidy, essential in the compact space, and he could locate the most obscure piece of information within seconds. 'There's nothing I'd like more than a den like this, but there may be something slightly more substantial in the offing.'

Scouring the familiar face in front of him, Joel was overcome with joy. There wasn't much he and Kurt didn't know about each other, and rarely a week passed without contact between them. The cameraman was his mentor, guide, and best mate, one of a handful of critically important people to appear in his life just at the right time (none of which were either his father or stepfather). From the comfort of his cabin, Joel lived vicariously through his friend's worldwide adventures, and he wasn't surprised that Kurt wanted to change direction. The work could be lonely, tough, and was often dangerous, and it challenged the hardiest relationships. 'You're roosting with Anya.'

'Yep. After a lifetime of gallivanting, it's time to put down roots. There's enough wildlife in Mull to keep me quiet for a week or two.'

Kurt's embarrassed blush was touching. He was by nature extremely confident, someone who had always known exactly where he was going and yet, Kurt was as nervous as the next person when faced with a big life-change. Anya Maclean was a steadying presence in his rolling-stone life: never restraining or holding him back, creating space in which they might make a home together, one day. Anya had quit her wildlife career and returned to Mull, her homeland. She was as committed to the planet's wellbeing as was Kurt – the only difference was that she no longer wanted to travel. 'I'm made up for you, mate. Don't forget to invite me to your *wee island* every once in a while.'

'Goes without saying. Talking of rare species, has anyone caught your eye lately, apart from Meg Swayne?'

'Meg is a constant reminder of why I choose to stay single. Our fling was shorter than a mayfly's mating ritual, but she can't stop fussing over me. I've got to sort it out. Thankfully, Gareth doesn't seem to mind. He's a good bloke.'

'The winning combination of cutie-pie face, unending optimism, and an annoying inability to lie makes you the perfect friend.'

'Compliments accepted. Now you mention it Kurt, here's a headline of a rare sighting. At the beach earlier, Meg and I were shielding a grey seal pup. A number of onlookers were taking photos, and while we were doing the usual, I heard someone say something like, *if you were vulnerable and scared, would you like strangers taking photos of you?* You can guess what happened next.'

'Out came the binoculars.'

'Not quite, as the object of curiosity was within sight.'

'Genus?'

'*Homo sapien*; female.'

'Height and weight?'

'One hundred and seventy centimetres; approximately one hundred and forty pounds.'

'Plumage?'

At this point, Joel was fit to burst. 'Chestnut cap, with a hint of fiery red, from what I spotted under her large straw hat.' When the friends finally stopped falling about at the silliness of it, Joel composed himself. 'Her name is Marianne, and her son is Zak. I asked them to the pub tonight. The boy, or should I say the young man, was interested in the Foundation. When I mentioned you, his enthusiasm levels spiked. It may be just the right time.'

'Marianne, eh? So, you still have a thing for the mothers. Safe ground, Joel?'

It was Joel's turn to blush. 'Maybe, but Marianne had a heady blend of wisdom and compassion behind those green-flecked eyes. I don't expect them to turn up, as she suggested he ask his father.'

'It's harder than ever to get into the industry, even with a good degree, but if the lad does show, we'll put him on the right track. There are plenty of other avenues if it doesn't pan out. Don't you love it when beauty catches the eye, Joel. It's why we do what we do.'

'You're so right about that. Every day brings a new wonder. Makes me glad to be alive.'

'It's a miracle there are any wonders left in this brutal world. We just don't know for how much longer. And don't get me started on the threats to Cuba's eco-regions. They may have declared biosphere reserves, but if the country succumbs to agricultural expansion, they'll lose even more of their precious habitat.'

'We've got things the wrong way around, Kurt. Half of the earth needs to be left untouched, but how likely is that? Most of the UK's Sites of Special Scientific Interest are underfunded, so how we go about protecting tiny eco-regions overseas is beyond me. Still, you filmed a bee hummingbird, and the sea turtles must have been something else.'

'They were, Joel, and I am grateful to have seen them, but we've got to face facts. It's taken programme segments like *Planet Earth Diaries* for viewers to see what happens behind the camera, and we're only now reporting on it. That doesn't exactly make me feel great. No wonder Anya bailed out early. Maybe I should have followed her.'

'No point in regrets, Kurt. It's done. What we do next is the only thing that matters. That's where the power lies, my friend.'

The men were silent for a while, allowing time for the other to mentally recalibrate. Sadly, this wasn't a new conversation. Kurt was suddenly dowsed by a huge dose of guilt. He had lived his dream, he had travelled the world, filmed untold species, and had a loving partner, and while he was bemoaning his lot, Joel made light of his 'faulty equipment'. He never once complained, blamed, or took advantage of any lack of physical vitality. His motto, that life is as unlimited as you want it to be, was inspirational, and his upbeat worldview was contagious. Everyone loved him for it. Shaking off his mood, Kurt rose, his gunmetal mop almost brushing the ceiling. 'Sorry, Joel. My outburst is over, and I'm ready for my first pint of refreshing Malt Coast.'

The spotlight bounced off the tiny diamond embedded in Kurt's right lateral incisor. Joel's heart lit up at the sight of the familiar star-studded grin. It was great to have his best mate back. 'Are we on for a visit to Keith's tomorrow morning?'

'Yep, around ten o'clock. I need a couple of prime lenses. He's got a Lavalier microphone for part-exchange but I've gotta keep an eye on the coin, now I'm going to ground. Anya is generous, but I can't expect her to keep me.'

'Keith's Camera and Kit Exchange saves us a fortune. He'll be pleased to see you again.'

'Likewise. You've got a splash of colour from this afternoon's session. The T-shirt's a nice touch, too. Ready to hit the town?'

'Do robins eat worms?' Joel tucked his wallet in his back pocket. 'We're looking, smelling and feeling *gooood*.'

The friends stood opposite each other, the cameraman a head taller than the ranger, and they made their customary Vulcan salutation. With great gales of glee resetting the starship's compass, Joel closed the cabin door and they beamed up to the pub.

It wasn't quite standing room only, but on his particular Saturday night at The Windlass, it had been a date on the calendar for a reunion of sorts. Several wanderers had returned to celebrate with friends, although no excuse was required for a fun night out. As soon as Joel and Kurt walked through the door, the decibels hit their eardrums, and that was before the music had started. Kurt wasn't the only one to be commandeered as, like a flock of returning fieldfares, friends and colleagues began the exciting migratory journey of reacquaintance. Before long, Meg and Gareth arrived and instantly disappeared into the rabble along with their fellow rangers, the squadron of volunteers, and faces that Joel hadn't seen for a while. As he waited for his round of drinks, Meg re-appeared to give him a hand.

'Kurt should have been in a band. Lori's face was a picture when he put his arm around her.'

Joel smiled to see Kurt happily ensconced. He was a local lad, but his future was in Mull. With luck, the island would weave its magic as it sounded as if he and Anya were ready to lay feathers.

'Joel, are you listening?'

'Sorry, Meg. How was your meal?'

Meg pulled a face. 'Gareth over-cooked the rice, and left the kitchen in a state, and before you ask, I didn't say a word, apart from 'thank you'. How's you? It's been a long day.'

'I'm fine, Meg.' Joel swiftly changed the subject. 'Looks like we're in for a crush. Maybe I shouldn't have invited those people on the beach earlier today.'

'Are they friends of yours?'

'No, but the boy wanted to meet Kurt, and I can't resist filling an open mind with wild ideas.'

'The Pied-Piper of Norfolk strikes again.' Meg sipped at her half-pint of cider. 'I can't imagine why they'd bother. The Windlass isn't exactly on trend, is it? Anyway, I promised Mitch a game of pool. He wants to win his money back, but I'm feeling lucky tonight.'

Meg bounced off to the far corner of the pub where the pool tables were under siege. Joel checked his watch. It was looking increasingly unlikely that Zak and Marianne would turn up. Disappointment blew up like a squall, so he battened it down and picked up the tray of drinks, ready to zig-zag back to his mates when suddenly Zak headed straight for him and was trailed by Marianne, her expression bemused. Without missing a beat, Joel welcomed them. 'Hey, you made it! Let me introduce you to Kurt before he gets stuck in for the night, then I'll get the drinks in. What'll you have?'

'Thanks, but my dad's at the bar. I'll bring our drinks over.'

'No need, Zak. It'll be good to meet him.'

Room was made for the new arrivals who were instantly absorbed into the conversation. With Marianne and Zak in good hands, Joel hustled through the mob to the bar where a rigidly immobile figure stared ahead, a lookout desperately seeking land. Joel's shoulders sagged. The last thing he needed was a disgruntled parent who'd been dragged out to a rowdy pub by his over-enthusiastic son. Oh, well, he was nothing if not polite, and could usually make even the surliest person smile. 'Hello, I'm Joel Midwinter. I met your son at the beach.'

'Yeah, I guessed. I don't know what you said to Zak, but he's stoked up about something.'

The men shook hands although Joel didn't feel much warmth in those cold, hard fingers. Not a man whose drink you want to spill. 'I hope I haven't spoilt your evening. Can I buy you a drink?'

'I've just ordered, mate. So, what's all this about, then?'

It took Joel two seconds to realise he'd made a mistake. The energy emanating from this man was as poisonous as a black legged dart frog. Was Zak really his son, and Marianne his wife? There was nothing else for it but to tell him about the Foundation as quickly as possible before getting back to great night out.

'Obviously I don't know Zak, but I can tell when someone is genuinely interested in our work. You can't hide enthusiasm, Mr er...'

'Armstrong.'

Joel bit back a laugh. *Mister Armstrong it is.* 'Well, Mr. Armstrong, you and Marianne have a fine son and you ...'

'Marianne isn't Zak's mother.'

Silence filled the space between the men.

'His mother is over there, by the jukebox, with my cousin and his wife. It looks as if their daughter has also been snapped by your cameraman's lens.'

Joel had met several objectionable people during his years as a ranger as it went with the territory, but he was rarely on the back foot as he was right now, and yet, there was an upside: Marianne wasn't his wife! It was like the pop of a champagne cork. He swung his head around to see who would have actually married such a sunless man. 'Wow, what a smasher! She's Zak's mother?'

It was Gil's turn to be gobsmacked. Such an outspoken declaration of admiration had the instant effect of cracking his shell, and he found himself smiling. 'Look mate, sorry if I was rude. This isn't our patch and – well, you know what I mean. Let me buy you a drink.'

'Yeah, I do know what you mean, and it's great that you care about your son. I'll have a cloudy lemonade, on the rocks.'

'Cloudy lemonade – what are you, twelve?'

54

The strangers laughed and were relieved to have broken the ice. 'I'm older than I look. Zak said you have a house and a beach hut here.'

'They've been in the family for donkey's years.'

'Did the hut survive the 2013 surge?'

'Only just. We bought the old chandlery way back.'

'I've often wondered who was lucky enough to get it. My gran worked at Ropemaker's Yard, before she married.'

'So did my grandfather.'

As the strangers digested this new information, a tower of a man with eyebrows like Fair Isle yarn appeared.

'Hi, I'm Spencer Armstrong, Zak's uncle once removed, and Esme's dad. You must be Joel. I could write a PhD about you, the Rose Foundation, and the famous Kurt Van Lynden's ecological exploits. He's already got our wives in a flutter and they haven't yet had the pleasure.'

The strong handshake was as warm as a winter fire. Joel was back on safe ground. 'If I can tear him away from his fans I'll introduce you. Thanks for bringing Zak and Esme along. Your cousin tells me you were responsible for saving the Ropemaker's Yard tower.'

Gil said, 'Joel's gran worked there.'

Spencer's astounded head swivelled between Gil and Joel. 'So did our grandfather! How about that. I wonder if they knew each other? Grandad Norman was born in Wells but left for London when the going got tough. He left his chalet and beach hut to the family. We've been coming here all our lives, haven't we Gil?'

A jubilant shriek drew the three heads in the direction of the jukebox. 'That's my wife, Nicole. Best warn your mates to take cover as she's settled in for the night.'

Joel said, 'We're a benign bunch of obsessive nature lovers so she'll be in safe hands. So, erm, where does Marianne fit in?'

'Joel thought Marianne was Zak's mother,' said Gil, his smile crooked with amusement.

Spencer threw back his head, revealing several impressive mercury deposits. 'Ha! Marianne has a son your age Joel. She's a family friend and is doing a spot of work for us at The Tower. I don't think she expected to be dragged out tonight, so let's hope the Norfolk hospitality is up to scratch.'

Shifting awkwardly, Joel prayed the cousins hadn't noticed his burnished cheeks in the dimly lit pub. He felt like one of those unfortunate crabs at Blakeney, lifted out in a bucket to be prodded and poked, before enduring the whole pointless process all over again. Just as he was about to make his excuses, a 'cuddly, cuddly' chant rose up amidst a storm of clapping and stomping. The karaoke was about to start.

'Sorry fellas, gotta go. It's time for the entertainment.' Joel put his hand out to the cousins. 'It was great to meet you. I appreciate you coming. Have a nice night.'

❀ GIL ❀

THE BEACH was almost deserted, apart from half a dozen or so regular dog walkers, of which Gil was one. He sat on beach hut steps, (one in a long line of brightly painted huts nestled between pine forest and the vast beach), holding a mug of tea, while the early morning sun warmed through his lightweight Harrington jacket. Rudy was charging up and down, tail flapping like a bedsheet on a washing line. Despite a rough night, Gil awoke early and crept out. He'd never been one for lying in, unlike Imogen, who loved lazing in bed on high days and holidays. It was good to start the day quietly, just him and the dog.

The Windlass hadn't changed much, apart from a lick of paint and new furniture. It was the only place in which to drown his sorrows on a wet Thursday evening four years ago, after yet another 'discussion' with Imogen about the future of their marriage. It was a period when a series of distressing and challenging events had stacked up: his sister Bonnie's death; Zak's over-emotional move from state primary to private secondary; Urbane's new contract with a countrywide corporate chain. Gil and Spencer had also argued, the first time ever. The cause of Spencer's peculiar mood was a mystery, but his suggestion to sell the company had knocked Gil for six. Rather than facing it, he had hightailed it to Norfolk, and the solace of The Tower.

Acutely aware of his alcoholic father's legacy, Gil's decision to get drunk was consciously made, provided he could find a down-to-earth pub in which to do it. No one had bothered him that night as he downed pint after pint until he physically could not take another drop. Gil had walked out of The Windlass' welcoming hearth into the cold Norfolk air, and weaved his way to the quay where he threw a handful of Bonnie's ashes into the water, fulfilling a promise to his mother. His sister lived at the Lee Morell Lodge for many happy years until a short illness took her. Gil was convinced that Bonnie's brain trauma was the result of his heavily pregnant mother's fall down the stairs. If it were an accident, why would Jimmy Knox have taken off? He must have known the extent of Bonnie's injuries but still never came back.

The replay of that awful night generally rose to the surface during times of stress: Aunt Jean comforting Lena while Uncle Lionel stands nose to nose with the old man, *Now Jim, the police are on their way so best you bugger off. If you ever show your face around here again, or lay a hand on my sister, it won't be them you'll have to worry about.* Lionel was a mild-mannered manager at the local building society. Maybe Knox was jealous. He'd often taunt Lionel and once, in a drunken rage, Knox almost dislocated his jaw. That was the only time Gil ever heard Lionel speak that way, and the last time he saw Jim Knox: market porter; bare-knuckle champion; violent bully; failed father.

The Windlass may have been overhauled, but it retained a warmth that only locals could bring. The buzz reminded him of long ago, when the sacred Saturday night partying was the one bright spot on his troubled teenage mind. He'd taken to bunking off school, rotating between geography and religious education classes so as not to get caught, but of course he did. Lena had properly whacked him just once, and the memory of it had crystallised in his cells. As she raised her arm that second time, they both realised the horror of it. What was to separate her from Jimmy Knox if she acted the same way? His mother never raised her arm again, and from that moment on, life improved dramatically. Uncle Lionel moved them into his house nearby. Spencer had made room in his bedroom for his young cousin, and henceforth he and Lionel became Gil's knights in shining armour.

Lionel had an extension built to provide Lena and Bonnie the space they needed; he organised specialist care; he discovered the Lee Morell Lodge in Epping which provided independent living for Bonnie when she came of age. When money arrived anonymously through the letterbox, his mother gave it to charity. Word got back that Jimmy Knox had lost his job at the Covent Garden flower market and was last seen bundled into a police van outside the local pub. Soon after, when the coroner stated the cause of death as brain haemorrhage, the family heaved a collective sigh of relief. Lena scattered his ashes in Victoria Park's boating lake on a Sunday morning at dusk, where they had their first date, when hopes were high.

Gil shivered. He rinsed the enamel mug and locked the beach hut. Rudy bounded over, ready to return home for breakfast and a tussle with Zak. As they made strides towards The Tower, he thought back to the previous evening. He had deliberately left Rudy behind as an excuse to leave the pub early, not that anyone would have noticed. The plan was to apologise to Marianne for hauling her out, but she was in conversation with Joel Midwinter. Gil was baffled by the ranger. He was nice enough, and the fact that their grandparents had worked at the chandlery was interesting, but there was something he couldn't quite pin down. Why was this guy so interested in Zak? Maybe he had a fancy for Marianne, hence the invitation. His colleagues were annoyingly friendly. A perky young woman called Meg Swayne seemed to think that Zak was genuinely interested in their line of work. The rangers weren't to know his well-mannered son was fickle: everything from drumming, to skateboarding to judo, each hobby jettisoned in favour of the next, just as this new interest would inevitably be. Football was the glue that bonded them. Zak was by no means the best player, but he was enthusiastic, and didn't mind his dad shouting the odds on the touchline.

Gil let himself into the house. Laughter and the smell of roasted sausages bombarded his senses. As he passed Marianne's room, he heard faint noises. Who could blame her for keeping out of sight? Nicole was so bloody rude, and Imogen's warm welcome act convinced no one, as she had always been indifferent to Marianne's presence. With Zak dragging her here, there, and everywhere, he resolved to make amends as soon as the moment presented itself.

'Great timing, Gil. Breakfast's ready.'

Gil filled Rudy's bowl with fresh water and pulled out a chair while Spencer placed a breakfast plate on the table. Such was the light-hearted babbling, he may as well have been invisible.

'I couldn't believe it when 'Cuddly Kurt' and Joel sang that eighties song, and the entire pub joined in. Some bromance! What was it called, Spence?'

'*Cuddly Toy*. Roachford.'

'That's the one! Those rangers know how to enjoy themselves, although Kurt was more 'flirty' than 'cuddly' from what I saw.' Nicole cackled. 'Gil, you missed a cracking night. We danced and sang all night long, didn't we, Imogen? My feet are killing me this morning.'

Nicole's dressing gown just covered her expanding chest. She pushed away a clean plate and moved a cup and saucer in its place. No apples for breakfast this morning, then. 'Good for you,' said Gil.

'I'd forgotten karaoke was so fun! I must tell Annette about it. Perhaps it's time for a revival,' said Imogen, as Esme slipped off her lap, feeling the texture of her ponytail plait.

Imogen picked up a tangerine. Gil watched her methodically peel the skin and every single strand of rind, before popping segment by segment into her mouth. She was still in her pyjamas and was unusually jaunty. A distasteful flurry swirled in his gut. 'Please don't tell me you got up to sing?'

'How could I refuse Kurt after the attention he lavished on Zak and Esme. In fact, we all had a turn – well, almost all.'

Zak and Esme were pulling one end of a toy bone while Rudy made pretend growling noises at the other. 'Hey, Dad, me and Esme sang, *I'm Forever Blowing Bubbles*. Practically the entire pub are Norwich City supporters, but everyone knew the words and joined in. It was the best night ever.'

Just then, Marianne walked into the kitchen with her bag over her shoulder, car keys in her hand. Gil's ill-humour was now too rooted to be shifted. 'Sounds to me like you all made fools of yourselves.'

'I beg your pardon?'

'Sorry, Marianne, I wasn't referring to you. Seems I missed a night to remember.'

Marianne ignored the remark. She wasn't about to get drawn into a family squabble. 'Zak, it's nine-thirty.'

Zak jumped up. 'I'm ready.'

'Where are you going?'

'Mum said I can go as long as my bag's packed. In case you're worried, Joel's had the CRB checks. He and Kurt are going to Keith's and they've got some things to give me. Joel said it's important to have a good pair of binoculars.'

'What's wrong with the ones we've got, and who the hell is Keith?' said Gil sharply.

'It's a camera exchange. I can pay for them out of my savings. Esme's offered to look after Rudy. Gotta go. See you at the pub.'

The front door banged. Gil pushed the uneaten food away. A conspiracy had taken place, and he'd been left out in the cold. Imogen said nothing further and swanned off for her shower. Nicole knew him well enough to sense another bad mood on the rise, so she quickly followed on with Esme and Rudy reluctantly in tow. Spencer was unusually quiet, which only increased his frustration. All this tip-toing around was driving him crazy. Did they think he was about to lose his rag? Gil rubbed his temples, the beginning of yet another headache. He walked over to the window and scanned the unending sky, wishing he were somewhere else.

🌹 JOEL 🌹

JOEL PUT the mug of tea beside the camp bed. He'd been up for an hour and had sat in the tiny Zen-styled garden, quietly observing his breath, and counting his blessings. Kurt was fast asleep. It was past midnight before they turned in. Joel insisted his inebriated friend drink a pint glass of water as he didn't do hangovers very well. Abstention had never been a problem for Joel. He was determined not to let the 'congenital heart disease' label define him or his future. Extensive research and meticulous care had so far resulted in sustained health. Alcohol, animal fats, and anxiety were out, while home-grown vegetables, regular meditation, and heaps of gratitude were in. Joel loved loud music, but silence was non-negotiable. He tuned in to its immense life-support system several times a day.

As a toddler, his mother and stepfather attributed his general lack of energy to a weak constitution, but their focus was fully engaged on his new twin stepsisters. Irene and Dudley Midwinter believed their grandson to be overlooked rather than neglected and proposed that Joel live with them until their daughter was better able to cope. It was assumed Joel would return home, and though family contact was maintained, his mother never asked for him back. Irene and Dudley were convinced that these early traumas impacted their grandson's health and were subsequently committed to providing him with a secure and loving home. A thorough medical examination revealed Joel to have a narrowed aorta. He was successfully treated with balloon angioplasty, followed by annual check-ups at the Royal Brompton Hospital, visits he had come to look forward to. Sabrina Cohen-Rockley was more than a cardiology consultant. She said he challenged conventions in an endearing, enlightened way and as time passed, his research into alternative healing modalities were of increasing interest to her. *'Whatever it is you are doing, Joel, your heart seems to be in agreement.'*

Sabrina's familial connections to Dorothea and Clifford Rose led to the ranger's role. With no enthusiasm or aptitude for the rigours and regulations of school, an informal meeting was arranged during which the professor's words gave Joel hope that there was something to live for. *Knowledge is important young man, but you can learn as you go. The ability to be still, to observe before reacting, is not so easy. In fact, this is by far the most important requirement of a ranger's role.* It was a match made in heaven. Not only was The Kedge situated in Norfolk, but he could choose the sorts of jobs to suit his energy reserves and skills. Joel had never looked back.

A prolonged groan announced Kurt's re-entry to planet earth. He pushed himself up, scratched his stubbly chin, and grinned.

'Morning, Kurt. Tea's on the table. Don't think you'd win the 'Cuddly Kurt' award this morning.'

'Surely it's not sunup? My mouth feels like the inside of a Bedouin sandal.' He drank the tea and the large glass of water in a continuous gulp. 'Aaahhh, that's better. Thanks, mate. Gotta go to the loo.' Kurt scrambled off the camp bed, grabbed his wash bag, and headed to the back of the cabin, ruffling Joel's hair on his way. In less than five minutes he was washed, dressed, and ready to go, not that there was a rush as they were equally content to sit still. It came with the territory.

Kurt unfolded the chair and sat opposite at the camping table. 'This looks good, Joel.'

Joel had laid out two bowls of fresh fruit, coconut yogurt, seeded bread, and a jar of almond butter. A pot of green tea sat in the centre, with two handless cups on either side. 'Grandad has offered to cook you a full Norfolk if you're up for it.'

'That's good of him but this'll do nicely. Apologies for talking rubbish when we got back.'

'In case you don't remember, it was a top night. You've bagged a few new friends.'

'The Armstrong kids are great, and if I rightly recall, Imogen Armstrong has fine pedigree. Can't be easy being married to such a head-turner. She enjoyed her moment in the karaoke spotlight.' Kurt fished in the back pocket of his jeans and passed a business card to Joel.

Imogen Marsalis-Armstrong and Annette Desai
'Urbane Event Management'
Is there another?

'Hmm ... think you got the better half of the deal there, Kurt.'

'Oh, well, it's not as if you'll bump into them any time soon. Norfolk's a big county, whereas Essex, with its curious inhabitants ...'

'I wondered when you'd get around to that. What did you make of Marianne?'

'She's more of a listener than a talker and was attentive to Zak and Esme. Lovely, though. What's the connection?'

'Family friend. The cousins weren't forthcoming when I asked about her but were pleased to tell me that Marianne has a son my age.'

'Skeletons, Joel. Don't open the cupboard. Remind me why we are meeting the family again in half an hour?'

'We're meeting Zak and Marianne in half an hour.'

Kurt's grin spread like sunrays over the valley. 'Oh, yeah? So, it's *more than a feeling* eh, Joel?'

Joel tried to keep a straight face while his best mate jumped up, air guitar swirling, and belted out their all-time favourite epic Boston tune before they collapsed under gales of laughter.

The server set down the tray carrying two filter coffees and two glasses of redcurrant cordial. 'A little birdie told me you had quite a time of it last night, Joel. Sure you don't want to change your order?'

'This'll do nicely, Dawn. Shame you couldn't make it. We missed your reedy warble.'

Smiling at the banter and feeling upbeat, Zak took his drink and sucked at the striped straw, then hastily took it out for fear of looking uncool. 'Thanks so much for showing me Keith's shop. We must have driven past it a million times before and I've never noticed the sign.'

'It's one of North Norfolk's best kept secrets, Zak.' Kurt cast his expert eye over the field glasses. 'He did you a good deal on the Bressers. You'll be amazed at the optics and wild field view. Technology moves so fast these days, so there's always a new 'must-have' bit of kit. Keith's exchange means we can update as we go without breaking the bank.'

Joel passed a folder to Zak. 'Here's your summer holiday homework. You'll soon regret ever meeting us.'

Zak opened it and read out the contents page: 'Neighbours First; How to build a pond; Know your invertebrates; Effective cover.' As his eyes widened at the prospect of what this might mean, Marianne came to his rescue. 'Don't panic, Zak. I'm sure the guys didn't mean for you to do it all in one go.'

Kurt and Joel tried to keep a straight face. ''Course not, but if you want to be a wildlife cameraman, you've got to know what you're filming, so it's best to start with the basics before enrolling on a course with Wildeye or any of the film schools. Tell us about your garden, Zak. What sort of things are going on in there?'

Sensing Zak's awkwardness, Marianne filled the gap. 'My neighbour had frogspawn this year but I've yet to see a frog. The Sycamore Crescent residents made a hedgehog highway through our fences and we've seen several hoglets. These things take time.'

'I didn't know you did all that, Marianne.' Zak turned to Joel and Kurt. 'To be truthful, I've been more interested in football and cricket than our garden's ecosystem. We've got a huge patio, a few trees, one of them has an order or something on it, and a lawn which is cut by the gardener. It's embarrassing.'

Joel's heart swelled for the boy. The last thing he wanted was for Zak to feel dispirited. 'Hey, you've got grass and a tree preservation order which is a bonus. You've not only got bugs, but lots of carbon capture …'

'… and with the help of your gardener, you'll soon get planting, and set up your camera traps and trails. We expect to see evidence of your endeavours before we can induct you into Nature's Hall of Fame,' said Kurt, ice-blue eyes twinkling.

'Tell them what's near your house, Zak,' prompted Marianne.

Zak's perplexed expression morphed into a grin. 'Oh yeah: Epping flippin' Forest!'

Everyone laughed. Joel pulled out a sheet of paper, a pencil and an apple from his rucksack. He drew a large circle. 'Let's get serious for a minute, and I'll show you the sorts of things I do with the schools. Here, Zak, take this apple and tell me everything that needs to happen in order for you to be holding it.'

For the next half an hour, four eager heads filled the circle with as many causes and conditions for an apple to grow: weather, soil, tree, pollinators, fruit pickers, packaging, supermarkets, transport. Joel sat back, grinning. 'This is awesome! It never ceases to amaze me what comes out of these sessions and I learn something new every time. I usually end with a question: What would happen to the apple under climate change conditions?'

Zak exhaled, long and slow. 'That puts a different spin on it altogether. Tell you what Joel, the first tree I'm gonna plant when I get back is an apple.'

'Epic! Now, let's do the same thing with your mobile phone.' Joel watched Zak's startled expression turn into a knowing smile. 'Save that one for homework. Joking apart

Zak, if you come back to Norfolk during the holidays, give me a shout. You can join the rangers for a day.'

'Can I? My grandmothers visit every summer. I'll see if I can hitch a ride, although we usually see the other grandparents in Fiskardo, or St Raphael, but maybe I can get out of that.'

'Zak, there are inverts in Greece and France.'

'But I'd much rather be here, Joel.' Zak looked at Marianne. 'I wish I could stay on with you this week.'

Kurt nudged his knee. Joel clamped his jaw to stop from laughing out loud. Then, 'How will you spend your holiday, Marianne?'

'Painting the living rooms in The Tower, Joel. If it goes well, there may be time to take my sketch book to Natural Surroundings. I've heard the wildlife gardens are special.'

'You've brought your sketch book!' Zak turned to his new buddies. 'Marianne's so fab at drawing. We used to jostle to sit next to her at Hazelwood Primary or during break as she always found time to help us. It was super exciting when the chickens and donkeys first arrived, and then the veg patch, wasn't it Marianne?'

'Hazelwood's head teacher was inspirational. When the school closed at the end of term and the head retired, I couldn't face travelling to the new one, so I handed in my notice, and am now self-employed.'

Joel was acutely aware of Marianne's discomfort. He raised his glass. 'Well, then, here's to a new start!'

They clinked cups and glasses and swapped phone numbers. Joel and Kurt waited until Marianne's car disappeared in the direction of Burnham Market.

'Have you got time for another coffee?

'Sure, Joel. Today's a light day. Got a busy week coming up, so why don't you and me make plans.'

While Joel was in the café, Kurt checked his phone. A quick scroll through the long list of messages revealed nothing that couldn't wait another hour. There was something going on with Joel and he wanted to know what it was. 'Hey, is that a coffee?'

'Yeah, with oat milk. My once-weekly treat. I'm feeling reckless.'

'Are you sure you don't want to come to London on Wednesday? The production team is based near the Wetland Centre, so we could check out my new lenses.'

'It's tempting, Kurt, but I'm washing my hair.'

'Ha! You're planning to rescue the maid Marianne from The Tower. Methinks this is quest worth pursuing.'

'Do you, Kurt? Could Marianne be interested in me?'

'Who knows, my friend? She didn't give much away. When Zak talked about her job and the sketching, she blushed like fury. She's no red breasted sap sucker, that's for sure. There was no mention of a husband, or partner, and no ring, which doesn't mean much. There's only one way to find out.'

'Aw, forget it. Marianne only came this morning because Zak asked her to. What the hell was I thinking?'

Kurt was despairing. He'd spent years trying to convince Joel there was room in his life for a partner. No human alive deserved to be loved more than he did, and who knew how long anything lasted. It wasn't for the lack of opportunity. 'Marianne is intelligent, easy on the eye, and possibly single. If not, friendship is a good second best.'

'Yeah, friendship I can do.'

'She may need a break from decorating. You could buzz over to Wishbone Heath. If lady luck is shining, you might find a Green-flowered Helleborine.'

'Hey, that's an idea! She must be a wildflower sort of gal from her description of Sycamore Crescent, and her proposed visit to Natural Surroundings.'

'Sycamore Crescent, eh?'

'Hedgehog corridors, too. I'll take a few books along for Zak, and if Marianne is busy, or thinks I'm a nut job, I'll slide down my rope and skulk off back to my brock.'

'That's my boy!' Kurt stood up. 'Thanks for the coffee, and for your marvellous hospitality. What an epic homecoming! We'll get cracking on the 'Day in the Wild Life' project before the nest building starts.'

'And I'll let you know how I fare with the fair maid.'

MARIANNE

BURNHAM MARKET was heaving. There was, however, an orderliness to the chaos as parking restrictions and a new car park took much of the strain. Earlier that morning Marianne was vaguely aware of a headache starting, but it was now squatting above her right ear, and had throbbed throughout the camera shop visit. Just as they were about to give up the search for a quick drop off, a convertible sports car whizzed out of a free parking space right in front of them. Who knew if traffic angels really existed, but Marianne thanked them anyway. With luck the handover wouldn't take long as she was desperate for a rest.

Zak ran on ahead. Rudy had spotted him and was yapping at full volume while straining at his lead, which was tied to a leg of the eight-seater pub bench. Marianne was too tired to care what sort of reception to expect as the ordeal was almost over. She was so grateful to live alone. Tension rippled through the Armstrong family with no attempt to disguise it. Nicole had done a fine job of acting as if she was invisible, and Imogen's attention span ended before it began. As Marianne approached the bench, the women were facing her, hidden behind huge sunglasses, no doubt scrutinising her daywear. Spencer was already inspecting the binoculars, while Zak's enthusiasm overflowed like boiling milk.

'Hey, Mum, Keith's shop is awesome! It's at the back of his house, and you have to have an appointment. He's got so much equipment, and not just cameras but also traps and tripods. If the binoculars aren't suitable he'll give a full refund. Kurt and Joel get their kit there. Oh, yeah, we did this apple test at the café, and I …'

'Slow down, son. We've got time to hear about it over lunch.' Gil made space for Marianne to sit. 'What can I get you to drink?'

'I've just had something, thanks. I was going to head back but I haven't got the keys.'

'Marianne, we are so grateful to you for accompanying Zak this morning. Please, help yourself to whatever's left in the fridge. The cleaning company will be in on Friday. No need to clean through.'

Gil and Spencer glared at Imogen who had remained seated during the cold dismissal. Even Nicole had glanced sideways. Spencer rose immediately and went to her side. 'Thank you so much for your company, the delicious food, and for your help this weekend, Marianne. Call if you need anything at all.' He pressed the house keys into her hand, holding his hand there for a fraction longer before returning to his seat.

Just as Gil was about to walk her back to her car, Zak and Esme ran over and wrapped themselves about her so tightly, she stepped back so as not to topple over.

'Thanks a million for the binoculars, Marianne, and for coming this weekend. It's been so fab!'

'Zak, please tell me you didn't let Marianne pay for those?'

Ignoring Gil's rebuke, Marianne took a package out of her bag and swallowed hard. The children's warmth had pushed her terrifyingly close to tears. 'Esme, this print is for you. Zak and I chose it from the Nature Shop. They'll change it if you don't like it. It's been so lovely to see you again.' Without another word, she got back in her car and drove away as steadily as she was able. As soon as she was out of eyeshot, Marianne pulled the car into a side road, and sobbed.

Like shallow beach water shelving into the deep, so the nap became a slumber which lasted into the early evening. Once Marianne had re-oriented herself, she lingered in a hot soapy bath, put on her pyjamas, and went upstairs to make tea. While it was brewing, she looked around. Without the family's occupation, The Tower's energy felt altogether softer, the structure secure, comforting even, against the sleek interior and stark décor. Marianne walked past the open plan staircase which led up to the main bedrooms (with no intention of taking a peek), and into the enormous living room. Several paintings depicting the coastline's various landmarks hung on the walls, but not so many as to look like a gallery. The L-shaped furniture was a pale oyster, while the only splash of colour came from a jute basket containing several colourful rugs, and a stack of magazines. Perhaps the idea was to let the landscape in.

Of the twenty or so books packed in underneath the television unit, Gloria Stenheim's *My Life on the Road* was the only one of remote interest. Marianne pulled out a dog-eared *Tatler*, which had fallen down behind the books. She checked the magazine's date. Ah, yes, the wedding. Flicking to the society pages, there it was: Imogen Alexandria Marsalis, granddaughter of Lord and Lady Keaton, daughter of grocery magnate Nikolaos Marsalis and Cilla

Octavia Marsalis. Married Gilbert Lionel Armstrong etc at Cleve Castle in the company of two-hundred guests and so on. The event was unlike anything Marianne had ever been to before and was ever likely to experience again. Lena had been stony-faced throughout, and had sat out her only son's celebrations in a plush guest suite while everyone else danced the night away to the eighteen-strong band, or was it a small orchestra? Freddie's puff had run out long before the never-ending wedding breakfast ended, so Marianne slipped out to drive him home. Spencer's mother, Jean, told her later that, as was Greek custom, the guests had pinned fifty thousand pounds to Imogen's exquisite silk chiffon gown! Marianne studied the pictures of Gil. Did he enjoy it? His frozen-faced grin must have ached by the end of the night.

The fridge was, as Marianne suspected it would be, bulging with food and drink, enough to last a fortnight. The Armstrongs were obviously not concerned about waste. She was suddenly reminded of her father's wise words, *it takes all sorts to make the world go round*, so swallowing her judgement, she put together a plate of leftover quiche and salad, poured a glass of *Pinot Noir*, and sat out on the balcony. The evening sky was rapidly changing colour. It was tempting to run downstairs for her watercolours in an attempt to capture the blushed grey and pink striations before they faded into deep umbers and blues, but that could wait for another day. Della had sent a text message. She'd know exactly why Marianne had been engulfed by the huge emotional wave: leaving the job; fatigue; missing her son; her complex relationship with the Armstrongs. Seeing Zak and Esme again was a painful reminder of the children she had left behind at Hazelwood Primary, but it was reassuring to see they were happy and were loved, even if their parents showed little affection for each other.

Marianne shuddered. The evening breeze was cool, and it was getting late. Reluctantly she went inside to wash the few pieces of crockery and cutlery. The pull-out larder revealed a box of hazelnut shortbread and pot of luxury hot chocolate, just the ticket before turning in. None of the DVDs tempted her to a night in front of the television. Maybe it was best to avoid all stimulus, to see what her mind brought to the surface. After all, wasn't she supposed to be in one of those transitions where you move from one phase of life to the next, and a period of quiet was just the thing? Marianne made her way downstairs and slid under the cool white cotton duvet. Zak had sent a 'goodnight' text, and she had finally replied to Della, and to Freddie, who remembered where she was. He actually wished her a happy holiday!

Knowing her loved ones were safe, she expected to drop off immediately, but sleep was a slippery as a March eel. Marianne rewound her thoughts to Wells beach, to the fates of the beautiful grey seal pup and his mother. She sat up, ashamed of her forgetfulness. Why hadn't she asked Joel if the pup had been safely returned? It was too late to send a message, although surely he would have mentioned it at the café if something bad had happened. Marianne flopped back down on the pillow. Her thoughts turned to the rangers. Joel and Kurt had been extraordinarily attentive to Zak. While she browsed through the rack of photographic prints, half listening to their conversations, they patiently explained to him the business of binoculars, film cameras, and photographic equipment. Later, at the café, she and Zak were amazed by the apple story. Zak's alert young mind was already joining dots, retrieving previously stored abstract knowledge which made practical sense when re-positioned in this way. In the space of a conversation, he understood how important his choices were, the difference he could make, and how empowering that knowledge was.

Although reluctant to go out, Marianne was glad she went. It was thoroughly entertaining to hear Joel and Kurt's stadium rock renditions with the crowd singing at the top of their jubilant voices. Swept up in the excitement, she had joined in with the *Cuddly Toy* song's call and response from her position at the back of the pub. It was lovely to see two grown men so openly affectionate with each other. Hazelwood choir was fun, but it was no match for The Windlass crowd. After chatting to the rangers, she walked back to The Tower under a twinkling sky in Zak and Esme's chattering company, while Imogen and Nicole clung to Spencer as he steered them safely along. No one seemed remotely surprised or concerned at Gil's disappearance.

At last, a rush of melatonin flooded in, weighting her eyelids like heavy velvet curtains. Just as she was about to drift off, the phone pinged.

Forgot to say pup and mum happily reunited.

Goodnight Marianne.

Grateful and relieved, Marianne's last waking thought was of the seal pup swimming contentedly with his mother in the cold, clear waters of Wells beach.

LENA AND JEAN

LENA ARMSTRONG lifted the gilt picture frame and kissed the sepia-tinted face of her beloved brother. After carefully polishing the glass, she returned Lionel to his rightful place in the centre of the walnut bureau, which was situated at the far end of the room by the garden, shielded from the sun by lined floral curtains. This used to be his favoured place on which to update his paperwork, do the crossword, or reflect in relative quiet. Now it was covered by a shoal of family photographs: Gil and Bonnie; the five grandchildren; Lionel and Jean's wedding day; Lauren and Spencer's graduations; Marianne and Freddie; Gil and Imogen's wedding – that one she couldn't bring herself to kiss. As much as she tried for her son's sake, Lena would never understand why he'd married her. Oh, Imogen was nice enough under the gloss, and she was a good mother to Zak when she wasn't gallivanting around hosting those 'events' as she called them, but there had been too much *Surprise Surprise*, and not enough traditional home making for her liking.

Jean accused her of being 'old school'. Why shouldn't women enjoy a career and children, especially when there were family to pitch in. She ought to be grateful to Imogen, as it was looking increasingly unlikely that Gil would ever marry, let alone have a child. Lena sighed. Now, that much *was* true, and she had been concerned. While Lionel and Jean clocked up a nice tally of grandchildren, she had watched Gil's long-legged fillies come and go like the changing of the guard. But as soon as he mentioned bringing his new 'partner' to meet her, Lena knew, in the way that only a mother can, that he would marry her. Even by Gil's standards, Imogen was a knockout, or that's the word Lionel had used. The young woman's sophistication was so far out of Lena's experience, her instinct was to withdraw. Jean hadn't accused her outright of jealousy, but so what if she was? It didn't change the fact that Gil and Imogen were a bad fit. Ambitious – yes, they had that in common, and as for a baby, they were never in one place together for long enough to do the necessary but against all the odds, Zak arrived.

Moving on to Spencer's photograph, Lena smiled. He'd made a fine best man, and his speech went down well, that much she remembered. Spencer was just like Jean: both were glass half full types. When Nicole announced her late-in-the-day pregnancy, he had stuck with it even though they'd only planned for Georgia, but now Spencer and Esme were as thick as thieves, bless them. Zak's final primary school photo was his best. Lena ran her thumb over his handsome face. He was the most sensitive of the grandchildren, a quality that cannot have come from Imogen's family as the mother was as cold as sheet ice. Admittedly, the father was warmer. Nik Marsalis had gone overboard to make her welcome during the pre-wedding lunch. He laid on such a spread, most of which she couldn't pronounce let alone eat, and it was served by waiting staff! Nik had taken a shine to Gil which was no surprise as her boy was also a self-made man, and he appreciated the hard work that went into building a business. Their giant of a house sat on the edge of Wentworth golf course and Gil had obliged his father-in-law by playing a round on the few occasions the jetsetters were home. Cilla Marsalis may have had the good fortune to have been adopted from a Malaysian orphanage by lord and lady, but she was a cut-glass tart who had brazenly flirted with Gil *and* Spencer during the spectacle they called a wedding!

'Lena, tea's ready.'

Happy that the photographs had been dusted to her satisfaction, Lena returned the polish and cloth to the enamel house-keeping tin. She was about to turn away, when an instinct to look at the only existing photograph of her ex-husband swamped her. She slid the back off of Gil's wedding picture and took out the faded photograph of her and James Knox, posing outside Shoreditch Town Hall just minutes after they were married. The navy two-piece suit and velvet pillbox hat with netting had felt so feminine, and Jimmy couldn't have looked more handsome in his single-breasted green tweed with a white rose buttonhole. A shiver ran through her at the memory of their first night in the bedroom above the saloon bar, after their meal with Lionel, Jean, and Jimmy's best man, Dino Scuderi. Jim's rough hands were electrifying, and the terrifying realisation that those hands could be used in such a brutal manner would be revealed in just a few months. Even Gil's happy arrival was short-lived. She wasn't to breast-feed him, it was wrong; she wasn't to pick him up every time he cried, or he'd end up soft, like Lionel; she hadn't the right to ask him where he'd been, reeking of booze and perfume. And yet, Jim's remorse was almost believable, as were his rough hands, pulling her back …

'Lena! The tea's going cold.'

A tear dropped onto the old photograph. Lena wiped it with her cloth, and tucked it back into the frame, behind the smiling faces of her son, and his wife. She locked the door on her remembrances, pulled a tissue out of her housecoat, and blew her nose. The mouth-watering smell of freshly baked rock cakes wafted around the kitchen. She'd never been much of a cook, apart from steak pudding, which Lionel had loved. In fact, the boys occasionally asked for it when they came for lunch, every first Saturday of the month, a long-standing tradition since moving to Epping. Lena winced as she lowered herself heavily into the chair. Jean kept on about getting the hip seen to, and the boys would pay for the operation, but unless her leg was hanging off, they'd have to drag her kicking and screaming. Bonnie's regular hospital visits and surgery were enough to put anyone off for life.

The immaculate countertops, oven, sink, and taps met with her approval. Jean always kept her domain in good order, no matter how many bodies needed feeding or taking care of. Was it sixty years ago they'd hopscotched outside the houses in Valance Road? Lena knew her brother would marry her best friend, much to their mutual parents delight. Not so when she married Jimmy Knox. Her mother was furious, said she always went for the wrong 'uns and she'd live to regret it. Lord knows what would have happened if Lionel and Jean hadn't taken her in. The children were treated as one big family with two mothers, and one father who was worth twenty.

'Try one of these, Lena. I've added cranberries. They've got vitamin C in them, which will help your hip.'

Lena took a cake. Jean was always trying something or other to improve their health. Monday's 'Shake and Rattle that Roll' class at the community centre was the best of their endeavours to date, as Nigel had them in fits. 'Gil's popping over after work. He sounded down in the dumps, although I can't think why. The boys love going to Norfolk.'

'It's the anniversary, Lena.'

'Eh?'

'Gil must have been thinking about Bonnie. I don't know why we insist on marking her death date. If you ask me its morbid.'

Although Lena struggled to recall dates, the agony of Bonnie's death day would be taken to her grave. There was someone who always remembered. 'Marianne is taking me to Lee Morrell Lodge to see the memorial trees. You can come but it might be a bit morbid for you.'

'No need for sarcasm, Lena.' Jean cut her cake in half and blew its hot surface. 'Well, it has been a while, and we don't see Marianne as much as we used to. She and Bonnie were so close. Yes, I'll join you. The Lodge gardens are lovely this time of year.'

'I don't know how Marianne finds the time to help with the fund raising. It's a shame that Nicole has never shown the same interest in supporting the Lodge.'

'Nicole manages the charity shop, Lena. It's a major income stream for the charity.'

'Nicole is *paid* to manage the shop, Jean. Anyway, Marianne accepted Gil's offer to re-decorate The Tower. I don't know how she'll survive without that teaching assistant's job. She's not getting any younger, and painting is hard work.'

'She's not forty-five yet, hardly fit for the scrap heap. I'm more concerned she's still living on her own. A woman like Marianne Bly deserves a good man, and not another Warren Silk. Freddie never wanted to keep in touch with his father, and who could blame him, although the boy sizzles with venom, and if he's not careful it'll poison him. I'd love to know what happened to Warren, wouldn't you?'

'When Ida Silk died, the history went with her. She suffered terribly from the shame. Warren could charm the birds from the trees. We used to love his silky ways. I'll never understand why he left her and Freddie in such a mess.'

'Jim left you and Gil, and you had a new baby.'

Lena reared. 'Warren Silk made bad financial decisions and should have stayed with Gil and Spencer in the business, but he was never violent. Warren will regret what he did for the rest of his life.'

The sisters-in-law were silent. Every once in a while the old conversations came up for air like mudskippers, and without Lionel's benign character to keep things smooth, the women occasionally raked up the murky past with no obvious benefits to either of them.

'I'm sorry, Lena. Let's change the subject. Why don't we pop along to the market. We'll finish the housework later.'

Lena hung her housecoat in the utility room. Jean would never know what it had been like to live in constant fear, to feel powerless, unable to protect her children. She had been cherished by Lionel and they had showered their love on Spencer and Lauren. Still, neither would understand the other's experience, so what was the point in trying? 'We'll buy Gil a quart of cockles from the fish stall. If the princess had her way last week, they'd have eaten everything but.'

GIL

GIL LOOKED out of the window, across to Spitalfields Market. Its renaissance never failed to astonish him. The fruit and vegetable market's relocation to Leyton's wider roads provided a fantastic opportunity for redevelopment on the old site. It hadn't taken long before the mix of urban and socially mobile had sparked a vibrant hub. Before property prices hit the stratosphere, Spencer proposed the company invest in one of the units nearby. The central address suited their clients, and the engineers could park their vans in the yard. It was a smart move. Armstrong Solutions currently employed ten full-time staff of whom the six highly skilled engineers were often sub-contracted out; they had an enviable list of private clients whose property portfolios increased annually, and they had earned industry-wide respect. The company was as solid as a rock.

It was a relief to be back in the office. The company's day to day scheduling ran like clockwork, enabling him and Spencer to take the same holidays when it suited them. The first week of the summer break usually meant quality time at The Tower, but this year it hadn't delivered the respite Gil had come to expect, and he wanted to discuss it with Spencer. It had taken the morning to work through the backlog with their indispensable assistant, Niall Osgood, whose father Clive, one of Gil's oldest friends, had worked for the company since it began.

Teenage Niall wasn't far off a spell in custody, and eager to help, Gil offered the wayward young man a job. Until then, he and Spencer had dealt with their own paperwork, but as Armstrong Solutions reputation and business grew, they needed someone to act as more than a secretary, and Niall had expanded the role, making it his own. Birthdays and anniversaries were no longer forgotten; gig dates and reunion venues were sourced, and coffee arrived just at the right time.

'Morning, Gil. You're booked to see Hugh Ridley at the Hatton Garden office. Dad said the van's suspension needs checking, so I called the garage. Oh, and Ashley's pregnant.'

Gil put down his coffee and hugged him warmly. 'Congratulations, Niall! How did you keep that from the old man?'

'We told him on Friday. First-time granddad. I may need some time off for appointments and stuff.'

'Sure. Take as much as you need. When is Spencer due back?'

'I'm back.' Spencer hung up his jacket. 'What's occurring?'

'Niall's joining the ranks.'

Spencer swallowed the slim man in his giant hug before putting the grinning assistant down. 'Lunchtime drinks to celebrate?'

'Sorry, Spencer, you've a meeting with Maurice Becker at midday. Let's make it Friday so the guys can join us.'

'Great idea. Has Gil told you about our karaoke night?'

'Yeah. Sounds like you enjoyed yourselves. What tune did you sing, Gil? *Too much, Too Young*? *Hands Off She's Mine*?'

'Not me mate. I scarpered as soon as the frolicking started.'

'How was Norfolk? Entertaining the kids in the rain must have been a challenge.' There wasn't much Niall didn't know about the Armstrongs. Zak and Esme's parties were more outlandish every year. Who else but Urbane Event Management would recreate the *Mad Hatter's Tea Party* at Hatfield Forest for Esme's eleventh birthday?

'Zak's got another new hobby. I'll give it a week.'

'He might surprise you, Gil.' Spencer took a sip of coffee before recounting the story. 'My nephew may be about to get his hands dirty.'

Niall couldn't quite picture Zak digging for worms. Imogen had convinced him to consider a role as a television sports presenter. From Gil's touchline accounts, a professional footballing career was never on the cards, but with Imogen's contacts, Niall wouldn't be at all surprised if that particular dream came true. 'I guess I've got all this to come.'

'Don't make the same mistakes as us. Zak doesn't know the meaning of hardship. Can you imagine him making do with a condensed milk sandwich for his tea? To be fair, it's not his fault. His mother and me can't agree on the best way forward. When your kids have everything, it all becomes meaningless in the end. This wildlife fad is just another of Zak's attempts to relieve his boredom.'

Gil's unprecedented confession stunned the two men. Niall was rescued by the phone and made a swift exit. Spencer sat at his desk and scrutinised his cousin. Since returning to the office, Gil had been unusually quiet. They hadn't discussed the holiday, and neither had mentioned

Marianne. 'I asked Nicole why she ignored Marianne. Do you know what she said? *You and Gil still feel guilty for Warren's behaviour and it's about time you let it go. She doesn't need this family, and probably never did.*'

'Maybe Nicole's got a point.'

'Marianne's a good friend. She visits our mothers more than our wives do, and she does her bit for the Lodge. She was great with the kids this weekend. There aren't too many people who'd be prepared to spend their free time in a pub, and a camera shop with total strangers. Nicole and Imogen might have had their noses put out of joint.'

Spencer's resumé sounded plausible. While his cousin gave the impression his attention was elsewhere, nothing much got past him. Gil walked back to the window. A homeless man was dragging a trolley loaded with his belongings and was hollering at the passers-by who were keeping their heads down. It was Ian Dunne, a face from the old days who had slipped through the net, but occasionally allowed the Armstrongs to arrange a night in the shelter when he was 'on his uppers.' Niall had gone down to give him a few notes. He was a good man and would make a fine father. Gil rubbed his temples. Everything Spencer said about Marianne was true. At no point had she discouraged Zak. She had accepted the ranger's invitation when she clearly didn't want to go out. Did his son know how fortunate he was to have her on his side? Zak was breaking away, and the pain was unlike anything Gil had experienced. 'What did you make of the ranger and his mates?'

'It's easy to see why Zak was impressed.'

'What d'you mean?'

'Apart from football, when was the last time you met a crowd as passionate? The atmosphere in The Windlass reminded me of university when we were bursting with enthusiasm and innovative thinking. Let's face it, Gil, we need environmentalists more than ever. You should be pleased for Zak. You missed a great night.'

The phone blinked. Gil sat back at his desk and picked up the receiver. This particular conversation with Spencer may have ended, but the churning in his gut had not.

'Another cup of tea, Gil?' Jean Armstrong refilled her nephew's mug without waiting for a reply, and went into the kitchen, leaving mother and her troubled son to talk.

'Thanks for the cockles, Mum. I'm not sure why we didn't get around to it last week. The rain kept us in most of the time.'

'Norfolk can be bleak when the weather's rough. Still, The Tower is cosy enough and you needed a break. How's Zak? I thought you might have brought him with you.'

'Don't talk to me about Zak. He's got another sodding hobby, and this one could be expensive, if it takes hold.'

'What's he doing this time?'

'Zak met a wildlife ranger and his mate who happens to be an award-winning cameraman, so now he wants to follow in their footsteps. He's already got a new pair of binoculars – in fact, Marianne bought them for him, and she also bought Esme a framed wildlife print which won't have been cheap. I was bloody furious. She'd only come to Norfolk to do a paint job, not to spend her pennies on our spoilt kids. You know she's been made redundant?'

'Nicole's friend is on the PTA.' Lena turned stiffly

towards the kitchen. 'Jean, your daughter-in-law has done it again. Nicole's been blabbing about Marianne, and how she's lost her job …'

'No, Mum, she didn't *lose* her job. Marianne chose to leave as she didn't want to drive to the new school, but what I meant was …'

'I know what you meant, Gil, and it was wrong of Zak to let her buy those things, but that's the way Marianne is. She loves the kids and with Freddie living in Liverpool, we mothers have to find an outlet. I just hope Imogen doesn't mind.'

'Why should she mind?' Their eyes locked. His mother was about to say that Imogen was resentful but had thought better of it. He'd long since given up telling her that Imogen had wanted to be at home with Zak for those first few months. Did it matter that she had worked right up until the week before he was born? Gil moved his tight jaw from side to side. The only time he had ever agreed with his mother was on the issue of childcare. What was the point of a nanny, a complete stranger, when Lena and Jean were willing to help out. Esme spent two days a week with them while Nicole was at the charity shop. Imogen had insisted her nanny was as good as family, but eventually she relented. Shortly after, her visits to the bungalow ended. Christmas and birthdays were the only times his wife and mother saw each other, and even that was an unbearable strain.

Jean returned with a fresh pot of tea and a cheery smile. 'Did your mum tell you that Marianne is taking us to the Lodge, to commemorate Bonnie?'

'That's nice of her Jean. They were good friends.'

'We're going to offer Marianne our car when the new one arrives. Her Fiat is on its last legs. Just about got through the MOT.'

'Please don't do that, Mum. Marianne won't take it. It was hard enough getting her to accept the going rate for the decorating job. She must be sick of our charity. If we're not careful, we'll chase her away.'

'Don't be daft, Gil. Marianne is as much a part of this family as Imogen and Nicole are, and what we do with our money is none of your business' said Lena, her face and neck flushing.

Gil pulled on his jacket. The visit wasn't going well. 'You're right. It's none of my business. Imogen's off to Singapore tomorrow, so I'd best get home.' He kissed his aunt, and his mother followed him to the door.

'Is everything alright, son?'

'Yes and no. To be truthful, it wasn't a great week away. Zak's growing up so fast, I hardly recognise him.'

Lena grabbed him for a brief hug. Apart from the grandchildren, she'd never been one for cuddles and alarmingly, Gil wanted to cry. As a kid, it was always Jean that hugged him, and that was only when Lena wasn't around. Gil had never been able to work his mother out. She didn't want anyone else to show him affection and yet she wasn't willing or able to give it to him herself. This was all down to Jimmy Knox. Gil never used the word 'father', and thankfully Lena had never judged him for it. He kissed her soft, powdered cheek and walked out of the cool hallway into the early evening sunshine.

MARIANNE

THE FRESH new morning poured through the balcony doors. Marianne laid down her breakfast tray of coffee and warm *pain au chocolat* and sat down. The blend of physical work and ozone-saturated air had the magical effect of great sleep and a re-emergence of energy. Gil and Spencer had thoughtfully moved the living room furniture away from the walls and had set up a step ladder. Once she had covered the sofas and the floor she immediately got to work, and on this, the third day, she was almost done. The pastry was delicious. Marianne tingled with pleasure at her good fortune to be here, right now. If her calculations were correct, by early afternoon the final coat of paint would be drying and she'd celebrate with a picnic at the beach hut, armed with sketch pad and pencils, and there she'd remain until sunset.

Looking out over Ropemaker's Yard, Marianne's imagination stirred into life. What must it have been like amidst the hustle and bustle, when Wells had been an important fishing and commercial port whose skilled shipwrights made ropes and sails in yards such as this? Like so many other coastal towns and villages, reinvention was essential to survival, although the cost to the locals was often high. Gil and Spencer must have felt some discomfort at owning a holiday home, despite family connections. Maybe their guilt, if any, was assuaged by using The Tower as often as possible and renting the holiday chalet cheaply to their employees. Gil had generously offered her an extended stay, as the next visitors weren't due for another week. Now here, Marianne wished she had accepted. The Tower's creaks and groans had fast become familiar friendly greetings, and its ambiance beguiling, but with a list of work commitments to be honoured, another Norfolk visit would have to wait.

Perhaps she could rent the chalet sometime? That's what she and Warren had done when Freddie was a toddler. It was a holiday of sandcastles, ice creams, and her 'boys' braving the shockingly cold water. That was before Warren had secretly second-mortgaged the house to invest in a Mediterranean holiday resort scam, only to file for bankruptcy before fleeing the country with debtors in pursuit. That was before her happy-go-lucky son crossed the bridge to introversion and sullenness and spite. There was so much love in Freddie, she was sure it would rise again to the surface. Acutely aware of how quickly her pleasant thoughts had been hijacked, Marianne finished her coffee and took the tray back into the kitchen. Didn't she promise herself to make new memories, ones in which she actually played the starring role for a change? Della would approve of that. Just as she was about to open a fresh tin of emulsion, her phone buzzed.

Morning, Marianne. Trust the job's going well. I think I left my black zip-up work folder behind. Would you mind having a scout round. I'll pick it up with the keys on Friday. Thanks, Gil.

Marianne walked through the various rooms but couldn't see anything resembling a folder. Did Gil mean for her to look in his bedroom? She sighed and climbed the stairs, pausing at the top. Directly ahead was a semi-circular viewing area with a padded window seat, and on either side were doors into what had to be Gil and Spencer's bedrooms. Marianne walked onto the landing and picked up the binoculars. The immense stretch of North Sea merged with the horizon with scarcely a join. She was no expert at bird identifications but was sure she spotted an arctic tern amongst the gulls as they circled and spiralled the skyline, while below was evidence of the town coming to life. After a while, Marianne turned around. No folder in sight. She was drawn to a triptych, 'The Hazelwood Oak' which depicted three aspects of the tree's life: an acorn, a detailed drawing of the tree itself, and a bench. It was hers! The great oak had suffered the ravages of a severe storm, and the local art group had staged an exhibition to celebrate its survival. How had the drawing ended up here? Oh yes, the artwork had been sold as part of a fund-raiser whose proceeds were used to plant a copse of oak trees nearby. Lena or Jean must have bought it.

The nostalgic pleasure of re-encountering her first serious attempt at illustration was uplifting. From way back, Marianne had loved everything that involved paint, crayons, and pencils. When she and her newly separated father traded the bleak life of indifference and neglect in their Ipswich 'family home' for an altogether more stable existence in their Wanstead flat, life improved exponentially. With the help of her aunt Sadie, they hung curtains and chose colourful things for her bedroom in which Marianne, hermetically sealed, spent hours bent over her small desk. Her father had taken a surveyor's job nearby, while she settled in her new school and perfected the art of lying about her family.

Marianne walked towards the bedroom door and there, resting on top of the bedside table was the folder. The enormous sun-filled room was in keeping with the understated colour and style of The Tower. Everything was a shade of white, from the blinds to the furniture, apart from the duvet which was a bleached wheat. No attempt had been made to straighten the bed or plump the pillows. A job for the cleaners. Above it hung a whitewashed framed seascape depicting a winter scene of pallid blues and greys and saved from sullenness by a fan of pearlescent sunrays which cast an ecclesiastical glow across the canvas. The only splash of colour came from Imogen's oriental silk kimono hanging on the half-open door into the ensuite. She had worn it on Sunday at breakfast.

On the chest of drawers stood a framed photograph of Gil, Imogen, and Zak, sitting on the beach hut steps. Next to it were Gil and Bonnie in the Lee Morrell Lodge garden. Darling Bonnie, with whom she had spent hours drawing houses surrounded by bold purple flowers under blue crayon skies and yellow pencil sunrays; Bonnie, whose expressions had a way of making Marianne laugh like no one else, and who loved having her thick carob hair blow-dried, and her nails painted flamingo, her favourite colour. No wonder Gil felt so sad. The tension between him and Imogen was palpable, despite outward appearances. Traces of her perfume and his aftershave lingered in the air and yet, this room didn't feel as if it were one for lovers. Instinctively, Marianne pushed open the huge windows before picking up the folder and making her way downstairs.

The kettle had boiled. Marianne dropped the banana skin into her own version of a compost bag and filled the teapot to the top. After a non-stop stint and a tummy rumble loud enough to bring The Tower tumbling down, it was time for a rest. Munching hungrily on the slice of honey-lashed toast, Marianne was once again drawn to the balcony whose open doors incited her to step outside and witness the magnificent summer day where squawking flocks of gulls were wheeling and diving like circus performers. She broke the crust in pieces and was about to put them on the hand rail when a human voice rose up from below.

'Ahoy there!'

Instinctively she stepped back. It took a while to register who the hat belonged to. What was Joel Midwinter doing here? There was a bag dangling from his raised hand.

'Morning, Marianne! I've brought some books for Zak, but if it's inconvenient, I'll leave them by the door.'

'I'll come down.' Flustered by the unexpected visitor, Marianne closed the double doors and went downstairs. Before the rising turbulence had time to submerge her, Joel's cheerful expression pulled her to the surface. 'Hello Joel. This is a surprise.'

'It's my day off. I was sorting through my shelves and came across a few things to keep Zak rooted to his wildlife quest. I wasn't sure you'd still be here, so I took a chance.'

Marianne wondered if she should invite him in. Would Gil or Spencer object, as the errand was for Zak? 'I've just made a pot of tea. Would you like to join me?'

'Sounds as if you're taking a well-earned break.'

Joel's gaze rested on her emulsion-splattered clothes. She smiled. 'I've been painting all morning. Come up.'

He left his boots by the door before following her upstairs. He paused at the top. 'Wow – what a space! The artwork is impressive.' A huge canvas displaying a tree, made from an OS map whose branches indicated the precise location of the Norfolk coastline, drew him towards it. After examining it, Joel turned to look at the watercolour of Blakeney harbour on the opposite wall.

'Do you know these artists, Marianne?'

'No, but the paintings may have come from local galleries.'

'The watercolour is by Keith Nash, and the 'Map Tree' is a Gemma Harwood. They perfectly suit the interior, not that I know much about these things.'

'Do you take sugar?'

'Nor milk, thanks.' Joel followed Marianne into the kitchen. 'How's it going?'

Marianne put the mugs onto the tray along with a plate of biscuits and faced her cheerful questioner. She took her cue from his infectiously, laid-back manner and relaxed. 'The interior was already painted white, so this hasn't been a difficult job. I was hoping to finish by early afternoon, but I put an extra coat on the utility area, and it was fiddly. Shall we have this outside?'

'Sure. Can I take the tray?'

'Oh, okay. I'll just give my hands a quick scrub.' Marianne buzzed down to the bathroom. As she nail-brushed the paint from her fingers, she checked her reflection. A streak of white paint ran across her dark hair, and spots of white peppered her cheeks. She rubbed the paint pimples off with a pad of cotton wool, but there was nothing else to be done without a shower. Joel hadn't come to admire her complexion, had he? She breathed out and joined him on the balcony.

'*Meles meles*,' said Joel, grinning at Marianne's quizzical expression. 'European badger.'

'Oh, yes, the hair. I forgot my cap. Do you name everything according to its scientific classification?'

'It's a bad habit. Kurt and I do it all the time. Sorry, I didn't mean to offend. It was good to meet Zak's family. If his enthusiasm follows through, their support will be key. What do you think, Marianne?'

'Me? I've no input into Zak's life. His invitation to visit was a surprise. We haven't seen each other for a while.'

'I got the impression you were really close.'

Marianne sipped her tea whilst contemplating this stranger who had appeared from nowhere and was now sitting comfortably as if he were at home. 'Our families go back a long way.'

'Did Gil tell you I thought you were Zak's mother?'

Marianne almost choked on her biscuit. 'No, but then again, Gil Armstrong is a man of few words.'

'And as chilly as the east wind to begin with. It turns out that his grandfather and my gran worked here, at Ropemaker's Yard.'

'Did they? It's a small world.'

'He told me about the chalet and beach hut. The huts are changing hands at sixty grand!' He whistled, as if to say how ridiculous the property market was. 'Spencer said they were in the security business.'

'My ex-partner was the third founder member.'

Joel finished his tea. This was as much as Marianne was going to share, and he had no wish to push his luck. He changed direction. 'Have you had much time to do any sketching?'

'Sadly no, but this afternoon looks promising.' They sat in silence for a while until Joel picked up the binoculars. Sensing that the visit was about to end, Marianne shifted forward in her chair to pick up the tray. Just then, Joel put the binoculars down, and passed her a book from his bag. It was an edition of botanical drawings by Marianne North.

'Is this for me?'

'Zak said you liked to draw flowers and suchlike, and I thought this might come in useful.'

Marianne held the book as if it were a precious object, and slowly flicked through the pages with the tips of her fingers. 'Are you sure you can spare it?'

'Only if you promise not to splash Little Greene paint over it.'

They smiled, and a tiny cosmic cog clicked into place. 'I'll take great care of it.'

'Marianne's not such a common name.'

'My father admired Marianne North. She and her father, Frederick were extremely close, and travelled extensively together. Dad was keen that I had an intrepid and talented role model. If he had lived, I'm convinced we'd have taken flight.'

'I'm sorry to hear that.' A flicker of emotion crossed her brow so quickly, Joel wasn't quite sure if he imagined it. 'Have you seen North's gallery at Kew?'

'Many years ago, but it's on my list to revisit, now I'm an adult.'

Joel smiled at that. 'How long have you been drawing?'

'All my life, but recently it's become more of a quest, although I can't exactly explain why. Also, it doesn't cost much apart from time, which I hope to have more of now.'

'Look Marianne, this may sound bonkers, so you can chuck me out if you like, but I've a proposal. Why don't I help you finish decorating, and then we'll go to Wishbone Heath. There's a rumour the Green-flowered Helleborine has escaped custody, and you won't see anything like her anywhere in the country. My camera's in the car, so we can take a few shots which will help with your illustrations.'

Marianne didn't know what to say. It was bonkers, but an afternoon out was also sorely tempting. Why shouldn't she go? Joel's manner was so disarming, just as he had been on the weekend, and to refuse somehow seemed wrong. 'Yes, I'll come, and thank you, but you're getting the short end of the stick here.'

'We'll see.' Joel clapped his hands. 'Right, let's start with the radio. Nothing revs up the reflexes more than a blast of stadium rock.'

So, for the next two hours, the decorators painted, chatted, drank tea, and sang their way through to the end of a fine job, before driving to Wishbone Heath in the hope of meeting the elusive orchid.

❦ JOEL ❦

IT TOOK just five minutes to drive from The Tower back to the cabin. Joel had a shower, changed into jersey bottoms and a fresh T-shirt, and sat on the sofa with a glass of lemon water. As usual there were a large number of text messages, Tweets and Instagram postings to respond to, but for now, to be quietly breathing was all he wanted.

Joel was accustomed to seeing wonder and delight on the faces of those who witness Mother Earth's treasures, so why was he so pleased to have seen Marianne's reaction to the orchid? She had knelt down to the flower so reverentially and touched the leaves so gently, he had been unable to move for fear of disturbing such a significant moment. It was as if she needed to absorb the intricate nature of the plant so that when she began her drawing, every detail could be recalled. After that, they had wandered through the heath while he pointed out the occasional tree, bird, and insect, taking care not to overload her with information, and waiting for her questions. As they walked back through the copse, Marianne had paused, and in a whisper, she wondered if these places suspended their breath until confident of the human interlopers' intentions before resuming activity. Then, right on cue, a roe deer walked across the understory, less than a hundred metres away. He had laughed at her wide-eyed reaction, and at several other remarks she made.

When they returned to The Tower, she invited him to

share a meal. It was, she said, the least she could do to thank him for an exceptional afternoon. While Marianne prepared dinner, he accepted her suggestion to look at the view from the top floor gallery as it was unlikely the opportunity would arise anytime soon. After several minutes of gorging on the new perspective through familiar eyes, Joel turned to leave and was stopped by the Hazelwood Oak drawing. The detail and colour were striking, particularly the stalk-less acorn: it was a *Quercus petraea*, a sessile oak, and not so common in the south east. In the bottom right-hand corner was a signature: M Bly. It was Marianne's work! There was no denying the latent talent and sympathy in the drawing.

Then, they sat outside with plates of beetroot falafel and mixed pepper salad. She talked about her son, and her summer work schedule; he told her about the cabin in his grandparents' garden, and she had said, *how lovely to live so simply*. Much of the conversation was devoted to Zak. They agreed that whatever the outcome from his toe-dip into the wildlife world, it was a positive thing, and who could predict where these things would lead. Joel thanked her for dinner, promised to post the photographs without delay, and wished her a safe drive home.

It was only nine o'clock – still light, and the night sounds had begun their customary lullaby, but Joel was ready for bed. Kurt's arrival was always a high-octane affair, as was the potential of a new recruit. Zak had already texted him with questions. It was unusual for a youngster to become so engrossed this quickly, but maybe he felt there was ground to catch up on. In any case, once Zak found a local tribe, he'd settle down, and perhaps they'd hook up the next time the family came to Norfolk. Joel lay on the bed. An early night would top up the reserves. Fortunately, tomorrow was a quiet day. He and Lori were scheduled to escort a group of student botanists to the wetland reserve, and Kurt was ready to start on their project. There was at least something of note to tell his friend. While not quite rescuing the maid from the tower, they had taken that first step into ... well, he wasn't quite sure what. Marianne hadn't mentioned a current partner, neither had she asked about his personal life, although Joel hoped to have made it obvious when describing a typical ranger's week. Yes, they could be friends although he had no shortage of those, but there was something about Marianne Bly that threatened to pull him out of a life-long hibernation. It was up to him to make the next move, and for advice, there was no one better than Kurt.

The Windlass was quiet, too early for the Friday crowd, and it gave the friends time to catch up. Joel and Kurt were the first diners of the evening, sharing a celebratory meal. The 'Day in the Wild Life' project was officially underway, and the first batch of film was safely in the can. With Kurt's encouragement and direction, Lori quickly overcame her timidity to reveal an infectious passion. The idea to showcase a number of professional, amateur, and enthusiastic people working and volunteering in the wildlife arena was as yet untested on the public as the focus had been solely on the animal kingdom, but people stories were popular, particularly those whose important work went under the radar. Joel was confident the networks would be interested, particularly as Kurt and Anya were respected, and the timing couldn't be better.

Kurt put down his pint glass. 'So, you helped Marianne finish the decorating, tip-toed around Wishbone Heath, returned for a bite, and waved the maid farewell having vowed to send her your snaps.'

'Yeah, as I said, it was a perfect day.'

Joel's expression was without irony or embarrassment. 'I've gotta hand it to you, mate, you are spectacularly easy to please. Next up, you're gonna tell me that Marianne also had a perfect day.'

'Maybe – I don't know, Kurt. We covered a lot of ground although not much on the personal front. I get the feeling she's happier in the company of children. Marianne's not one for hyperbole – mistress of the understatement, the exact opposite of me.'

'No one alive can match your fizz. Mr Joel Midwinter, king of the exclamation mark.'

They laughed. 'Anyway, we had a chuckle and a singalong, and boy can this bird sing. She's a member of a rock choir – if that's not a sign, then I must be scratching up the wrong bark.'

The bartender brought their food and chatted for a minute before leaving the hungry men to their curried vegetable pie and chips.

'You like rock music, she sings in a rock choir; you're Mister Outdoors and she can paint a nice acorn. That's a start, I guess.'

Joel laughed out loud at his own naiveté. It was at times like this he felt blessed to have a friend like Kurt who was honest, funny, but never unkind. It had been agonising, trying to decide whether or not to drive back to The Tower before Marianne left. She wasn't likely to return any time soon, as much as the Armstrongs insisted she was a 'family friend', but the moment came and went. He wanted to know her better, but the fear of being labelled a stalker was not a risk he was willing to take. 'Look Kurt, I admit it's a tenuous link, but something's going on under my ribcage, and it's nothing to do with my dodgy arteries. You must know what I'm talking about. Tell me what makes Anya so special.'

Resting his knife and fork on the side of his plate, Kurt was uncustomarily serious. 'Anya doesn't need me, but she would like us to know each other, deeply, honestly. She is serious and light-hearted, but always steady – it's me who's moody and can't settle. It's as if there is something eternal running through her veins. I wish I could explain it better Joel. We have our moments, but Anya is always on my side.'

In all the years they had known each other, never had Joel heard him talk about a human being with such tenderness. He slugged a mouthful of apple juice to quell the lump in his throat.

'Joel, when it comes to the natural world, you have passion, curiosity, and a lion's courage. Marianne may turn out to be the greatest love of your life, a pleasant distraction, or a case of mistaken identity.' Kurt raised his pint glass. 'Whatever happens, it's time to go boldly, my friend: to new frontiers!'

The friends raised their glasses and returned to the serious business of being the first to reach the curried vegetable pie summit.

Hi Marianne. How are the drawings coming along? Hope the photos were helpful. Just seen a Banded Demoiselle butterfly at Gosling Wood. Totally awesome! Give me a shout if you'd like a peek. Joel

It was done. Joel put his phone on the side table and sighed. Messages usually flew from his fingers like swifts on the wing, so why this one to Marianne had caused so much consternation and angst was baffling – he'd have taken less trouble texting Sir David Attenborough. The distinct rhythms and beats of his heart were no longer a concern, yet this churning came from his gut, like seasickness, and he'd experienced plenty of that living by the coast. Unsure what to do, Joel lay on his bed and contemplated the blue-green planet poster on the wall opposite. Instantly, calm restored itself. The image of earth taken from space was the first thing he saw when the morning arrived, and the last before he fell asleep. Of the billions of people living on her surface, Joel knew he had found someone with whom he could deeply connect with, but he had no idea if Marianne felt the same. His text was friendly definitely, tentative maybe, but it was a first step.

Ping!

Slowly, Joel. The photos and the book are brilliant aides. I'd love to see the Demoiselle. Merci mille fois! Marianne

Instinct propelled Joel out of bed to pace the floor. She replied! What to do next? *Check the diary, you idiot. Send dates. Offer an overnighter.* Oh, crap: where will she stay? The hotels and guest houses were expensive and in any case, were probably booked up. Maybe he'd try Airbnb. He couldn't suggest his camp bed – well, he could, but he wasn't about to do that at this stage, but what about his grandparents' bungalow? They often put his friends up, and Marianne more than met the criteria. There was also Kurt's Fakenham flat. Joel had a key as he checked the place over during his friend's regular absences and he'd get the green light there. In a nervous frenzy, he scrolled through the Foundation's work schedule. If the dates didn't match Marianne's, he'd either swap with one of the rangers, or offer her different days.

> Fab! How about next Friday or Saturday? If you'd like an overnighter, grandparent's' spare room and Kurt's flat are at your disposal. If not, I'll send other options. Joel

Twenty minutes later, Joel stopped pacing and slid despondently under the duvet. He had to get some sleep and could no longer stare at his phone, willing a reply. If Marianne wanted to come back to Norfolk at such short notice, she'd have to re-arrange her own commitments, so what was the hurry? She agreed to return, and it was so totally miraculous, he could scarcely get his head around it. He turned off the lamp.

Ping!

> Sorry for the delay, Joel. Friday's best for me. I accept your gran's generous offer. Goodnight!

There was nothing else for it. Joel dived out of bed, put his ear plugs in, and belted out one of his bust-a-gut rock songs in sheer, consummate joy.

MARIANNE

MARIANNE TIPPED the new potatoes into a dish, added a knob of butter and a sprinkle of fresh parsley. Supper was ready. It was tempting to eat outside, but the evening had turned chilly and there were wasps on the prowl. It was not a great combination for Della whose fear of flying insects was too ingrained to shift, and she felt the cold like no one else. So, the kitchen table had gone rustic: a bright gingham tablecloth, matching napkins, the best from a mismatch of crockery and cutlery, and a vase containing the last of her farewell floral gifts.

So much for the kitchen. Della wouldn't approve of the living room, so she closed the door on the orchid photos which were white tacked to the walls, the botanical books spread out on her desk, and the discarded sketches scattered like leaf litter. The decision to use Freddie's bedroom for her artwork was postponed. It would mean splashing out on a sofa-bed for the living room which was disruptive in such a small house. Besides, there was now Rachel to consider. During their last conversation, Freddie suggested they meet. He had mentioned various women in passing, but this was the first time a serious contender for his heart had been declared. The least she could do was to offer privacy by way of her son's double bed, and a fresh new duvet cover. The current configuration would have to remain awhile, and anyway, Della could turn her nose up all she liked. Marianne was content with her efforts, and her uncustomary disorder felt reckless, as if school really were out, and she was letting her hair down. She had finally unpacked her eighteenth-century folding botanical microscope from its tiny mahogany box, a present from her father. It was thrilling, as was the faintest scent of their Wanstead home, releasing a log jam of happy memories.

Joel's invitation to Norfolk was too important for a five-minute text exchange. It required a face-to-face conversation during which she and Della could dissect the unprecedented turn of events over a glass of wine. What to make of it? Joel Midwinter's motivation was to encourage Zak, or that's what she believed, until they went to Wishbone Heath. He had stood nearby, as still as a stork, while she knelt down next to the orchid, soaking up its essence. There was magic on the heath, no question. When she stood, his shining eyes met hers, and she had floated along in a haze, barely registering his comments. Her spontaneous offer of dinner ended a sensational day.

Della wouldn't mince her words. Did she fancy Joel? Was there a relationship in the offing? Spencer's comment about the ranger and Freddie being the same age irked her. Joel had mentioned a thirtieth birthday celebration on Mull the previous year. The thirteen-year tally that separated them wouldn't be a barrier for her. Marianne's speculations had strayed into the misty world of relationships, and it was unexpectedly enjoyable to give free rein to her imagination. Further rumination was halted by Della's arrival. Marianne passed her a glass of wine and watered the potted geraniums while her friend unloaded the weekly stockpile of Chickadee shenanigans.

'Hmm, smells grand. Reminds me of Wanstead Hall's kitchen. The boys are playing snooker, so dinner with you was not to be sniffed at. It's been a manic week. Using the house for business may save on the tax bill, but you never get away from it. Anyway, enough of my claptrap, how was your week? I haven't had the chance to ask you about Norfolk.'

'As predicted: frosty on the women front; warm hugs from the children, and a generous bonus for a straightforward job. Nicole and Spencer were there, which wasn't a nice surprise, although seeing Esme again made up for it.'

'Ah, well, I'm glad to hear it. How was the princess?'

Marianne laughed. 'Imogen was perfectly cordial, for all we saw of each other. My low-key tactic was working well until Zak and I met a ranger on the beach. He and a colleague were protecting a seal pup which had drawn a crowd. Don't ask me how it happened, but the ranger invited us to meet his cameraman friend at their local pub.' She got up to fetch the dinner plates while Della kicked off her usual run of questions.

'Bet you're glad you took the linen trousers, eh, Marianne. Tell me about the evening. No, let me guess: shriek-a-minute Nicole made a splash while Spencer mopped up after her. The spuds smell delish. Is this parsley?'

'Fresh from the garden. Actually, it was an interesting night. The Windlass has a great atmosphere. A huge roar went up when Joel, I mean the ranger, and his friend sang on the karaoke.'

'Joel, eh? Is that a blush you're wearing on those pale cheeks, Ms Marianne?'

Marianne recounted her Norfolk adventures in as much detail as was insisted upon. 'Who knows where this will lead, but it's about time I made new friends, and I'm not going to do that stuck in Hazelwood.'

'I like the sound of Joel Midwinter. Whatever happens between the two of you, the fella's had a good influence on Zak. Even Gil and Imogen must approve. Show me a parent who doesn't want to see their kids meaningfully engaged, however long it lasts.'

'Gil came over to pick up the keys. He looked worn out. I don't think the holiday was as restful as they'd hoped for. Apparently, Zak's garden project is already underway.' Marianne had said nothing to Gil about Joel's helping hand, nor of her imminent return to Norfolk, although why she should have kept it to herself was more out of habit than subterfuge. In any case, she was unlikely to return to The Tower, so what was the point. 'Changing the subject, Lena and Jean offered me their Renault Clio at a ridiculously low price.'

'Please tell me you said yes. I love mostly everything about you, Marianne, except this awful habit of blocking other people's generosity while you go around spreading goodwill like a farmer on muck day. Just for once, I'd like to …'

Marianne leant over and placed a finger on Della's thin lips. Della pushed back her chair and grabbed Marianne for a hug. 'I've not seen you like this since we lived at the Hall. Do you remember that night when Terence took us to Charlie Chan's night club to celebrate his thirtieth birthday? The bouncers were friends of his, so we got in buckshee, *and* they threw in a bottle of fizz.'

'How could I ever forget the night I met Warren Silk and the Armstrong cousins.'

'How indeed. Gil was wearing Stay Press trousers and a button-down shirt, looking like he was in the wrong nightclub, while Spencer and Warren joined us to dance like mad things before going back to party at the Hall. If Peter Llewellyn had caught us, we'd have all got the push.'

Marianne laughed. 'Peter would have been the first to dive into the scrum.' Wanstead Hall had given her sanctuary, and the staff were her salvation after her father's death from pancreatic cancer. His end was so sudden and shocking that sitting A levels seemed so irrelevant and going back to Ipswich to live with her aunt felt like a retrograde step. Finding a new roof was of far greater importance. Who could have predicted that a tiny postcard in the local newsagent's window would have resulted in those blissful years as the Llewellyn's live-in housekeeper. It helped that Marianne spoke French as Malika Llewellyn was a Seychellois, and when she wasn't travelling with her diplomat husband, she initiated regular conversations around the kitchen table while her chef brother Gerard, made the most delicious meals Marianne ever had the good fortune to eat.

Gerard Lionnet. He had crept into her room in the wee small hours to relieve her of her virginity and returned once more before he was quietly dispatched to the Seychelles, back to his family. Malika was so ashamed of her brother's behaviour, desperate to make amends, afraid of losing her goodwill. For Marianne, however, the clandestine encounter was wondrous, the memory of it tucked away with Wanstead Hall's box of secrets, never to be mentioned – not even to Della.

'The Llewellyns appreciated their staff, eh, Marianne. Marianne? Earth to Marianne Bly.'

'Sorry, yes they did.'

'You were a gilt-edged housekeeper, and Terence was a valet-butler like no other, or so Peter Llewellyn used to say. He and Malika have been divorced for years now, and he plans to settle in Thailand with Terence. I wonder what happened to Gerard. Do you remember him? Didn't stick around too long, but oh, the food! By the way, Terence is coming over in August. We'll sing our version of *Lola* in his honour.'

Not a peep from Number 7. The tenant was either on holiday or had moved out. The pneumatic thump that usually seeped into the brain despite ear plugs was conspicuously absent, and in its place was the reassuring blackbird and robin chatter, drifting in through the window. Marianne leaned back in the chair and stretched. After a superb night's sleep, she had risen early, eager to return to the orchid drawing. This was no easy flower to tackle with her inexperience, but as she wasn't being judged on performance, did it matter? The pencils felt comforting between her fingers, and the electric pencil sharpener's purr sounded like a contented cat.

As she waited for the tea to brew, Marianne checked her phone. Until last weekend, this hadn't been a habit, but now the urge to look for Joel's messages had insinuated itself into her day. His mobile phone was constantly buzzing. Twice he had apologised and switched it to silent mode. Marianne wondered how he found time for quiet with the amount of people he knew. *Ah, that's easy. I've taught myself to stay in touch with the soundscape. I also set aside specific times of the day to do nothing. Without that, I couldn't engage in the same way.* Della had urged her to enjoy the return visit without trying to work out Joel's motive. He was a nice guy who made friends easily and they'd have fun.

Marianne put down the phone and poured the tea. Excitement flowed through her, and she liked the feel of it. In five days from now, she'd drive her new car to the Midwinter's bungalow on the coast road, opposite the allotments, and there she would meet her hosts. The ridge of high pressure over East Anglia was forecast to continue indefinitely, which was a mixed blessing. Marianne was neither sunbather nor swimmer and took shelter under her trusty hat and sleeves. Joel was an outdoors man. It could be tricky. Oh, well, if she had to bail out early, home was just a two-hour drive away.

 ZAK

NEVER IN his short life had Zachary Nikolaos Marsalis-Armstrong been so stoked. Since returning from Norfolk, he was riding the crest of a wave, and every new discovery catapulted him into another mystery in which to delve. The first stage of his 'Go Wild!' project involved checking out the front and back garden with Shane Bennett. Once the gardener got over the shock of his personality transplant, they hatched a plan for parental approval: the installation of a pond and water butts; planting several mature trees; introducing pollinator plants, flowers, and shrubs in the new borders; fit a feeding station and possibly a hedgehog house and highway. As it was midsummer, certain things would have to wait but if they kept on top of watering, there was every chance of success.

Apart from the early birds, there was nothing else on the camera trail to warrant a cartwheel, but as Joel and Kurt emphasised, it was a waiting game with no end – rushing was for the rest of the world. Zak closed the lid on his laptop and went into the garden. Every time he finished one job, another took its place, like the thing had a life of its own. Stage One had also included a survey of local flora and fauna, and what a result that had been! After walking up and down Grove Road and seeing disappointingly little greenery on his neighbours' large concrete front gardens, Zak decided to knock on a few doors. He was embarrassed by the number of residents who knew who he was, but that soon disappeared as most of them invited him into their gardens and were generous with their knowledge. By the end of the quest, he had amassed a great deal of information and had made several new friends who wanted to see his endeavours. Shane calculated it would take four weeks to finish the first stage. Maybe Zak would ask his mum to organise a celebration?

Next up was a visit to the local wildlife reserve to get a feel for what was going on in the area. Joel had put him in touch with a friend at the Epping Wildlife Trust. There were heaps of volunteer projects and groups to join. Joel said it was important to meet like-minded people as it would grow his network. It was a familiar word in the Armstrong house. Even his dad had a network, although it was nowhere near as big as his mum's. Zak began raiding the stack of spectacular wildlife programmes on his laptop before crashing into sleep. After one particular film whose content was disturbing, a realisation came like a burst of light: he could help to make the difference between a species' extinction and survival! There were brilliant initiatives underway in the UK, and countries like Puerto Rico had done so much to protect the leatherjack turtles, the parrots, and the manatee. A group of young people from the west of Scotland called the Ullapool Sea Savers were raising awareness of marine life – imagine being a turtle ambassador! So many youngsters had already joined this critically important movement, and he had to be a part of it.

Typically, his parents were ambivalent, but this time Zak was determined to prove them wrong. It was true, he had been flaky, but this was too important not to take seriously. Joel and Kurt didn't need to point out the dire planetary predictions, as school had covered a fair bit about that, and who hadn't heard of the 'Greta Effect'. Two students had been given permission to join the Fridays for Future protests, which at the time, Zak thought was just a way of dodging classes. How wrong could he be! He'd begun filming each stage of the garden makeover and had started a blog with several responses already posted. Esme had wanted to be a zoologist forever, and shamefully, he'd only recently taken notice. She offered to help, but he wanted to wait just a while longer to see what he could do on his own. The neighbours hadn't exactly said 'no' to his suggestion of a hedgehog highway, but his dad said they were being polite, so not to get his hopes up or pester them. Zak ignored his pessimistic view: he knew all about the power of persuasion, especially when it came from a sincere fourteen-year-old kid who was doing his bit. The old 'uns would be eating out of his hands.

With his daily jobs finished and Rudy happily napping after their walk, Zak decided to cycle to Marianne's house. Her message said she had some books for him, and that was a few days ago. With any luck, she'd be free to take him to a local nature reserve. As Zak approached the house, his grandmothers' car was outside with the boot open. He punched the air. Lena and Jean were expecting him, but he'd been so busy lately that a number of commitments had to be shelved. This was better as he'd update them in one go. As he rested the bike against the hedge, Marianne came out of the house, carrying a holdall. 'Hey, Marianne! Going somewhere nice?'

'Hello Zak. You're up early. How are you?'

Zak put out his hands. 'Blistered and bruised, but apart from that I'm good, thanks. Can't wait for you to see the garden. Shane is teaching me all sorts.'

'It sounds terrific.' Marianne put the holdall in the boot and closed it. 'Have you got a minute?'

'Sure. Don't let me hold you up.' Marianne almost hurried into the house, embarrassed about something. Zak's stomach lurched. Maybe she was annoyed he hadn't come over for the books. He followed her into kitchen. His grandmothers were nowhere in sight.

'Would you like a drink?'

Zak pointed to the water bottle in his rucksack.

'I promise there's nothing wrong – in fact, it's all good. Lena and Jean sold me their car, which is why it's outside. The thing is …'

Marianne's face blushed bright pink. Zak felt the knot in his stomach untie itself and smiled right back. He wasn't in trouble.

'Joel has invited me to Norfolk. I've started my plant illustrations and he wants to show me some wildflowers and rare orchids. He stopped by The Tower with these books for you.'

Zak took the books. Mental cogs were turning as fast as bike wheels. Marianne had seen Joel – without him. And she was going back!

'There are two reasons why I haven't told you. The first is that I didn't want you to feel left out, and secondly, this may be a one-off visit.'

'Are you kidding! Joel likes you, even I could see that. You'd be nuts not to go.' He gave Marianne a hug. It was as if he were the grown up, and it felt weird but good. 'I'll keep *schtum* until you tell me otherwise. Can you imagine Aunt Nicole's reaction? It'll be all over Epping before lunchtime.'

They laughed, relieved that neither were upset, and also to share a secret. 'I'll send Joel a text to thank him. We've been messaging like mad. He's quicker than Wiki when it comes to nature questions.'

'I'll bet. I'm sorry, Zak, you wanted to ask me something.'

'Oh, yeah, I almost forgot. This gardening malarkey is so tiring, I've been crashing out early every night. Would you come with me to the Roding Wetland Reserve next week? There are kestrels, kingfishers, and wild flowers. Mum is super busy and it's not Dad's idea of fun.'

'If they agree, I'd love to join you. Shall we take a picnic?'

'Great idea! Gotta go. Say 'hi' to Joel for me.'

With his new books stored securely in his rucksack, Zak cycled the longest route home. There were important things to think about. Marianne and Joel! What a super-cool couple they would make. It was top news to add to his growing pool of exciting things and the timing couldn't be better. His mum was working all hours and sleeping in the guest bedroom, and his dad was extra moody. Oh, well, he couldn't do much about that. At least they weren't shouting at each other. Shane was due in the next hour. The new apple and hawthorn trees were ready to go in, and it was his turn to dig the holes.

JOEL

AFTER ANOTHER round of pacing up and down, Joel pulled back the curtain and peered hopefully at the road.

'Sit down, Joel. You'll wear out the carpet. What time is your friend arriving?'

Joel sank into the well-worn sofa. It was perfect for lying out and watching the occasional programme with his grandparents or snoozing after a belt-expanding Sunday dinner. 'Any time now unless she's hit traffic at Swaffham. It's good of you to let her stay, Gran.'

'Dudley and I like the company. Your friends don't usually make you this twitchy. What's her name again? You know so many people, I can never remember who's who.'

'Marianne Bly. I met her and Zak at the beach. His great-grandfather, Norman Armstrong, worked at Ropemaker's Yard.'

'Oh, yes, now I remember. 'Gorgeous Norman'. He got us girls in a tizz, but then he disappeared down south.'

'Zak is interested in doing what Kurt does.'

'Everyone is interested in what Kurt does.'

'I don't think Marianne fell under his spell.'

'Looks to me like you fell under her spell.'

They were silent for a while and once again, Joel jumped up to look out. His grandmother was as sharp as a razorbill especially when it concerned her 'precious cargo', as she called him.

'Where's Gramps?'

'Give you three guesses. Oh, here comes Dudley now with his basket of muddy veg. I told him to be back in good time.'

Joel grinned. His grandparents were the equivalent of mandarin ducks, (Dudley definitely the more flamboyant), and you only had to step into the bungalow to feel the love light. The cabin met his basic needs, but he was in the bungalow most days, either sharing a meal, taking the occasional bath, or helping out. Taken together, Irene and Dudley, the cabin, the Foundation, his friends – all were ingredients for a fulfilled life: almost. His gran, however, was onto him. 'It's the strangest thing, Gran. I've spent less than one full day with Marianne, yet I find myself thinking about her more than is good for me. Maybe she has cast a spell, but it can't have been intentional. I'm convinced she didn't expect to hear from me again, let alone to be invited back.'

'It's a long time since you've mentioned a girl, although it would take a saint to put up with your lifestyle.' Irene pushed herself up from the table to greet Dudley. Apart from Joel's friends, people didn't understand the obsession. His job wasn't a nine-to-five. She had hoped that Meg Swayne, being a kindred spirit, would be a candidate for her grandson's affections, but that fire had blown out as soon as it was lit. Unfortunately for Meg, she made the mistake of fussing over Joel as if he were an invalid, or about to have a heart attack which was ridiculous, and he couldn't stand it. Irene didn't blame him for staying on his own, but Joel was such a loving, caring boy, and everyone deserved to be loved.

'A saint is just what I'm looking for, Gran.'

'Who's a saint? Are you talking about me again, *Peggy-Day*?' Dudley kissed his wife and pulled up a chair. 'Your friend has arrived. I saw her car pass by the allotments.'

'Joel says her name is 'Saint Marianne'.'

Joel kissed his gran's curly grey hairdo as he walked past to open the door. 'Best you watch that sense of humour of yours. You know how sensitive these holy folks can be.'

'Gran loved the herb pots and the Essex honey, and Dudley will make short work of the wine. That was thoughtful of you, Marianne.'

'It's the least I can do for them. I can't tell you how nice it is to eat a meal made by someone else. Is there anything else I can get for them while we're out and about?'

Joel turned off the main road and into an untarmacked area bordered by wire fencing and a metal gate. He parked next to a single vehicle and switched off the engine. 'I'll have a think. I take it for granted that Gran will cook for me, although as you saw earlier, throwing a dish together on the stove is no problem.'

'In my entire life, I've never seen a cabin like yours. It's just as well Zak hasn't been here. He's already making serious inroads into his inheritance with the Go Wild! project.'

'Zak's fortunate to have parents willing to fund it, in view of his self-confessed tendency to change tack. I love his project name. Says a lot about his confidence and humour. Have you seen the garden yet?'

'No. Before I left this morning, he cycled over to ask if I'd take him to the Roding Reserve. He wanted me to thank you for the books.'

They pulled their rucksacks from the back seat. 'Zak has calmed down with the messaging, but I don't mind in the least. Engaging with nature is not for the fickle, and I suspect he's already sussed that out. With busy working parents and a remote support group, it'll take time to find his people. Having you close by will keep him anchored.'

'I hadn't thought of it like that. Anyway, where are we, and why have we come?'

Marianne's directness took him by surprise, but he liked it. They had picked up where they had left off, as if they'd opened a book at the next chapter with barely a time lag. Joel could tell right away that his gran approved of her. Maybe it was because they were mothers, or they enjoyed house and garden tasks, or simply that they were equally good listeners. Marianne talked about Freddie, and how he had chosen to stay in Liverpool after graduating with a social work degree and was managing a residential home for young people coping with mental illness. Although Irene and Dudley had heaped their love on him, Joel acknowledged the inevitable imprint of parental abandonment. It had to be the same for Freddie, even though Marianne said she was lucky to have had good people to help her. Was this root of the melancholy he'd detected that day on Wells beach? Did she still carry a residue of anger, or worse, for her ex-partner? Joel laughed to himself. He was so accustomed to playing nature detective, he had leap-frogged a species and was now scrutinising Marianne's psychological make-up with the same gusto.

'This is Gorse Wood, and we are here because I want to show you something I hope you've not seen before.'

Marianne followed him through the gate. A faint drone

from the main road traffic accompanied them along the wide woodland path for a while. 'Is it a bird? Is it a bug? Is it a super-furry mammal?'

Marianne's eyes glinted from under the wide brim of her hat, and he found himself laughing. 'It's a tree. A type of copper beech.' Joel stopped for a moment. 'Can you hear that, Marianne?'

She cocked her head. 'It's as if we've climbed through the wardrobe into Narnia, but without the snow.'

'So it is! You should see the white woodland when the winter sun glints like treasure tumbling from a chest.'

'A poet and a ranger – two for the price of one.'

Joel's bubbling-brook chuckle echoed around the woodland. They paused for a moment before moving off in a southerly direction, through a densely planted area. Marianne came to a halt. 'What's that, over to the left?'

'It's a muntjac carcass. If this were a public forest or wood, it would be cleared away for health and safety reasons. We've become too tidy. You'd be amazed at how many species a carcass will provide food for. It's the same with trees. There's no such thing as a dead tree.'

'I can imagine the complaints. If we knew this sort of information, we'd be less fearful.'

'I couldn't agree more.'

They walked on for a while longer, tuning in to the sounds and space until Joel paused at the foot of a tree. 'Ta – da! This is *Fagus sylvatica* 'Purpurea Tricolour', the only one of her kind in this woodland.'

Marianne ran her hand over slim trunk's smooth grey bark and stepped back to admire the leaves. 'Three colours – native?'

'Originates from Europe. We're not sure how she got here, but she'll be fully grown at over a hundred feet and is nicely shaded. The bark can get scorched.'

'Do you think *Madame Tricolor* would mind if I took a leaf?'

Joel was touched by the request. 'I believe the lady would be honoured, especially if you drew her portrait.' He picked a leaf and passed it to Marianne whose eyes were as wide as saucers. She pulled a small wooden box from her bag: a palm-sized microscope. It was fascinating to watch her study the leaf under the lens. 'The leaves are pink in the spring. The creamy margins are striking against the purple red.'

'Yes. The shape is ovate to elliptic. The prominent parallel-veined leaf is a characteristic feature of the *monocots*. I read that in your botanical book, Joel.'

While Joel's expression changed from surprise to elation, Marianne raised the leaf up to the sun. 'Almost transparent. It would be a pleasure to try and capture her character on paper.' She ran her thumb over the surface and edges, just as she had done at Wishbone Heath. Then, she took off her rucksack and lay down under the tree to look up through the elegantly poised branches. 'Will you join me?'

Joel shrugged off his backpack and lay down next to her. Splinters of ethereal sunlight pierced through the branches creating a mosaic across their supine bodies. He often stretched out under various trees to get a different perspective, and while out alone on a job, occasionally he'd have a nap if he needed to reinflate his energy supply. Joel was acutely aware of Marianne's proximity and felt an overwhelming urge to hold her hand. Did she feel it too?

He got up and took his camera out of his pack. Marianne stood and brushed herself down.

'I'll bet that happens a lot, Joel.'

'The kids usually want to climb upwards. I wasn't sure which direction you'd choose.'

As Marianne tipped back her head to look up, her hat tumbled to the ground. Her dimpled smile revealed a glimpse of the lovely young maiden who had matured into a *bona fide* beauty. Brushing the woody debris from her hat, Joel passed it back.

'Thanks.' She put it back on. 'I choose *terra firma* every time. I used to spend the summer holidays at my grandparents' cottage in rural Suffolk, walking in meadows and making daisy chains.'

'A contented childhood?'

'Yes and no … but I'm happy now.'

Joel was vaguely aware that if this were a film, he'd take her in his arms and, against the backdrop of a stirring soundtrack, they'd kiss. But this was no fiction, and before he could consider such intimacy, he had to talk to her.

The Outlander set off in a westerly direction to Salthouse Beach. Joel was aware of time passing, and while he had so many places to show Marianne, he needed to sit somewhere spacious, and talk. He'd booked a table at Creake Abbey Café for eight o'clock. The live music on offer was either a jazz trio, or an acoustic guitarist and singer. Either way, it wouldn't be a rerun of The Windlass, which wasn't appropriate for tonight. With only a few hours remaining until dinner, Joel suggested they spend an hour on the beach before heading back for a wash and brush up. As they made their way across the shingle ridge, Joel was stopped several times for a chat. He kept the conversations brief before finding a suitable spot close to the shoreline from where they could watch the sea roll and taste the salty air. Opening up two camping chairs, he passed one to her. 'Do you like swimming, Marianne?'

'I don't swim.'

'Do you mean you can't swim, or you don't like to swim?'

'I swam as a toddler, but something happened.'

'Listen, Marianne, you don't have to tell me.'

'There's not much to tell. When I was five, my legs were burned in an accident. After that, I stayed out of the water and out of the sun.'

For a while, neither spoke. Joel poured two cups of tea while Marianne unpacked the fruit buns. To an onlooker, the couple might have been lifelong companions enjoying a well-rehearsed ritual. 'I hope you like jasmine tea. It's usually keeps its flavour. If not, there's water.'

'I'll drink anything Joel: hot or cold, fruity or herby. The bun tastes good. I can't quite make out the flavour.'

'Lime zest. Gran likes to keep me guessing. It's a game we've played forever, and a great way of widening the palate. She puts interesting combinations together.'

'This one works'. Marianne pulled off her boots and socks and wiggled her toes. 'Thanks so much for taking me to Gorse Wood. I'd never have found it. My camera should give me what I need. Oh, I almost forgot, I must pay you for the prints.'

'They're a gift. A buddy of mine has a shop. He uses FSC paper and vegetable-based ink free of VOCs, if you're concerned about that sort of thing.'

'Yes, I am. I'll pay for dinner. Della, my best friend, says I give too much without allowing the same in return. So with that in mind, I accept your gift without fuss, and so you must accept mine.'

'Thank you.'

Marianne smiled, feeling lighter with every second in the company of this fascinating man. 'In fact, I've Della to thank for being here. It would have been easy to talk myself out it.'

Joel turned his chair to face Marianne. This was the moment he'd been waiting for. 'Why might you have done such a thing?'

'I thought you were focused on encouraging Zak in what might turn into a lifelong passion, which by the way, makes our meeting with you and Kurt the most fortunate of events. But then, you turned up at The Tower, and you asked me to come back. I may be out of touch, but isn't it natural to wonder why?'

Squalling seagulls flapped overhead, instinctively drawing Joel's gaze upward. He thanked the birds for those few precious moments to formulate his reply. 'It was – is about Zak, but on the beach that day, something made me want to see you again.' Joel took a deep breath. 'Marianne, I'm as out of touch as you are. I don't date. My last girlfriend was eons ago, and I had no intention of getting involved with anyone after that.' Joel's heart was beating so wildly, for a moment he was afraid for himself, but he did what he always did, and closed his eyes, let his breath fall back into its natural rhythm. 'When I was a kid, I had a heart operation. The condition has a name, but I'm not going to tell you what it is as the last time I did that, my potential girlfriend mutated into an over-zealous nurse who was convinced I was going to die at any moment.'

'And are you?'

'I'm thirty-one, and according to the medics my life expectancy is way above average. I've learned how to take excellent care of myself in a variety of ways. I decided not to have a family – too much anxiety all round – I've a tiny treasure chest, no ambition, and a job which is a way of life. The only plans I make are via the Foundation, the next pub night, or the occasional visit to Carrow Road, to watch Norwich City. It's not a question of making room for a partner, it's more that I'm not exactly a good catch.'

'You are so right about that. Guess I'll be off home.' Marianne pretended to stand, and soon they were laughing wildly.

'I'm so sorry, Joel. I don't know what came over me. It must be your gran's buns.' She put her hand on his strong sun-warmed arm and was serious. 'Already you've shown me places and things I've never seen, and I'm so grateful, and as for the jaw-dropping double act at the pub, I can't wait for the next performance.'

'Let's learn as we go. Forgive the clichés, but neither of us has a track record and we've got off to a flying start. As for the duo, you'll be bowled over by our *Islands in the Stream*. Is it a deal, Marianne?'

Marianne offered her hand to shake. Joel pulled her up, and wrapped his arms around her, trying to contain his euphoria, while the gulls whooped applause, and the sea rippled.

IMOGEN

At four-thirty, Imogen was ready to call it a day. The extra hours had paid dividends as she had completed the last phase for the Singapore Expo project. For the first time in Urbane's successful partnership, Annette declined to be a part of the venture. The commission from an existing client to launch a new product in the Asian market was, she said, *too big, it's way outside of our remit, and what's the point when we've two years of bookings in the diary.* Imogen suspected that Annette had other plans, namely, to take her foot off the corporate gas and try for a baby before her clock ran out. As frustrating as this lack of enthusiasm was, how could she blame her friend for wanting what she had. So, while Annette and the team continued with the existing schedule, Imogen dived into the unknown: alone.

To begin with, it was exhilarating. Armed with her mother's connections, she was shown the best that the forward-thinking, vibrant sovereign island state of Singapore had to offer before knuckling down. Imogen quickly readjusted to the different set-up, using her resourceful, can-do attitude and excellent people skills to get results. Then, there was Kiran Lin, her client's business partner, whose appearance added another interesting dimension to the project. Social invitations went with the territory, so a late supper was nothing out of the ordinary. What Imogen hadn't anticipated was the long-forgotten thrill of being wined and dined by a super-attentive, potent, thirty-something man. It was a welcome, albeit brief interlude in a manic timetable, the outcome of which was left open-ended. The Singapore Expo was sold as an unmissable event, but ultimately it was a job like any other. There was, however, the opportunity of a sensational new role which Imogen had every intention of accepting, and it had given rise to an inspired idea to make life easier for Gil and Zak in her absence. It simply had to lighten the increasingly heavy mood between them.

Right from the get-go, Gil had unequivocally supported her endeavours. Urbane's debut foray in the business sector took the form of a black-tie security industry awards ceremony to which Armstrong Solutions were invited. Their business was riding high: a stable market position, peer respect, and plaudits for best practise, with more to be awarded that evening. During her pre-event research, Imogen's interest was piqued after seeing Gil's striking profile on his company website. As soon as she saw him by the bar, hovering on the edge of the conversation – aloof and alluring – her mission was clear. It had been fun to wrong-foot the group of engineers, of which he was one, as they clearly hadn't expected to engage in technical conversations with her and Annette. Gil's coolly detached manner offered little resistance when faced with Imogen's siren song, and sensing the strong sexual undercurrent, Annette scooted swiftly on, leaving her partner to close the deal. The heady combination of explosive sex, Gil's inability to fawn, and a shared business vision propelled Imogen into staking out the most important event of her twenty-four-year-old life.

Gil's working-class background was no barrier to the marriage. Her darling Papa had worked his way from nothing to grocery magnate in his adopted England, and his mentorship scheme had been rewarded with an MBE. As his only adored child, Imogen might have easily swanned through life, but Nik Marsalis' prodigious work ethic was in her genes. While he wept openly on Marlborough College's sweeping gravel drive, his precious eleven-year-old daughter skipped ecstatically into the illustrious boarding school for seven productive and lively years after which, at Bristol University, Imogen met Annette Desai, fellow Events Management undergraduate, and soon-to-be best friend. They plotted their route to the glass ceiling with the skill and pluck of Himalayan mountaineers. Imogen had no wish to emulate her glacially elegant, aristocratic mother who used her beauty as power. This was a new era. She wanted success in her own right, and if her so-called 'exotic attributes' influenced the clients, that was their affair.

Nowhere in the ambitious young women's career plan did marriage and children feature. Imogen's shock announcement might have stopped the partnership in its tracks, but she had figured everything out. With a tweak here and there, Urbane's trajectory continued as planned, and during the subsequent years, the company had done extremely well, but Urbane's most fruitful and fulfilling days were behind them. The clients' expectations were often grossly inflated and the events increasingly extravagant. The Singapore Expo was Imogen's way of gently uncoupling the partnership without damaging the friendship.

Imogen's impressive roster of former school and university acquaintances were useful, but close friends had been hard to come by. Annette Desai was the only person she had ever confided in. The Armstrong family had proved resolutely inaccessible, apart from Spencer, intellectually progressive and always genial. Nicole was bearable in small doses, and Jean was amenable, but Lena Armstrong had been openly hostile from their first disastrous meeting. Despite several attempts to befriend her mother-in-law, Imogen had finally given it up as futile. As long as Lena had access to her beloved grandson, the wheels just about rolled along but of late, the wish to be away from it all nagged at her like a dull toothache.

There was a light tap on the door. 'Thought you might need a cuppa. Mint, without the bag. Dinner's in an hour.'

Imogen stretched her long arms upwards and outwards in an arc. 'Thanks, Gil. I'm finished for the day. Is Zak outside?'

'He's soaking in the tub. Have you seen what he and Shane have been up to? They roped me into digging up the patio.' Gil rubbed his lower back. 'I could do with a hot bath myself.'

'I had a peek earlier.' Imogen's smile contained a healthy dose of pride. 'The transformation is quite remarkable in so short a time, don't you think?'

'Zak wants us to go the garden centre with him tomorrow. Something about picking out our favourite plants. Have you read the email from his house tutor? Our son has told the school he's swapping music and drama for Spanish and geography.'

'They want to confirm we are happy with his option changes, nothing more. I can't see a problem. Zak is simply substituting two GCSE's. It will make little difference in the long run.'

'I agree, but Zak didn't talk to us first. What's he up to?'

Imogen sipped her tea. This really was no big deal, considering the unsavoury people their teenage son could be involved with. Zak was beginning to make his own decisions. Did it matter if they slightly diverged from their original agreement? 'He's not 'up to' anything, Gil. Our son is growing up. Anyway, if you've got a moment, there's something I'd like to discuss.'

Gil perched on the arm of the sofa, his expression unreadable. 'Are you coming back to bed tonight?'

'I didn't want to disturb you, Gil, that's all.' Imogen talked through her blush. 'Do you remember when Annette and I hosted the women's enterprise events at The Southbank? Apparently, my name was mentioned to a woman called Malika Lionnet. She heads up a mentorship organisation supporting Asia's brightest businesswomen. We met last week at the Expo site where she is preparing to host a series of dialogues. To my utter astonishment, Malika wants me to join her team!'

'What does that mean, exactly?'

'It's a senior advisory role to begin with, so I'll continue with the business as is. Annette's been making noises about having a baby, you know, clock ticking and all that, so this will be a neat segue into an infinitely more interesting and rewarding role.'

'I thought you loved Urbane.'

'Things change.'

They both sensed the importance of the conversation and while this wasn't the best time to discuss their future, there was an inevitability looming. Annette's new relationship and the speed with which she and her partner had set up home to prepare for a family had left Imogen feeling unexpectedly envious. She hadn't quite given up the idea of having a second child at some point, although with her relationship as it currently stood, it wasn't the best moment to raise the subject. She had maintained low visibility since returning from Singapore. To expect Gil to understand her workload as the reason for sleeping in the guest bedroom might have been stretching it, but he was a troubled sleeper, often shouting and kicking out, which was disturbing and frightening, and so difficult to broach without creating further enmity between them.

'Sounds as if you've already made up your mind. What will this new role mean to the family? How much less of you will we see?'

'Don't be silly, Gil. I'll be away for short periods only and will help set up a London base as soon as it's feasible, all of which brings me on to the next incredible thing to have happened. In fact, this could be key to maintaining our family's well-being while I'm engaged elsewhere.'

Gil was beginning to feel as if he were in one of those meetings during which a string of really bad ideas were touted, and he had to refuse them without dampening enthusiasm. 'Surprise me.'

'During my lunch with Malika, it transpired that she used to be married to the diplomat, Peter Llewellyn. They lived at Wanstead Hall. Their staff included butler and nanny – the Carthy siblings – and a housekeeper called

Marianne Bly! Malika was delighted with Marianne's input, and the children adored her. There is so much more to her than I had ever believed possible. So, I had the inspired idea to hire Marianne as our housekeeper.' Imogen smiled triumphantly.

'No.'

'What do you mean, 'no'? It's the perfect solution, Gil. Didn't you say Marianne is unemployed? She can help Zak in all manner of ways. According to Malika, she speaks fluent French, and is skilled at art. She'll keep the house running smoothly, cook, ...'

'You don't know anything about Marianne. In fact, when have you ever had a real conversation with her? You and Nicole were unbelievably rude at The Tower. I expect that sort of behaviour from Nicole but you, Imogen, with your education and breeding?'

Imogen's cheeks flushed. Gil was only ever a stone's throw from the prehistoric and she was too tired to be polite. 'I've no idea what you are talking about. I was perfectly welcoming and offered our hospitality during her stay. I admit we may not be the best of friends, but that's not to say Marianne and I couldn't get to know each other better.'

'I realise you're used to getting your own way but let me save you the embarrassment of being refused.' He shifted to the edge of the sofa, ready to spring. 'There's something missing here, don't you think? Our son is entering the most challenging period of his life, and you want to absent yourself for longer than you usually do for the sake of what, exactly? Surely your career can wait. And to clear up any confusion, Marianne isn't 'staff'. She was an important member of my family long before you arrived and will be there long after you've gone.'

Gil's vehemence was so shocking, Imogen immediately left the office and sought refuge in the bathroom. His coldly cruel behaviour had pierced her shell, but she would not break down in front of him, despite the slow, inexorable rise of emotion. She ran the tap and soon the cold water rinsed away her tears. In the next breath, indignance set in. Why shouldn't she accept the once-in-a-lifetime role? She'd been head-hunted by a forward-thinking and respected woman, the honour of which was overwhelming. Was Zak really at such a crucial stage he needed his mother at home seven days a week? Admittedly, Gil had always kept the house running smoothly, but wasn't that what women had been doing forever and a day without complaint?

As for Marianne Bly, clearly she meant more to Gil than ever suspected. It was true: Marianne had been in his life long before their marriage, but she'd only ever floated in the background. They'd exchanged brief conversations, but as pleasant and well-mannered as Marianne was, no friendship had materialised, and neither had courted it. Although she never attended Zak or Esme's birthday events, there were occasional reunions at Lena and Jean's bungalow, and it was no secret the grandmothers thought highly of her. Freddie had remained on friendly terms with Zak, another connection to the Blys. During the Norfolk holiday, Marianne's effect on the children was notable, and there was no denying they were fond of her, but hadn't she been their teacher's assistant for many years?

Then there was Bonnie to consider. There were few people Gil's sister had felt at ease with, and yet Marianne had been one of those few. Imogen's visits to Lee Morrell Lodge appeared to cause more strain than pleasure despite her gargantuan efforts, and her success at transforming the charity shop's fortunes. A shudder rippled throughout her. Was it possible Gil was no longer in love with her? Was the marriage finally coming to a conclusion? No, it couldn't possibly be that. She was simply worn out, and her imagination had got the better of her. In any case, she wasn't ready to let him go. Those blissful all-consuming months during which Gil had been generous with himself may have faded into memory, but her yearning for their reappearance had never waned. A rekindling of their former spark was within reach, she was certain of it. With the Expo about to be concluded, the family could relax together in Daddy's Fiskardo house. Imogen longed to see him, and for Zak to reunite with his adoring grandfather. Feeling somewhat recovered, she pinched her pale cheeks, flicked up her hair, and made her way downstairs.

'Nice dinner, Dad. This garden work is giving me an appetite. Are we on for the garden centre tomorrow morning? Shane thought it'd be a nice touch if you each chose a plant or shrub, so we made a list of the best ones to attract the pollinators.'

'Sounds fun, Zak. Why don't I book a table at the Smoke Shack? It's your favourite eatery.'

'Sorry, Mum, I've got a shed load of things to do. Anyway, I thought Spencer and Nicole were coming over. Esme wants to talk to me about making a raised bed. She reckons home-grown veggies are the way to go, but I don't want to overload myself.'

Imogen's heart sank. Did this mean she had to organise a meal?

'Spencer is coming for tea, not dinner. We'll eat before they get here, but if you're not up to it, Imogen ...'

'What do you mean by 'tea', exactly? A cup of tea? High tea?'

'You know what I mean. Nicole has baked a cake and Esme wants to see her cousin. They'll be here at four.'

Zak banged the table with his cutlery. 'Hey, listen, Ma 'n Pa, I wanted to talk to you about Fiskardo. You don't mind if I skip it this year, do you? It's just that I'll soon be back at school, and there's so much to get done before the autumn season kicks in.'

'Your grandparents are expecting you, Zak.'

Gil ignored her. 'By the way, Zak, we've heard from your house tutor. It's good to see you making your own decisions, son.'

Imogen shot him a look. This was too important to be brushed aside. 'My father is growing old. He enjoys the company of his only grandchild, but if you don't want to go, I am not about to force you, although I am disappointed. As you wish to be treated as an adult, Zak, you can tell him yourself.'

'Why don't we invite them to stay? I know you're too busy to help me organise a garden party, but Grandpa is always interested in what I'm doing, and he'll be so pleased to see my efforts.'

Imogen's protean mind shifted into gear. Perhaps this wasn't such an issue after all. She could use the time to discuss Urbane's future with Annette and the team. Her parents hadn't visited Epping in ages, and while they wouldn't want to stay over, her father would enjoy seeing his grandson's extraordinary new talents. 'Okay, Zak, we'll make a deal. You plan the celebration, work out a budget and a guest list, and I'll sign it off. It will take place on the Sunday before you return to school. Your grandparents will have returned from Fiskardo and can join us here. At October half-term, we'll arrange to see them in St. Raphael.'

Zak punched the air. 'Yay! I've already started a guest list. Joel, Kurt, and Marianne are top, although Kurt may be filming somewhere. I'll invite the neighbours, and the Bugspotters. Oh, Dad, I meant to tell you I've dropped out of football. Mason was really angry and called me an unrepeatable name. He accused *me* of losing the plot!'

Despite their current mutual antipathy, Imogen was sorry for Gil. He and Zak shared so little together, and football was an important bond. 'Will you relinquish your West Ham season ticket, Zak?'

'Of course not, Mum. I've just got to the point where it's no longer fun to play. I only kept it going because Dad and me could spend time together. Let's face it, I was never going to be a Lucas Pérez, was I?' Zak slid of his stool. 'Do you mind if I take off?'

'What about Rudy? He's been waiting around for you all day', said Gil, attempting to keep his emotions in check. Was that really the only reason Zak had kept going with the football?

Rudy reappeared from his place of refuge with a spring in his step. It had been a sorry time since returning from Norfolk, with only the occasional park run and no rough and tumble.

'Okay, I'll take him out. Come on Rudy, let's go get 'em.'

The front door clattered. As Gil cleared the plates away, Imogen put her hand on his arm. 'I am sorry about the football, Gil. It means a lot to you. The GCSEs are inconsequential, you know.'

'What about your folks?'

Suddenly they laughed. A rare light moment. 'You said our son was coming into his own. Neither of us can complain, can we, Gil?'

'No, Gen, we can't, but with Zak's track record, he's bound to change his mind, so be prepared.'

The tiniest glow lit Imogen's heart. Gil had called her 'Gen', and she couldn't recall the last time he'd said it.

MARIANNE

THE WAITER set down a huge earthenware tea pot and two dark chocolate mints in between the diners. Mack's Jazz Trio were on their second interval of the evening, and a gentle buzz of voices drifted up into the café's huge oak atrium. It was a full house, but with the tables well-spaced, conversations were hushed. Marianne lifted the teapot.

'Do you want help with that?'

'I can just about manage, thanks. Are you sure you don't want dessert, Joel? The puddings look good.'

'I've not much of a sweet tooth, but don't let me stop you. The main course was big enough for two.'

Whilst sipping the camomile tea, Marianne scanned the unfamiliar figure opposite. Joel had changed into a check shirt and jeans and had tied his fair hair in a half up pony tail. From around his neck on black cord hung a silver feather and a vaguely familiar mystical symbol. 'Your grandparents are so hospitable. Their guest bedroom will be a fine place to rest my weary head tonight.'

'Oh, I'm so sorry for dragging you around. I get over-excited.'

She grinned at Joel's hangdog expression. 'I'm not one for lying in, and my guess is that Irene and Dudley will be up with the larks.'

'That's for sure. I've suggested they postpone their early morning song-and-dance routine, otherwise you'll have the pleasure of *Nashville Skyline* for your breakfast.'

'*Nashville Skyline?*'

'Bob Dylan. That's where Dudley got Gran's pet name 'Peggy Day' from. She likes it, even though she pretends otherwise.'

'Dudley must have some entertaining stories up his sleeve.'

'And some! Gramps used to take me to the saltmarshes and the woods. He got me started, both musically and naturistically. I liked the idea of playing in a band, but it would take a lot of practise, and I wanted to be outside more, so that was that.'

'So, what's with the stadium rock? I'd have thought Crosby Stills and Nash would be more in keeping with your gentle life.'

'The rock music initiation happened during my only trip overseas. When I was twenty-one, a group of us went to New Zealand's North Island – the Coromandel – to volunteer on various projects, one of which was to plant the *kauri*. It's the world's second largest tree after the giant Redwood. Left alone, it can live for up to two thousand years, but the tree has been logged, sawn, and burnt to within an inch of its life. Its biggest threat today is die-back, but as a climax species, which basically means adaptability, the *kauri* is making a comeback.'

'I thought New Zealand fiercely protected its ecosystems?'

'They have the same challenges as the rest of the planet, but their biosecurity is light years ahead of ours. Everyone is urged to wash their footwear when entering and leaving forests and national parks. The *kauri* would be a great tree to draw, Marianne.'

'My list is growing by the day. What were the stand-out memories of your trip?'

'Oh, where to start? Kurt managed to get a rare pass to Codfish Island where a breeding programme for the *kakapo* is established. That was special as was sleeping in an authentic *bach*, the Kiwi equivalent of a beach hut, but not like those on Wells. These are uniquely quirky and are disappearing fast as developers eat up the coastline.'

'That is so depressing. Everything has a commercial value these days, doesn't it?'

'Yeah. We've a way to go before we understand that economic growth is only a part of the picture. Coming back to your question about the music, we used to spend our evenings at a ramshackle place called The Boot Wash Café. The owner played it loud: Bryan Adams, REO Speedwagon, and suchlike. Those Coromandel nights were crazy, wilder than The Windlass by a country mile.' Joel paused, aware of talking too much. Then, 'Have you heard of a singer songwriter called Jane Gregory? She lives in your territory.'

'Sorry. Is she on YouTube?'

'Not at the moment. She's low key. A friend sent me a recording. Jane's music is the equivalent of a sweet summer day.'

'Sounds amazing. You said you like the quiet. Is that what your Zen garden is for?'

Joel nodded. He wanted to ask Marianne about her, but maybe tonight wasn't the night. She'd open up when she was ready. 'How about this for synchronicity – a few years before the New Zealand trip, I met a group of Buddhists visiting from the North Island. They said that if I ever

143

ventured that far, I should stay at their retreat centre. Two weeks was all I could get with the schedule, but I'm so glad I went, as it was awesome.'

'Are you a Buddhist?'

'I don't follow any organised religion. Wisdom can be found in many places, but there is so much that is useful and practical in Buddhist philosophy and psychology. I meditate every morning when the air is at its cleanest, before industrial and human activity pollute it.'

Marianne was quiet for a moment. Joel's world view was so unlike anyone else's she had encountered. Although unaccustomed to dating, she was aware of bombarding him. They were both flagging, so she called for the bill. 'Would you ever go back?'

'Probably not, although green fuel can't be too far away.' Joel looked wistful. 'There was one place I'll never forget. It's a look out point near Lake Taupo. Standing up there alone, feeling like the only human on the earth, my mind and body atomised. The experience changed me forever.'

Marianne's imagination summersaulted. 'I'd love to see the photos sometime.'

'Sure, but you might run for the hills. I'm a bit of a nerd.'

'It'll take more than a few holiday snaps to chase me away.'

'That's good to hear. You know, Marianne, the UK is a remarkable island and is often overlooked. Kurt's partner lives in Mull.'

'Kurt has a partner?'

'Doesn't look the type, does he? The 'Kurt the flirt' moniker is a tad unfair, as to my knowledge he doesn't play around.'

'Do you, Joel?'

For what seemed like an eternity, neither said a word. Marianne was mesmerised by this stranger who, without knowing how or why, had begun to dismantle her armour. Joel Midwinter was a man whose very existence was programmed to kindness. She paid the bill, and as they walked to the abbey ruins, a barn owl's hiss slashed the black sky. Joel held her face in his gentle hands. *No, Marianne, I don't play around.*

'Morning Joel. There's tea in the pot. We were just telling Marianne about the old days, when Gramps used to wait for me outside Ropemaker's Yard, and we'd scuttle over to Gorse Wood, before it was taken over by the Trust, that is.

'The Trust only bought it to stop you young rascals from disturbing the wildlife.' Joel pulled up a chair amidst the mirth. 'Morning, Marianne. Did you sleep well?'

'Yes, thank you. It took me a while to remember where I was though. How about you?'

'Joel's a creature of habit. As long as he gets his eight hours, the world's the right side up, eh, lad? What are your plans for today?' said Dudley, who was sporting his weekend best 'Cambridge Folk' T-shirt.

'The weather's good until late afternoon when there's the chance of a rogue shower. I thought we might go to Weybourne for a beach walk and lunch, unless you've a special request, Marianne?'

'I'm happy to be guided. Irene, let me help with the dishes.'

'That's kind of you dear, but I'll have a clear up when you've gone. Go and enjoy yourselves.'

As the Outlander drove away from Wells along the coast road, there was a moment of awkwardness as neither were sure how to greet the other, but Joel's laid-back manner reignited Marianne's confidence. She had fibbed about sleeping well. Her thoughts had swirled like a snowstorm until the early hours when fatigue dragged her into sleep. Joel's kiss couldn't have been less playful, as were his words, *No, Marianne, I don't play around.* Her earlier excitement had morphed into trepidation, as if she were about to enter into a situation which required great care. Beneath Joel's upbeat, hyper-friendly exterior she detected a reticence, a weighing up of just how much of himself he was willing, or able to reveal. In such a short space of time, they couldn't claim to know the other, but if feelings were Marianne's guide, there was nowhere else she wanted to be. Joel was as deep as the ocean, and she felt compelled to dive in, despite the risks. Perhaps it was because she was older, or simply fed up being single, or that he was the most interesting man she'd ever met. Her inspirational quotes book said that every moment was perfect, and she was determined not to jump ahead.

When they arrived at the quay, Joel switched off the ignition and turned to her. 'Marianne, I've a confession to make. I didn't want to say this in front of Gramps as he's a worrier, but I didn't get eight hours last night. You were so near, yet so far.'

'That's exactly what I was thinking at three o'clock this morning!'

'What a pair! So, I haven't put you off?'

'Let me see: you are good company, knowledgeable, and fun, but your kissing technique could do with buffing up.'

Joel pulled her towards him and as their eyes met there it was, another knot tied. They got out of the car and walked hand-in-hand to the shoreline.

'Marianne, do you trust me enough to tempt you into the water?'

'How d'you mean?'

Joel told her about the professor's property, and his open-ended access to the pool. How to reply to such a startling request? She didn't even own a swimsuit. 'May I think about it?'

'Sure. What time are you heading home?'

The thought of home was like the sun disappearing behind a cloud. 'I'd like to get back before dark.'

'After lunch let's have a rest in the cabin, then we'll make a date for our next adventure.'

'Yes, let's do that. At least now I get to choose my hours.'

'The rangers are happy to swap, which makes life easier. Did you get a message from Zak?'

'The invitation to Go Wild!?' She nodded. 'I can't wait to see what he's achieved. Can you make it?'

'I'll confirm it when we get back. C'mon, let's eat before I run out of puff. I owe Gramps at least two hours' sleep to keep him happy.'

Marianne's reluctant return to Sycamore Crescent was eased by the jubilant news that the tenant in Number 7 was no more. Several notes had been posted through the door in addition to numerous telephone messages confirming celebratory drinks on the communal lawn, tomorrow afternoon at three. Without turning on the lights, Marianne opened the living room window into the garden, and sat beside it. It was tempting to sit outside under the balmy night sky, but she didn't want to draw attention to her return. She had almost fallen asleep at the wheel on the motorway, the shock of which had acted like a freezing shower and was relieved to be home.

The warm lemon water was refreshing. Irene had made her the same thing just this morning, before breakfast. *We always start our day this way, Marianne. It clears out the clutter.* Irene and Dudley Midwinter were good people. After another inspiring morning, she and Joel returned to the cabin. Laying on his bed, his wiry frame softened into her curves through their clothes, and there they slept, wrapped up in each other. Two hours later, over tea and toasted sandwiches, it was decided that she would return the following week for her first swimming lesson. Then, work rota permitting, he'd drive to Sycamore Crescent and accompany her to Zak's garden party. They had burst into laughter as it seemed so silly to think that with a combined age of seventy-five, they were tentatively making a date to get under the covers. Marianne smiled at the thought as she went upstairs for a bath. Without having to spell it out, they both knew that Joel's reaction to her scars would determine the next step. It was exciting and unnerving in equal measure.

'You'd think that after all these years of wiping snotty noses my immune system would be robust enough to keep the germs out.' Della blew into the tissue through red nostrils. 'Anyway, enough of my blather. What do you mean, *help me choose a swimsuit*? OMG! Don't tell me you are at long last getting in the water?'

Della's legs were resting on the sofa. She was wrapped in a blanket and nursing a tumbler of medicinal brandy. The cold had affected her ability to hit the high notes, and the Guildhall performance was coming around fast, so desperate measures were in order. Della had no trouble accepting her best friend's solicitous ministrations. Now snug, she grinned at Marianne's startled expression. 'Nothing doing, friend?'

'These swimsuits are cut so high they wouldn't cover a freckle, Della. Whatever happened to the good old-fashioned Speedo?' Marianne closed the laptop lid and picked up her tea.

'Times have changed. What I am busting to know, Marianne, is how, in just twenty-four hours, you've agreed to expose your most intimate and painful secrets to a stranger.'

Marianne had thought of nothing else since returning home. The disturbing memories of her childhood accident had settled into the furthest reaches of her unconscious mind until Warren arrived on the scene, so funny and so kind. *It's a tragedy that a treasure like you has been hidden away for so long.* After Warren left her and Freddie, Marianne's habitual tendency to hide had reasserted itself. Joel's well-meaning offer to swim had reignited all manner of past fears which she was determined to overcome. 'Am I making a mistake, Della?'

'Who knows, but this is the first time since Warren you've thought about you. Joel deserves a medal, even if he is a flash in the pan.'

'He doesn't feel like a flash in the pan. I trust him. Joel's professor friend has a shallow rainwater pool, perfect for a test run. After years of worrying what others might think about my scars, who knows how many loving encounters I've missed. By the way, Joel's coming to Zak's garden party. You'll meet him then.'

'What a shame! We're off to Cork for Mam's birthday. Did I tell you that Terence will be staying with her before coming to Epping? I don't know who'll be the first to explode, but we'll be sure to hear all about it on the six o'clock news.'

'Good luck with that. Anyway, if the pool session is a disaster, at least we'll have seen each other with our kits off. I've an idea – why don't you and Terence come for dinner, and you can give Joel the once-over.'

'That sounds grand! We'll have napkins and candlesticks and port – show my hoity-toity brother we know how to do things in style.' Della sneezed, blew her nose and laughed. Finally, her best friend had a romance on her hands. 'As long as Joel's not stringing you along, Marianne, I'm happy you're happy. Okay, now I've finished my brandy I'll pick you out suitable bathing togs, although from what you've said about the professor's private pool, you may not be needing any.'

❀ ZAK ❀

IT WAS seven o'clock and the sun was already warm. Zak finished watering, taking particular care over the newly planted *Salvia* Woodland Sage, his dad's choice. It was Bonnie's favourite. His mum had picked a native honeysuckle called Graham Thomas, which ticked all the bee and bug boxes, and she liked its scent. Shane had praised his enthusiasm and growing knowledge. They had worked out a weekly schedule although there wasn't much to do this time of year. Esme's idea of a raised bed was put on hold as they now had a veg box delivered, and the waste went into the new hot bin for compost.

Zak took the apple diagram out of his folder. Looking at food, clothes, and products in this way was addictive. If everything that was grown or manufactured used cause and effect as a first principle, the planet wouldn't be in this mess, even he could see that. Zak had reorganised the weekly shopping delivery to include as many ethical products as were available and sourced the rest online. As for clothes, Imogen pointed out that she already had a number of Stella McCartney pieces and 'might consider' changing her brands. Gil said he had enough clobber to last a lifetime anyway. At least they had thought about it, and Zak took it as a step in the right direction. Identifying the various insects and bees was occasionally tricky. Thankfully he could ask Joel or his new friends, Nina and Benedict, who had set up the Epping Bugspotters What's

App group, and they were in touch almost every day. Nina Kossi. Epping Bugspotter. Totally fab. Zak couldn't stop thinking about her. Esme had grilled him, as if Nina were a rare specimen, but in a way she was, as he'd never met a girl who talked about twelve-eyed caterpillars, and who had protest marched to protect the endangered stag beetle. She and Benedict were chuffed to be invited to his party, and if it went well, he'd ask her over for tea.

Life was moving so fast. When was the last time he'd played on the Xbox? He missed Mason but not the football team, although he felt guilty for disappointing his dad. To make amends, Zak invited him to the water meadow. Marianne hadn't minded, and Rudy didn't make a fuss about staying on the lead. The kestrel was the highlight, and the Devil's-bit Scabious had hypnotised Marianne. All in all, the summer was turning into the best ever. The only fly in the ointment was his parents' relationship. They were still sleeping in separate rooms. Zak had given up hoping things might return to normal, as they hadn't been 'normal' for ages. Mason had two sets of parents and he enjoyed the tug-of-war as at least he was getting attention.

With the watering finished, Zak called for Rudy. If his parents did split up, there were lots of people to talk to. Fortunately he had a lot to think about and was able to side-line the 'what-ifs.' With a bit of luck it might not affect him at all.

🌸 GIL 🌸

GIL HUNG his jacket on the back of the chair. The tube train had been stifling, and the headache pulled like a rubber band across his skull. Hugh Ridley's back-office air conditioning unit had packed up, and the jeweller moved at a snail's pace, which was one of the reasons his exquisitely crafted jewellery was so sought after.

'How was the meeting?' asked Spencer.

'Long, hot, and surprising. Hugh's brother moved to Auckland three years ago. Roger Ridley wants us to project manage a new fit for his warehouse and shop in conjunction with the local engineers.'

Spencer passed Gil a glass of cool water and two painkillers. 'What's the timeline?'

'No later than Easter. The Ridleys know it'd be much less expensive not to involve us, but money's not the issue. I said we'd talk it over. What d'you think?'

Spencer gave his glasses a polish, something he did when ruminating. He'd never been to New Zealand and knew for sure that Gil wouldn't go. It would mean at least a week away. Once Nicole got wind, he'd have to fight her off. Business and family were best kept separate in his view. 'I love an excursion, but it'd be tough to do it in a week.'

Gil swigged the last of the water. 'This is your call. Long haul, even in business class is a last resort for me. The question is, do we need the contract? It's flattering to be asked, but what is the benefit?'

'The Ridleys are our oldest and most loyal clients whose recommendations constitute a third of our turnover. It's a favour, pure and simple. When does Roger want an answer?'

'End of the week. You'll think about it Spence?'

'Yes, and let's not mention it to Nicole. Talking of wives, any news from Imogen? The Expo must be in full swing by now.'

'She called last night. Zak was out with his new Bugspotting buddies. It's full-on as expected, but she sounded happy enough. Imogen's been offered a job. The CEO is Malika Lionnet.' Gil waited for the penny to drop. Spencer was nothing if not sharp.

'Marianne's former employer from Wanstead Hall! What are the chances of that.' Spencer tapped on the keyboard and read out her impressive CV. 'Phew, that's some gig. Malika has long since left her old man's Foreign Office shadow by the looks of it. So, what's on offer?'

'Senior advisor or something. To be honest, I didn't take much notice. Imogen can't take the job.'

'Why not?'

'It's obvious why not. She has a fourteen-year-old son who lives in Epping, and the office is based in Singapore. The only reason she's interested is because Annette wants to start a family. Urbane's days are numbered, and she's lining up a replacement role.'

'Wow, that's a huge change. The job sounds interesting, though. If Imogen were to accept it, the family will pitch in. Lena would be only too happy to do your washing.'

'No need, mate. My wife also has the answer to that. She wants to hire Marianne as a housekeeper – you know, keep things 'ticking over' whilst she's absent. I kicked that one into touch. When has Imogen ever been interested in Marianne? She's got some nerve. This Expo has kept her up late, so she's been sleeping in the spare room.'

'Flippin' heck, Gil, no wonder you've been quiet.'

Gil suddenly felt guilty. No matter what was happening in Spencer's life, he was always upbeat. 'Sorry, mate. I should have told you. With Imogen's workload, and Zak hell-bent on this wildlife palaver, I've become the invisible man. He's even chucked in the football. Said he only did it so that we'd spend time together. What kind of a father does that make me, Spencer? Have I neglected Zak?'

Spencer walked over to his cousin and put a reassuring hand on his shoulder. 'No. Zak's a great kid, and he must have got that from someone. I'm sorry about the footie. Maybe he'll change his mind.'

'I'm not so sure. This thing has really got hold of him. Shane said he's a different boy. You know I took Tuesday off so we could spend the day together? He'd already made arrangements to go to the Roding Wetland Reserve with Marianne. Me and Rudy ended up tagging along like a couple of sad plonkers.'

The cousins chuckled, and the mood brightened. 'Looks like you're developing a taste for the outdoors, Gil. You must have had a nice time over there.'

Actually, he did have a nice time, once he got over the shock of being out with Marianne in such circumstances. She was just as surprised when he arrived to pick her up, picnic basket, hat, and all. While Zak skipped off after a kestrel sighting, they had sat in the picnic area, and Marianne passed him an orange to peel as if she did it every day. He found himself confessing a few home truths while she listened attentively. Her reaction to the wildflower was unexpected. What had she called it? A Devil's bit or something, and she had knelt down to take photographs. When Zak said she'd been drawing plants and flowers, the impulse to mention her illustration couldn't be held back. *Your Hazelwood Oak sketch is hanging in The Tower,* to which she replied, as quick as lightning, '*I hope it isn't painful Gil,* and they had laughed. He told her he bought it from the fund-raiser exhibition, and she said, '*I saw it when I went in search of your folder*' and his face burned, caught in the act. Later, sitting on Marianne's bench with tea and cake, he watched Marianne and Zak go in search of bugs. That night's sleep was the most restful he'd had in months.

Niall came in with a tray of sandwiches and coffee. 'Cheers, Niall. Just what I need. How's Ashley doing?'

'The morning sickness has passed, so yeah, all good thanks Gil. Zak's Go Wild! jamboree sounds fun. Imogen will have booked an uptown funky band and ordered ten crates of the best champagne.'

'Zak is calling the shots on this one. Could be an interesting afternoon with Lena and Cilla Marsalis sharing the same space. D'you fancy overtime as a bouncer?'

'I'll pass on that guv, but I'll order in extra headgear for you. By the way, your meeting with Darren Turner is confirmed.'

'Thanks. Have you got a minute, Niall? Spencer and I want to talk to you about something.'

Niall moved further into the office while Spencer closed the door behind him.

'Your dad said he's got room for you all at his house when the baby comes, but you're not keen to move in.'

'Ashley's willing, Gil. She'd do anything to get out of the flat, but I don't think it's the best way to start family life, as much as me and Dad get on. I've been looking at two-bed flats in Woodford, close to the tube station, but they're pricey.'

'How do you fancy a two-bedroom cottage in Hazelwood? One of our tenants has moved out, and let's just say it wasn't a good match for the community. A friend of ours lives next door. She'd be willing to show you around, help you to settle in.'

Niall's face was crimson. 'It's good of you Gil, but there's no way we can afford to rent a house in that area.'

'Look Niall, you'd be doing us a favour. Marianne had a rough time living with the noise, and it was only committee pressure that made her call us in. There's no deposit, and the rent will be the same as you're paying now. Perhaps later on, you might want to buy it if you like living there, that is.' Gil stopped speaking. Niall's eyes were about to spill over. 'Have a chat to Ashley, and if she's interested, we'll give you Marianne's number. The cottage is in good nick, and will be nicely decorated before you move in. Ashley can choose the colour for the baby's room.'

'The only catch is you might already have a lodger,' said Spencer. 'Apparently, the Sycamore Crescent residents have a hedgehog highway which runs through your garden: an eco-version of HS2.'

The men laughed, and all was well.

'Ashley loves all that caper. Do you mind if I call her?'

'Course not. Number 7 is yours if you want it.'

Gil waited for the door to close. 'Niall was made up, eh? I can't think Ashley will refuse, and they'll make nice neighbours. How did you know about the hedgehogs?'

'Esme and Zak were talking about it. Anyway, well done, Gil. We owe it to Marianne, don't we? She'll also have another decorating job, and an easy one at that.' Spencer didn't need to point out that once again, Gil had added another notch on his safety belt, keeping his people close. 'So, Darren Turner's been in touch. It's been a while.'

'Four years, to be exact. He'll put forward another takeover bid for sure. How do you feel this time around?'

Spencer was thoughtful. He was ready to cash in his chips back then, but things were different now. The European client work had livened up the calendar, and this potential New Zealand trip would be something to look forward to. 'I'm okay at the moment. You?'

'I don't know. The company would be in safe hands, you'll get a five-year consultancy role which takes you to sixty, and we'll negotiate as much security for the staff as we can.' Gil rubbed his brow. 'To be honest Spence, I'm at a crossroads, but what would I do? I've got no hobbies or interests apart from running, and Imogen is hardly waiting in the wings for me to pack it in, is she? If anything, she wants to rev up her working life which will dig an even bigger hole between us. Even when Imogen is at home, she's not there, and cosying up by the fire was never her bag. Let's see what the meeting brings. My immediate focus is on Zak's garden party, and Imogen's fortieth bash. By the end of the year, we'll have a better handle on Armstrong Solution's future.'

'Sounds like a plan. Why don't you go for a walk? Shake

the tube dust from your soles. There's not much going on today.'

'Why not? I'll pop over to the nursing home, see how Dino's getting on. Mum will be pleased about that. I might have a whizz round Vicky Park, feed the ducks with the sandwich crusts.'

Spencer opened a drawer, took out a book and threw it over. 'Here, take this. It'll be better for you than bird-watching.'

Gil smiled at Spencer's reference to the long summer Sunday afternoons by Victoria Park's boating lake, when the frisky East End boys used to scout for girls. Gil glanced at the title, *Emergency Poet*, and slid the book in his jacket pocket. 'Right, then, I'm off. Don't tell the boss.'

Dino Scuderi's frail frame was bent and brittle, but his mind was as sharp as a tack. As soon as Gil walked into the day room, the old man waved him over, gave him a fatherly hug, and sweet-talked the duty nurse into making tea. For the next hour they reminisced about the good old days, and the fun they'd had selling women's clothing on his market stall in Roman Road. No one smooched the ladies like 'Dino the Scud', and women flocked to his stall in their droves. *Will this colour suit my complexion, Dino? Won't I look like mutton, Dino? Can I pay you next week, Dino?* When Nicole and her crew turned up to mingle furtively amongst the rows and racks, Dino would nudge him to be on guard against their thieving fingers, but come the end of trading, he'd often let the girls have unsold items at knockdown prices. *Dressing nice when you're hard up ain't so easy, Gil.*

He'd lost count of the number of times they were propositioned. It wasn't surprising Dino was three-times divorced, and now living out his days in a peaceful nursing home. Market trading had taught Gil important life lessons, and his boss was always generous. *Your fine face pulls in the customers, 'caro amico'.*

'How's Lena. Still as beautiful as ever?'

'Prickly more like. She'll be over the moon when I tell her you haven't lost your twinkle.'

'I keep the staff on their toes. See Muriel over there? She's got her eyes on me. Now, what d'you wanna know?'

'Mum never talks about the old man. With Zak growing up, I've been thinking about family, but ...'

'Jimmy always dressed smart, just like you. He wanted to see you, but Lionel said if he showed up, he'd call the boys in blue. Jim's real name was Flowerberry, but after one too many pastings at school, he took up boxing and changed his name. Used to keep an eye out for me, being so skinny. He was a prize fighter, back in the days: Jimmy the 'Knockout' Knox. He had the swagger, no doubt about it.'

Torn between wanting to know more but fearful of the outcome of such knowledge, Gil was quiet. Sensing his agitation, Dino placed a transparent, liver-spotted hand on his.

'*Mio figlio*, Jimmy Knox loved you as much as he could. His old man was a docker, hard as nails. Used to knock him about. Jimmy left as soon as he could. Wasn't much psycho help back then, and even if there was, he was a proud man. Once he came over, sober, said he was sorry, and could I tell Lena. Poor man died soon after.' He put his hand up to Gil's face. 'You are nothing like him. *Sei un angelo, mio figlio.*'

After gently embracing Dino's fading frame, Gil sprinted across the road and into the park. He sat on a bench by the boating lake and blew his nose. Dino had called him an angel ever since he could remember. *Your father loved you as much as he could.* Wasn't that all anyone could do? Feeling the colour return to his face, Gil surveyed the grounds. He couldn't remember the last time he'd been to Victoria Park, yet the terrain was stamped on his soul like a sailor's tattoo. A sequence of grainy images instantly flickered through his mind: His old man giving the merry-go-round a running spin, *best you hang on boy*; in the rowing boat, *don't grip the oars too tight, boy*; walking away from the ice-cream van, holding two cones, Gil's one topped with hazelnuts and sticky strawberry sauce, *mind you don't spill it down your clean shirt, boy.* Afterwards, they'd walk the never-ending trail along Bishops Way and into Old Bethnal Green Road towards home. Gil would count the pavement cracks, praying for even numbers, as there was a chance that after the roast dinner, the snooze, and the boozy night at the pub, his old man would go straight to bed without walloping his mother.

Gil bought a cup of hot sweet tea from the café and sat at the empty table by the side of the lake. He pulled the book out of his pocket: *Emergency Poet: An Anti-Stress Poetry Anthology.* Spencer had one of those brains that absorbed everything, which was useful in quizzes, and at other times slightly annoying. Gil opened the book at random. *Leisure: W. H. Davies.* He scanned the poem and was surprised to find that not only was it familiar, but he agreed with the sentiment. Who actually had the time to take a breath and look around these days?

His mother's words were engraved in his seven-year-old brain: *Now he's gone, you're the head of the family, Gil. Don't let me down.* Lionel and Jean knew he wasn't destined for a desk job, so the opportunity to join Brett Alarms was encouraged. He, Warren, and Clive traded their childhood skirmishes for serious money as enthusiastic alarm engineers, working six days a week, sometimes seven. When Lionel moved the family to Epping, Gil had bunked down at Mrs Silk's house until he had saved enough for a deposit on his first flat. Within five years, he had upscaled to a warehouse development on the Isle of Dogs, and Strong-Arm Security was doing well. It didn't take long before Warren started grumbling: *you cousins don't think big enough; you've no ambition, and we'll get left behind while everyone else makes the big bucks.* Fortunately Gil and Spencer were able to buy him out. Soon after, the newly branded 'Armstrong Solutions' were wearing suits and winning awards, Gil had met Imogen, and the world was his oyster.

Two women passed nearby with their prams, chatting and laughing. Gil glanced up. 'Would you like the table?'

'Only if you're staying.'

They laughed, and after a fruity exchange, Gil left the women to their sunny afternoon, their thick black lashed eyes lasering his back. It used to drive Warren crazy. *I just don't get it, Gil. I do all the talking, while you just stand there like Richard soddin' Gere and watch the women fall at your size nines.* Even Imogen had engineered their business lunch, and the sub-text couldn't have been clearer. His stomach rolled. This new job would mean weeks away from home. Gil had always admired her independence but now, fifteen-years on, what did they have in common? At the time, he was elated to have met his professional and sexual match, but the lack of intimacy hadn't occurred to him until recently. Perhaps he had accepted that this was the closest he would ever get to a loving relationship.

Gil had seen men and women crane their heads to gaze at Imogen whose elegance flowed like liquid gold. It was the same at the wedding, when he and Spencer stood with two hundred guests in Cleve Castle's grand reception room, waiting for the stunning bride to arrive. Spencer said their romance was like an upside-down urban fairy tale, and for a while the spotlight was enjoyable. Even when Imogen's ignorant, chinless wonder pals enquired after his educational status, it didn't bother Gil too much. Telling them he'd been to borstal, usually did the trick. Soon though, the constant round of parties wore thin. The last straw was listening to a gaggle of drunken dinner suits commenting on his jolly good fortune for making history by 'wedding and bedding the lynx-eyed Venus.' This had tightened his jaw and his fists. Thankfully not all of Imogen's circle were forgettable. While not quite his intimates, several had become clients, and occasional sporting event companions.

Soon after came the children's parties, and while neither he nor Imogen wanted a family, it wasn't long before it became a question of why not. After all, they were committed enough to marry so surely a child, just the one, would enhance their lives. Looking back, he could see it play out like a business transaction during which they discussed the pros and cons of having a baby. His mother, however, hadn't held back. *It won't last. Your backgrounds are too different; business is the only thing you've got in common, and once the physical attraction wears off, there will be nothing left. Imogen is no homemaker, and the child will suffer for it.* How he had hated her for that. Imogen had tried her best to win his mother over. The fund-raising auction for Lee Morrell Lodge was a success, as was the charity shop's revamp, still the recipient of a stream of pre-loved designer clothes canvassed from her circle. Lena's furious reaction to Imogen's 'brazen interference in our family business' affectively ended the relationship.

Gil drove away from the nursing home towards the office. He thought of Imogen, and how, after their last argument, she had returned to their bed for a single night. The sex was urgent, desperate. It had always been a physical, straightforward affair – that was what Imogen wanted, and that was what she got, but that night she had clung to him, something she'd never done, and he didn't like it. In a rare moment of openness, she confessed that his nocturnal lashings out were the reason for sleeping next door. When he said he was afraid of becoming like his father, Imogen suggested he have another try at counselling, 'for himself.' Did she also believe their marriage had run its course? Something in him was shifting, and the recognition was both alarming and liberating.

Spencer was right to have chucked him out of the office as he felt much better. Gil replayed a conversation he'd had with Shane recently. The gardener had suffered with depression after a protracted and messy divorce. Help came in the guise of a 'natural running' group who met regularly in Derbyshire, and it was the best thing he'd ever done. After seeing Gil's alarmed expression, Shane grinningly suggested he look them up online, which he did, and he was impressed. It was good to have another ally at such an unsettling time.

JOEL

JOEL CLOSED the steel gate, grateful to have completed the repair job alone. He climbed into the Outlander and drove to the Rose's farmhouse. Marianne had arranged to meet him at the swimming pool, and he could barely contain his excitement. His absences at The Windlass had drawn suspicions which, when confronted over lunch at The Kedge, led to a red-faced confession. The rangers (apart from Meg) had crowded him in congratulation: *it's about time; Marianne's a lucky lass; there'll be more overtime for us now*. Later that afternoon, Joel had tackled Meg head-on. She stopped short of accusing him of betrayal. *Just because we didn't get it together, Joel, I'm not going to apologise for caring about you.* He was sorry for giving her the wrong impression but if she didn't love Gareth, she should let him go. Then, Meg tearfully apologised for her misguided actions. Whatever he might think of her, she only wanted what was best for him.

His grandparents had guessed. When Joel side-stepped their offer to put Marianne up, his blush gave the game away. *Nothing ventured, Joel* was Dudley's comment. If he hadn't plucked up the courage to ask Irene to go dancing, they might never have married, and look at them now. His gran had held him tight, and said he was in safe hands. Kurt was due back in a few days by which time Joel was confident he'd have an announcement. Marianne's image filled his waking moments and disrupted his sleep.

The subsequent energy nose-dive prompted a call to his consultant, Sabrina Cohen-Rockley. She insisted he contact her in an emergency, no matter what time of day or night, and their regular exchanges were always playful.

Rose Ranger to Doctor Sprockley: Disturbance recorded on the heart-o-meter due to unexpected fly-in of fabulous female. Do I require medical assistance? Over.

Doctor Sprockley to Rose Ranger: Probably not, but I sure do! Do the usual. Call back if needs be. In the meantime, keep calm and carry on. Over.

Rose Ranger to Doctor Sprockley: Message received loud and clear. Will continue investigation. Over and out.

Joel re-read the messages. He could see Sabrina laughing in relief. Her first question was always the same: have you fallen in love yet? The GP confirmed that his symptoms were indicative of fatigue, but all was well. Once again, Joel checked the time. The closer it got to one o'clock, the more his nerves fluttered. After Marianne's swimming lesson, they agreed to go back to the cabin for a quiet afternoon, followed by dinner. She didn't want to impose on Irene and Dudley's hospitality, so Joel reminded her that Kurt's flat was available should she want it, and they left it at that.

There was just enough time to buzz around the grounds before walking over to the pool. The approach to the swimming hut was through the ancient orchard, Joel's imagined version of the Garden of Eden. In amongst knee-high grasses, lichen-covered boughs displayed ripe fruit of every variety, and all was overseen by two majestic limes whose delectable fragrance filled the air. The wild raspberries and strawberries were too tempting to resist. Joel picked a handful and delighted in the texture and taste of each one as they melted on his tongue. He picked up a punnet of windfall cherries from the long grass and left them with the raspberries on the wrought iron table outside the pool along with a picnic, and his backpack. As he pushed open the doors, warmth poured over him. Joel rolled back the cover to reveal crystal clear water. There were clean towels, floats, and goggles on the poolside and as he bent down to feel the temperature, he was reassured: twenty-eight degrees Celsius. Today was monumental, so everything had to be right. He couldn't believe Marianne had agreed to join him in the water, and he was prepared for every eventuality, although he was convinced her limbs would instinctively remember how to move, and at no point would he leave her. All was ready. Joel walked out to the front of the house and waited.

'That's it, Marianne, keep moving your arms and ankles in small circular motions. My hands and the water are supporting you. Try not to hold your breath, and I'll try not to hold mine.'

Step by slow backward step, Joel led Marianne's body through the water, holding her head and shoulders as gently a five-day-old chick. Everything had happened so quickly since her arrival. After an awkward hug, it was obvious she wanted to get on with it. As soon as Marianne walked around the shallow pool and tested the water temperature, she took her bag into the tiny changing room, and emerged wearing an orange swimming cap and a towel wrapped around her. Joel waited nearby as she made her tentative steps down the ladder to join him in the pool. They stood for a while and without prompting, she dipped her shoulders underneath and came back up, after which he took her hand and they walked together, up and down, while he made small talk, gauging her fear responses which were minimal. Marianne's confidence was infectious, but he didn't want to push it. As her body floated close to the water's surface, Joel could easily make out the scars on her thighs as the sunlight revealed their colour and texture, stark against her alabaster skin. He set aside his instinct to empathise with her traumatic history as there was time for that later. For now, he was keen to bring the session to an end. 'Marianne, in a moment I'll ask you to bend your knees and allow your body to come into an upright position.'

'Do I have to? This is so relaxing, just like soaking in the tub but with the added bonus of a lovely man to sweeten the water.'

A peal of laughter bounced around the corrugated roof. Joel was elated. In the next second Marianne stood, grinning. Emboldened by her confidence, he asked her to lie back once more.

'I can barely feel your hands Joel, and I'm not sinking. Instinctively, I want to turn over and kick my legs.'

'Are you sure?'

'Yes, but please stay close to me.'

'Marianne, my middle name is 'barnacle'.'

In a flash, she rolled over and doggy-paddled to the side of the pool. Then, she threw her arms in the air. 'I did it!

Joel swam over, grateful that the water masked his tears. He wrapped his arms about her. 'Yes, you did. You're amazing!'

'Can I come back tomorrow morning?'

'Your wish is my command.'

Joel rinsed the last plate and passed it to Marianne who wiped it and returned it to the rack in the tiny kitchenette. He couldn't help but grin. Being with her was as natural as being in the woods, or by the sea, places that felt like home. It was early evening, warm and light, the kind that draws you outside to enjoy its splendour as it begins its own end. Joel longed to remain in this bubble of present tense, but his mind zipped ahead to the moment when Marianne would walk away from the cabin, and drive away from Wells, until the next time. He acknowledged the uncustomary sensation of separation and shook himself up. 'Would you like to see the sunset?'

'Yes please!' Marianne hung the wet tea-towel on the rail. 'If you were an artist Joel, how would you paint today?'

'With the most vibrant colours in the palate, using big bold strokes and with a theatrical flourish – like this.' He swung out his arm to demonstrate, then he wrapped it around her.

'Sounds like Hockney, swimming pool and all. When you were holding me, I realised that my fear was never about swimming *per se*, as I swam as a toddler. The fear came from being exposed, of not wanting to uncover my body. That must be why I feel so euphoric.'

'There'll be no stopping you now. Is there a pool nearby?'

'Yes, near the town centre but the Rose's rainwater pool

is so special, I don't think I could face the noise and the chlorine. Oh, I just remembered Hilda Paxton's pool. I house and cat sit when she visits her family in Lincoln.'

'Will she let you use it on a regular basis?'

'I'm there Friday week. I'll ask her.'

Joel was quietly calculating dates. 'That means we won't see each other until Zak's Go Wild! party. The Foundation's schedule is swamped next week, and this time I can't swap.'

'Well then Ranger, there's no time to waste.'

Joel's cloud of disappointment dispersed as quickly as it arrived. Marianne grabbed his hand, and they swiftly exited the cabin in search of the miraculous.

Late evening birdsong, melodious and heartening, floated through the window. Joel felt Marianne's quiet breath synchronize with his own. He'd been awake for a while, ecstatically reliving the afternoon in the pool, and the wonderful picnic under the lime trees. Later, they had silently and painstakingly undressed each other before sliding under the duvet. Making love with Marianne was so much more thrilling than he could ever had imagined. He had searched out every landmark, and as he tenderly traced the silky-smooth scar tissue from lower abdomen to mid-thigh, Marianne yielded with barely a flinch. She had endured unimaginable physical and psychological pain with immense courage. Joel studied her peaceful sleeping face. Marianne didn't need to be noticed: she was willing to take risks in her own time, and tempo. Now that this burden had been lifted, like a song canary released from its cage, life would welcome her in unimaginable ways.

And what of him? There was no question he loved her.

It was as clear and as strong as his love for all of the earth's treasures. There was time to discover if Marianne felt the same, but would that truly matter? At last he had finally given himself permission to love another human in this way. Gratitude and humility engulfed him. Sabrina, Kurt, his grandparents, the Roses, everyone he held dear had wished this for him, but he'd been unable to allow himself the experience as he had considered the risk too great. What if he was hurt? What if his heart were broken? Joel smiled to himself. His heart was already broken, but hadn't he proved to trust it? He was young, strong, healthy, happy, and was experiencing the joy of his boundaries dissolving as he and Marianne spent time together, grew together. Who knew if the exhilaration would last for a day, a week, or decades? Life was movement and change; he was meant to know happiness, to be present to each experience, and to welcome the next one without grasping, craving, or reliving the past. He simply had to trust there were more to come. But in this moment there was nowhere else, and with no one else Joel Midwinter wanted to be.

'What d'you think, Joel? It needs editing, but I thought we might leave in some of the out-takes as it gives the piece humour and authenticity, like the wildlife. The French call it *Cinéma Vérité*.'

'Get you, Luc Besson. This filming lark is going to your head. In all seriousness Kurt, you've done a fine job. Lori's quietly passionate manner really shines out.'

Kurt pulled the cushion from behind his back and threw it at Joel. 'Get you, John flippin' Keats. This falling in love malarky is making a poet of you.' The old friends chuckled at the rapid-fire wisecracks which were customary whenever they reunited. As usual, Kurt's appearance lit a fire under everyone although there had been a significant change in him since returning from Mull. Joel had registered it within that first hour, and they finally had quiet time during which to talk. He put the kettle on the stove and sat opposite. 'It seems we've both got a dose of woman trouble. I'm having a tough job stopping myself counting down the days till I see Marianne again.'

'I'd be doing the same, Joel, but if Marianne Bly is in the running for the perfect mate, what then? How will you react if she wants to settle down, get a place together? She may want another child. Where will that leave you? What about your freedom?'

'Steady as she goes, Kurt. Marianne is mature enough to see how it pans out. As for kids, you know it's not what I want, and anyway, she has a son. Meeting her feels pretty miraculous. She's got an eighteenth-century botanical microscope and she talks to her plants! I'd say that qualifies Marianne as more than simply an object of desire. After all, it's my cerebral cortex that distinguishes me from the animal. If it were just sex, I've no trouble meeting that need.'

'Sorry mate. Didn't mean to bombard you. You're right not to look ahead, and to enjoy it for what it is. I'm just having a wobble. Anya and I talked through the practicalities of living and working together, raising a child, having a routine, however loose. Then it hit me. She said it was a healthy response but at some point I'd have to face myself, as no one else can work out where the uncertainty is coming from.'

'Anya will never hold you back, but what if you enjoy staying in one place long enough to watch your child grow. Your dad was an important role model, and so will you be. To quote you Kurt, there's only one way to find out.'

Kurt turned off the kettle and poured the water in the teapot. 'Yeah, stupid me hadn't considered it. Too busy thinking about what could go wrong. All I know is that when I'm in Mull, the less I want to be anywhere else.'

'That's a start. Let's celebrate with a slice of Gran's fruit loaf.' He took the cake out of its box. 'It's a shame you're not around for Zak's Go Wild! wingding next Sunday. He's logged a shed load of inverts, insects, and birds. I think it's put the wind up his parents, but isn't that what children are meant to do?'

'I'll let you know when it happens to me. So, you're staying at Marianne's house. Will you meet her son?'

'Freddie arrives as I leave, which is a good way of breaking the ice. Shall I mention the Mull trip to Zak? He'll need to ask permission and get organised.'

Kurt nodded. 'Anya can't wait to meet Marianne.'

'Oh, I hadn't thought that far ahead … I mean, yes, I must ask her!' He slapped his forehead. 'I'm such a *dik dik*. She'll definitely want to come. We'll spend a whole week together! That'll be something to look forward to. Can we stay in Anya's cottage?'

'Of course, you dummy. If Zak can come, he'll want to camp out with the group. Just make sure you keep yourself fit and well. Remember what traditional Chinese medicine says about *Jing*. All this sex will be leaching your life energy. Best not mention that to Marianne at this stage, though. It'd be a real shame to nip it in the bud.'

MARIANNE

THE SWEET sounds of domesticity rose from the kitchen and into Marianne's happy ears as she marvelled at the turn of events. It had taken Joel less than five minutes to make himself at home. After a quick orientation, he dived into the garden and immediately identified a bullfinch, five species of bee, three butterflies, and a water cricket pond skater, all before finishing his iced tea. The post-lunch walk in search of the Hazelwood Oak was followed by an afternoon of blissful lovemaking and ended with a deeply restful night. Marianne had no idea at what point Joel went outside to meditate earlier that morning. She wanted to know more. He had gathered much of what was beneficial and practical from various spiritual traditions and age-old healing systems which, along with conventional medicine, supported his wellbeing. Knowing this afforded an intriguing glimpse into his *modus operandi*. As Marianne propped the pillows behind her back, a grin appeared from behind the door.

'You're awake! I've made hot water and lemon.'

'Lovely. Are you coming back to bed?'

'Try and stop me.' Joel put the mugs down, slid back under the duvet, and immediately drew Marianne to him. 'I could get used to this. Your south-facing garden is perfect for early morning meditation. Next door's wind chimes added to the atmosphere, and several bees were making moves on the lavender. I had a high old time.'

'When the new neighbours move in there will be a different song to be heard, much sweeter than what we've had to endure recently.'

'It was good of Gil and Spencer to rent it to the expectant parents at a reasonable rate. I'm so lucky in that respect. I can live in the accommodation block at The Kedge for free, but Irene and Dudley only want a small sum to cover electricity and water, and I prefer to be near them. How long have you lived here?'

'Sixteen, seventeen years. After Warren left, Freddie and I moved in with Della and Sean. When the Armstrongs heard about our predicament, they offered to rent me this house, but I was lucky enough to buy it. Warren's mother was ashamed that we'd been left in the lurch, so she paid the deposit, and Gil's uncle Lionel arranged a mortgage.'

'It's comforting to keep loved ones close.'

Joel was referring to Gil and Spencer. Slightly miffed, Marianne reached for her lemon water. It suited her to live at Sycamore Crescent, making her own decisions, answerable to no one. Niall and Ashley's occupancy was a business decision: landlords needs tenants, particularly those who don't upset the neighbours. She elbowed the unpleasant feeling aside. 'When will you know if Zak can go to Mull?'

'This afternoon, with luck. I hope Freddie doesn't feel awkward with me in his mother's house.'

'Freddie will have to get used to it. My son's moods are his responsibility but be prepared for an interrogation.' Marianne sounded more confident than she felt. Freddie's temperament was unpredictable. She was still adjusting to the speed with which she and Joel had got together, so it had to be difficult for her son. The colossal swimming weekend already felt like a lifetime ago. Hilda was happy to see the pool in use, provided it was an early morning dip. Marianne's first length of front crawl might not win prizes for technique, but she was overjoyed with her progress. With so much going on, there was barely a moment to pick up her pencils. After accepting the job to re-decorate Number 7, Gil had called to ask if she'd like to meet her new neighbours. Niall and Ashley were delighted with her artistic efforts in the baby's bedroom. They were ready and willing to muck in with the community projects and apologised in advance for any disturbance once the baby came.

Gil had made a quip about her amazing maternal instincts and it had chaffed. Did he expect her to be on call? Joel's 'keeping his loved-ones close' comment stubbornly resurfaced. If Gil were attempting to match-make her with Niall and Ashley, he might be disappointed. After waving the couple off, Marianne insisted Gil pay her decorating fee directly into her account – no more cash jobs. Since then, she scrutinised her connections with the cousins and was more determined than ever to go her own way.

While Joel showered and changed, Marianne held her dress up to the light. The muted calico print had kept its freshness, despite its thirty-year vintage, and needed only the smallest alteration. It had been tucked away in the wardrobe, a present from Aunt Sadie, for her sixteenth birthday. The prairie style might be dated but the only people who would notice were Imogen, and Nicole. Marianne glanced down at her bare legs, finding it hard to believe she'd waited so long to uncover them. Would Freddie notice? His arrival generally fluttered her motherly heart. To see him with Rachel was something to look forward to. There was no easy way to tell him she had met a *really nice man*, and predictably he had been silent on the phone before changing the subject. While Joel would never expect to be a stepfather to Freddie, there was a relationship to be had. It was an incredible position in which to find herself after living alone for so long. Joel's gently reassuring proximity gave her courage. No, he wouldn't kiss her in front of Freddie; no, he wouldn't mention the swimming lessons; yes, he must return to Norfolk after the party. He had to get back for work and in any case, their relationship might be difficult for her son to accept. With these thoughts on her mind, Marianne stepped into the dress, tied the sash, pinned up her hair, and finished tidying the bedroom.

'What's so special about my mother that you'd drive two hundred miles to see her just for one day? Just so you know, she's got no money.'

Joel and Freddie stood like sentries on either side of the living room window, watching Marianne and Rachel admire the garden. Joel studied the serious face of the younger man and was sympathetic. 'I've no money either, now you mention it. Look Freddie, you don't need me to list Marianne's qualities. I believe you know the circumstances in which we met, and as we're both single, I can see no earthly reason not to spend time with her.'

Freddie coughed in embarrassment. 'Fair enough. So, erm, is it a rewarding job, being a ranger?'

'Yeah, it's terrific. I brought something with me on the off chance you were interested in what we do. You're a Liverpool fan, right?'

Freddie nodded. He was trying to come to terms with the fact that a) his mother had met someone b) that 'someone' was just six years older than he was and c) Joel Midwinter seemed like an okay bloke. He'd entertained them with his tales of Foundation life over lunch, and once Freddie had overcome his resentment to find that a stranger had hijacked his family and friends, he found himself warming to the bright-eyed man who fancied his mother (who was actually wearing a dress!) 'I used to support West Ham, but I moved away and … why do you ask?'

Ruffling through his rucksack, Joel pulled out a pack of playing cards. He already knew Freddie's team and had prepared a game which was always a hit with the kids, while the adults found it both disconcerting and funny, once they overcame their initial embarrassment. 'Humour me for five minutes, and I'll guarantee that by the end of our game, you'll have a better idea of what a ranger's life is like.'

Freddie pulled up a chair opposite and watched the ranger shuffle the pack of cards before splitting the deck into two halves with the expertise of a professional croupier. He was intrigued.

'The game is called '*Snapperwhipper!*' – it's basically 'Snap', but when you get a matching card, you have to shout '*Snapperwhipper!*'

Freddie chuckled. It was too ridiculous to take seriously, and this fella was clearly not your everyday sort. He took his half of the pack and slowly they laid alternate cards.

After a short while, Freddie saw a match and banged his hand down. '*Snapperwhipper!*' He and Joel burst out laughing.

''Fraid not, Freddie. Take a closer look.'

As he laid the cards next to each other, Freddie quickly spotted the Liverpool F.C. cosmetic kit trim was different. 'Oh, this must be the 1980's kit.'

'Good spot! Let's continue.'

A few more seconds passed. Freddie's hawk-eyes scanned each card, slower now. He shouted out once again. This time, it was an image of a flock of black-legged kittiwakes.

'Take a closer look.' Joel waited.

'There are fewer birds on my card.'

'That's right. The image on your card was taken last year whereas mine was taken twenty years ago. Their numbers have reduced by 50%. These sea birds spend most of their lives on the ocean, apart from nesting time where the most successful breed as established pairs. With climate change, plastic pollution, and less food, particularly the sand eel, they are now critically endangered.'

At this point, Freddie was on high alert, and as the game progressed, a natural conversation struck up between the players during which Joel talked about Mother Nature's huge environmental losses and her miraculous gains, alongside obscure facts concerning Liverpool F.C. By the time the game ended, Marianne and Rachel returned to find their men engaged in ardent conversation.

'Hey Mum, have you played '*Snapperwhipper!*'?'

'I've not yet had the pleasure. Sorry to break up the fun but it's time to go. Joel will drive us over as he's going home after the party. As it's such a nice day, we can walk back.'

'I hope Zak likes our frog and toad abode. We got it from the RSPB, didn't we Freddie?'

'He'll love it, Rachel. We've a surprise for him, too. Zak's itching to learn about wildlife camerawork so he's been invited to join a group of us on Mull, to film otters and other delights. His parents haven't yet agreed, and Zak doesn't know, so keep it to yourselves.'

Freddie stared at his mother's crimson face. 'You're going to Scotland, Mum?'

'Aren't I the lucky one!' She picked up her bag. 'Shall we go? Zak wants to give us a tour before the other guests arrive.'

Before her son could say another word, Marianne ushered the group out of the house in the direction of Flaxfield.

GO WILD!

FLAXFIELD WAS one of ten mid to late twentieth century houses built on a private road, and within a short distance of Epping Forest. Its name, redolent of bygone days of swaying meadows and damselflies, was a case of wishful thinking by its original occupiers. By the time Nik and Cilla Marsalis bought it as a surprise wedding gift for Imogen and Gil, it was just another in a tradition of makeovers. The multiple additions were the aesthetic equivalent of corpulent cosmetic surgery: a nip here, a tuck there, the bruises and swelling visible forty years on. The interior had received similar treatment: extra reception rooms, ensuite bedrooms, the ubiquitous walk-in wardrobes, and quartz worktops glinting under a planetary window. The present incumbents had added two home offices and a compact gym, everything to suit the modern family's requirements for essential contemporary interior living. Sadly, the neglected afterthought, formerly known as a garden, had fallen victim to these invasions, eroding as fast as the coastline at Robin Hood's Bay.

There was nothing outside to indicate a celebration, apart from a number of cars parked on the huge block-paved drive and further along the road. Upon entering the house, an unexpectedly mean-spirited hallway gave way to a gargantuan kitchen/diner whose bifold doors opened onto a recently reduced patio area, but roomy enough to support a large number of people. From this vantage point, Marianne spotted a group of guests clustered like a conspiracy of ravens on the lawn, while the real stars of the show were conspicuously absent. The feeding station was deserted. The Armstrong clan were in host mode while Zak and Shane were talking to an upright, polar-white-haired gentleman wearing a bowtie. He had to be *the* Mr Goodchild.

Marianne was relieved to have got to this point in the day without a fuss. Freddie's introduction to Joel wasn't too painful, and he now had the opportunity to reunite with the Armstrong family, particularly his good friend Georgia, in cordial surroundings. While he wasn't much of a drinker, his mood generally improved after a beer or two. Rachel was lovely and might even help Freddie to change his bitter tune. He continued to believe that Gil and Spencer were in some way responsible for his father's bankruptcy. There was no concrete basis to this supposition, only that in these cases it was easy to blame the other as a way of avoiding the painful fact that his father had abandoned him. Gil and Spencer were aware of this. Marianne was confident that conversation between them would remain on the relatively safe ground of Zak's achievements, football, and Freddie's job.

With the potential for a tense afternoon receding, Marianne decided to enjoy herself. This was Zak's big day, and she was honoured to have played a small role in this chapter of his young life. Her fingers were crossed for a positive response to the Mull trip. She and Joel would soon be together on a gorgeous island, and if Zak could join them, they'd meet inspirational people and have a memorable time.

Out of nowhere, Zak rushed towards Freddie and after a hug, made a beeline for Joel. The poor boy's adrenalin was on overdrive.

'Marianne, you look fab! It's super exciting and everyone is coming, even Ms Werner my biology teacher. Esme's made a vegan cake especially for Joel and Nina. Are you still up for a visit to Chigborough tomorrow, Freddie?'

'Rachel and I can't wait. C'mon, let's have a look at your garden.'

Zak's twitter led them around the island countertop, laden with trays of glasses, ice-bucketed bottles, and cake domes and into the garden where more visitors had arrived through the gate. Marianne took a glass of fizz from the tray. It was fascinating to watch Imogen weave her way through the crowd with the finesse of a professional who had done this a million times. Alarmingly, she appeared to be heading in her direction! As Imogen approached, looking sensational in an off-the-shoulder dress, Marianne was struck by the fabric design which depicted a variety of wild cats amidst tropical foliage, the perfect choice for the afternoon. Her lightly made-up face, however, couldn't hide exhaustion.

'Marianne! I'm so happy we can chat before the fun starts. You look divine. Is the dress an original?'

'A gift from my aunt.' Marianne was dumbstruck by the sudden interest and couldn't think of anything else to add.

'This is a super important day for Zak, and I must thank you for having a hand in it. Gil and I scarcely recognise our son these days, but it's all to the good. How are you?'

'I'm well, thank you. Was the Singapore Expo everything you hoped it would be?'

Imogen smiled at the skilful but not unkind question. 'I'm still processing the experience, so I'll come back to you on that. I had the great good fortune to meet Malika Lionnet. She expressly asked me to give you her warmest regards and would very much like to see you again when she returns to the UK later this year.'

Silence.

'Oh, I hope I haven't said anything untoward. Malika spoke so highly of you and ...'

'That was good of her.'

With nothing further forthcoming, Imogen found herself uncustomarily blundering on. 'Gil and I haven't had a moment to decide whether Zak ought to go to Mull. I understand he is due to return on the day of my party ...' Her flow was halted by the realisation that Marianne, whose self-contained manner was having a disconcerting effect on her, hadn't been invited.

'I'll make sure he's back in time.'

Imogen's attention was instinctively drawn towards a noisy influx of new arrivals. She turned quickly back to Marianne, her gaze focused, eyebrows slightly arched. 'How extraordinary! I wasn't aware you are one of the Mull party.'

As the realisation dawned on her host, Marianne was mesmerised by Imogen's eyes, like fossilised amber. How to paint such an unusual colour? 'Joel and I, well, it's too early to say ...'

Suddenly, Imogen threw her arms around her. 'I'm delighted for you, Marianne! From the little we know of Joel Midwinter, he appears to be a most engaging and interesting man.'

Nicole zigzagged towards them carrying an empty tray, her cheeks the colour of sangria. Imogen was desperate to avoid her increasingly bad humour. 'I'm so sorry, Marianne, it's time to meet and greet. Look, this trip will cause consternation within the family. Zak has already cancelled one holiday, and it will upset Daddy enormously.' She threw a glance in her father's direction, his silver-grey head nodding enthusiastically at Zak and Joel, before composing herself. 'Marianne, if you can return my son in good time to join the party, I will be grateful.'

Imogen's transformation from disturbed parent and daughter to efficient host was incredible. Her effusive welcome had almost knocked Marianne off her sandalled feet. Imogen's concern for her father was understandable, as hadn't she loved her own dear dad more than anyone else in the world? Marianne hadn't anticipated announcing her new relationship this afternoon, but hearing Malika Lionnet's name had wrong-footed her, particularly as the context in which her former employer and Imogen had met wasn't disclosed. Marianne sighed, and sipped her champagne. Now that Freddie knew about her and Joel, there was no longer a reason to keep it secret. She walked across the garden towards Lena's animated wave, ready for the volley of questions.

Within half an hour, the remainder of the guests arrived, bearing gifts of plants, wooden bird boxes, and nicely wrapped presents in exchange for glasses of champagne, beer, and sparkling elderflower. There was no opportunity to talk to Joel, but Marianne had expected it. It was gratifying to see Freddie in an extended conversation with Spencer and Gil. At one point, the cousins glanced in her direction and she looked away, her face flushed. Then, Zak's finger whistle brought everyone to attention.

'Welcome everyone to Go Wild! especially the blow-ins from Greece and Liverpool, and the all-important pond squatters whose arrival have given me more pleasure than West Ham beating Liverpool (loud cheer). I'd like to thank Mum and Dad for letting me raid their pension pot (more laughs), Shane, Mr Goodchild, Marianne, and my Grove Road neighbours for their generous input.

'But none of this would have been possible without Norfolk's most inspirational ranger, Joel Midwinter, who for some unhinged reason, believes that one day, I'll be inducted into Nature's Hall of Fame (laughter). So, as an expression of my gratitude to him, may I introduce you to a migrant Canadian songbird who has, luckily for us, remained on our shores. She is Joel's favourite species of singer songwriter, and Epping's best-kept secret. Give it up for Jane Gregory!'

A tall, hickory-haired woman dressed in a mulberry linen smock, and carrying an acoustic guitar stepped out from the crowd to an enthusiastic welcome. Marianne hadn't met the singer songwriter in person, but they had talked on the phone. She was inspired by Zak's enthusiasm and agreed to sing a few songs. As Jane lived just ten minutes away, it was no bother at all. Marianne and Zak stood with their arms around a flabbergasted Joel as they listened reverentially to three songs, the last of which was *Back To The Stars*.

I'm back to the stars
That's where I'm going
Back to the stars
Where you're never alone
Back to the stars
That's where we'll meet again
When your blue green days end

After the performance, a crowd quickly formed around the singer. Joel dried his eyes with a napkin. 'How did you find her?'

'It was Marianne's brilliant brain-wave. When we told Jane about you she was only too happy to come,' said Zak, bursting with pride.

'It was one of those serendipitous moments, Joel. She and my choirmaster teach at the same music college' added Marianne.

'I've got to hand it to you both, this was an awesome surprise. Would you mind if I have a chat with Jane?'

They grinned as the ranger hot-footed it across the lawn. Marianne turned to Zak. 'Your speech was wonderful. Everyone is so happy for you.'

'Life's good for both of us, isn't it, Marianne?' Esme called to him. 'Don't go without saying goodbye' and he was off.

Marianne wasn't the only one to have wiped away a tear that afternoon. It was anyone's guess just how far Zak would go. The celebration was almost over, and time for Joel to head back to Norfolk. They walked out to his car, and he drew her to him.

'Marianne, it's been an epic weekend! Even Gil thanked

me, although the Mull holiday has put the cat amongst the pigeons.'

She was tempted to tell Joel about her conversation with Imogen but chose to wait. 'What did he say?'

'Zak can go – isn't that great?'

'Yes it is, Joel. Will I know anyone?'

'Larry is bringing his son, Travis. Larry is divorced, so this is an important yearly fixture for them. I've got a feeling we'll see Nula Buchan and her kids. She and Larry met last year, and they hit it off. You and Anya will get along, and I for one, can't wait.' Joel kissed Marianne a final time and climbed into the Outlander. 'I'll call you when I get home. Freddie and I got off to a good start but let me know if I'm wrong.'

Marianne waved at the car until it disappeared before returning to the dwindling party to retrieve her son and his partner. So, Zak had been given the green light, although Imogen told her they hadn't yet decided. Gil had looked decidedly uptight. She didn't envy the couple's evening. Marianne suddenly felt weary. Rachel was far too nice to mind if she excused herself for an early night. More than anything, she wanted to lay in bed and relive the weekend. Joel's reaction to Jane Gregory was priceless; her son was in love and appeared to like Joel; Zak and Esme were flying high. For once, everything in her garden was rosy.

GIL

'I CAN'T BELIEVE it's over Zak. It was so fun. Are you going to open your presents now?'

'Why don't you give me a hand, Esme?' Zak passed his cousin a package. Rudy had settled next to them on the rug between the sofas while Gil and Spencer wearily observed their offspring.

'It's an RSPB membership and bird book!'

'Wow! Don't lose the tag, Esme, as I have to write my 'thank you' letters after. These presents are fab: a suet feeder, a robin nester, seed from Cumbria Wildflowers and Dara McAnulty's book.'

Gil forced a smile. He was pleased for his son, and the afternoon had gone well in spite of the last-minute scramble to get organised, but he was so glad it was over. Ordinarily, Imogen would have had an event like this sewn up, but since returning from the Expo she'd been lethargic, which was hardly surprising as adrenalin will get you only so far. He'd done his best to speak to everyone and had expertly avoided his mother-in-law. It was comical to see Cilla with Shane. She could take an elbow as though you were the most important person in the world. Gil apologised to his father-in-law for the holiday postponement. While not his usual ebullient self, Nik Marsalis was impressed by his grandson's efforts and enjoyed his speech. There was always another holiday, but times like these were important.

The afternoon had ticked along until Gil's conversation

with Freddie who was uncharacteristically upbeat, and actually enjoyed Spencer's 'Red Fred' football jibes. He even made a self-deprecating comment about Rachel's interest in him. *I don't know what she sees in me, but there must be something appealing about the Blys right now.* Marianne must have felt the powerful six-eyed stare hit her as she had turned away just as quickly. Freddie hadn't needed to say more as there was a lightness to her, and she was wearing a summer dress of all things. Yes, there was something appealing about the Blys.

The clack of Nicole's slingbacks announced her arrival. With a glass of champagne clutched in one hand and a generous slice of lemon cake in the other, she groaningly manoeuvred herself onto the sofa beside Spencer. 'Can someone remind me why we didn't have serving staff this afternoon? I am cream-crackered.'

'Oh, don't complain, Mum. It was so nice for the whole family to be together. Hey Zak, it's a bee brick.'

'What a great idea.' Zak pulled the paper from another parcel. 'Dad, Mr Goodchild gave me a Swiss Army knife!'

'Just don't take it to school, eh?'

Imogen sank into the empty two-seater sofa nearby. Gil had never known her to be so exhausted. He was about to suggest they call it a day when Nicole started her usual post-party swipe.

'I loved Cilla's two piece. Your mum is super stylish, Imogen. Marianne should take note. Where did she dig that frock up from?'

'It's a vintage Marion Dugdale prairie dress. I thought it suited her very well.' Imogen's tired eyes lifted towards Gil. 'How wonderful to be wanted.'

'What d'you mean? Who on earth could want Marianne Bly?'

Zak reared up. 'Please Nicole, can you for once not start a post-mortem. You'll spoil my big day.'

Spencer shifted forward to the edge of the sofa. 'Let's make a move. Everyone's tired and we've a busy week ahead.' He shook Zak's hand. 'Well done, mate. It was a fine afternoon. How did you find Jane Gregory? Great musical chops. I captured all the good bits on the camcorder, which is set up and ready to roll, by the way.'

Zak's bubble was about to burst. He hugged his cousin. 'Nina loved your courgette cake, Esme. Come to Chigborough tomorrow.'

Esme turned to her mother. The champagne and lemon cake were in the process of being hastily dispatched, and she was in no position to answer.

'Dad, can I go?'

'Sure. Make the most of your freedom before school next week.' Spencer was itching to go home. It had been a long day, and neither Imogen nor Gil were in the mood to dissect the event. Nicole's snout had caught wind of something going on, and she wouldn't let up until the truth was out. 'I've a nine o'clock in Bishopsgate, Gil. I'll see you in the office.'

After collecting various belongings, leftovers, and waving the family off, Gil followed Imogen and Zak back into the living room. 'What do you want for tea?'

'I'm too excited to eat, but pizza's always good.' Zak gathered together his mound of presents. 'It was great to see Joel again. He was chuffed to bits at the garden and teary-eyed when Jane Gregory gave her terrific performance.'

'Hmm. Whose idea was that?'

'Marianne's. Even with your connections Mum, you wouldn't have found her. Jane keeps her talent under the radar which makes a nice change, don't you think?"

Gil pulled down the gate on his thoughts. 'Your mother and I have something for you.' He passed an envelope to his son. 'It's from Joel.' As he watched Zak read the invitation, it was impossible not to be pleased that such an opportunity was on offer. Even Imogen was lost for words. Annoyingly, she had given Zak permission to go without finalising it with him but considering her current state, he wasn't about to make a fuss. It was difficult enough for her to accept Annette's sole charge of her birthday party, but Zak's absence would be too much. He'd thought of a contingency plan, and at some point would discuss it with Joel, but right now, his son was about to explode.

'A week on Mull. OMG! Seven days of camping out and filming otters with Kurt, Joel, and a whole bunch of wildlife nuts.'

'Marianne is joining you,' said Imogen.

'Marianne's coming – even better!' Zak caught his father's stony expression. 'What's the matter, Dad?'

Everything was changing so fast, Gil felt the ground fall away. He looked at Imogen. 'Joel didn't mention it.'

'He must have other things on his mind.'

Gil said nothing, his mind whirling.

'Marianne assured me she would bring Zak home in good time, which is why I agreed to the trip,' said Imogen, who was now totally flat and ready for a long hot soak.

Zak was exasperated. 'Well – can I go?'

'Yes, you can go.' Imogen stood up from the sofa.

Zak punched the air and lifted up his dog for a cuddle. 'I'd better whizz Rudy over the park before tea.'

Imogen was on her way out of the room. 'I'm exhausted, Gil. Would you mind if I went up? An early night will restore my spirits.'

'Why don't you take tomorrow off?'

'I may do that.' She walked back to him, desperate for a hug but too proud, or too emotionally wrung out to initiate it. 'We had to let Zak go on this trip, didn't we?'

Gil nodded. 'I just hope that when he gets back to school, everything calms down. We've missed two holidays so it's no wonder we're worn out. Why don't you see your parents at half-term?'

Imogen straightened up. 'Yes, a few days in France might be just the thing. I'll call Mummy tomorrow. We'll have time to talk, Gil.'

Gil flushed. 'Shane's asked me to go to the Peak District and one of us should be in the country while Zak's away.'

'Oh, I hadn't considered that.'

'A few days in France before the party will stop you fretting, and hassling Annette, come to think of it.'

'You're right, Gil. Well then, I'll be off for my bath.'

Gil crept down the stairs and into the kitchen, closing the door softly behind him. Not that the kettle would wake anyone up, but he needed a cup of coffee. It was four o'clock, and the birds were shaking their feathers. He was edging close to another bout of insomnia, and last night's dream was more of a nightmare. Marianne and Zak were trapped in The Tower which was ablaze, and he couldn't get to them. Just as Spencer pulled him back, Zak jumped.

Gil had sat bolt upright, heart racing. He was desperate for human warmth, but Imogen was next door, and the dream state was too terrifying to risk another encounter.

He padded into the darkened living room. Zak's bounty was piled up near the camcorder. The family usually watched the recordings immediately after their frequent events, but this one was a casualty of the severely edited evening. Gil muted the sound on the remote-control panel and sat on the sofa. It was interesting to see the guests' reactions without the soundtrack. While Spencer 'interviewed' each guest, their expressions ranged from incredulity to joy. As someone who had been self-conscious all his life, Gil was much more comfortable as an observer. His son, however, was a natural public speaker. Zak had his mother's confidence in that respect.

Peppered throughout the film were shots of Marianne: chatting animatedly with Lena and Jean; with Zak's biology teacher; her rapt expression as she watched Jane Gregory's performance; her arms around Joel and Zak. The ranger must have spent the night with Marianne! That was what Imogen had alluded to. *How wonderful to feel wanted.* That's why Joel would have had other things on his mind. Gil rewound the film, reeling from the gut punch. The intimacy between her and Joel, and their mutual affection for his son, was undisguisable. They were a gang of three, with secrets and stories and adventures, none of which included him. Marianne had several opportunities to tell him but then again, why the hell should she? What exactly were they to each other?

Gil switched off the television and took the rising nausea onto the patio. He breathed deeply. The sky

195

was brightening with every passing second against the crescendo of the avian orchestra. Since Zak and Shane had put in the feeding stations, there had been so much activity. Historically the early mornings were his, but often he'd return from running to find Zak checking his camera traps and making lists. His son's language had also metamorphosed: Binoculars were now field glasses; beetles and bugs were inverts; eagles were apex predators, and idiots were *dik diks* (an insult to the poor antelope, in his opinion). In the space of the summer holidays, Zak had become a budding naturalist, brimming with knowledge and facts which spilled out in a torrent, and all the while he and Imogen ashamedly pretended to be interested, although she was much better at acting than he was.

As for the Mull trip, at least Marianne would be there to keep an eye on Zak. To Gil's knowledge, she hadn't been in a relationship since living with Warren. It was naïve to expect her to remain single for the rest of her life. Several times now he'd seen her in a different light, as if a long shadow had finally lifted. The realisation struck like a lightning bolt. Why else would he feel so gutted? Of course he loved her! He had loved her ever since their first encounter in the nightclub, when he could have punched Warren's lights out for trying to embarrass him in front of her. Gil had always hated his name, Gilbert, ever since they were snotty schoolboys kicking footballs around the flats, and Warren knew it.

Warren: So nice to meet you, Marianne. This is my best pal Gilbert 'workaholic' Armstrong, and his brainy cousin Spencer.

196

Marianne: Gilbert's a fine name. You're in exalted company: Gilbert White; Gilbert and Sullivan; and the brilliant Gilbert Scott-Heron.'

For once, Warren's smooth-talking gob had slammed shut. (Spencer's encyclopaedic knowledge had later filled him in as to who these famous Gilberts were). Marianne had lit up that dark night club, and for a glorious moment they had been intimates. Soon after, Warren and Spencer had followed her to the dance floor while he grappled with the thunderbolt. The next thing he knew, they had piled into taxi cabs at Terence Carthy's invitation to continue the party at Wanstead Hall, while the family were away. Warren's beady eyes were on stalks at the finery, the history. Marianne Bly, well-spoken, educated, and quietly lovely worked with these people! It was too big an opportunity to miss. After lavishing her with what he called *the gold-star treatment*, within six months Marianne was pregnant, and that was that.

Not long after Warren left the company, Gil had met Imogen. So all-consuming was their relationship, any feelings for Marianne became sediment in the pool of his unconscious until several years later when Warren left her and Freddie, and the Armstrongs cast their safety net widely around her. If Gil had called time on his marriage after Bonnie died, he might now be in Joel's shoes, but he had hung on for Zak, who ironically had also nailed his colours to the ranger's mast – great for his son, but it felt like another right hook. Gil sighed heavily. He was so glad to have signed up for the running workshop. The Tower seemed cruelly inappropriate now that Marianne and Joel were in such close proximity. Offering Niall and

Ashley Number 7 was motivated by keeping his 'family close', but it was painfully clear that he couldn't keep Zak, or Marianne for that matter, by his side forever.

It was time for his run. As Gil tied his laces, he was aware of the golden sun rising majestically before him, and all those clichés about a new dawn evaporated. What could only be described as joy poured into him, and the chronic tension in his neck and jaw miraculously eased. His love for Imogen had evaporated drop by drop below his conscious awareness, like perfume from a forgotten bottle. There was no way of getting it back. He didn't want it back. Their paths were diverging, and however uncertain was this new trail, follow it he must. With the weight momentarily lifted from his shoulders, Gil put in his earplugs and quietly left the house.

❦ JOEL ❦

JOEL WIPED his sodden face. It wasn't exactly embarrassment, as he was often moved to tears by events in the natural world, but this was unknown territory. He waited for Marianne to return the DVD to its box and join him on the sofa. Her eyes were moist and merry.

'I warned you the film was a tear-jerker Joel, but you specifically requested a romance.'

'Yes, and the title, *The Bridges of Madison County* sounded really interesting, but I didn't expect to be traumatised by it.' Joel held Marianne close, their bodies shaking with laughter. 'At least I can now tick it off my *no longer new* list.'

'What happens once you've ticked everything off? You'll be searching for another chestnut capped specimen with a hint of fiery red.'

'You're not on this particular list, Marianne. I've another one and it's called the 'R List'. Everything on it requires repeat experiences.' He reluctantly released her after a passionate kiss. 'Clint Eastwood makes even carrot scraping look sexy. Watching him and Meryl Streep playing house gave me another idea. Shall we share a candle-lit bath?'

Marianne laughed at the thought of them wedged into her tiny tub. 'Are you serious about trying new things?'

Joel nodded.

'Well then, I'm duty-bound to help, especially as you've shown me so much already.'

'Seriously though, I hear friends talking about everyday things they do with their partners – shopping, dinner parties, watching movies and such-like – and until I met you, it never occurred to me that I would want to experience these things.'

'But you cook with your grandparents, and you watch the occasional programme together.'

'This is different. You'll just have to humour me.'

'Actually, the last time I gave an official dinner party was twenty or so years ago.'

'Really? Sorry for making assumptions, Marianne.'

She kissed his troubled brow before continuing. 'Warren and I hosted the occasional evening for the Armstrongs and their clients while Lena and Jean had the kids.'

'You were all so close. Why did Warren break off contact?'

'There was an argument, and he left the company. He wouldn't talk about it, and he didn't want me to see the family. Anyway, this dinner party will be as exciting for me as it is for you. There's a farm shop nearby and if we need extra, there's the market. Della isn't fussy, but Terence Carthy – let's just say that his palate is considerably more refined. What's your specialty?'

'Chickpea curry. Works every time.'

'For Kurt, you mean. Let's see what's available. Niall and Ashley will join us for a drink but not dinner. They've been swept up by the Sycamore residents, and we don't want to overdo it. We're so grateful to have neighbours who want to be part of our community.'

'So, Niall works at Armstrong Solutions.'

'As does his father, Clive, as project manager.'

'The Armstrongs strike again. How are the cousins?'

'I don't know. According to Zak, Gil has been away with Shane.'

'Is that unusual?'

'Barefoot running in the Peak District doesn't sound like Gil's style at all. It's good of you to agree to talk to Zak's class. He invited me, but I'm not sure I should go.'

Joel wanted to ask her what she made of Zak's cryptic text message, but Marianne seemed unwilling to talk about the family. Maybe Zak needed to confide in someone. *The winter season has arrived early at Flaxfield, and not in a good way.* His return to school may have come at the right time. Maybe his parents' marriage was in trouble. Joel sighed. Kurt had been right about skeletons. 'You have to come to Noke House, Marianne. I need an assistant to hold my magic markers.'

'Why didn't you say so.' Marianne led him willingly upstairs.

'Between the eye-wiping and nose-blowing, I picked up a handful of helpful tips from Clint,' said Joel mischievously.

'Excellent. I'll let him know how you get on.'

The early evening traffic was light. In no time at all Joel turned off the A11 towards Norwich. Overhead, unruly grey clouds had joined forces to knock the warm September sun from its perch and bold blobs of rain splatted on the Outlander's windscreen. He'd be lucky to get back to the cabin before the deluge, but nothing could dampen his soaring spirits. For two glorious days, Joel's list of new experiences had escalated: the wet-eyed movie night; shopping; afternoon undercover delights; cooking with

Marianne in her galley kitchen while garden sounds and smells drifted through the back door (Joel had laughed when she tied an apron on him as if he were an infant); the hysterical dinner party. Della and Terence Carthy shared the same humour, outlook, and genetics, and their raptor eyes missed nothing. Terence was worldly wise in ways Joel would never be, and his evocative and hilarious descriptions fired the imagination. The siblings adored Marianne. Joel had to choke back a sob when Terence described her arrival at Wanstead Hall, *a sad-eyed orphan carrying two suitcases and a mournful heart*. Within months, it was the family and staff who fastened their ropes to her loving raft. At one point during the raucous evening, Terence had winked conspiratorially. *Our Marianne has a wild side beneath the halo, so have your wits about you on the full moon.*

During the hour with Niall and Ashley, Joel discovered more of the Armstrongs' good deeds which left him feeling slightly anxious. Terence had enquired after Gil, 'the broodingly handsome engineer', and made an offhand comment about the cousins' velvet-gloved grip on the family. For a split-second, Joel sensed a change in Marianne, a discomfort. Whenever he asked about the Armstrongs, her answers were perfunctory, at odds with her passionate way with him. The facts were undisputable: her ex-partner was in business with the Armstrongs after which he hit the skids; Marianne had bought Number 5 to be independent; she accepted the Armstrongs job offers as her employment circumstances had changed. But as Joel reflected on that first meeting at The Windlass, when Gil and Spencer declared Marianne to be a 'family friend', it occurred to him that whether she was aware of it or not, she was a part of 'the family', and the cousins' philanthropy, particularly Gil's, might have an ulterior motive. As Della and Terence emphatically concurred, Marianne was a dark horse. There were doors to the past she obviously wished to keep bolted, and who was he to want to open them. Kurt was right: what if he didn't like what came charging out?

Joel pulled up outside his grandparents' bungalow and sat in the car. This stream of consciousness had sparked an uncustomary sense of insecurity and it was troubling, but this wasn't the whole story. Marianne had instantly absorbed his routines and health regimes as naturally as if they had been together for years; she was the inspiration behind the meeting with Jane Gregory; she was overjoyed to see him again, and when they parted, hugged him just as tightly. Not once had Marianne lamented the long gaps apart, nor had she suggested spending more time together. She accepted their relationship with no apparent wish to change it.

Thread by filamentous thread, his love was spreading like mycelium through his veiny networks. Marianne was his counterbalance: quietly funny, subtly attentive. Somehow she knew what was going on under his skin. When she slept, her hand found its way to his wrist, his radial pulse, resting there unconsciously, connecting them through his blood flow. It was profoundly life-affirming. Never in his wildest dreams did Joel expect to feel so intensely, the speed of which was stupefying. He took his bag from the boot and went to the cabin, in need of an evening's reflection.

LENA AND JEAN

'How LONG will the toad be, Jean? You know Gil doesn't like his food too hot, and the boys will be here any minute.'

Steam misted Jean's spectacles as she lifted the baking tray from the oven. She opened the top half of the stable door and a huge gust of wind knocked Esme's puzzle from the worktop. With infinite patience, Jean picked up the pieces before walking into the living room to find Lena fiddling with the cutlery on the dining table. 'I don't know why we aren't eating in the kitchen, Lena.'

'Gil and Spencer haven't been to lunch since July, so I thought we'd make a special effort.'

'They never come during the summer holidays.' Jean led her to the armchair and sat opposite. 'Come on, tell me what this is about. I don't want to get caught in the crossfire while we're eating, and I know how you and Gil can go at it.'

Lena was worried. Zak had said something disturbing, which she'd kept to herself. Bemoaning the unsuitability of her son's marriage was one thing, but a divorce would be devastating – a failure, and a reminder of her own terrible past. At Zak's garden party, Imogen had looked gaunt. She had disappeared from sight at various times that afternoon, and at no point had she and Gil stood together, not even when Zak made his speech. Lena had quizzed her grandson as subtly as she was able. There was tension at home, and while he was in Mull, Gil was going away with

Shane, and Imogen was flying to France to see her parents. Lena was convinced that this signalled the beginning of the end. Maybe Gil would have something to say over dinner.

'Look Lena if you won't tell me I can't help.' Jean adjusted her spectacles, a nervous habit that usually gave the game away.

'Have *you* something to tell *me*, Jeannie Armstrong?'

Jean sighed. 'While I was at Spencer's house last week, Nicole let it slip that Urbane Event Management were winding down.'

'Surely Gil and Imogen aren't trying for another baby?'

'On the contrary. Imogen is considering a new role which involves a lot of travelling – and she has moved out of their bedroom.'

'How would Nicole know that?'

'Julie Brooking. Nicole usually has a cup of tea with Julie after her cleaning session, and you can imagine the conversations. If Gil knew, he'd probably let Julie go', said Jean, indignant at the gross indiscretion from the reputable cleaning company boss.

'I thought Julie only cleaned downstairs, and even that is too much of an intrusion for Gil. Why didn't you tell me?'

'Lena, have I ever passed on Nicole's fake news? She may be my daughter-in-law but ...'

'Nicole may be right.'

'Whatever do you mean?'

'Zak told me that his mum and dad are spending the half-term holidays apart, and Imogen was sleeping in the guest bedroom. I'm sorry I didn't mention it as I wanted to find out for myself when the boys get here. Gil couldn't lie to save his life.'

'So, that's why you've been uptight. I hope he and Imogen stay together. It can't be that bad, can it? Will you ask Gil outright?'

The back door clattered, and Lena straightened up. 'They're here. Let's have lunch and see what happens.'

'Thanks Mum, that was delicious. No one makes toad-in-the-hole like you, and the buttery mash was perfect.'

'Well said, Spence. That'll save me making dinner tonight, not that Zak would eat it.'

'What are you on about. Zak loves a banger.'

'Yeah, but only if it's made from lentils. I thought you knew your grandson is a vegetarian.'

'Since when?'

Gil walked over to the sofa. 'Since he met Joel Midwinter. In fact, my son has reinvented himself as saviour of planet earth. No more unethical clothing, products, or meat.'

Spencer followed Gil to the sofa and sank heavily into it. 'Esme's the same. She and Zak have set up an eco-club and have a fistful of projects on the go. Esme's got her mother into composting after convincing her the hot bin doesn't attract rats. Shall I make tea, Mum?'

'It's ready. I've made a custard tart for pudding.'

Gil groaned at his burgeoning stomach.

'Just a small slice for me, Jean. Are there any rooms going at this hotel?'

As if struck by lightning, Jean and Lena stood quite still, both staring at Gil.

'What did I say?'

'Nothing, son. You are welcome to stay here whenever you want, and for as long as you want, if needs be.'

Spencer's mind clicked. Family talk was the norm over the monthly meal — after all, this was the hub, the place where you discovered what was going on. Nicole had weaved her own version of events since the garden party, and Gil had been subdued at work. It was no secret that Imogen had been under par since returning from Singapore. If there was something to say, this was the time to say it. Gil wasn't able to hold back where his mother was concerned. All Spencer had to do was wait.

'Look, Mum, I'd be lying if I said everything was fine at home, so a few days of being spoilt by you and Jean is tempting, but it's not that bad. Imogen's still dragging herself around while Zak's doing the opposite. Even Rudy's confused, so I've been taking him to work. Shane asked me to join his running group in Derbyshire. I'll hardly be missed.'

'Shane never mentioned it, and he was here yesterday.'

'He doesn't gossip, Mother.'

'But you never go away on your own.'

'No, and it's about time I did, don't you think? Everyone else has something to look forward to except me.'

'Marianne is doing all sorts of things with Joel. She deserves a nice fella. You should be pleased she and Zak have found such a good friend,' said Lena.

'Marianne's been over?'

'That's hardly news, Spencer. She took us to the Lodge. We've never seen her look so well.' Jean passed around mugs of tea. 'Marianne's excited about her holiday. Mull is a long way away, but she's promised to get Zak back in time for Imogen's party, although she was supposed to stop in the Lake District with Joel.'

Spencer frowned. Gil hadn't said a word about Mull, or running in Derbyshire, and they usually shared everything. 'Isn't Marianne coming to Imogen's party?'

'She hasn't been invited, Spencer.' Lena stared at her son, arms folded, ready for an argument.

'Of course Marianne's been invited. Why would you say such a thing, Mum? Oh, yes, another excuse to criticise my wife.'

Jean was compelled to step in. There were occasions when Lena was wrong, but not today. Marianne hadn't been in the least upset, as she and Imogen were hardly friends. 'Actually Gil, it is true but there's no need to make a fuss. Marianne didn't expect an invitation, and she is happy to come back with Zak.'

Gil jumped up. 'Right, I'm off home. Thanks for dinner, Jean.'

'Wait up, Gil.'

'Stay and enjoy the pudding, Spencer. I'll see you later.'

Lena sat back in her armchair. Her nephew was unusually tense. 'Let him go, Spencer. He needs to sort this out. Imogen may be many things, but I never thought she was cruel. Zak is a different boy these days. Marianne and Joel have had a lot to do with it. Imogen should be happy there are people looking out for Zak, especially when she starts this new job. It's a miracle he hasn't gone off the rails.'

Jean's heart sank. She was in for a rough night. Spencer was never agitated, but even he wasn't immune to the effects of Lena's virulent speculation. 'So you were also in the dark, Spencer?'

'I was aware that Annette wanted to start a family, but I was, as you say Mum, in the dark.' Spencer finished his tea. He needed air, and if he stayed any longer his mother would start asking questions. 'I'd best make tracks. Thanks for dinner, ladies.'

While Jean accompanied Spencer to the door, Lena fought back her tears. Why couldn't Gil be more like Spencer. His contemptable expression was exactly like his father's. Anger smouldering like that was just waiting to boil over, and it terrified her. Maybe this running weekend would lift the lid on it. For once, she actually felt sorry for Imogen. Her business was ending, and Lord knew how much she'd sacrificed for that. Zak was flourishing of his own accord, so that must have hurt, even though she'd only got herself to blame. And now Gil was taking flight, the biggest surprise of all. He never did anything outside the family.

Habit drew Lena back to the bureau, to take solace in the faces of her loved ones. If Lionel were here, he'd give her a cuddle, pour her a brandy, and tell her it would all work out in the wash. She took two cut glass snifters and the decanter from the drinks cabinet. A nip would settle her nerves and might stop her worrying about the confrontation at Flaxfield.

❧ ZAK ❧

ZAK PADLOCKED the shed. According to Mr Goodchild, there had been a spate of garden thefts, so better safe than sorry. The elderly neighbour had become something of a regular visitor, probably because he'd been widowed for several years and was lonely. Grandma Lena had told him off for saying Mr Goodchild was 'elderly' after spending most of the garden party in his company. What he didn't know about gardening wasn't worth knowing. Not only had he suggested removing the row of six-foot fence panels separating their gardens, so that everyone could enjoy his beautiful beech hedge while the new one grew to size, but Mr Goodchild was happy to ensure the smooth continuation of food supplies to the steadily increasing bird population in the family's absence.

With the nights drawing in, the turtle doves had already left for the Sahara, and the forest dormice were in hibernation. The temperature had dropped at least five degrees in the south east, but fortunately the forecast for Mull was better. With just one more evening to go, Zak had no idea how he was going to sleep. The thought of camping under the stars on a remote Scottish island after mammoth days filming the wildlife was too much to contemplate. His dad volunteered to drive him and Marianne to Peterborough Station where they'd meet Joel and Larry for the onward journey. His mother couldn't understand why they didn't fly, as surely that was the quickest way, but what was the point of talking about carbon footprints and the world's obsession with speed if she weren't on board. To be fair, until July he hadn't given it a moment's consideration either and as Joel reminded him, there were more inventive ways of changing minds than blaming everyone else.

Zak had never been so pleased to be in school as it insulated him from the strained atmosphere at home. It was unrealistic to expect his parents to roll happily along without arguing. They never traded insults – well, not in front of him, but after their almighty row the other week, the silences were excruciating, especially at dinnertime when the conversation was punctuated by stilted, polite exchanges. Grandma Lena said that a good old holler was healthy, provided you kept your hands in your pockets. At least his list of new friends was on the up, one of which was Nina Kossi. Except he wanted her to be much more than a friend, and he was sure she felt the same.

Nina had been totally impressed to hear about the Mull trip and had lent him her copy of *Ring of Bright Water*, a classic story about otters. Zak desperately wanted her to join him, but he was Joel's guest and anyway, she helped her mother in the café after school and during holidays. His heart ached to think of how hard she worked, and how much she cared for the earth. Esme had urged him to ask her out: *Nina Kossi is the best thing since sliced bread*, and they had fallen about laughing at yet another of Grandma Lena's expressions which had insinuated itself into their *patois*. Zak suspected he was in love, but without Mason to talk to, he had an idea to ask Joel while they were away.

He and Esme had really clicked. Dinner at her house was much less stressful than at home. They agreed to share Rudy if the worst happened. Nicole was much more creative than Zak had previously given her credit for. She and Esme had sewn the bunting for his garden party: green and yellow triangles embroidered with different birds, bugs, and trees, as well as the variety of delicious cakes they baked. Nicole was so different when her sisters or Jean and Lena came to dinner and her airs and graces disappeared in the reminiscing of *On Mother Kelly's Doorstep* and *Roll Out The Barrel*. Zak wondered why his father was so hostile to Nicole. One day he'd pluck up the courage to ask. Joel suggested he should form his own opinions rather than adopt those of his family, teachers, and society in general.

Zak stepped into the kitchen and slipped off his boots, Before washing his hands, he bent down to stroke Rudy who was glued to his legs. A week at Esme's would do him good, especially as he was allowed on the sofas.

'There you are. Nut cutlets okay?' Gil pulled the cap from a bottle of beer and poured it expertly into a long glass.

'Did you make them?'

'The farm shop. Steamed broccoli and cabbage on the side.'

'Nice one. Mum sent a message. Don't forget my padded fleece.' Zak laid the table. He'd packed his own clothes for a long while now. With his mum out of the way, tonight was the night to find out what was going on. 'Can I have a beer?'

'No, but I'll make you a very weak shandy.'

Zak slid onto the stool and waited for his father to fix the drink. For as long as he could remember, his dad had been in charge of the kitchen. It wasn't that his mother couldn't cook as she made lots of salads and stir fries, but it was the one place where his dad was skipper, in total control of the pots, pans and baking trays, and everyone had to be out of the way. The meals were plain but always filling. Grandma Jean had taught him and Spencer the basics, which was just as well as cooking wasn't one of Grandma Lena's skills. Zak sipped the pale golden liquid and immediately set it down, his face contorted.

'It's an acquired taste. I don't know what your itinerary is for next week, but if beer is on offer…'

'Don't worry, Mum's given me the talk. At the very least I've to send her a text, but I'll probably call.'

'She'll appreciate it. Best you get an early night as we're picking Marianne up at five-thirty. Cereal and toast okay?'

'I might be too fizzed to eat. Marianne is bringing a picnic.' Zak held his father's gaze and plunged in, his words tumbling like rockfall. 'Mum is okay, isn't she? I mean, she's been acting weird for weeks. Nina says her mum and dad get on much better apart and she's a lot happier.'

The timer buzzed. Talk was suspended in the clatter of colander, baking tray, and plate, after which father and son settled at the breakfast bar to eat. Zak said nothing further as when it came to talking about serious subjects, his dad usually took a while before answering. Sometimes it was infuriating, but right now Zak could pretend everything was okay because soon, he might regret ever having asked. Gil put down his fork, and Zak's stomach backflipped.

'Every couple goes through tough times. Your mum's a bit run down, that's all.'

'Dad, just for once, tell me the truth. I bet Grandma Lena didn't treat you like a kid when you were my age.'

'You want the truth, son?' Gil breathed deeply. 'I was seven when my old man left, so I had to grow up sharpish. Grandma Lena had her hands full with Bonnie; Jean and Lionel were working to support two families. I had to do more than my bit: paper and milk rounds before school; Saturdays with Dino on the clothes stall; clean the house; wash the neighbours cars. At your age, Warren, Clive, and me were on the tools at Brett Alarms. I'm knocking on fifty, so you do the maths. There wasn't time to be a kid.'

Zak was floored. His father had never said anything about his past. 'Grandma Lena talks about those days as if they were happy.'

'They were, compared to her life with Jimmy Knox, but she never talks about the details because it was a terrible time. Dawdling and dreaming were foreign words in my mother's limited vocabulary. So was affection. If I am awkward with you and your mum, there's a reason.'

The hefty confession winded Zak, but an unknown force compelled him to press on as this opportunity might not come again. 'Why didn't you go to France with Mum?'

'Because we agreed that one of us should stay in the UK in case something happens.'

'To me, you mean. Why would anything happen to me? Marianne and Joel will be there.'

'Which is why we agreed to this trip in the first place.'

'Is that why you had a blazing row? I heard you, *and* I was wearing ear plugs.'

'Look Zak, I didn't want you to go. In my opinion, you get your own way far too much, and your mum caves in every time you ask for something. She believes the opposite is true, so from time to time we're bound to argue.'

'Oh! Well, why didn't we discuss it together as a family, rather than leaving it to the last minute. I'll stay at home if ...'

'It's too late for that. Arrangements have been made.' Gil picked up his cutlery. 'You're right Zak, we should have talked about it. Your mum needs a rest, and she also needs to spend time with her parents. Grandpa Nik is getting old, and we hardly saw them this summer, did we? I'll be in the Peak District with Shane. It's no big deal.'

It suddenly occurred to Zak that while he was intent on getting what he wanted, his parents had made sacrifices without complaint. They'd missed two summer holidays, and they always spent them together. A mixture of frustration and guilt galloped through him, uncustomary in its strength and shocking that it was there at all. His sanguine nature was disturbed. It felt awful. Zak slid off the stool, walked over to his father and put his arms around him, resting his head on his father's back. Gil patted his hands. It took just five seconds, but it was enough.

MARIANNE

Yarrow Cottage was located to the east of Calgary Bay, on the north-west coast of Mull, and typical of many other Inner Hebridean island dwellings constructed to withstand all weathers. Its stone rendered walls, slate roof, and industrial strength windows were further shielded by a densely wooded area without which the wind, according to its owner, would whip the chin hairs off a giddy goat. Sustaining a living was a challenge, although the indomitable island spirit burned bright.

It was Thursday morning. Within Yarrow's bright yellow rustic kitchen walls, the animated conversation of ten hungry breakfasters infused the convivial atmosphere. Marianne refilled the twelve-cup cafetière while the toaster popped its light brown seeded contents, ready to be halved and slotted into the glazed toast rack, which she'd found tucked away at the back of the old pine dresser. She smiled with pleasure. It reminded her of Wanstead Hall, when the family and staff (minus Peter Llewellyn who was often away), sat together while she ministered to their varied culinary wishes: high fibre muesli and yoghurt for Della; fresh fruit for Mrs Llewellyn and Terence; soft boiled eggs and soldiers for the children. Sundays was blueberry pancake day, everyone's favourite. Yarrow's guests were so obliging: porridge, toast, and coffee.

Within minutes of meeting her host, Marianne knew they would get along. Anya Maclean was unlike any woman she'd ever met. Was it her Gaelic ancestry, her experience of different landscapes and cultures, or simply a clarity of purpose? Whatever it was, they were a magnet for the other's experiences. Whilst directing a film shoot in Namibia, Anya had sustained a leg injury after falling from scaffolding and had limped home with a gut full of travel and a head bursting with inspirational ideas to implement closer to home. Blair, her only brother, lived and worked in Tobermory, and was without the financial means to update their deceased parents' rundown cottage, but there was no reason why his globe-trotting sister couldn't buy his share. So, with his help, and the sale proceeds from her West London terrace, Yarrow's reinvention began. A no-frills campsite offering wildlife tours provided an important income stream alongside the administration role earnings from Blair's yoga centre. With Kurt's flat sale funds to reinflate her dwindling savings, the couple planned to extend their small holding, run residential wildlife courses, and start a family.

While the men and boys were on their overnight campout, Marianne and Anya spent the drizzly Tuesday afternoon reorganising the linen cupboard and food store, sharing stories and drinking fruit tea behind steamy windowpanes. Anya's unambiguous affection for Joel was heart-warming, and she wanted to know how they had found each other (not Kurt's abridged version). Marianne could have delved into his romantic history, but that wasn't her way. Anya told her that of the several friends Joel had brought to the island, Marianne was the only one to share his bed. They had burst out laughing at that. It was a busy life, but from what Marianne had seen so far, an enviable

217

one. The island scenery couldn't help but enlarge the spirit: vast skies, abundant flora and fauna, and a strong sense of community, sprung from the ancient need to survive. Apart from the campout, she and Joel had been together the entire time: looking out over the Atlantic Sea from the Glengorm Estate's highest point; exploring Lochbuie's Moy Castle; picnicking in secluded corners; wandering along Tobermory's colourful harbour. Evenings were an eclectic mix of stories and song, although Yarrow's creaky pine bed and cosy eiderdown tempted them back before the revelry ended.

The early morning October sun filtered through the kitchen windows onto the heads of the breakfasters, breaking Marianne's recent recollections. She put the cafetière and toast rack in the centre of the table where hungry fingers swooped in like a flock of starlings.

'Come and sit, Marianne. We were discussing the merits of Irene Midwinter's mulberry jam,' said Anya.

Larry tipped a huge spoonful of jam onto his half slice of seeded toast. 'Yeah, nothing to beat it. We're off to the headland in search of bottlenose dolphins, Zak. D'you want to join us?'

'Will we be out all day?'

Laughter ricocheted around the table. Zak had been bouncing like a basketball and had now, inevitably, hit a wall. Joel rescued his young friend. 'Marianne and I are having a quiet day. You're welcome to hang out with us at the bay or take a time out.'

Larry said, 'Travis and I will be back after lunch, Zak. To tell you the truth, I'm flagging, too. An afternoon kip will see us rejuvenated in time for tonight's fire circle.'

'Don't forget, Larry, it's yours and Kurt's turn to prep for dinner,' reminded Anya. 'My brother and his clan are joining us. Blair has threatened to bring the bagpipes. Fortunately he plays well.'

'Great! An authentic taste of Scotland. I've got a killer chilli recipe to keep the fires burning.'

Travis nudged his father. 'Save it for home, Dad. I'm sure the others want to keep their salivary glands intact.'

'Take it easy today, Zak. We've the closing fire tonight, and the interview to finish. Your story will fit perfectly in the series. Can you spare an hour before dinner?' asked Kurt.

'Sure, no problem.' Zak's sigh was despondent. 'I can't believe the trip is almost over.'

Kurt put a comforting arm around his drooping shoulders. 'Buddy, this is just the beginning.'

The day was placid, made for hushed voices and light footsteps. Marianne sat on the beach mat, next to Joel's sleeping body. She pulled the rug over him and leaned into the soft, sandy bank, listening to the quietly comforting waves as they ebbed and flowed, incessantly, timelessly. If only she felt as calm as the water. Like Zak, she was bereft at the thought of going home. This time tomorrow, they'd be at Peterborough Station, ready to catch the train into London, after which she'd leave Zak at the gallery and would catch another train to Hazelwood.

She was so grateful not to have been invited to Imogen's party. The combination of noise, flashing lights, and brash colours would be too great a contrast to bear after Mull. Zak was going to suffer. His senses were already overloaded, and he had valiantly said 'yes' to everything while the occasional 'no' might have been wise. As a member of the community, he had rolled up his sleeves to clear tables, make sourdough, and had revelled in the outdoor activities. He and Travis had hit it off during the long road trip to Mull. The older boy was eager to show him the ropes as this was his fourth year, and a great opportunity to spend a meaningful week with his divorced father.

Marianne studied Joel's restful face. Neither had actually said the word 'love' out loud, but did it matter? He was so attentive, a marvellous companion throughout the week, subtly creating space for her to be alone if she wanted, which she hadn't. Joel insisted they amble around the island as until then, they had spent *so little time together.* So little time together – did he want to see more of her? If he asked, what then?

Joel stirred, and drew her under the blanket where they snuggled. 'Sorry for falling asleep.'

'Don't be. We're all tired. What will happen this evening?'

'Another social gathering around the fire, but this time everyone has the space to talk about their week: to read something, to sing, or to sit quietly. We offer our gratitude and our wishes to the fire, along with gains or losses, insights, that sort of thing.'

'Losses?'

'Losing our anger, letting go of a past hurt, lamenting the loss of a woolly hat.' Joel's dazzling smile instantly dissolved her anxiety. It was beginning to sound a bit heavy, but as long as there was no pressure to speak, she'd keep an open mind. After all, the group were friendly, and they shared the same concerns.

Just then, a familiar voice rang out across the bay. 'Hey love-birds! Mind if I join you? I've brought a flask of tea.'

They sat up. Zak approached with a basket and a grin and was so much brighter. Marianne budged up to make room. 'Great timing, Zak. Have you had a good day?'

'Awesome! We spotted a hen harrier *and* a pine marten.' Zak knelt down, skilfully filled three cups and passed them around. 'After a snooze, I finished my interview. Kurt talked me through his 'end of shoot' schedule, so we've charged batteries, checked and backed up the film, and logged it on a spreadsheet.'

'Hey Zak, you sound like a pro. I'll be asking you for framing tips before too long.'

'Travis and I know all about the rule of thirds and triangles. My brain cells want to blow, but in a good way.' Zak unclicked the lid from a sealed box. 'Biscuits are from Larry. I've road tested them, so your teeth won't fall out.'

Their laughter was conspiratorial, as people who have come to know something of each other's peccadillos. 'Thanks for the warning. Larry's cooking has always been innovative. He's more Heston Blumenthal than Delia Smith if you know what I mean.'

'Yeah, I get the drift.' Zak finished his biscuit. 'Joel, you've been coming here for years. Do you feel gutted when it's time to leave?'

'A little, but now that Kurt is hanging his field glasses at Yarrow, I'll come back more often. Norfolk life is pretty special, so it's not as if I've got to go back to a job I don't like, or to a boss I don't respect. There's not a massive gap between here and home ...' Joel trailed off, as if he'd suddenly had a thought, or an insight, but he wasn't ready or prepared to share it.

'And you, Marianne? Are you as sorry to go back as I am?'

She nodded. 'What makes you sorry, Zak?'

'Lots of things: the terrain, the community, the wildlife. The campout was super special, and I met a group of really interesting guys of all ages who had come to Mull especially for the gathering. Everyone is so switched on, and not afraid to speak the truth. When I asked my dad what was going on with him and my mum, he just couldn't bring himself to talk about it. What I discovered instead was how rough it was for him growing up, and there wasn't time for fun. It got me thinking how good my life is. I felt so bad, I gave *him* a hug.'

Marianne studied Zak's mournful expression. He had never spoken like this before. Since his return from the campout, he appeared to have leapfrogged adolescence for adulthood. At sixteen, Travis possessed a maturity lacking in most men she knew, including Freddie. Joel had explained that at specific times of the year, grandfathers, fathers, brothers, and sons gathered together to camp, eat, and share their stories around the fire. Anya did the same with women and girls. It was an ancient custom, one that was being revived throughout the world, although their circles contained neither initiation nor ritual. Marianne wondered what would Freddie make of it all? Would he find such a rites-of-passage interesting, or dismiss it as an irrelevant new-age custom?

Apart from Freddie's humanities tutor, whose gentle

222

nature may have influenced his switch from politics into social work, there was not a single man who had been either mentor, or role model during his adolescence. He had consistently rejected his father's overtures until they stopped arriving altogether. She prayed that Zak would never have cause to react so strongly. 'I also feel a dose of the lonesome holiday blues coming on, but Sycamore Crescent is a nice place to live. What we don't have is space, dark skies, and the profound silence. You'll have to visit The Tower more often when you have time. It'll help you stay connected to the big picture.' She put a reassuring hand on his back. 'Take care not to burn yourself out, Zak.'

'I'll try, but until July, I had no idea there was such a fascinating world going on under my nose. Esme and Nina knew it all along.'

'Have you been in touch?'

'Every day.' Zak blushed. 'I asked Nina to come with me next year – if we're allowed, that is. How do you pay for someone without offending them? I feel guilty for having so much when she has so little.'

Joel got up and stretched. 'Turn it into a blessing, Zak. Take the Rose Foundation: they use their money to do amazing things such as investing in people like me and Larry to become rangers, and so much more besides. Join forces with Nina, Esme, and your friends.' Joel twirled in a circle, arms outstretched. 'Break the mould! Step into the unknown! Live like Larry and Travis, Anya and Kurt ...'

'You and Marianne.'

Joel held out his hand to Marianne and waltzed her across the beach as their giggles floated across the water. 'Yes, Zak: like me and Marianne!'

The group sat in chairs around the fire circle which had been built in the centre of a spinney of silver birch. Beer, hot chocolate, and warmed apple cinnamon were the drinks of the evening. The house and shower block had been cleaned, the wood store restocked, and rucksacks were packed. Marianne had sailed through the house like Mary Poppins, doing as much as Anya would allow. The women had found a moment to talk, thanking the other for mutual kindnesses, promising to reunite. It had been another boisterous meal, but this time imbued with the sadness of the final evening. Joel was unusually subdued. The night before, whilst wrapped up as close as two human bodies could possibly be, they reviewed the week-long highs, ignored the low of her imminent departure, (he was staying to work on the film editing), and said nothing about the future. They'd return to their respective homes and continue to see each other as before.

Now, Marianne was wrapped up warmly in a rug and hypnotised by the contrast of orange flames flickering against the black night. While Travis and Zak helped Blair and Nula's children to toast their marshmallow sticks, Nula shared an ancient Celtic folk tale. Then, Zak and Travis requested Larry play *Teach Your Children Well*, as he'd done at the campout, and Marianne pitched her harmonies to the Crosby, Stills and Nash song along with everyone else. Kurt read a thought-provoking chapter from Ron Dennis' book, *Cottongrass*, while Anya sang a haunting rendition of *The Ark* with her brother on the bagpipes. Travis and Zak settled for short speeches of gratitude, with particular thanks for Anya and Kurt's hospitality. That left Marianne. A growing sensation to add her voice to the chorus could no longer be quashed. Whether it were the ghosts of the ancient island's past, the camaraderie, or simply the need to speak the truth, a wistful voice rose from the depths of her soul.

'Once upon a time in the delightful English countryside, there lived two sisters, Lily and May. Their father was kind and loving, but their mother only had eyes for her first-born, Lily, who was as bright as the night stars and destined for great things. May's light dazzled in the garden amongst snapdragons and honeysuckle, where faeries and unicorns, and all of Earth Mother's adorable creatures lived. May tried everything to win her older sister's affections, but her gifts of caterpillars, tiny frogs, and weary bees were squealed away, and her angry mother would send her to bed, even if the sun were still shining. And there May would remain until her father came to her rescue after his long daily toil.

'On May's fifth birthday, Lily gave her a tea party, just for the two of them. It was the happiest moment of May's young life. But the east winds blew brisk that afternoon, and her painful screams brought her father running. How the pot of boiling water ended up in May's lap remains a mystery to this day. When she left the hospital many months later, the world had forever changed. Her mother had taken Lily away to school, while she and her father moved to the city. From that day on, May no longer sang, or swam, or skipped with the faeries, but chose the silent, safe world of crayons and pencils. She covered the monstrous scars, but a deeper wound sank into her heart.

'Years passed and the memories faded. On her thirteenth birthday, May's father gave her a botanic microscope, a precious gift with which to reveal the mysteries of the natural world. The teachers said she was a bright as the night stars and destined for great things. But the east winds blew cold, and May's father died suddenly. The grief-stricken young student put the microscope back in its box along with her dreams. She found a job as housekeeper to a grand family where the winds changed direction, and so with it her fortunes.

'One fine day, Mr Flynn arrived. He cheered her with his swashbuckling tales of derring-do, and when the grand family left for different shores, Mr Flynn offered her home and hearth. Soon, she had a beautiful son, and a job in the small school where fairies and unicorns were the children's friends. But Mr Flynn was an ambitious man. He traded his trusted business partners for grander schemes, only to lose everything, and to disappear in a puff of smoke. Good friends came to the rescue, but a heart can take only so much beating, and May withdrew once again to live quietly, until something deep inside her began to stir.

'It was a Saturday: the arrival of summer, a day fit for miracles and warm west winds. May was beach walking with her dear young friend and his charming dog when they were befriended by an angel with a lion heart, disguised as a ranger. Step by step, he showed the friends a different way to live, and May came to understand that it is as wonderful to receive love, as it is to give it.'

The pine logs cracked and hissed in the firepit, throwing glowing cinders into the charcoal sky. Marianne held Zak's quivering body while the silent group brushed away tears. After a while, Joel led her away from the circle and they walked along the path to the shore's edge, lit by the stars and the half moon. She breathed the last painful traces of that time into the crisp, clear air. Could the earth have been any more sublime, as starlight reflections glistened in the water, and words were superfluous against the celestial canvas?

Joel turned to face her. 'Marianne, I ...'

She kissed him, and for an eternity they stood in silence by the water's edge, before returning for their final night in Yarrow Cottage.

GIL

THE DULL throb had by increments screwed itself so tightly across Gil's temples he could stand it no longer. He swallowed the pain killers, the second lot of the day. Earlier that morning, Spencer came over to confirm the timings for the party and urged him to eat something. That was his cousin's answer for everything, as if the accumulated psycho-physical tension could be magicked away by a cheese and pickle roll.

After returning from the Peak District, Gil expected to find Imogen preparing for her celebrations. Apart from jointly received messages from Zak, there had been no contact between them. In retrospect, he regretted confronting her after discovering the party snub, what he believed to be yet another act of unkindness towards Marianne. The result was a massive row during which Imogen denied all knowledge, and that only an overactive, sleep-deprived imagination could possibly conclude she was maliciously motivated. He accused her of not wanting to be at home; she countered that he no longer wanted sex; he couldn't stand Flaxfield, she couldn't stand Epping, and on it went.

It was under this heavy cloud that she left for St. Raphael, only to find her father seriously unwell with suspected pneumonia and refusing to go into hospital until the matter was taken out of his hands. Nik Marsalis had never been ill. Inevitably, his unrelentingly industrious and globetrotting lifestyle had overtaken him. Until Imogen's return, Gil had no real idea just how important Nik was to her. She had been remorseful, guilty, tearful, helpless. When she calmed down, he suggested she cancel the party, but after an hour on the phone with her mother, it was agreed that so drastic an act was quite unnecessary. After that they declared a truce of sorts, but a showdown was threatening, and it had to be faced.

Imogen appeared in the kitchen, ready to go out. He poured her a cup of tea. 'What time's your hair appointment?'

'Midday. The salon squeezed me in for a manicure. Mummy and I had to cancel our spa trip. I've never seen her in such a state, much worse than I was yesterday.' She sipped the tea. 'We've just had a chat. Daddy is so much better. Heaven knows how she'd survive without him. Underneath her cool, super-flirty manner, Mummy really does love him.'

Gil held Imogen's intense gaze for as long as could before changing tack. 'Zak's on his way.'

'That is tremendously good news. If there is an upside to this ghastly week, I've had no time to speculate on his island experience. Do we know if Zak had a good time?'

'No, but I took the lack of contact as a positive. I can't imagine he'll want to spend many more holidays with his parents.'

Gil turned away from her unsteady expression. He was determined to keep everything smooth for the next few days, but it was obvious they were teetering on the edge of another emotional outbreak.

'Forgive me, Gil. I haven't asked about your running workshop. Was it fun?'

'Not sure I'd call it fun – unexpected, maybe. Anyway, best get cracking. The cars are coming at five. I'll have a snack ready for when you get back.' As Gil picked up Imogen's empty cup, she rested her slim, cold hand on his.

'Gil, we need to talk. We've been estranged, and that hideous argument has shaken us to the core.'

'I agree, but not today.' How could he tell her that three days of running had changed him. Was it even possible to begin such a conversation when he was still trying to process it? The man who left Epping on Monday was no longer the same man who had returned on Thursday. The visceral sensations of connecting to the land through bare feet had left him shattered, exposed, vulnerable, ecstatic. Mercifully, he had shielded himself from the others during one particular wet and windy run, when he slunk down behind a boulder, his body shaking, his eyes streaming. Memories flooded his mind while running and during sleep. Shane's company had steadied him, as did the group. They shared their stories, listening without judgement or worse, offering advice.

To begin with, Jonty and Kath's introductory chat had sounded so outlandish, Gil's instinct was to take off. Talk of increasing sensory awareness, unlocking the mystery of the self, and bridging the great disconnect – they may as well have been speaking Tibetan. There was no mention of timed runs, optimum footwear, or goals. But by the end of the second day, as he sat around the fire with his cocoa, Gil felt that first protective layer drop away. Those seven people were the same: each navigating the rapidly changing landscape of family, work, identity, the planet. The group had been meeting for some years, providing a support system through which deep friendships had been made. Gil was invited to join them: no membership, no pressure.

He was suddenly overcome with sympathy. It was Imogen's fortieth birthday on Sunday, her father was ill, her son was away, and their marriage was in trouble. Arriving at an unknown venue to hear music and eat food she hadn't chosen would make anyone nervous, especially Imogen, whose expertise lay in hosting the ultimate event. The least he could do was to make sure she had a good time. 'Annette is as capable as you when it comes to throwing a great party for her best friend. She has confirmed everything with me so if you're unhappy, the buck stops here. Now, enjoy your pamper and look forward to a top night.'

Gil hovered inside the gallery's basement doors. He'd been monitoring the rail network throughout the afternoon, and all was well until a train derailment outside Peterborough Station pushed back Zak's arrival time from five to eight o'clock. A number of coaches were laid on for the stranded passengers, but that would make him later still. After speaking to Marianne, they decided the best option was to take a taxi direct to Hanover Square where a fresh set of clothes would be waiting at the gallery. Fortunately, Imogen had been swept up by her friends, many of whom she hadn't seen for years. Once reassured that her son was on his way, she went back to the throng. Annette had come up trumps. *The Narrative*, south west London's premier über-stylish art gallery and exclusive party venue was currently displaying a collection of indigenous women's art, a piece of which Imogen was to choose for her birthday gift, courtesy of her guests. The eight-piece band's universal playlist had already filled the floor, while cocktails and freshly prepared sushi were disappearing as fast as they materialised.

Spencer whizzed down the stairs. 'Any news?'

'Five minutes away.' Gil nodded in the direction of the gallery. 'What d'you think?'

'Fantastic venue, great vibe, fab food, and cool sounds. Annette has never been so nervous. I've persuaded Esme to stay upstairs. She's desperate to give Zak his surprise. It was her inspired idea to bring Nina along. We've not had a chance to catch up since your running trip, Gil. How's the headache?'

'Almost gone. Work feels like a lifetime ago. Niall's got nothing to report, which is good news under the circumstances.'

'I can't see Ashley lasting the night with those swollen ankles. Maybe Marianne will travel back with her and Niall.'

'We'll soon find out – here they are.' Gil pushed open the glass doors and stepped into the cold, musty, October night, instantly tasting the metallic city air, a far cry from the clean White Peak skies, dew ponds, and the anciently rugged terrain of just days before. He paid the driver while Spencer opened the cab door to lift out the luggage. Two weary bodies tumbled onto the pavement. While Gil's brain readjusted to the vision of this lanky boy/man wearing a top knot ponytail and a black cord necklace, his son came forward to hug him and his uncle.

'Hello Dad. Sorry we're late.'

'You made it, son, and that's all that matters. I've a clean shirt and jeans for you to change into.'

'Thanks, but I had a shower this morning and a brush up on the train. Mum won't mind.'

'Oh – no, 'course she won't.' Marianne was so altered and in the dark city light, her eyes shone like beacons. Her embrace surprised him. 'It's good to see you, Marianne. I can't thank you enough for getting Zak here in one piece. Will you join us for a drink? Niall and Ashley are going home soon. They've offered to take you.'

'That's so kind of them, Gil, but I've run out of steam. I'm heading straight home.'

While Marianne and Zak hugged in farewell, Spencer flagged down a black cab and gave the driver the destination before passing him the fare. Gil was grateful for the gesture as he was about to do the same. Zak slid Marianne's bags inside the taxi, closed the door and waved until it disappeared from view.

'It was good of you to do that, Spencer.'

'No worries, Zak. It's great to see you. Now, let's get up there. Esme's got a trick up her sleeve.'

Gil cracked two eggs in the pan while Imogen sat at the kitchen table, working her way through a huge pile of birthday cards. A cheerful voice floated down from the landing, followed by human and animal footsteps.

'Morning! I must thank Mr Goodchild for keeping the feeders topped up. I can't wait to check out the traps.'

'Do it later. I had a chat with him earlier this morning, and all's well. Rudy was desperate for a wee, so I let him out of your bedroom. I'm surprised you didn't hear me.'

'What time is it now?'

'Eleven.'

'Twelve hours! That's got to be a record. By the way Mum, Grandpa sends his love and will talk to you this afternoon.' Zak kissed her cheek and sat down. 'Wow! Don't think I've ever seen so many cards. Must be nice to be so popular.'

'Just like my darling son. Nina was certainly pleased to see you again. So, how is Grandpa?'

'Disappointed to have missed your party. He wanted to know about my trip. I told him we'd visit as soon as they get back. We've an important plan to discuss.'

Imogen and Gil exchanged a glance. 'A plan might be just the thing for Daddy right now. Is it a secret?'

'Embryonic stage. Did you enjoy yourself, Mum? The venue was super-cool. Interesting artwork, from what I could make out.'

'It was bearable until eight o'clock and then it was fab. I scarcely recognised you. Another growth spurt?'

Zak laughed. 'Must be the porridge. Marianne took on breakfast duty and on the last morning, she caved into group pressure and revealed the secret ingredients: half oat milk, half water, spoonful of honey, and lots of love.'

'I want to hear every detail of your island jaunt, but first you must eat. Your dad has made brunch.'

Gil put a steaming plate under Zak's nose. 'Hope you're still eating dairy: Poached eggs, *haloumi*, and spinach on sourdough.'

'Hey Dad, you've gone all Shoreditch hipster.'

'No, son, real EastEnders eat black pudding. We can take Rudy to the forest later if you like.'

'Okay. I'll make you porridge tomorrow. May I have coffee?'

234

'Coffee?'

'It was our morning ritual: porridge, lashings of toast and jam, and coffee. You wouldn't believe the things we talked about, and the noise we made! Joel and Kurt's arena rock songs had us falling about.'

Gil brought the cafetière over with two mugs and a jug of milk. 'Did you get to film much?'

'Did we! Kurt took Travis and me out and about. He's Larry's son and they spend every October half-term at Anya's. We shared a tent, which was great fun.' Zak guided the fork to his mouth, swallowed and was off again. 'We filmed two young otters while their mum was grooming them. So much has to be right: keep moving into the wind, so it blows your scent away from the water; look for otter spraint, which in fact, smells quite sweet; check out the otter highways and holts. After all that, you get into position and wait.' Zak gobbled the rest of his food so he could talk some more. 'Oh, yeah, I'm appearing in Joel and Kurt's film, A 'Day in the Wild Life.' Anya is producing it and the BBC might option the series. Sorry Mum, it's not quite a *Match of the Day* presenter, but this is so much better. Oh, I forgot.' From his rucksack, Zak pulled out a packet of milled oats, two jars of honey, a litre of oat milk, and several nicely wrapped parcels. 'Happy Birthday, Mum!'

Imogen carefully opened Zak's present, and held the brooch up to the light. It must have been difficult to see through her dewy eyes.

'Made on Mull: topaz and silver dolphins,' said Zak proudly.

After a hug, she immediately pinned the brooch to her dressing gown. 'Your necklace looks interesting.'

Zak put his hand up to his neck 'Oh, yeah – the lads gave this to me after our campout. It's a silver sparrow feather. Look, Dad's got something for you.'

Gil was amazed at how quickly his son changed the subject. As Imogen unwrapped the Mulberry document bag, he felt a mixture of embarrassment and guilt. In different circumstances, it would have been a piece of jewellery, but he just could not bring himself to make such an unauthentic gesture. 'It's not exciting, but with the new job …'

'Thank you, Gil. Just what I need.'

Imogen's smile was almost convincing.

'I've done extremely well. My guests' generosity paid for a painting, and a donation to the indigenous art organisation. Spencer and Nicole gave me this dressing gown, and Niall and Ashley gave me a bottle of perfume. I may drop in tomorrow as Ashley is now on maternity leave, and perhaps Marianne might be available. I'd like to thank her for accompanying you, Zak. Give her a gift of something.'

Gil was stunned. Imogen hadn't taken any interest in Ashley before. She obviously wanted to talk to Marianne. Surely she wasn't about to resurrect her idiotic housekeeping idea. He ignored the churning in his gut and picked up the wrapping paper.

'There's an art shop on the high street, Mum. How about a box of watercolours, or acrylic paints? Ask Ashley to show you the woodland scene in the baby's bedroom. Marianne painted it. Fly agaric toadstools, fairies, fawns, and all sorts of magic – just like appearing in your own fable.'

Zak was quiet for a moment. 'So, Mum, you're taking the job.'

'Yes darling. It's such a worthwhile role, and your father will be here to look after you.'

'It's okay, no need to explain.' Zak got up from the table and had a play with Rudy. 'Hey Dad, we could spend more time at The Tower while Mum's away. Travis is coming to Norfolk soon for a reunion. Can Nina come with us?'

'I don't see why not,' said Gil.

'Perhaps she'll have an idea for your birthday party, Zak.'

'I've had enough parties to last a lifetime, Mum – no offense, but I'd rather spend the weekend in Norfolk with my real friends.' He gawped at his father's naked feet. 'Dad, what happened to your socks? Oh, I just remembered your holiday. What was it like?'

'Unlike anything I've ever done before. I'll tell you about it over the forest. Get your skates on. Rudy's desperate for a ramble.'

Imogen suddenly pushed back her chair and stood. 'Would you mind if I joined you for that walk? I could use some fresh air.'

'You don't have to ask, Imogen. We all need a restful day.'

'Erm, I've arranged to see Nina this afternoon – if that's okay.'

'Why don't you invite her for dinner, Zak. It's about time we got to know her, don't you think, Gil?'

Gil nodded. 'Nina will love my beef casserole.'

'Beans on toast is fine. She's not fussy.'

While Zak bolted off to get changed, Gil pulled on a pair of socks. The freedom that came with bare feet was so enjoyable, it felt wrong to imprison them. He looked up at Imogen. 'You'll be busy with your 'thank you' cards for days.'

'It's not as bad as it looks. Annette has put the addresses on the envelopes along with a list of who gave what. I'll nip upstairs and get changed.' Imogen paused. 'Nina is his first girlfriend. I hope she doesn't break his heart. I can scarcely believe how grownup Zak is. We always said we wanted him to be independent didn't we? Now the day has arrived, it's much harder to accept than I ever anticipated. In no time at all, Zak will be gone.'

Gil stared incredulously at his wife. She couldn't see what was under her nose. He mothballed his comment about the demands of her new role taking her away from home, and said diplomatically, 'All the more reason to enjoy his company while we can.'

JOEL

THE TEMPERATURE had bombed overnight, revealing a harsher, adversarial side to the island, and heralded the coming of winter. Ashen clouds brooded over the bristling hills, setting the tone for the day, although the morose colour scheme did nothing to veil the land's innate beauty. Joel had almost completed his morning walk. He paused to watch a curlew dip its slender downcurved bill into the muddy bank while overhead, the black-headed gulls' harsh trill was music to his ears, particularly as these birds were an amber list species. Along with the wagtails, song thrush, and redwings, it was a fine farewell performance. Shivering, Joel pulled his jacket hood over his thermal Beanie hat and drifted along Calgary Bay. Was it just last week when Zak brought tea for him and Marianne? Seductive as the island was, he was impatient to return to The Kedge, to his rituals – to see her again.

Joel paused by the dune, in the exact position where they had embraced, after the final fire circle during which Marianne had unveiled her harrowing past through the haunting fairy story. She loved him, and he was so happy to have heard it whilst sitting around the fire, where truths are told amongst friends. He was desperate to tell her he felt the same. As Joel approached the cottage, the heartening sight of washing blowing on the line, chimney smoke, and chickens roaming here and there warmed him. The Land Rover was loaded and ready. He and Kurt had arranged a pit-stop in the Lake District to complete their interviews and catch up with mutual friends. Kurt waved at him from the porch.

'Coffee's ready, then we'd better hit the road. Nice walk?'

Joel slipped off his padded coat but left his hat on. 'Bittersweet if you know what I mean. Something smells good.'

'Anya's frying blueberry pancakes.'

'Ah, Marianne's recipe. I miss her porridge.'

'Yeah, she definitely upped the ante this time around.' They sat at the table. Kurt poured a half cup of coffee into a mug before passing it to Joel who topped it up with oat milk. 'I wonder what Zak's re-entry was like. Travis has learned to keep his head down after our campouts. Zak may need help with that.'

'Zak messaged me. He lasted an hour at his mother's party before conking out, but he must have recovered quickly as he's got an idea for a first-class project involving his grandpa.'

'Any ideas?'

'The family is wealthy. It wouldn't surprise me if it were some kind of charitable trust. Zak asked if he might meet with Professor Rose during his next Norfolk visit. There's a clue for you, Kurt.'

'There's never enough money to do what needs to be done, is there? Zak has his parents' potential marriage breakdown to face, though. Whatever the age, it's a huge deal.'

'He's got good people to support him, and these circles are an essential resource.'

'Once we add the camping pods and extend the facility block, we'll run more of them – with help, of course.'

'Larry and I are handing in our notice as soon as we get back.'

'You may jest, Joel, but I reckon that as soon as Nula and Larry hook up, they'll consider relocating. If Travis comes with him, Zak won't be far behind and we'll have ourselves a tribe.'

'Gil and Imogen may have something to say about that.'

Anya brought a plate of hot pancakes to the table and sat down. 'Zak is so charismatic, a natural in front of the camera. I can't imagine many people would say 'no' to him.'

'Me neither. I can see him fronting any number of programmes.' Kurt speared another pancake. 'These are tasty, Anya.'

'Marianne's talented, and not just with the housekeeping.' She reached over and picked up a framed picture. 'Her yarrow plant is incredibly detailed, and the watercolours so subtle – the perfect 'thank you' gift. We talked about careers, university, and suchlike. The teacher's assistant role enabled her to help extend the children's natural sense of wonder without being hamstrung by the curriculum, as she would have been as a teacher. We agreed that a new subject, 'earth matters', needs to be taught alongside English and maths, and not as a GCSE choice.'

'Sharing the Foundation work with the schools is as rewarding as being in the field. The kids I meet have no shortage of ideas. If we can catch them while they still have a light in their eyes, there's a chance we might realign humanity's trajectory.'

'That echoes Marianne's view. It's an uplifting philosophy to have in common.' Anya put another pancake on his plate. 'I asked Marianne what she made of island life. She said that a happy home could be made almost anywhere with the right companion.'

Joel put down his fork. 'I can't believe you asked her that, Anya. She must have known you were fishing.'

'We talked about many things, Joel, including co-habiting. Marianne knows you better than you think. She said, and these were her exact words: *Joel will never leave Norfolk. It's his safety net, and in it he feels free. Who am I to disturb the status quo?*' Anya paused to let Joel take this in. This was important, and they didn't see each other as often as she would have liked. 'I wanted to challenge Marianne's statement, but something in her manner prevented it.'

No one spoke. Soon, the pancakes disappeared, along with the coffee. 'Marianne is right. That's why I'm with her. She gets it. She gets me. There is no point in discussing a hypothetical future.'

'Why ever not, Joel? Hypotheticals become real. Marianne loves you, she told us at the fire. Unless I'm mistaken, you feel the same way. Kurt, what do you think?'

'It doesn't matter what I think, does it? If Joel and Marianne are happy with their relationship, why change it?'

Anya's passion was too great to hold down. 'I'll tell you why, Kurt. We don't choose who we fall in love with. It just happens – it's like grace. But if we're lucky, a few of us will share a lifetime of love, long after the thrills and spills are over. When I look at Marianne and Joel, that's what I see: a togetherness that goes way beyond sexual attraction. They are two halves of the same coin.' She looked at Joel, her pale eyes shining. 'Tell me I'm wrong, and I'll change the subject.'

Joel's mind flipped back to the night of the fire when the group had silently travelled through the vicissitudes of the heroine's tale and were overwhelmed when they realised it was Marianne's story. When they returned to the cottage for a last night of love, he saw Marianne in her true light: courageous; radiant; released. While she slept, he silently wept for a life he would never have. In these gatherings he'd become accustomed to hearing tales of love and heartbreak, but never from someone whose very existence was bound to his own. Joel's sigh was deep and despairing. His meticulous efforts to avoid such feelings were in shreds.

'Anya, I think of nothing else, and Marianne is right. I will never leave Norfolk, the Foundation, and my grandparents. But let's imagine for a moment that she and I decided to live together. The cabin is just about big enough for me, and I'd never ask her to sell up. In any case, you seem to have overlooked the most obvious fact: If Marianne gave up her home to live with me and my heart gave out, what then?'

Anya and Kurt were silent. Joel rarely discussed his condition, but those closest to him understood this was a possibility, no matter how much they ignored it or pretended otherwise. While he was working and socialising, it was easy to see Joel as an enthusiastic, upbeat man engaging fully with life. As soon as he arrived, however, Anya saw the seismic transformation in him, and as the week progressed, she understood why he and Marianne had fallen in love. Marianne and Joel had transcended the legacy of maternal neglect which would have sunk other people, and they had done more than simply survive. Somehow, they had found each other, so to squander this opportunity was incomprehensible to her.

The friends stood outside the cottage. Kurt wrapped his arms around Anya. It had been an emotional week. He wanted nothing more than to see Joel and Marianne make a home together, wherever that happened to be, but he understood why his friend had never undertaken a relationship or had a child. Joel had set Marianne on the path to a different life, and that was enough for him. It was time to leave. After a poignant farewell, the Land Rover rolled slowly out of Calgary Bay, and followed the winding road towards Craignure as Anya's wistful image slowly faded from view.

The downhill slide began on the journey home. Thankfully, Kurt's chat was focused on his flat sale and the film, while the Lake District offered Joel a temporary hiatus before his darkening mood descended. Historically, autumn was his most challenging season, as not only were the educational visits at their busiest, but the change in weather affected his finely tuned body clock. Instinctively Joel wanted to hibernate. The aim was always to reduce his working hours during the dormant seasons, but with so many eco-web strands to weave together, and a sense of duty to his colleagues, Joel never got around to it. The professor and his wife often invited him for a post-swim cup of tea, which was generally the best time to discuss such things, but as yet he hadn't felt like swimming.

Marianne had postponed her planned visit to Norfolk. The talk at Noke House was just two days later, and she wondered if it were better to wait until he came to Essex, when she would accompany him to Zak's school. It was a sensible, practical idea, but the delay added up to a fourteen-day gap since Mull – fourteen days! He couldn't bear the separation from her. Neither had sufficient steam to drive those long miles to see each other for a single night, as they were both catching up with the backlog and anyway, seven nights hadn't been enough time together. Joel's gloom increased exponentially. Phone calls and messages were meant to bridge the gap, but there was always so much to say and never enough time to say it. The fabulous island holiday was by now the stuff of photograph albums and past tenses.

When it came to the business of expending energy, Joel was a master. The act of thinking could be as tiring as physical exertion when thoughts ran out of control, as they were now. Marianne's words appeared randomly, day and night. *Joel would never leave Norfolk. It's his safety net, and in it he feels free.* But hadn't she also said that with the right partner, a happy home could be made almost anywhere? Wasn't that worth a conversation? If nothing else, it gave him the opportunity to talk about his fears. He had let her into his life, but he hadn't anticipated being engulfed by despair. It was time to pull down the shutters.

'We're about to have our tea, Joel. I've made a pearl barley stew. Shall I fetch you a dish?'

'No thanks, Gran. I'm off to bed. Feeling whacked after the trip.' Irene came towards him, but he stepped back. 'It's okay, honest. I just need to rest for a couple of days. Please don't panic or call the doctor. I've switched off my phone, so you may get the odd call on the landline.'

'But how will we know if you're alright?'

'There's food in the cabin.'

'Joel, can I make a suggestion?'

'If it's the only way to stop you worrying, Gramps.'

'We'll leave a parcel of food outside every morning. If you don't pick it up, we'll come in.'

Joel nodded, and walked to the cabin, his place of refuge. He was sorry for causing his grandparents anxiety but there was nothing else to be done. After drawing the blinds, he undressed and went to bed. In bursts of fitful sleep, shadowy figures flew around him, dismantling his neatly controlled existence, piece by piece. Why was he, Joel Midwinter, worthy of Marianne's love? His father was unknown; his own mother had given him up; his stepfather was indifferent; his teachers had written him off as a day dreamer with zero academic aptitude, and his colleagues pitied him. Friends were free to make plans, to have children and grandchildren, to live their dreams while he, Joel Midwinter, 'Great Guy and Best Buddy' endlessly, frantically, pulled his mind back to the present, to focus on all that is good and loving and true. It was exhausting.

And then there was Marianne, whose mother and beloved sister had acted so violently, almost crushing a life through bitterness and ignorance. If that weren't enough, Warren Silk's greed had pulverised Freddie, robbing him of his father and his confidence, all of which had shaken Marianne to the core. The cruelty was overwhelming. Joel willed his heart to stop beating, to bring this egoic superstorm to an end but it would not, so he let his thoughts hurtle on. Slowly the anguish blew out, after which came sleep, deep and disturbing, until it transformed into calmer, windless waves, lulling him back to the shore, back to familiar ground.

The following morning, Joel brought in the soup. Then, he sat in meditation as the morning broke. His thoughts continued to rampage, so he roped his mind to a still point, and let it run as if breaking in a wild horse. Gaps appeared, the speed dropping to a canter, then to a trot and finally rising and falling: weightless, spacious, peaceful. Joel drank the soup before going back to bed, where he slept soundly until another disturbing dream woke him up, drenched in sweat. He had no idea of the time, although the dawn chorus gave him a clue. Sliding out of bed, he brought in the parcel of freshly baked rolls. Irene and Dudley were a comforting presence, just yards away. Throughout the day he alternated between sleeping and sitting quietly in the Zen garden, clearing the mental debris, and bring his mind into a pure resting state.

On the third day, Joel awoke with a stillness permeating his mind and body, and his heart was bursting with love for all beings. He climbed out of bed and brought in the pastries. A raging thirst drove his weak body in search of fluid. The jasmine tea had never tasted so refreshing; the cup in his hands had never felt so lovingly crafted; his gratitude for the miracle of life was never so all-encompassing. Reflecting on the episode, Joel accepted he was no different to anyone else on the brink of major change. If he wanted to be with Marianne, he simply had to ask her. He stood and after a while, his body became steady. Before anything else, he needed a shower.

They sat together on the sofa, their hands firmly clasped. Somehow she had known. He had kept radio silence for too long, so she called his grandmother. When he came out of the shower and saw her making tea he jumped back, believing her to be an apparition but no, Marianne Bly was real, she was here. They hugged, cried, talked, drank tea, and were now reconnected.

'Irene has made your favourite mushroom and chestnut tart for tea. If you feel up to it later Joel, why don't we walk up to Gun Hill. Do you remember telling me about the Dark Green Fritillary? My botany book says the Rosebay willowherb attracts the butterfly, and we might be lucky enough to see one.'

'Yes please! Have I told you how grateful I am to see you?'

'Only a trillion zillion times. Irene didn't need to ask twice. Any excuse to put down my brushes. You'd have done the same for me.'

'No question, although I can't imagine you'd ever need rescuing, my darling Marianne.' He kissed the back of her hand. 'I had to let these crazy, overblown thoughts pass, despite Irene and Dudley's concern. To have been so afraid of falling in love sounds so stupid. I mean, my middle name is 'love': every tree, every bird, every fungi.'

'Aren't we supposed to enjoy the thrills, as Anya calls them. After that comes the really good part. It's tremendously healthy to have things to look forward to. That's why gardeners live so long. You of all people should know that.'

'I must have bunked off from school that day. So, you'll seriously consider my proposal?'

She nodded. 'We'll look for a two-bedroom house in a similar price bracket to Number 5. The Armstrongs can have first refusal. If there is a delay, I'm sure they'll let me pay rent. You'll use the cabin as often as you want. I'm confident of finding work and anyway, I'm an expert at making ends meet.'

'What about your friends, your community – Freddie?'

'You think I'd pass up an opportunity to be with you for my neighbours' sake?' Marianne placed her hand on Joel's forehead. 'No, raging fever. Back to bed with you.' His smile was as wide as the blue yonder. 'Della has been waiting for years to see me settle. As for Freddie, I've been soft-soaping him for far too long. I shouldn't hide my feelings from him. In fact, it's deceitful to do so. My son's only concern is that you might be after my huge pile of treasure.'

'He already told me you are a woman of no means.'

'Did he now? My mother left him a legacy. He wasn't interested. Didn't even ask how much it was. Freddie can't forgive her for what she did to me, and never wanted anything to do with her.'

'Freddie's got a loving heart in there somewhere.'

'That I know for sure. So, Joel, in answer to your question, no one is standing in my way of happiness.'

'I feel a song coming on.' Joel launched into his version of *Nothing's Gonna Stop Us Now*, and Marianne's laughter was sprinkled with relief. The storm clouds had passed.

'Let's do a duet at the next karaoke night. Without Kurt, I need a new partner who can hit the notes.' Joel grinned at the thought. He was coming back to himself, and it felt great. 'Isn't this fantastic, Marianne? We have faced our fears and look at us now. With my contacts, I'll find us a suitable nest. Hey, I just thought of something. A friend of mine has a cottage in Syderstone, by the common. It's tiny, and it may need an update but there's land, about a quarter of an acre. Andie's talked about selling for years but doesn't want it to go to the developers.'

'Will she consider selling to us?'

'I think so. She currently lives in Totnes, making pots. In fact, why don't we drive by before you leave tomorrow?'

'Perfect. While you're casting about for dens, I'll talk to Gil and Spencer. It may take a few months, so let's get the ball rolling.'

'Early Spring is fabulous here. There's so much I want to show you, and it'll be much easier when we're together.'

'Mustn't let my excitement get out of hand.'

'Why not?'

Marianne's heart skipped and jumped. Joel was right. They had earned the right to be excited. 'Why not indeed. We'll probably see more of Zak now that Imogen is taking the job with my former employer.'

'I wonder how Gil will cope with the change. It's no coincidence he chose to build a security company. From what Zak told me about Gil's childhood, keeping his pack protected makes sense.'

'I've never thought of it that way. Even so, Gil can't stop the world from turning. Do you think we should mention our plans to Irene and Dudley?'

'Yes, but only them for now. Once it's legal, we'll surprise everyone. How does that sound?'

Marianne kissed his face all over. It was a marvellous way to agree.

GIL

GIL PULLED off his soaking running kit and climbed into the shower. The warm water pummelled his exhilarated body. Of all the years he'd been coming to Wells, not once had it occurred to him to run barefoot along the beach. At dawn, he had followed the sea as it weaved along the shoreline until he reached Holkham. Then he rested, made an about turn and ran back to the beach hut. The experience was so unlike the Peak District runs but he was equally as euphoric. This morning's session was better still, as the fear of being judged had disappeared and an overwhelming sensation to shout had almost won out, were it not for another runner who had passed him, pointing to his bare feet. 'Hey fella, I like your style!' Yeah, he liked his style, too.

A grin had invaded Gil's habitually taciturn face. Had he ever really smiled from inside, a smile that actually felt genuine? Apart from the joy that Zak and Esme brought, the only other person with whom he was truly himself was Spencer. They shared the same humour, values, and outlook. Inexplicably, Gil was reticent to talk about the running workshop and the counselling sessions. Did he think his cousin would make fun, or belittle him in some way? He still hadn't talked to Imogen. They were moving further away from each other, but Gil's unanchored boat wasn't unhappy to be pushed and pulled. During one of the running workshop's evening chats, a good-humoured man called Marcus Frobisher had mentioned his work as a psychosynthesis counsellor. The group practice was based at Limehouse, just two miles away from Gil's office. Without prompting, he scoured the website and, liking what he saw, booked an introductory session with one of Marcus's colleagues. A week later, in what he could only describe as an art-studio-come-relaxation-suite, Gil sat opposite the affable therapist whose account of this particular counselling style appealed to him. Olivia Donahue described the founder, Roberto Assagioli's philosophy using an analogy of a house in which each floor represented an aspect of the personality. By building an elevator, it was possible to move out of the limited-view basement and reach the rooftop terrace, where the view was infinitely more creative, interesting, and optimistic.

Next week was his fourth session, and they had covered a lot of ground. Gil was better able to grasp how his preoccupation with the outer world of goals, ambitions, and over-identification with his head had led to a serious neglect of his inner landscape, notably his heart. It was as though he'd bypassed childhood for the grown-up world of responsibility and duty. Through a blend of dialogue and guided imagery, he was learning to recognise his stress drivers, and was taking those first tentative steps back to himself. After reluctantly setting aside the iPod in favour of a total sense experience, Gil realised how much the music disconnected him from the environment in which he was running. It was an epiphany. What was becoming increasingly clear was that he needed time alone to reflect and to befriend himself. There was no turning back. The process of untying himself to Imogen had begun years before, so slowly as to be imperceptible, but was now gaining momentum.

With every passing day, Gil let himself release a fraction more into the space around him, not unlike his son's parallel journey. When Zak announced his plan to forgo higher education, Imogen had reacted angrily, accusing Zak of squandering his opportunities which he would live to regret. Gil wasn't so sure. Zak's plans were sound enough. During the last family visit to Wentworth, his father-in-law was energised by Zak's charitable trust vision. Nik had no concerns for his grandson's education either: Zak was embarking on a life-long learning as a ranger, and formal study could be undertaken later, if at all. His boy was flying high. Nina Kossi was a solid, kind-hearted girl and they were good together. The break-up with Imogen wasn't going to be easy, but there was a fair chance Zak would hold his own.

Gil started the breakfast. The kids had arranged to meet Joel and Marianne to visit some site or other. Imogen and Nicole had left for a spa day, and Spencer was beach-kayaking. The Mull reunion was at eight o'clock. He and Rudy would have a quiet day, and he'd think about the right moment to tell Imogen he wanted to separate. She'd never return to The Tower. It had never been her holiday of choice. She only came this weekend because Zak and Esme were here. Marianne had asked to meet him and Spencer at the beach café tomorrow morning. With a bit of luck, he'd catch her at the pub, to try and find out what she wanted. Gil ignored the stomach cramp and continued to stir the porridge.

'Any idea what Marianne wants to see us for? I could have done with a lie in this morning.'

Gil turned a deaf ear to his cousin's morning after grumble and scanned the outdoor café. A number of dog walkers had stopped for a cup of tea before the afternoon drizzle arrived. The family were still in bed. The Windlass had been ramped up for a crazy night of rowdy pool games, and karaoke songs. By the time they arrived, the party was underway, and the kids were gobbled up by their friends. Marianne was nowhere in sight. Soon after, his attention was drawn to the stage where the crowd had gathered noisily. Nicole spotted her first. '*OMG, that's Marianne up there, with Joel! Hey, Imogen, check her out!*' Marianne's hair was a mass of cork-screw curls, and the sheer black silk shirt and hipster jeans were like nothing he'd ever seen on her. He was vaguely aware of Nicole and Spencer's attempts to identify the Bryan Adams and Tina Turner song, *It's Only Love*. Gil left the cheering behind and walked back to The Tower, sober and disturbed.

Spencer was half-way through his third cup of coffee. 'The girls will have sore heads this morning. You took off smartish, Gil.'

'It was impossible to talk in that racket. Good time?'

'To be truthful, I don't remember much, apart from being grateful The Tower was within walking distance.'

'Maybe Marianne's looking for more work. Did you know Joel gave a talk at Noke House?'

'Esme said the hall was packed, Joel got a huge cheer, and the spike in eco-club membership uptake was impressive. Apparently Marianne was with him, and also had interesting things to say. Joel Midwinter is quite the fella. That was a performance and a half last night. Did you know Marianne could sing? Zak said she's a member of the Hazelwood Rock Choir … hey-up, she's here.'

Marianne walked towards them and sat on the edge of the bench. The remnants of curly hair were tied back, and the light residue of black kohl gave her a sultry air. She didn't want a drink.

Gil said, 'Looks like you had fun last night, Marianne.'

'Joel's very persuasive. Thanks for coming out so early. Sorry for the cloak and dagger, but I'd appreciate it if you kept this conversation between us for now.'

The cousins glanced at each other. 'Is everything okay?'

'Everything's fine, Gil. I'll get to the point. I'm selling Number 5 and I want to give you first refusal to buy it. If you're not interested, I'll do my best to find a good neighbour for Niall and the community, but it might be out of my hands. If you are interested, can you let me know by the end of the week? I'd like to move out by February.'

Silence settled over the table like a cold snow flurry. Gil's brain was frantically forming questions: why was she moving; where was she going; how had this happened? Then, an unrecognisable voice filtered into his eardrums.

'No can do. It's unlikely we can finance it, and in any event, we wouldn't know for certain until next summer.'

Gil stared at Spencer, and then at Marianne's flushed face. She was about to stand when he rediscovered the ability to speak. 'Can you give us a few days to confirm? How much of a rush are you in?'

'Not a rush as such Gil, more an eagerness to start a new life with Joel, here in Norfolk. Look, there's no problem. I just thought I'd ask.'

'Best you have a good long think beforehand, Marianne. You don't want to make another mistake like you did with Warren.'

'I beg your pardon, Spencer?'

'Well, we had to bail you out of that mess, didn't we? After all, you've only known Joel for five minutes. You've a lot to lose.'

Marianne shot back. 'I'm not asking for permission. I've spent too long being grateful to the Armstrongs, but that ends right now. I'll contact the agent tomorrow. Thanks for your time.'

Gil followed Marianne's double-quick step to her car. 'Hey, wait up! Spencer's got a hangover. He didn't mean it. Let me call you tomorrow, Marianne. You can give me a day, can't you?'

She turned to face him, eyes blazing. Then she nodded, and he watched her drive off before returning to the café. God knows what she thought of them. The scarlet heat of shame and anger tore through him as he walked back to the café. 'What the hell was that about? You've really upset her.'

'I don't see how our concern for Marianne's welfare could upset her. Anyway, we can't handover potentially a quarter of a million quid or more just like that. If she's serious, the estate agent can sell the house.'

'And she'll have to pay the agent's fees. It was a gesture, Spencer. Marianne wants to make sure Niall gets a good neighbour. We let that idiot make the Sycamore residents' lives a misery for months.'

Spencer finished his coffee. 'Look, Gil, I may have overdone it and I'm sorry, but your philanthropic ideas stretch way too far. Maybe now is a good time to talk. For weeks now you've been distant. Something's happening, and you don't usually keep me out of the loop. We haven't even discussed Tanner's offer. If you want out of the business, there's a lot to work through.'

'I'm leaving Imogen.'

Silence.

'I'll tell her when we get home. I've also begun counselling.'

'Flippin' heck, Gil, why didn't you say anything?'

'I'm telling you now. My main concern is Zak, but I think he'll be okay. This thing with Joel, the eco-club, his new mates – Zak's no longer a kid. I can't make a decision about the business yet.' Gil's eyes filled. 'I should have ended the marriage when Bonnie died, but Zak was having a melt-down, and you were in a slump ...'

Spencer's eyelids flickered. He looked away and, like a burst of sunlight, it all dropped into place. A paroxysm of fury instinctively tightened Gil's fists but Spencer's fire blanket hands immediately immobilised them.

'I'd rather not have a fight in the café, but if that's how you want to play it Gil, then go ahead, punch my lights out. In any case I'm going to tell you what happened, so hear me out.'

Neither man moved, poised on the tightrope of their lifelong friendship, impossible to take a safe step either way. Spencer relaxed his hands and when Gil's remained still, he spoke. 'It was just after Bonnie's funeral. I went to Marianne's house, to give her a present from Nicole, something from Lee Morrell's shop. When I got there, Marianne was tearful, and I was concerned. I made tea, and we talked. Bonnie's death had knocked her for six; Freddie wasn't coming back after university; Zak and Esme were leaving Hazelwood Primary. She had no direction and couldn't see the point anymore. I hugged her, and you know …'

'No, Spencer, I don't.'

'We – I kissed her. I told her I had loved her since that first night in the night club. I asked her to start a new life together. She pushed me away – she didn't love me, she was lonely and had made a terrible mistake. Marianne asked me to leave and to never bother her again. After that, I went downhill. Maybe it was a kind of depression, I don't know, but it passed, and I picked myself up. I've not seen her until recently. Haven't you noticed that she only ever deals with you, and avoids me like the plague?' Spencer breathed out. 'Gil, it's all in the past. Marianne has found happiness with Joel and is leaving Hazelwood. She doesn't need us and as Nicole said, she probably never did. We've got to let her go.'

'Stay out for half an hour. When you get back to The Tower, I'll be gone. You can take the kids back with you.'

'Gil, wait a minute …'

'I trusted you, Spencer. Have you any idea how important you've been in my life? There is no one I've respected and loved more than you, and in the blink of an eye, you'd have broken up our entire family, and you didn't have the guts to tell me.'

Gil's arctic expression may have frozen the hardiest soul, but Spencer's constitution contained enough kindness for them both. Now that the burden was lifted, relief spread through him like molten lava. 'I didn't say anything because

I knew you'd react exactly as you have. You've always put me and Marianne on a pedestal, and there is only one way for us to go. The reason you feel betrayed is because you also love her. If it hadn't been for Warren, you and Marianne would be together.'

'Yeah, and you'd have done the exact same thing to me. Do me a favour, Spencer, stay out of my way.'

So emphatic was his grip on the steering wheel, Gil had to shake his hands before he could open the front door and punch in the alarm code. The morning's elation had been scorched by a ball of flame, intensified by the increasingly dank weather. Fury rebounded through him like a deranged pinball machine. In a desperate bid to release it, he went into the gym and punched the boxing ball until his arms gave out. Then, he sprinted at full pelt on the running machine until he collapsed, his lungs screaming. Spencer had kept his secret for years, and yet, hadn't he done the same? Yes, they both loved Marianne but they had married other women, and had children, and now she was with Joel and was leaving Hazelwood. She must have been at such a low point back then, and his cousin had taken advantage. Had she encouraged his or Spencer's feelings towards her? The only thing that had stopped him from punching Spencer's face to a pulp was the thought of his old man.

The freezing shower literally knocked Gil into his senses. Mid-way through rubbing his skin as if it were the enemy, he stopped. Where was the self-acceptance, the self-care now? He was on the verge of calling Olivia as this was a crisis, but the intensity subsided as he focused on his breath. How he wanted to hate Spencer and Marianne, but he couldn't be sure they'd done anything wrong. His reaction was so immature, so primal, and yet it was the only reaction available. Gil knew one thing for sure: he *had* to buy Marianne's house. He didn't need Spencer's approval and to hell with the motivation. She had come to her senses. *It was a mistake. She didn't love him.* But she loved Joel, and it was time to let her go. Spencer was right about that.

Zak and Imogen were in the hall. Gil took a deep breath and went downstairs to greet them as best he could. 'Sorry I shot off. Had a migraine starting. Did Nina get home okay?'

'Yes thanks, Dad. She had a fab time. Spencer was quiet, though. He and Nicole must have had a row. Esme chirped away, bless her. I'll let Rudy into the garden.'

Gil switched on the kettle and wolfed down a banana. He hadn't eaten since breakfast. As his precious son fiddled with the feeding station with not a care in the world, a stab of guilt pierced his chest. This was all about to change.

Zak walked back in. 'Marianne was incredible last night. She and Joel have total chemistry. Nina said they were *cookin' on gas*.'

Imogen was already at the kitchen table, logged into her laptop. She answered without looking up. 'Marianne is fortunate to have met such a vibrant, attentive young man. To use your naturalist terminology, Zak, she's undergone a metamorphosis. It's called 'lust'.'

'No, Mum, it's called 'love'.' Anger flared in his cheeks. 'I've never seen two people so happy together, and no one deserves it more than Marianne. She's been on her own forever and must have been so lonely. Joel isn't afraid to show how he feels. It's great to be around them.'

Gil shuffled in the fridge. With nerves stretched to the limit, he was hanging on by a thread. 'What would you like for dinner?'

'I'll make chickpea curry if you like. When we were on Mull, Joel said it was the easiest and most nutritious meal ... what? Why are you looking at me like that?'

'Like what, son? I don't fancy a curry. Imogen?'

Imogen continued to look at the screen. 'Anything will do.'

'I don't understand why you're offended because I choose not to eat meat, Dad. I'm not asking you to do the same. Jeez, I'm almost fifteen, and old enough to decide for myself. Joel says ...'

Gil slammed the packet of pasta on the worktop and faced his son. 'I'm sick of hearing what Joel says. Are you sure he isn't making the decisions for you? What does Zak Armstrong say?'

'Do you wonder why I don't talk to you? The fact is, Dad, I've never been happier, or more certain of what I want. Look, I'm not blaming either of you. I'm simply pointing out that my life is my responsibility. It's not about what you want for me. Joel and Marianne are available – they ask *me* what I think. I have to make an appointment to talk to you, as you're either on the computer, like right now, or you've got the phone stuck to your ear.'

'Now wait just a minute, Zak.' Imogen closed down the screen. 'Your father and I ...'

'There is no 'your father and I', is there? When do you ever do anything with Dad, apart from buzz off on holiday?

Come to think of it, when is it ever just the three of us? What does that tell you about our family unit, Mum? It's dysfunctional, that's what.'

Zak slammed the kitchen door while Rudy ran for cover into the living room. Imogen attempted to hide her shock. 'You shouldn't be so hard on Zak. His influences could be so much worse than Joel Midwinter. At least our son is not afraid to show his emotions. Maybe he has a point about our family being dysfunctional. What was the last thing we did together.'

'So I should follow my son's lead?'

'Zak is a teenager. This is how he is meant to behave, Gil. Now more than ever, he needs his father to guide him, not someone he is afraid of.'

Gil's jaw instinctively tightened in a desperate effort to suffocate the volcano that threatened to erupt. Who the hell was she to lecture or criticize him? They were the mirror image of each other, and until that moment, he hadn't grasped just how ugly it was. 'Zak knows I love him. I don't have to give him untold back-stage passes or over-the-top presents to show it.'

Imogen's eyes narrowed. 'I'm sorry, Gil, it's me who is being unrealistic. How can you show love if you don't have any to give?' Her voice began to crack. 'I know exactly how Marianne feels. I am lonelier than ever, and too bloody young to be invisible.'

'You've no idea how Marianne feels. Your lives are the polar opposite. She would never break a vow.'

Silence.

'I wasn't born yesterday, Imogen. You're seeing someone else.'

Gil's unnervingly quiet demeanour was disturbing. She expected him to lose his temper, but this was a million times worse. 'It isn't what you think. Kiran and I worked together in Singapore and had supper. It happens a lot in business, you know that. After all, that was how we met.'

'How can I forget. The only other woman who circles her prey as efficiently as you is your mother. It's quite a skill.'

'Gil, I have no plans to leave you and begin another relationship, but you could scarcely blame me if I looked for comfort elsewhere.'

'For a woman with your communication skills, I'm staggered you found it so hard to tell me you've had enough. We promised we'd never cross the line.' Gil walked towards the hall. 'I'll move out tomorrow. At least the divorce should be straightforward – that is, if you decide to stay in Epping. In any case, I'll be here, so Zak can finish his education while you rebuild your flagging career.' The realisation of what was happening struck him like lightning. Imogen came towards him, but he held his hand up. He had to get out.

'Gil, please don't leave like this. Surely we can discuss it?'

He walked out of the house and closed the door quietly. Moments later, the BMW's quiet purr faded, and Imogen's self-assured face crumpled under a cascade of silent tears.

Gil parked by a clearing at the heart of the forest. The early evening air was chilly, so he opened the boot and pulled out his thick Puffa coat. Watching his son play football was a cold business but, like his marriage, and his relationship with Spencer, that too had come to an abrupt end. All the touchstones in his life were disintegrating. Gil pulled on the woolly hat. His breath was steamy against the soft dark night, and the stars were out in force. Apart from seasonal seven-a-side football and the recent running club fire circles, nocturnal wanderings weren't his idea of fun. He had never camped. It seemed like unnecessary hardship, as if his upbringing weren't tough enough. Gil unconsciously rolled the platinum wedding band around his finger. Fifteen years was remarkable by any standard, but even his son could see through them. It was laughable.

A couple walked by with their dog. He murmured a reply to the 'nice night' comment and checked his watch. It was now a half-past eight. Gil was tempted to drive to Bethnal Green, to Lionel and Jean's old house, but quickly changed his mind. Recollections of his drunken father banging on the door shouting abuse while he, a helpless kid unable to protect his mother and sister, wasn't exactly nostalgic. During that single marriage guidance session, Imogen couldn't wait to expose his emotional unavailability. He had angrily replied that, given she'd had a life of plain sailing and was universally adored, what could she ever know of suffering, or fear? The only good thing to come out of that miserable hour was their honesty. Gil felt as if he were standing on the edge of a cliff, and the only solution was to step back. To stay with Imogen was to dive into the void. Far better to suffer short-term pain than to prolong or postpone the agony, for all their sakes.

As for Spencer, it was impossible to think about him without going to pieces. It was his own stupid fault for elevating his cousin to the status of a god. Maybe it was time to sell the business and go their separate ways? The takeover would make them considerably wealthy men. Gil shuddered. At least he didn't need to make a decision on that just yet as ending his marriage was all he could deal with right now.

Zak walked into the kitchen, sullen. 'Where's Dad?'

Imogen closed her laptop. She looked at her son, her heart breaking. The inevitability of what was about to come in no way diminished how devastated she felt. 'He's gone to see your grandma. Can I get you something? A milky coffee perhaps?'

The dark smudges under her eyes immediately set off the alarm. 'No, thank you. What's happened, and please don't lie?'

'Your father and I had an argument, that's all.'

'It's gone nine. Dad never goes to grandma's this late.' Just as he finished his sentence, Rudy ran to the front door, barking. His father walked to the kitchen without taking off his shoes, with an expression that raised the hairs on Zak's neck. 'What's happened to Grandma Lena?'

'She's fine. Has your mother told you?'

'Told me what?'

'We've decided to separate. I'm moving in with Gran and Jean. You'll go to school, see your friends, just as you do now.'

Gil's brutality poleaxed her. He was every atom the hard businessman and Imogen hated him for it. She grabbed her son's hand. 'Darling, you are upset, which is to be expected, but we'll ...'

Zak pulled his hand away. 'No, I'm actually okay. Have you any idea what it's like to live in this house with people who don't know how to communicate? It's a miracle you lasted this long. Please don't worry about me. I'm much more resilient than you think.'

As they watched Zak walk upstairs, Imogen and Gil were united in their anguish. This was the worst way to tell him, but the outcome would have been the same, however they approached it. Imogen could have slapped his cold, stony face as he stood there, his arms hanging uselessly by his side. 'Do you want your grandmother's engagement ring back?'

'I don't want anything back. Can you call the school? They'll need to keep an eye on Zak. I'm going upstairs to check on him, then I'll be out of your way.'

Suddenly Imogen began to cry. The effect was so startling, Gil instantly walked over and pulled her to him. 'I'm so sorry, Gen. I didn't mean for it to come out like this, but it's for the best, isn't it?'

Despite her anger and her sorrow, the truth was undeniable. 'Yes, it's for the best.'

LENA AND JEAN

THE LAST of the Christmas decorations fitted snugly into the large storage box, ready for Gil to lift it into the cupboard. In less than an hour, Lena and Jean had dismantled the festive season so effectively, the annual event might never have taken place. Why Jean insisted they follow the 'Twelve days of Christmas' palaver was beyond her, so as soon as that last day had gone, the decks were cleared of their holly boughs, and the clear up began. Satisfied that all was in order, Lena put her housekeeping coat and tin back in the utility room and sat in her nicely upholstered chair. Jean had set down the tea and a plate of shortbread biscuits on the side table and was settled beside her. Sofas were all well and good for the young ones, but you'd a devil of job heaving yourself out once you were in. 'Wasn't that the strangest Christmas we've ever had, Jean?'

Jean groaned inwardly. The post-mortem was coming, and she steeled herself for it. At least Lena had waited until the holidays were over before raking over the coals. Spencer had been uncharacteristically quiet, and it was troubling for Jean to see her son like it.

'Gil's glad to be back at work. The tradition to close the firm over the holidays is fine and dandy, but with everything that's happened, he'll have missed going in. I thought we'd see more of him once he moved into the loft. Do you know where he goes, Jean?'

Jean shook her head.

'Marianne's moving soon. I could cry at the thought of it, but I am pleased for her. Joel's a good man. He got stuck in when we were over there for dinner, didn't he? She'll miss baby Pearl but at least Ashley and Niall are staying put. It's been a long while since we had a new-born. Pearl is adorable, isn't she Jean. Jean?'

'Sorry – yes she is, Lena.'

'It was a shame Gil didn't join us for the New Year's Eve do. He probably wanted quiet time on his own at The Tower. With such a crowd, he wasn't missed, was he? Zak doesn't seem too upset at the break-up, but he's loved up with Nina. I just hope she doesn't take advantage as he's such a generous, loving boy, and according to Nicole, there's not much in the way of home comforts in her family, eh Jean?'

More nods and shakes.

'I had to laugh though. Nicole's got a cheek. I just about stopped myself from reminding her about the shoplifting, the truanting, and her over-easy ways, as she's been so good to Zak since the split. Wasn't it good of her and Esme to make him up a bedroom? Still, when all's said and done, Nicole's lucky to have Spencer, and they've been married nigh on thirty years, which counts for something in this day and age eh, Jean.'

'Did you think Spencer was quiet?'

'I do love a shortbread.' Lena dunked her biscuit in the tea, and swore under her breath when it dropped in.

Jean flinched. She couldn't abide bad language, and one of the few positive things to have happened since Lena moved in with her and Lionel was that she had curbed her vile tongue.

Lena fished the biscuit out with her spoon and put it on the saucer. 'What do you mean, quiet? There was so much racket with the kids, I can't say as I did. Why are you asking?'

'The boys usually play cards, but Spencer and Nicole left early. He and Gil are due for lunch next Saturday, although Gil said something about another running weekend.'

'The last thing Gil wants is more time in our company. He and Spencer see each other every day. He'll move into Marianne's cottage once she's gone.'

'I wouldn't have thought so. It's far too small, and it's a terraced. He's used to living at Flaxfield.'

'Gil will be glad to see the back of that eyesore. What does he need all that space for? Number 5 is perfect. There's a bedroom for Zak; Niall and Ashley live next door; it's five minutes from us, and he owns it. It makes sense. Zak's got another three years at Noke House, and there's every chance Imogen will sell up. It's her house, after all, and she's never liked living in Epping. Gil never wanted it. He's got his own money.'

'Gil bought Number 5?'

'Of course he did. You were here when he said it, Jean.'

'No, Lena, I wasn't, and there's nothing wrong with my memory. Spencer told me they couldn't buy Number 5 as they might need the capital for the takeover.' Jean got up to refill the pot and left Lena to the Radio Times. Her mind was whirring, and she felt quite sick. Spencer and Gil must have argued over it. For as long as she could remember, the boys had been exceptionally close. Spencer had taken Gil under his wing, introduced him to his university friends and widened his horizons. It was Spencer's idea to design their own access control systems, and to focus on private clients rather than fight for a share of the corporate market. Without his guiding hand, Gil would never had achieved the levels of success alone.

There was no doubt her nephew was undergoing a significant upheaval, maybe even a breakdown. Jean's bedroom was directly beneath the loft conversion. She'd become accustomed to hearing the grandchildren's giggles over the years, but her nephew's strangled sobs broke her heart. She kept this to herself as Lena wouldn't want to hear this from her sister-in-law. Living with Jimmy Knox had made Lena thick skinned, and she had little in the way of tenderness for Gil. She had encouraged him to toughen up, mistakenly believing it was the best form of self-protection, and his unyielding expression gave the impression of confidence, but Gil's true personality was empathetic, sensitive. In another life, he'd have been an artist, or perhaps even a therapist. Jean bit back a sob. She would never forget holding his thin shaking body after the school bullies had cornered him. Lionel's advice was to either learn how to run or fight, and mercifully Gil chose running. Scores of track wins had earned him respect. He reminded her of the Colin Smith character played by Tom Courtenay in the *The Loneliness of the Long-Distance Runner*: defiant, autonomous, and ultimately, a survivor.

It suddenly occurred to her that Spencer was the more dependant. Gil was now undertaking counselling; he had left his wife; he was reconsidering his working life and was building a relationship with his son. Spencer on the other hand, was desperate to keep the business going. He had taken to travelling more but had stayed with Nicole who had been reliant upon him since the beginning, and all the while his best friend was breaking away. No wonder he was subdued. And of course, in the middle of it all was Marianne. Although she and Lena had never discussed it, Jean had known for many years that their sons were in love with her. Spencer's confident and friendly manner had never effectively masked his feelings. Gil may have possessed a different character, but he, too, felt the same. When Warren left, they had closed ranks around her, and whether Marianne had deliberately courted it or not, she became an integral part of the family. Now she had found someone to love her, and they would all suffer her absence in their own way. Gil *had* to buy Number 5. This was as close to Marianne he'd ever get, and if her relationship with Joel failed, he would give her the house back. But if his dream came true, Gil would move in with her. That was it! How would Spencer stand it? He must have considered it a possibility, which was why he had blocked the purchase in the first place. That was the fuse that burnt the friendship!

Fresh tea made, it was almost time for *Cash in the Attic*, one of Lena's favourite programmes and it would keep her quiet. Jean needed time to digest these disturbing deductions and prepare for the fall out.

 ZAK

THE CAR TOOTED. Zak pulled on his jacket and flew down the stairs, his bag banging against the bannister rail. He hadn't combed his hair but then again, did it matter? There were so many more important issues to be concerned with rather than hairstyles, and school ties. Nicole had already tooted her arrival. He was running late again. It was impossible to get to bed earlier, as apart from the mountain of things to do, his mind had been hijacked by thoughts of Nina. She loved to slide off his headband and run her hands through his hair when they were geeking out in his bedroom. Travis had his own opinions and warned him to be prepared. Nina was six months older, and much more mature. Zak waved the disturbingly delicious thoughts away before saying goodbye to his mum who was outside, talking to Nicole.

Far from the separation being disruptive, life had gone on as it had before. The transformational visit to Mull had helped to prepare him. Marianne's tragic history was shocking, but not only had she survived, she and Joel were together. By all accounts, he also had it tough, growing up without a mum or dad. Put into perspective, Zak was grateful for his lot. As jewellery wasn't allowed at school, every morning he'd hold the silver sparrow feather and do as Joel suggested: sit quietly, observe his breath, listen to the sounds and feel of nature around him. Next, he was to send himself and his loved ones a bucketful of loving kindness before sending it to the world. He wanted to make a Zen garden, just like Joel's, but was mindful of his father's accusation, *'What does Zak Armstrong say?'* As much as it annoyed him, his dad had a point. It was so hard not to think about the camera traps rather than his breath. Still, he wasn't to judge himself, but to give it time. He was steering his life in the direction he wanted it to go.

Noke House was a great school, but Zak had no intention of staying until he was eighteen. Several people he admired the most hadn't even got A levels. The family's wealth was no longer an embarrassment. Nina pointed out that he was in the enviable position of not needing to earn a big salary, so he was free to follow his heart. Professor Rose had counselled patience, but when the time came, and with parental support, there was every possibility of a ranger's role. The professor was supportive of his idea to set up a trust, much like the Foundation. Grandpa Nik was willing to start the fund with a large donation, so there was a mega amount to be excited about.

Rudy had settled down to his 'job-share role', as Spencer called it. Any doubts about Nicole's ability to care for his dog properly were unfounded. The other day, Zak noticed Rudy curled up next to her on the sofa while she was knitting and watching the telly. Nicole's guilty look made them both laugh. He told her she looked so much nicer without make up as her skin was like a peach, and she welled up at that. His mother had been away but bizarrely, they spent more time together. Nina said she needed his company. Apart from Annette Desai, Zak had been really sad to discover how few good friends Imogen actually had. Spencer and Nicole invited her for dinner, but she was yet to take up the offer. She tried her best not to cry in front of him, but he told her to let it out. They had established a weekly routine whereby they'd watch a wildlife programme together, and chat about his discoveries and her work.

Although his dad's absence in the house still felt weird, they saw each other regularly and talked every day. Gil was doing much better. Last week, they took Rudy for a forest ramble during which he described how the bare-foot running had led him to Olivia Donahue (maybe his mother should see a therapist?) Over lunch, Zak told him about the Sparrow Feather Manifesto (this world is *our* world; tread lightly; my life is *my* responsibility) and how the sparrow symbolised love, joy, self-worth, and community. His dad said he'd like to join them sometime and had smiled, but not sarcastically. Apparently, the running group talked about similar things. It seemed to Zak that no matter who you were, if you didn't come to terms with the childhood baggage, or talk about your worries, they got bigger and bigger until they swallowed you up, so to hide or ignore them was counterproductive.

Zak climbed into the back of Nicole's car. Esme immediately bombarded him with suggestions for the eco-club while Rudy jumped on his lap and gave his face a wash. As Zak turned to wave at his mother, he was so grateful for all the people in his gang, and his heart ached for her loneliness.

MARIANNE

'WOULD YOU like these, Della? They were a gift from someone whose name I've forgotten. Never been used.'

Della held the purple wine glass gingerly by its stem, her nose crinkling. 'They're not quite my thing, but I know just the person who'd appreciate them.'

Marianne smiled sadly. In a few weeks' time, she and Della would no longer share the minutiae of daily life, or sing together, or work together. On the map, a hundred miles was no distance, but it might as well have been a thousand for all the time they'd actually see each other. In spite of that, Della was so happy for her to have found love. It was a pity there wouldn't be babies, but there were always chickadees to cuddle at the centre.

'How's Freddie taking it?'

'Fine, once he got over the shock of his mother actually having a life, and also that the deeds to the cottage will be in my name.'

'Why ever would Joel do that? What if you break up?'

'Joel insisted I own the property outright as he's got the cabin, and he says it's only fair. You know me, Della, I always pay my dues.'

'You do and ignore my eejit comment. Now, have you any idea who the new tenant might be? Ashley and Niall have settled in, and she'll be working with us part-time in the Spring, after her training. I hope Gil and Spencer find someone nice.'

'Gil is buying the cottage out of his own money. We're due to exchange contracts soon.'

'Really! I thought …' Della's mouth hinged, hovered, and finally gave in to gravity. 'Surely he's not going to live in it?'

'Think about it Della. It makes sense.'

'Location; family; needing his own roof. Yes, it makes sense, but don't you think it's creepy? Gil will be here, in your home.'

'Except it won't be my home anymore. I'm creating a new one with Joel, in Norfolk.'

'What will you do for work? If you want to help out with holiday cover, you're welcome to stay with Sean and me.'

'I'd love that. Do you remember when I told you about the professor and his wife? Dorothea has offered me a part-time housekeeper's job. She could use someone to keep the farmhouse ticking over while they're away, and to help with the family's regular reunions. I'd like to focus on my drawings, at least for a while. Joel's wages will cover the bills. He says I should think about staging an exhibition, but I'm not really bothered about that sort of thing.'

'You've the knack for making a bob or two, so I shan't worry about you. Shall we break for tea? I brought doughnuts. This may be the last time I'll see you scrape off the sugar and scoop out half the jam.'

The friends smiled. These might have been the sorts of details that only close friends know about each other, but Marianne decided not to tell Della about Joel's recent emotional downturn. While certain she loved him there were, nevertheless, nervous stirrings. Joel was much more

276

aware of how his mind worked than she. During those few sequestered days, he saw clearly how a deep-seated fear drove him to live in such a disciplined way: strict health regime; the exact amount of rest; being outdoors; helping every sentient being apart from himself. Whatever Joel's spiritual practices were, he had forgotten to include himself as beneficiary of goodwill, as had she. A loving relationship was fundamental to well-being: to care and be cared for, not as a duty or a burden, but as a gift, a privilege, was the only basis on which to begin a life together: in theory, at least.

Spencer's harsh words had, however, troubled her. Marianne thought back to that unhappy time when she was lonely, bereaved, depressed. In all likelihood, Spencer was undergoing a similar experience, but she had stopped it in its tracks. Perhaps he harboured a sense of guilt, or anger, but what could she do about it, and if Gil chose to move in to Number 5, that was his affair. It was an unsettling time. Imogen's unexpected visit to Sycamore Crescent the day after Zak's garden party had resurrected memories. The women had sat in Ashley's kitchen talking babies, and briefly touched on Imogen's new role. So, Malika Lionnet was Imogen's new employer. Why did it feel as if the past was encroaching on the present?

The need to move on was growing, and the meeting with Andie Lawton had come at the right time. Marianne liked the vivacious ceramicist who wanted the family cottage to go to good people. Irene and Dudley were overjoyed to find they wouldn't be far away and had grabbed her tight, *He's been waiting for someone like you all his life. We know you'll take care of each other*, another sign she was embarking on the right course. Anya acknowledged her elation and trepidation but was confident. *As long as you and Joel continue to be open and honest, all will be well.*

Winter's slow withdrawal allowed Spring a tentative entrance, although ringlets of cold clung to the mornings and evenings. Through the dark, Marianne could make out that the blackbirds and magpies had devoured the fat balls and seeds, so she ventured outside in the freezing air to refill the feeders. She was glad to do it. The birds needed all the help they could get, and the sensor lights made the job easier in the dark. Whoever the new occupier of Number 5 was, the Sycamore residents would have something to say about continuing the bird-feeding tradition. Marianne glanced down at the frozen pond. She reminded herself to ask Joel what the impact of the weather would mean for next season's frog spawn. There were still so many practical things to discuss but Kurt had arrived in Wells with an armload of work, and they'd had only the briefest conversation the day before.

Joel's next visit to Hazelwood was his last. Everything was now couched in terms of finality, but Marianne was determined to make every last gathering a celebration. When Zak, Esme, and Nina came to lunch next week, she planned to invite them to the housewarming party. Larry's fire-pit and shelter would be ready in time to celebrate the Spring Equinox. It didn't matter that her illustrations had taken a back seat, as Marianne had heaps of new plants to draw. Just thinking about the south-facing lean-to, the space where Andie used to paint her ceramics gave her shivers of anticipation.

After closing out the cold, Marianne made a mug of hot chocolate. It had been a busy week. Hilda Paxton had overpaid her for decorating the dining room during the winter house sit. Anyone who could control her crazy cat deserved a bonus. It was heartening to know that Hilda would always welcome her help. As the warmth of the mug spread into her cold hands, Marianne swung her legs onto the sofa and sat back amongst the growing tower of boxes. She and Joel had made a pact that if the item wasn't useful, it had to go. His possessions consisted mainly of books, files, photographic equipment, and his precious collection of shells, fossils, feathers, and animal bones, most of which was to remain in the cabin. Apart from her treasured botanical microscope and Freddie's baby box, there wasn't much of sentimental value, and much less in the way of clothes and shoes.

Hot chocolate finished, it was time to pack the last box of the day, and then treat herself to a good long soak. As Marianne got up from the sofa, she heard a car door slam. It was either the veg box or another member of Ashley's family, frequent visitors since baby Pearl's arrival. Oftentimes she heard their joyful exclamations through the walls. The happy couple hid their disappointment when she told them about her house move, but they'd see each other on Wells beach, and when she visited Jean and Lena. With Gil as the new owner, they wouldn't have to worry about unruly neighbours. He had proceeded quickly with the purchase as promised, and she had thanked him for it.

Marianne answered the doorbell, and there, huddled under the front porch, were Professor Rose, Dorothea, and Kurt, whose wretched expressions were heightened by the sensor lights' eerie glow.

THE FINAL MIGRATION

CERTAIN DAYS of the year contain the four seasons. Joel Midwinter's farewell gathering was such a day and began with the tail end of a storm whose remnant gusts measured thirty miles per hour. By ten o'clock, the rain was forecast to fade, and brighter skies would grace the afternoon. The temperature was unseasonably mild for early February, not that anyone attending the service was remotely interested in the weather, as so many hearts were still shredded by Joel's unexpected death. Few people knew about his heart condition. He'd done such a good job of keeping it a secret, the shock waves had been all the greater. When Irene and Dudley gave permission for Kurt to release the devastating announcement, within hours a large group of mourners made their way to The Kedge to light candles, and to console each other at the loss of a unique individual.

Before the news spread through the technological tendrils of social media to Zak's sensitive ears, Kurt called Gil. Soon after, in the living room of his former home, with his soon-to-be ex-wife sitting close by, Gil told Zak. He was inconsolable. There was nothing the distraught parents could do to comfort their grief-stricken son, barely holding back their tears as they endeavoured to absorb the shock. Esme ran from her house to be with her cousin, while Nina's mother drove her to join the heart-broken young souls who together, in the safety of Zak's bedroom, tried to make sense of it. Imogen had made tea while Gil,

Lena, Jean, Spencer, Nicole, Niall, Mr Goodchild, and Shane congregated in the kitchen, not knowing what to say but each of them thinking about Marianne. No one knew where or how she was, and Freddie's phone calls went straight to messages. In a light bulb moment, Nicole suggested they try Della Carthy, the result of which revealed Marianne's whereabouts. She was in Norfolk and would return home the following day. No one was to visit, not even Freddie. He would come back the day before the funeral, although it wasn't to be a funeral in the traditional sense as Joel followed no formal religion.

That was three weeks ago. Marianne had worked it out exactly, and of the six months she and Joel had known each other, sixty-one wonderful days were spent in his company. Now, every second was like wading through a swamp, her reactions running on automatic pilot: brush teeth, eat, sleep, delete phone messages, sleep some more. Only once had she collapsed in Della's arms. Further tears would not come and any suggestion to call in the doctor was dismissed. *I don't want to feel anything, Della. It's better this way.* A pile of letters and cards sat on the hallway table while the flowers wilted in their vases, but the feeders had remained full. Later she would discover it was Shane who had taken care of the important things.

Joel's final wishes were carried out with the precision of a cormorant diving for fish. Kurt was his sole executor. He and the Roses had taken her to the cabin where she kissed Joel's radiantly peaceful face, and now he was dust in Irene and Dudley's safekeeping, until scattered exactly where he had requested. Marianne assured the devastated couple she wanted nothing more. The cabin was to be rebuilt in the gardens of The Kedge to provide a library and study area, and a list of items were set aside for specific individuals. Before any more personal belongings were given away, Kurt invited Marianne to spend time alone in the cabin, to take as long as she needed, to choose whatever she wanted, without question or explanation. Joel's New Zealand folder and his beloved poster of the blue green earth were enough. Marianne sat on his sofa, breathing in his scent from his football scarf, reverently leafing through the folder's pages, following the trail of Joel's too short existence. There was a section containing photographs of her, extensive notes of sites they had visited, and those to come later that year.

Then, within the dark mist of Marianne's grieving mind, a tiny beacon glowed, hinting at an escape from this desolate place: *Follow Joel's trail; visit the places he visited; meet the people he met; know what was in his heart.* The details were in the book: photos, maps, sites – it was all there, a pilgrimage only she could undertake. As soon as she arrived home, Marianne began her quest. After a phone call with Kurt, and a short email exchange with the owner of a small apartment block in the Mercury Bay area on the North Island, her offer of housekeeping and cleaning services in exchange for a reduced-priced six-week stay was agreed, and her plane ticket booked.

While Marianne and Freddie were on their way to the funeral, Gil was almost ready to leave. Zak and Esme had been given permission by their house tutors to take time off for the funeral and nothing was going to stop Nina from accompanying her stricken boyfriend. After the service, they would stay at The Tower for the weekend. Niall and Della arranged to meet them at The Kedge, where a marquee had been set up for the farewell. Gil persuaded Imogen not to cancel her business trip. They were united in their support of their son, but in all other respects, they were as strangers. Jean and Lena reluctantly stayed behind with Spencer. Conversations between the cousins were still strictly work and family related, although Gil had thawed. There were sufficient members of the Armstrong family attending the service, and by all accounts it might end up standing room only. In light of Marianne's wish to stay out of reach, Gil was relieved to have spoken with Freddie. The poor man was in pieces, overloaded with regret at his selfishness, and ready to do anything for his desolate mother. Gil wondered if he and Marianne might join them at The Tower after the funeral, as to drive back to Epping after such a day might be too much and Freddie agreed. Andie Lawton had delayed the purchase until Marianne felt able to make a decision. When Gil insisted on paying for any incurred costs, Freddie thanked him for being such a good friend.

Gil climbed into the driver's seat. He squeezed Zak's hand, and was reassured by his son's weak smile. They'd had a long talk the night before, during which Zak spoke of his love and respect for Joel. So much had passed between the ranger and his son, and Gil was genuinely sorry for the traumatic ending of what would have been a unique friendship. By the time the car reached the M11, the sun had burst through the thick sullen cloud, casting brilliant shadows across the wintry landscape, lighting their way.

When Marianne retrieved the memory of that day, she would remember just two things: the tremendous outpouring of love from three-hundred mourners, and her conversation with Joel's doctor. Marianne had initially taken a seat next to Freddie, Della, and Niall at the back of the marquee, away from Joel's family and close friends. Everyone appeared to know each other, but few knew of their relationship which justified her choice of semi-visibility. Minutes later however, Irene had walked over, taken her hand and led her to sit with Dudley, Kurt, and Anya. A wet-eyed woman who had to be Joel's mother sat with his half-sisters in the row behind. When the *Back To The Stars* song finished, Kurt began a moving, oftentimes hilarious and entirely appropriate eulogy, which set the tone for the afternoon.

The tension that had gripped her body for weeks did its best to let go. Marianne listened in awe as people from all areas of Joel's life shared their memories and stories of his far-reaching influence. Dr Cohen-Rockley's daughter worked as a marine biologist, due in large part to Joel's passionate encouragement. The consultant's tribute summed him up perfectly. *Joel challenged me from the first moment we met. He encouraged me to extend my horizons beyond science and to embrace ancient healing wisdoms, but he did this with his unique blend of humour, insight, and charisma. Without realising it, Joel crept into our family's hearts and there he has remained.* When Sabrina spoke of his condition, there were intakes of breath, but it was the testament to Joel's character that he had lived happily and healthily for so long. Later, she had taken Marianne aside. *Joel asked me if falling in love would be detrimental to his health. I told him that on the contrary, it was the best thing he could ever do. He was elated. He said that there was no one on this earth he'd rather give his heart to for safekeeping than a woman called Marianne Bly.*

Still reeling from the consultant's account, Anya arranged tea and brandy for her, and they tearfully held hands. She was invited to stay in Mull indefinitely. Irene and Dorothea Rose also offered sanctuary. Kurt gave her a package containing Joel's iPod, a wishing stone, and another botanical book. He was no longer 'cuddly Kurt', but a vulnerable man devastated by the loss of his best friend. Meg Swayne's anguished hug was almost the last straw, but it was Zak's tearful collapse in her arms that tipped Marianne over the edge. Freddie instantly came to her aid. Yes, she was ready to leave; yes, she'd stay overnight at The Tower.

Gil had never been to a funeral in a marquee before. A rough headcount revealed at least two hundred and fifty people with more arriving, all of whom had a place to sit under what could only be described as an oversized bell tent. To one side, a large hospitality area was set up, whilst opposite sat the stage with the ubiquitous karaoke and microphone stand, ready for the huge celebration that would take place throughout the afternoon and evening, and entirely fitting under the circumstances. Above the speaker's platform was a banner showing Joel wearing his Foundation T-shirt and hat, and a huge grin, much like the one Gil had seen that first night in The Windlass. Other images of Joel with friends, trees, and animals were pinned to the tent walls. There was no coffin, and no flowers. Mourners were encouraged to tie their tributes and personal messages to the branches of a large potted tree. From his position at the back, Gil could just about see Marianne's frozen profile, seated beside Joel's grandparents. Zak sat between him and Freddie. His mental state continued to cause alarm and the house tutor, teachers, and the family were keeping a close watch. Right now, though, after reuniting with his friends, Zak appeared to be hanging in there – just.

As the afternoon progressed, Gil discovered just how cherished Joel Midwinter was. After a slow start and with guidance and mentorship, he evolved into a dedicated and passionate naturalist, environmentalist and conservationist. He had set up an extensive network of groups, and inspired thousands, many of whom had come to pay their respects in person, or by letter. Gil could not imagine anyone speaking of him in the same way, let alone leaving this kind of legacy. Joel's footsteps were impossible to follow, but the fact that the ranger had spotted potential in his son was a reason for gratitude. When the service ended, Gil and Niall went to the bar to organise drinks. Marianne was in quiet conversation with the doctor after which Kurt, Anya, and several other people took care of her. She agreed to meet them at The Tower at six o'clock. With luck, the evening would be a calming end to a fraught day.

'That was the best Thai meal I've had, Gil. Thanks for organising it. Mum only had a cup of tea earlier on, so it was good to see her eat something. Have you ever seen so many people at a wake?'

'No, but from what was said today, Joel Midwinter was an extraordinary man, so I'm not surprised.'

'You can say that again. I'm so grateful you invited us to stay.' Freddie looked about him. 'Mum was right about The Tower. It's quite a building. We had a walk along the beach and sat at the hut, before coming here. Do you still have the chalet?'

Gil sat back while Esme and Nina cleared the table, their friendly chatter infusing the atmosphere with light and hope. 'The staff and their families use it every year. You and Rachel are welcome to stay there, or here, anytime.'

'Really?'

'You've always been family, Freddie.'

Freddie coughed. 'Thanks. Rachel would love it here.'

'How do you think your mum coped?'

Freddie glanced over his shoulder towards the balcony where Marianne stood with Zak. 'To be truthful, Mum hasn't said much. Apart from Della, she didn't want anyone to visit. I called every day. Sometimes she'd pick up, sometimes not. She told me not to feel guilty, as Joel liked me, and believed me to be a fine young man. You can imagine how I felt after that. How well did you know him?'

Gil topped up Freddie's wine glass. 'I met him maybe half a dozen times, but never for long. The first time was in a local pub. I'm ashamed to say I acted like a complete pratt. It didn't take long before I realised he was one of the good guys, and a positive influence on Zak.'

'You can say that again. I can't believe how much the boy's grown into himself.' Freddie sat forward on his chair. 'I was sorry to hear that you and Imogen had separated. That can't have been easy. I also want to apologise for being so hostile to you and Spencer. What my father did was nothing to do with either of you. You've only ever been kind and generous, but I got a bit stuck.'

'Doesn't it go with the territory? Not everyone has the good fortune to have a decent father, or mother, for that matter.' Gil was suddenly aware of Warren's happy-go-lucky features shining out of his son and felt compelled to repaint the picture of his old friend. 'You know Fred, Warren won us several important contracts which we've still got today. He had the gift of the gab – the ultimate salesman. His dad had a fabric shop in Petticoat Lane. That's where he met your nan.'

'I didn't know. I just about remember my grandmother.'

'Ida Silk was my surrogate mum. I lived with her and Warren in Bethnal Green for two years when my family moved to Epping. She was so warm and generous, and always interested in us.'

'She must have been gutted when he …'

'Look, Freddie, no one is perfect. Warren got carried away and was too ashamed to ask for help. Money burned a hole in his pocket. He loved a nice watch, a new car, and was incredibly generous: always the first at the bar, always gave the down and outs a few quid.'

Freddie was silent but not upset, so Gil continued.

'Warren, Clive and me had great times together. As we worked on Saturdays, Sunday was our day, so we'd take off for Brick Lane. Warren knew the owner of the bagel shop, which meant free grub. I can just see us now, strutting our stuff. We used to call ourselves The Three Wise Men – more like the three cocky idiots.'

Freddie found himself laughing. He was intrigued. 'Where was Spencer during your Sunday escapades?'

'Chatting to the Socialist Workers Party. Before university, he went to several Rock against Racism rallies, but I was too young to go. After my growth spurt, he used to smuggle me and Clive into Ska and Two-Tone all-nighters. Your old man never came with us. Teddy Pendergrass, Luther Vandross, lover's rock – that was Warren's bag. He met your mum at Charlie Chan's night club in Walthamstow.'

'Those were the days. I don't even know if he's alive.'

'Would you like to know?'

Freddie drank a mouthful of wine and was thoughtful. 'I'm not sure, Gil. Funerals throw up all sorts of emotions, don't they? It's not the best time to make such a decision. Mum actually shouted at me yesterday, can you believe. Her mother died last April, and I found out recently she left me seventy grand. I told Mum I didn't want the old woman's guilt money. She told me to grow up, drop the political bullshit, and if my girlfriend agreed, I should give the money to one of my causes. Rachel was of the same opinion as Mum but said we should put a deposit on a house as that was also a good cause.'

'You can always rent out a room if you feel guilty.' Gil was serious for a moment. 'Can we ever know why people act the way they do? Marianne and Joel's mothers practically gave them away, and my old man – well, the less said about him the better. Marianne never stood in Warren's way when it came to you. It was always your decision. She and Joel are two of the finest people I've ever met, the sort that bring goodness into the world. We can choose to be different.'

'Blimey Gil, that's quite an insight.'

'Ha! I can't quite believe I just said that. Must be the counselling sessions.' Gil blushed. 'To tell you the truth Freddie, it's the best thing I've ever done. That, and bare-foot running.'

'What's the best thing you've ever done, Dad.' Zak walked back in, pleased to see Nina and Esme laying out cheesecake, serving plates and forks, just like a proper family.

'Having you as a son, that's what, Zak. Now, why don't you make a pot of tea while I take a blanket out to Marianne. After pudding, we'll play a game of something, or watch a film, if you're up to it.'

Freddie took a pack of cards out of his pocket. 'Hey, why don't we play *Snapperwhipper!*'

Zak pulled his own pack out of his rucksack. 'Snap!'

Gil stepped onto the balcony and was greeted by an icy blast of North Sea air. 'Here, Marianne, thought you might need this.'

Marianne turned to face him. Her eyes glistened, and the wind blew her hair this way and that. She wrapped the blanket around the shoulders of her coat.

'Zak was about to make tea, but they're playing Joel's card game.' He shivered. 'It's a lot colder than the last time you were here.'

'Seems like a lifetime ago. I never told you this Gil, but when I stayed on to do the decorating, Joel came to see me. He called my name, (she pointed below) as if he were an old friend, popping in. I invited him up, and he helped finish painting so he could take me to see a rare orchid at Wishbone Heath.'

Gil was momentarily lost for words. Far from being annoyed or surprised, the confession warmed him. Marianne pulled the blanket tightly around her. She had never looked so lovely. 'That was a generous thing to do.'

A single pear-shaped tear crept slowly down her cheek. He passed her his handkerchief. 'Shall we go inside?'

'Before we go in, there's something I have to tell you.' Marianne dabbed her eyes. 'I'm going to New Zealand on Sunday, for six weeks. Would you mind if we delay the house sale until I get back? You've been so kind, but it's impossible to know what to do.'

He swallowed his surprise. "Of course. Where will you stay?'

'A beach apartment on The Coromandel. It's a trade: apartment cleaning for a reduced-rate stay. The owners were incredibly generous. I told them about my circumstances, and they insisted I take the first week and the last few days as holiday. Whether it was pity, or they are genuinely short-handed, I'll find out soon enough.'

'Lucky owners. You'll have everything organised within a week. Just don't offer to paint the walls.' Marianne's misty smile lifted him to the heavens. 'Is there anything I can do for you, while you're away?'

Marianne's hand brushed cold against his cheek. 'Look after our boys.'

PART TWO

MERCURY BAY

HAL HOPKINS parked the Mazda outside the art gallery. He could sense the elements with the expertise of a sniffer dog: yes, perfect conditions for sailing. More than anything he wanted to be out on the boat, but he promised to help his wife unpack and rehang her unsold paintings from last weekend's exhibition. It was well attended and rewarding – financially and artistically – which accounted for Pippa's good mood. The official holiday season was slowing down, and Hal was grateful. Upkeeping six beachfront apartments wasn't exactly onerous, but after fifteen years of welcoming worldwide travellers, honeymooners, wildlife enthusiasts, and native retirees spending their savings, attending to their comfort was losing its gloss. Sundown Apartments were the only holiday accommodation on their particular stretch of the bay, and that alone made them exclusive.

When the tired apartment block on the plot next to their house came up for sale, Pippa saw it as a golden opportunity to convert the building into unique holiday accommodation. Hal had been terrified to take on the debt, fearing they'd be tied to the business for the rest of their lives, but he underestimated his wife's business acumen. Going that extra mile with the renovations hit the jackpot. Every modern convenience was catered for in the white walled, open-plan, king-sized, sea view apartments. The bathroom and kitchen products were made by Mercury

Bay's artisans, as were the rugs, paintings, linen, napkins, and crockery. Guests returned year after year, particularly during the quieter season when the rates were more affordable for the Auckland and Wellington townies. There wasn't quite enough cash in the coffers to officially retire, but these next five years would pass quickly enough. Pippa's artistic reputation was secure, and Harlequin Gallery enjoyed a steady income. It kept her pleasantly occupied which left just enough time for him and Arnie to indulge their aquatic obsession on the Mary-Lou, their hand-built wooden pilot sloop.

'There you are Hal. I thought you'd forgotten.'

Hal kissed his wife's dusty cheek. 'And miss the chance to spend a fine morning disrobing art treasures from their bubble-wrap overcoats?'

'Irony aside, how does it feel to be two thousand dollars richer than you were last week?'

Pippa's grin cast a fan of creases over her sun-stained face. She was dressed in her favourite tangerine dungarees, and her arm bangles jangled like kea birdsong. The ravages of coastal living had aged them both, more so for Pippa, a decade older than he, but she was essentially the same quirky personality he'd fallen for all those years ago, albeit less patient, and more likely to holler at him these days. Arnie said it was his own fault for hitching up with a sheila sailing too close to the menopause. Hal didn't bother to point out that in the last three years, Arnie had been ditched by two women half his age. If Pippa hadn't given up her career in graphic design for the Coromandel's artistic allure, Hal would still be kicking the traces in Auckland's fair city. He wasn't a brave man, but the combination of

Pippa's limitless energy and fearlessness was enough for him to tailgate. The businesses were flourishing, and they were buoyed by a great bunch of mates. He could put up with her mood swings right enough. 'Let's celebrate at the Cabbage Tree.'

'Good idea. We'll invite the usual suspects. Vera will come. Her paintings sold well, so she can afford to treat herself. The Colville Festival's coming around fast, and we can plan ahead. Are you joining us this year, Hal? You know that Bluegrass band you like – Hotdog? They're topping the bill.'

Hal pulled the wrapping off of the acrylic seascape and stood it alongside the others. He had no intention of going to the festival. It was the same crowd every year, and besides, he and Arnie had already scoped out their trip to Matarangi with some of the guys from the sailing club. Backing out was not an option. As was his custom, Hal changed tack. 'Marianne has settled in alright. I wondered if we were too hasty in agreeing to her coming so soon after her bereavement, but she's not half-way through the second week, and it's as if she's always been here.'

Pippa scrutinised her husband's expressionless face. His evasiveness drove her nuts. Still, there was plenty of time to twist his arm with regards the festival. Humping boxes filled with artworks to and from the various venues was getting harder each time. 'Beattie is singing her praises. Your mother's high standards are being matched and they've hit it off. I heard them laughing over a cuppa yesterday. Marianne's appearance on the balcony that third day was a relief, wasn't it, Hal. I had visions of the police kicking down the door.'

'Me too. I like your idea of showing her the sights. She won't get far on the bicycle, and the town isn't the most stimulating of places after the second visit.'

'Beattie has offered Marianne the use of her car. She can take herself up to Opito Bay later on.'

'That was nice of Mum. Oh, I just remembered something. During this morning's clean, Marianne spotted the wear and tear in *Hebes* and has offered to decorate. What d'you think, Pip?'

'All the ground floor apartments need a lick of paint. I don't mind doing it, but it'd be nice to take a breather as I've been flat out. We can either pay Marianne cash or deduct it from the balance of her stay, but let's not take advantage, Hal. After all, she's here to recover.'

'Yeah, you're right. We'll look out for her. Here's the last picture. Shall I unpack the ceramics?'

'Not if I want to stay in credit. Why don't you go for a spin in the boat, and I'll see you at home.'

In a flash, Hal whizzed off in the direction of the harbour. Pippa's hearty chuckle reverberated around the whitewashed gallery. It was hard to be annoyed with him, well, not for long anyway. Hal had considerably more physical energy than her these days, but the weight of his insecurities continued to push on her like a pile-driven anchor. He could cope with the apartments and doing the books, but it had taken years before he was confident out front. She'd never been able to work him out: on the surface he was approachable and went the extra mile, but underneath it … Pippa sighed. Hal Hopkins and change were unhappy bedfellows. Arnie Wilkes was a pain, there was no denying it, but he had done the impossible and had got her bloke involved in a hobby, and the Mary-Lou lit up Hal like nothing else.

Marianne's arrival had been an unexpected boost. The fact that Beattie was pleased with her temporary assistant was the best news as it could have been a disaster, knowing her formidable mother-in-law's blunt manner. But far from needing a shoulder to cry on, Pippa found herself unburdening her own concerns to the soft-spoken woman during their tour of Whitianga town. At the gallery, Marianne had studied each work of art with genuine interest, asking questions only an artist would ask. Clearly there was more to her self-deprecating 'doodler' than met the eye. After a gentle prod, she obligingly revealed a previously drawn illustration brought from England to be included in a memorial project. Pippa was impressed. Marianne's interpretation of the Helleborine revealed so much more than what was on the surface. Finding talent was like mining for gold, and nothing pleased Pippa more than to encourage and support emerging artists in any way she could, however short their stay.

With the ceramics back on display, she washed her hands, closed the gallery, and prepared to walk back to Sundown. Instinctively it had felt right to invite Marianne to join them at the forthcoming art festival. You never knew where these connections would lead. With a bit of luck, Arnie wouldn't have her running for the hills, and Hal would catch on that she wasn't a damsel in distress. Beneath her reserved exterior, (and notwithstanding the tragic circumstances that brought her across the water), Marianne Bly looked like a woman who could take care of herself.

MARIANNE

FROM HER seated position on *Poroporo's* balcony (every apartment was named after native flora), Marianne watched the morning light rise across the bay. The view, the sounds, the scents, and the kaleidoscope of changing colour poured over her wounded soul like healing balm, and the soft woollen rug tucked over her legs kept away the early chill. She sipped the English Breakfast tea, noting how quickly her taste buds had acclimatised to its slightly bitter taste, and how easy it had been to establish a new routine twelve thousand miles away, in a world where everything and everyone was, as yet, unknown. But the mending of her shattered heart would not be hurried. It was as if the last seven months belonged to someone else. Marianne let out a long, weary sigh. Joel had led her out of a prolonged inertia, and had catapulted her into every conceivable experience, only for his death to plunge her into the worst kind of darkness with only a pinprick of light to lead her out.

The journal lay open on the table, daily ritual over. Freddie had given her the notebook before dropping her off at the station. *Write it all down, Mum. It'll help you to recover.* Marianne finished her tea. Yes, she was writing her grief on the page when she was able, although the introspection was uncomfortable. At any rate, it was good to be here, and not to have to explain or remember. She could pretend she was someone else until a new sense of self appeared. Marianne picked up the journal and flipped the pages back to the beginning.

Day One: Two G&Ts in the waiting lounge. Ate. Watched 'Friends'. Slept. Dubai airport. Another G&T. Ate. More sleep. Mini bus, here, bed. It hurts, Joel.

Hal Hopkins' greeting was mercifully brief. After carrying her suitcase up the single flight of stairs to the apartment, and pointing out the emergency telephone number, she closed the curtains and went to bed. Finally the anguish erupted. Her desolation soaked into the saturated pillow until her wailing stomach called for sustenance, forcing her out of bed and into the kitchen area where a bounty of bread, cheese, eggs, milk, salad, tea, and biscuits provoked another river of tears. There was fruit in the bowl, wine in the cupboard, and an aloe vera plant housed in a vividly painted ceramic pot on the table, none of which she had noticed, but was now so grateful for.

On the second day, Marianne had ventured onto the balcony and was relieved to find her apartment the last in the row of three, and next door currently vacant. After a morsel of lunch, she unpacked her case. Seeing the carefully folded contents reminded her of those too recent dreadful days when darling Della was there to cook, cancel her work commitments, wash her hair, pack her case. Marianne removed each item with a growing gratitude for her friend: straw hat; microscope; Joel's digital camera and binoculars; sketch pad and pencils; prairie dress, (and a new, tissue-wrapped dress of the palest lemon); condolence cards. The rest of the evening was spent scrolling numbly through hundreds of channels, settling for the BBC Earth series.

Day Three: How could you leave me?

Self-pity charged through her like a freight train and properly derailed her. Joel's desertion felt like an assault, and no amount of punching the pillows reduced the intensity of this perceived injustice. The sole consolation was that she hadn't moved to Syderstone, as to have been abandoned in that tiny cottage, in an unknown village without him, was too awful to contemplate. But he hadn't left her. He was here, in her battered heart. From Marianne's vantage point on the balcony, a streak of moving colour caught her eye. A cropped dandelion haircut and a marmalade dress waved to her. Later, she would discover it was Pippa Hopkins, her benefactor.

On the afternoon of the fourth day, she had crossed the garden and onto the beach, walking the length and breadth of the bay until the sun set. Of the handful of people taking an evening stroll, only one had come near to retrieve her curious dog, and they exchanged pleasantries. That evening, Marianne ate salad, cheese, and biscuits, and poured herself a glass of *Sauvignon Blanc*. She took out Joel's iPod. He had sub-divided his playlists to include 'arm wavers', 'tear-jerkers' and 'bust a gut' collections. After two hours, Marianne had emptied the contents of two tissue boxes and her entire internal water supply.

Day Five: Couldn't write yesterday as your sad songs took every last drop. Today was better. I had tea with Pippa and Hal. They live next door. They've given me a bicycle with a basket and have offered to take me on an island tour. Tomorrow Pippa will show me around Whitianga Town and her gallery, where she shows and sells mixed media artwork. The kindness of these strangers is too much. She said I mustn't batten down my life again – how can Pippa know that about me so soon? Do you know how much I miss you?

Whitianga was the perfect harbour town, a blend of everyday shops, arts and crafts, and historically interesting pit stops on a manageable scale. Harlequin Gallery was a treasure trove, Pippa's creations especially. Her style – bright colours, graphic shapes, and off-kilter compositions – was in stark contrast to Marianne's minutely detailed drawings. A large display board listed a full programme of exhibitions, workshops, and open studio days. It was a true artists' hub. She had taken Beattie's advice and had coffee in Tarragon's Café. It was busy, which was no surprise as the freshly made savouries and sweets were tempting, a sign that her appetite was returning. She sat in a quiet corner, a baby step into a life without Joel, and though she desperately wanted the pain to fade, that would mean she had moved on, and she never wanted to move on. Meeting Joel Midwinter would always feel extraordinary.

Day Seven: I swam this morning. Were you impressed with my backstroke, Joel? As I floated, your cloud-face cheered me on. I checked the messages on the tablet Freddie gave me. Love has been sent across the miles, and I am grateful. My loving son has come back, just as you predicted. Zak and Kurt are writing a book to celebrate your life. It's called 'Wild at Heart: The Remarkable Life of Joel Midwinter.' They've asked me to provide the illustrations. Pip and Hal have invited me for dinner, to meet their friends. I'll be glad to start work tomorrow. By the way – I love you. We never told each other anywhere near enough.

'That's a good morning's work, Marianne. *Karo's* guests left an un-opened pecan and chocolate torte, a box of mint creams, mushrooms, salad, and four bottles of Tui. Some combo, eh?'

Marianne took the shopping bag from Beattie's work-hardened hands, astonished by the unanticipated windfall.

'What people leave behind. There's no point in wasting it. Open packets go for compost, or if it's meat and fish, my Busby's dinner. That dog's a fussy bugger.'

'Thanks so much, Beattie. I'll pop into town for lemonade and make a shandy. By the way, the sink is blocked. I left the windows and doors open. The aftershave was potent.'

'You've got the hang of it already, lovey. He was a hairy beast. It wouldn't be the first time a fuzzball like that blocked the pipes.'

Laughter erupted from the rough and ready woman whose generous heart was never far from the surface. After the death of her husband, Beattie had accepted Hal's invitation (at Pippa's urging) to move to Whitianga and had taken charge of Sundown Apartment's well-being like a military nurse on a mission. Marianne knew exactly how to fit into her way of doing things, and they immediately got along. She followed Beattie's sturdy gait to the utility area located behind Hal's office and immediately loaded the bedding into a large collection sack while Beattie emptied the recyclables, sorted the biodegradables, and put the kettle on. In double-quick time, the women sat on the tiny patio, warmed by a comfortable mid-morning temperature of twenty degrees. Two apartments had been vacated early, allowing Marianne a head start. By the time Beattie arrived to help remake the beds, she had almost finished the second job. The work was easy, the backdrop exceptional, and her boss was great. Marianne had fallen on her feet.

From the road, the holiday block was unremarkable, but as soon as you walked into the garden, you had arrived at your exotic holiday destination. The borders were filled with magnificent hibiscus, ferns, and grasses, and several huge trees provided shade. At the far end to the left stood the barbeque area, with several high stools lined up alongside the breakfast bar, the perfect position from which to look out to sea or to toast the sunset. To the right, four loungers circled a hot tub, although as yet, no one had used it. The gap between these areas led directly onto the beach. This was Marianne's view as she tasted the pecan torte. 'This is yummy. Did it come from Tarragon's?'

'The best café in town. Now, what are your plans for the weekend? It's a good time for a coastal drive.'

'I'd like to finish my current illustration this afternoon.' Marianne licked chocolate from her fingers. 'Tomorrow I'm helping Pip at the market. How far is Opito Bay?'

'Less than an hour. Early is best, but not because the beach gets crowded as there's hardly ever a soul on it, even in the season. You'll have it to yourself.' Beattie scanned the face of her new friend, confident that whatever she said wouldn't cause offense. 'It's good of you to help Pippa, but don't overdo it. When my Wyn passed away, I threw myself into work, but it didn't do much good. One day I stood in the queue at the Pak'nSave, tears dripping onto the conveyor belt, and dear old Dickie Hirsch who was on duty that day gave me his hanky. What man carries a clean, pressed handkerchief these days?'

All of a sudden, an image of The Tower's balcony under freezing skies flashed into Marianne's mind. Gil had passed her his handkerchief. That was a different century, a life that no longer existed. She had kept her replies to Zak's emails brief but not unfriendly. Gil must have told him not to bother her. Any further contact would drag her back to those devastating weeks, whereas sitting here with Beattie, drinking milky coffee and overlooking the bay, this was the present moment she wanted to dwell in. 'Thank you so much for the food, Beattie. This holiday may not turn out to be as expensive as I anticipated. Hal said he'll reduce my bill in exchange for decorating.'

'As long as you're happy, lovey. My boy still hangs on to Pippa's coat tails after all these years. Always was more of a follower than a leader, but he's ever so helpful, and good-natured. A fine front man. He'll often take the guests out on the boat. I'm sure he'd take you for a tour.'

'I'm afraid I left my sea legs at small school. I've only recently learned to swim, Beattie.'

'You look like a mermaid out there. What got you back into the water?' Beattie took one look at Marianne's expression and grabbed her hand. 'It was your man, Joel, eh? If you want to talk, I'm a good listener, despite what Hal says. Mothers and sons, eh? You're young enough to start again. I was forty-five when Coral came along.'

'I thought Hal was your youngest?'

It was Beattie's turn to dab her eyes. The women were quiet for a while, absorbing the other's heartache. There was no escaping it. She heaved herself up and stacked the crockery. 'Take yourself off somewhere nice, Marianne. Get out and about.'

Marianne threw her arms around the stoutly affectionate woman. 'I will Beattie and thank you.'

The Mazda hugged the curving road as it travelled towards Mercury Bay, passing another 'no mining' sign along the way. A flicker of environmental concern nudged at Marianne, but a yawn, too impressive to ignore, postponed her question about the protests. She was done in. It had been an incredible day, and she understood what Joel had meant by the mind-blowing coastline. The unending space, and lack of human existence was overwhelming. She would never have ventured out to these places alone. Pippa had ducked out at the last minute, and after an initial awkwardness, Marianne found herself enjoying Hal's company as they went from Cathedral Cove to Cooks Beach, and everywhere in between. Over lunch they sat on the deck of a beach-front café while he talked about the business, his boat, his dreams. He didn't mention Joel, and the breathing space was welcome. With the apartments just minutes away, Marianne looked forward to watching the sunset before turning in early.

'Pip was sorry not to join us. She's never been good at taking time off, although she'd tell you that making art is restful.'

'Maybe we have to be still to begin with before attempting anything, let alone a work of art.'

'I've never thought of it that way.' Hal pulled over to let another car pass. 'Stress and sailing aren't a good combo, but you've got to have your wits about you. Mum said you're not one for boats. If you change your mind, Arnie and me will whizz you around the bay.'

'Walking along the beach, or just sitting on the balcony is more than I could ever have wished for, Hal. You are so lucky to live here. I'll bet you never take it for granted.'

Hal's habit to agree was so strong, he was on the cusp of saying no, he didn't take it for granted, but that was untrue. When was the last time he walked the length of the beach, or visited the sights? There was always a booking, or paperwork, or something to fix, or trailing behind Pippa on her unending list of events. He was suddenly aware of Marianne's gaze. There was something in her manner that made him want to tell the truth. She hadn't said much throughout the day, but she didn't seem bored. 'I guess I do take it for granted. I've got used to hearing our visitors talk about the wonder of the place and must have stopped looking.'

'But when you're out at sea, the coastline gives you a different perspective. That alone will change your sensory register.'

'Yeah, I guess so. I feel alive on deck with the sails flapping, the wood creaking, the wind whistling.'

'It must be exhilarating to experience something new each time.'

'Well, Marianne, there's nothing to match the solitude and the elements. Archie says it connects us to our waterborne ancestors. I could go on all day, but that would be boring for you. By the way, Pip's friends are coming over to talk about the festival. Why don't you join us?'

'That's good of you, Hal, but I'm wiped out. It's a bath and – oops, I mean shower and bed for me.'

Hal pulled up outside the apartments under a silver-streaked sky. He opened the passenger door. 'We've three bathrooms at our place. You're welcome to a soak any old time. Special staff rates.'

'It's a risky invitation, Hal.'

Hal looked confused.

'Didn't Beattie didn't tell you? I've won awards for my professional cleaning skills and if the bath doesn't pass inspection, I may have to blow the whistle in the Whitianga Chronicle.'

Hal's deep-chested laugh was infectious. Marianne thanked him for the day, and once back in *Poroporo*, she took out her journal.

Day Fifteen: What a day! Hal kindly took me to Cathedral Cove and around the coast. Joel, you were right about the colours, the vastness, the terrain. To use your description, it was epic! I may even take the plunge and try a spot of sailing with him and Arnie. Do you remember your list of new experiences? Carrots and Clint Eastwood will never be the same, you said. My courage is growing, too. Did I tell you my apartment is called Poroporo *– a native shrub, purple in colour, otherwise known as a kangaroo apple. Tonight, I will read the condolence cards and letters over a glass of wine. Your 'bust a gut' songs which will keep me from sinking. Kurt told me that your spirit will be close by, so I should try not to disturb your journey with too much grief. If you are near me, I'd give anything for a sign.*

In the meantime Joel, I will write to you, and talk to you, as that way, you are still here.

 ZAK

Zak collected together his cards. It had been a birthday unlike any other, and he did his best to hide the ever-present sadness. Everything on his wish list had landed: waterproof hiking boots; extendable gib pole; tripod; extra memory media; first aid kit. Imogen took him to Wentworth to celebrate with his grandparents. Nicole and his grans gave him a dinner party, but the best of all was the weekend with Nina and Esme at The Tower, courtesy of his dad. Travis was visiting, which provided the perfect opportunity to talk to the rangers about the book project. Joel's cabin had already been rebuilt in the grounds of The Kedge, and a 'topping out' ceremony was arranged. Gil had put the finishing touches to the electrics, while he and Travis helped to plant the garden.

The candle by Joel's photograph flickered. Zak closed the window. Adjusting to his friend's death was all the harder because the one person who would understand how he felt was on the other side of the planet. At the service, Kurt suggested he and Esme send loving thoughts to Joel, and if possible, light a candle. It would not only ease their suffering but would help his onward journey. Zak had no idea what this meant so he looked it up. Joel's consciousness could be travelling through a forty-nine-day *bardo*, the intermediate state between life and death, before taking another birth. What an incredible thought! Joel never said he was a Buddhist or anything like that, but as Zak thought about him every day, it was an easy request to carry out.

Marianne must be doing the same on the other side of the globe. She was almost half-way through her holiday, and Zak couldn't wait for her return. His dad made him promise not to bother her, which he hadn't, apart from asking after the illustrations for Joel's book. Money raised from the sales would be donated to the Rose Foundation. Professor Rose was really pleased and agreed to help Zak with his charitable trust scheme. Providing funds to support wildlife rangers was a fitting tribute to Joel, the professor said. Not only had Gramps and his dad agreed to be trustees, but his mother said she'd raise awareness and funds through her networks. This was the one positive thing to come out of the divorce, and a reason to be at least a teeny bit cheerful.

Zak had mixed feelings when Imogen mentioned selling Flaxfield, even though the garden was his sanctuary and training ground. Gil wasn't surprised, as it was natural to want to move on and start afresh after a break-up. Living with Lena and Jean wasn't a long-term solution as he was considering moving into Number 5, or into The Tower, although Spencer would have something to say about that. The tense atmosphere between Gil and Spencer hadn't gone unnoticed in the family. They hadn't been to see West Ham play for ages and were rarely in the same space at the same time, although Spencer was as helpful as he'd always been. The counselling session with his dad's new running friend, Marcus Frobisher, was useful. It was important to express his fears, and anxieties, and to be reassured the divorce wasn't his fault.

Preparations for the end of term presentation to the Noke House students and families were coming along nicely. Zak had previewed his 'garden renaissance' film to Nina and Esme, and they had laughed out loud, which was a good sign. If the book was ready in time, he planned to launch it that afternoon. Zak couldn't quite work out at what point Ms Werner had become his favourite teacher, and biology his favourite subject. She was super impressed by his Go Wild! event, the eco-club, and his hike in grades. Joel's wildlife talk had been the turning point. Zak had never been so proud. His fellow students were amazed by Joel's world view, as rather than creating anxiety or apathy, he was funny and inspiring, and Ms Werner said it was empowering. There were rumours she had put him forward for the 'student of the year' award.

At long last, there was a result on the trail cam. A vixen and her cubs were captured several times crossing the garden. Mr Goodchild confessed to feeding Mrs Foxy but had kept it hush-hush as not everyone liked that sort of thing. Apparently, he'd been to tea with Grandma Lena! Nina had a go at him for laughing. She made him promise that when they were Mr Goodchild's age, he would take her to Paris on Eurostar, and at the Jardin des Tuileries, he was to give her a single red rose (locally grown, obviously). The thought of it kept Zak awake at night. Somewhere deep inside he knew they'd be together for a long, long time.

MARIANNE

Day Twenty-two: Hazelwood feels like a dream, Joel, but you are so real. I could have sworn you were beside me in bed last night, although it may have been alcohol-induced wishful thinking. I had so much fun with Pip and her friends. Vera Winiata cut my hair, so I'm now a henna-tinted pixie! Vera can trace her ancestors way back. As well as a hairdresser, she's an artist, a jewellery maker, and a tour guide. She took me to see a Maori village and has invited me to spend the day at her loft studio. The Coleville festival sounds interesting. I've never been to a festival before. One of Pip's friends has a 'bach' – and it's mine to sleep in for the weekend (OMG!) Vera asked me how I washed up at Mercury Bay, so I told her about you. It sort of come out over the second bottle of wine. Thankfully, I didn't ball my eyes out, but I may have inflated your exceptional qualities. The crying came later.

Reading the condolence cards broke me up. So many heartfelt words and offers of help – even Hilda said I was welcome to use her house as a retreat. There were two unexpected letters: the first from Nicole. She was sorry about the misunderstanding and had repaid the money. (I caught her putting several items aside at Lee Morrell's charity shop). The blue linen trousers were her way of apologising, but at the time, I was having a meltdown, and she took it as a snub. Anyway, Nicole wanted me to know how much she liked you and wants to take me to lunch. The second letter was from my sister. My instinct was to rip it up, but I thought of you, and how you said that forgiveness was good for the heart. Aunt Sadie told her about you. Claire wants to see me, to put things right. What would you do, Joel? Maybe it's too late for that now.

Exciting news – my 'Joel Midwinter Pilgrimage' begins in earnest this week. After the kauri *plantation, I'm going to Opito Bay. Vera said the Boot Wash Café was still in business, so I shall stop for a coffee and a hazelnut croissant, your favourite. The illustrations are progressing. I've decided to include a Kiwi plant to mark our connection to NZ. Oh, I've got to go. Hal's here. He and Arnie are taking me for a short tour around the bay on the Mary-Lou. Gaps are now appearing, Joel. You are always here but it feels a fraction less painful. I never thought it would.*

'That was bloody good, eh?' Arnie banged the empty beer glass on the bar mat and wiped his wild moustache with the back of his hand.

Marianne grinned at the burly, flint-eyed sailor whose body could stop a steam train. Arnie Wilkes was not your slippers and early nights type. The harbour tour exceeded her wildest imaginings, and after just two hours, she had an inkling why Hal and Arnie enjoyed being on the boat so much. They had let her steer while they fiddled with the mainsail, jib, and boom, and the ancient language filled her with pleasure. At one point, the sloop sailed into the wind at a rate of knots, and the three of them had burst into gales of laughter. Arnie's seadog looks were deceptive. He was a decade younger than Hal, and since his wife left, every spare moment was devoted to the Mary-Lou.

'I reckon Hal was spinning me a yarn about you being a sailing virgin, Marianne. Got a good pair of sea legs there.'

Marianne blushed. 'I'll add it to my long list of firsts. Can I get you another beer, Arnie? It's the least I can do for the terrific afternoon.'

'No, ta. I've an aerial to fix on the neighbour's roof so steady as she goes. I hear you're off to the Colville Peninsula. Don't forget your togs for Otautu Bay. Hal and me are headed for Matarangi.'

'May have a change of plan there, mate. Pip reckons I should go to the festival. She needs my muscle. The line-up's good, and the beer tent will be well-stocked.'

'Hotdog playing?'

Hal nodded.

'Lead singer's worth a look. Ah well, cheerio, Marianne. *Pipsqueak* won't let you leave without a send-off, and I'm buggered if she'll keep me away.'

His thick-armed hug all but winded her, and in the next second, he was gone. Marianne rubbed her itchy cheek, the damp remnant of his moustachioed kiss.

Hal laughed. 'Pip and Arnie aren't what you'd call best mates. He's a bad influence and leads me astray.'

'Does he?'

'Erm, well, no, but if it weren't for Pip's hawk-eye, I wouldn't fancy my chances. Arnie likes to paint the town red.'

'Will he come to the festival?'

'He has a way of turning up when you least expect it.' Hal looked at her hair. 'Nice hair-do.'

'Vera cut it.' Something in Hal's expression prompted her to change the subject. 'It was so generous of your mum to lend me her car. I'm looking forward to driving out to Opito Bay. Anyway, I've finished painting *Hebes* in good time for the next visitors. The low-emission paint is excellent. We use something similar at home.'

'Home. Won't be long before you make tracks, eh? We've got used to you around here. Mum says you're a bright spark.'

'Beattie is a treasure. Would you like another drink?'

'That's good of you Marianne, but I'd better get going. New arrivals to book in, and a busy evening with the accounts. Give us a shout if you'd like another tour.'

Four down, four to go. Marianne stepped back from the drawing for a critical appraisal. The Whinchat was a charming bird. Yes, that's enough, any more titivating would spoil it. Joel would approve. They had seen an orange-chested male last September, at Cley. After persuading her to draw animals and insects as well as plants, he had produced several highly detailed photographs which included a four-spotted Chaser dragonfly and a Chalkhill Blue butterfly, insects they had spotted while out and about. The butterfly was her choice for the fifth illustration.

Marianne took her tea and nervous flutter onto the balcony. Tomorrow was the first pilgrimage. Why did she feel trepidation? No one had said it was a bad idea. After all, it was her reason for being here. Meeting Pippa, Vera, and the art crowd was wonderful, and there was always a get-together with an open invitation to join in, but she didn't want to get distracted from her purpose. Since the boat trip, Marianne had kept a healthy distance from Hal. He hadn't said or done anything untoward, but his look reminded her of that awful time with Spencer, when she had mistakenly bared her soul and caused untold damage. Pippa had jokingly offered him for sale at a knock down price, but even so, Marianne took the hint seriously.

The sea water was crystal clear, and the gentle surf was perfect for body boarding, but not today. Opito Bay was deserted. Beattie advised her to take it slow after Kuaotuna, and she had held her breath on the hair-pin bends, thanking her lucky stars for the lack of traffic, as there were few passing places and no railings around the cliff-edge drops. At the end of a long gravel road, she parked the car. There were several picnic tables, a loo, and no shops. Soft, pristine white sands curving between the rocky headlands rooted her to the spot. After a while, Marianne made her way onto the beach, and after walking the three-mile stretch, she set out her mat, took off her hat and dress, and stood at the water line where her feet sank into the shelving sand. She swam close to the beach, aware that the sharks had season-tickets, and after clambering out, she carved hers and Joel's initials into the wet sand and took a photo. As the mellow sun dried her skin, Marianne ran her hands over the jagged strips of shiny scar tissue. *Befriend your skin, Marianne. It has made you who you are.* And who am I, Joel?

The jasmine tea had become something of a ritual. Marianne balanced her cup on the mat and unwrapped the seeded humous sandwich. Her holiday was halfway through. Was it just five months ago, when she and Joel had sat together at Calgary Bay, feeling the ache of parting, and by a cruel turn of events, had been taken away from each other forever? Joel wouldn't look at it that way. He accepted karma as naturally as the sunshine and lived each day authentically, as if it were his last. Sadness washed over her. There hadn't been enough time for their experiences to become memories, but Joel used to say that memories could trap you in the past if you weren't aware of the nature of your mind. If that were so, how could she honour their love without replaying specific times, places, and events?

Tired of searching for answers, Marianne brushed the crumbs off her lap and rubbed a handful of moisturiser on her skin before pulling on her dress and gathering her things together. Across the dunes, several *baches* stood out amongst the low-key holiday homes – a heartening sight. A woman in her front garden waved to her, and she waved back. With the picnic over and photos taken, as reluctant as she was to leave, it was time to go in search of the *kauri*.

The Boot Wash Café was as exactly as Joel described it. Set slightly back from the road, the wood-constructed building had the appearance of an age-old collection of garden sheds and weatherboard, cobbled together with crossed fingers. Various beer barrels were filled with splodges of plant colour, while a flock of tiny birds hopped on and off the empty picnic tables in a post-lunch clear up. It was now well past three o'clock. Marianne got out of the car and did her best to breathe out the tension that was surging throughout her body. It was ridiculous. What on earth was there to feel so nervous about?

She walked into the café. As if on cue, Bryan Adams' live Wembley performance of *Heaven* sang out in the background. She had replayed that very song on Joel's iPod night after night, and knew every heart-felt chord, every bar of audience participation, the final emotional cheer. She and Joel had slow danced to it in his cabin, and she had never felt so loved. Marianne turned down the volume on the painful recollection and scanned the scene in front of her. In the dark interior, tables and chairs of various shapes and sizes formed small clusters, while to the right was an information area, where piles of leaflets, magazines and newspapers were stacked high. A tea-light flickered on a shelf, above which were pinned hundreds of photographs on a huge cork board. Marianne's attention was drawn by the sound of activity behind the food counter, where a long, lean woman with cane row hair tied with a psychedelic scarf looked up.

'What can I get you?'

Marianne glanced at the blackboard. 'An *Americano*, a glass of water, and a hazelnut croissant, please.'

'Take a seat. I'll bring it over.'

As the woman continued singing along to whatever it was she was doing behind the counter, Marianne walked back to the candle and the pictures of grinning faces, some holding spades and standing by trees, others at various wildlife sanctuaries, wearing 'Save The Kauri' and 'Kakapo Recovery' T-shirts. There were photos of monks and nuns in red and maroon robes, standing outside a building whose strings of flapping prayer flags were forever freeze-framed. And there, in the centre, was a photograph of Joel. He was standing alongside Kurt and Larry and a beaming gaggle, each raising a glass to the photographer. Marianne dropped onto the seat, her breath a pant, her mouth dry. This was real. Joel had been here, and the fact of it was overwhelming. After a while, the wave subsided, and the clatter of cups brought her over to the table where the woman was conspicuously eyeing her.

'I brought you extra hot water. Our coffee can be on the strong side for the uninitiated. Hey, are you okay? You look a little pasty.'

Marianne sat on the chair and sipped the tepid water. 'I must have a touch of sun-stroke. Stupid me has been out all day, and I left my sunhat at the *kauri* plantation.'

'Easily done. Mind if I join you?'

Without waiting for a reply, the woman sat opposite. 'Ah, you'll be right in a minute or so. I love this time of day – a few hours' let-up before the crazies fly in. It's pizza and quiz fund-raising night.'

Marianne stirred a spoon of sugar in her coffee. Without needing a formal introduction, she knew it was Toni Roebuck. There was no mistaking her from the photos in the folder, even though the image was ten years out of date.

'Feeling better? Mad dogs eh, you Brits. I'm Toni, and this is my café. Here for long?'

Something about the woman's over-easy manner irritated Marianne. 'I work in Mercury Bay. It's my day off. A friend suggested several places of interest, including Opito Bay and Kauri Hill.' The women's eyes held fast. 'He also said I should try the hazelnut croissants. Apparently, they were the best he'd ever eaten.'

'He wasn't wrong. Is that why you were looking at the photos? Joel Midwinter was quite a guy.'

It was over.

Toni reached across the table and gripped her hand. 'We've been saying prayers ever since we heard. You must have been a good mate to have come all this way, but then again, Joel Midwinter was worth it. Look, eat up, while I grab a coffee. You'll feel heaps better when you've got that inside you.'

Marianne felt her shoulders drop. Her hostile reaction was uncharacteristic, but these were strange times. She bit into the ice-dusted croissant. *Thank you, Joel, you were right again.* Toni reappeared with a large steaming mug.

'Sorry, these past few weeks have been a rollercoaster. I'm Marianne, by the way. How did you find out about Joel?'

'The conservation world is tight-knit. The team were around for weeks and Joel was popular. He and Kurt were a fun double act. Did he get around to building a cabin in the old folk's garden? Joel took to meditation like the proverbial when we were on retreat. We've arranged for prayers at the *stupa*. If his consciousness reincarnates on earth, the parents will be lucky buggers alright.'

Marianne couldn't quiet grasp what Toni meant but had no energy for a full-on theological discussion. Instead, 'He used to sit quietly every morning and evening.'

'Oh – you were together! Jeez, that's tough on you. I must say I'm surprised. Joel didn't seem the type to partner up, more the lone ranger sort. Did he say anything to you about ...'

Just then, animated voices burst into the café, and a curly, treacle-haired boy flew straight into Toni's arms. '*Kia ora*, Mum! I had a great day at school. Miss Young said my story of the Sherpa and his dog was *extra-ordinary* and she asked me to read it to the class and pinned my drawing up and everyone apart from ...'

The boy chirped away while his companion bent to kiss Toni's cheek. Suddenly he stopped, aware of a pair of eyes staring at him.

'This is our boy, Eli, and this is Daryl, his other mum.'

Marianne was thunderstruck. If it hadn't been for the chair, she would have crashed to the floor. It was Joel! His eyes, his expression, his sizzling energy... The boy turned away from her startled expression and sat on Toni's lap, wrapping his arms tightly around her waist.

'Daryl, be a sweetheart and take Eli out back.'

Mother and son disappeared, leaving the women to face each other. Toni jumped up and returned with a bottle of *Rescue Remedy*. She had turned the music off. After putting several drops into the glass of water, she held it out. 'Look, Marianne, why don't I come over to Mercury Bay, and we'll talk. You're in no fit state to hear ...'

'I want to know.'

Toni's chest swelled like a puffin about to jump off a cliff. Marianne fought the urge to either laugh hysterically, or scream. Whatever happened, she was not leaving until she knew every last detail. After what felt like an eternity, the standoff ended.

'Daryl and I knew as soon as we met Joel. He was our first choice for biological father. I don't need to tell you he was hardwired for joy. You can imagine the conversation – he was twenty-one: naïve, but not a virgin, open-minded, and willing to help. The only condition Joel made was that he played no paternal role, although he didn't mind the child knowing who he was, if that was good with us, and if we were ever strapped for cash, to give him a shout, although he didn't have much, that we knew for sure. Joel told us about his non-hereditary heart condition. He was in good shape and fit enough to travel. Kurt confirmed it, so we were good to go. We couldn't believe our luck.'

'How did it – I mean ...'

'Joel and I had sex. Daryl and I got lucky. We told him all was good with the birth, and after that, we cut our ties. Eli knew about Joel, and that he's passed on. That's what the candle is for.'

Toni sat back and sighed, story over. Suddenly, Marianne got to her feet, heat rampaging through her, suffocating, constricting. She had to get back to Sundown, to the safety of her apartment. Fumbling in her bag, she pulled out a twenty dollar note.

'Aw, look Marianne, Joel would have had his reasons for not telling you. It doesn't have to be a big deal.' She scribbled a number on her pad. 'As I said, I'll come to the bay ...'

Marianne took the piece of paper, dropped the money on the table, and stumbled blindly out of the café. She drove back to Mercury Bay with barely a pause for breath.

🌸 GIL 🌸

ARMSTRONG SOLUTIONS' steady metronome was as soothing as ever. Gil was under no illusion how much of a wrench it would be to leave it behind, but at least there was sufficient time to step away without creating unnecessary disturbance. He and Spencer had almost reunited, but their relationship could never be the same. He wasn't the same. They had talked long into the night about marriage, family life, the business, wanting to do new things. Gil was shocked to discover that Spencer had a lover whom he met whenever he was in Europe. The woman (Gil didn't want to know the details) was also married, and neither had any wish to live together. Nicole had turned a blind eye, but at Christmas, she told Spencer the arrangement no longer suited her, and it was time to make up his mind. After an emotional few weeks, they decided to stay together. Initially Gil was appalled. Was he naïve? How could Nicole have allowed it? But who was he to judge his cousin?

Imogen had met him in London with the divorce papers. It was so weird to sit in a bar opposite her, where for two hours, they actually listened to each other. For a moment, he wondered if she was going to ask him to reconsider as she had steered the conversation towards it, but he redirected it elsewhere. He just could not tell her he no longer loved her even though she must have known it. It was cowardly, and he was ashamed of how he had brought the marriage to an end. What he said instead was

Just make sure Kiran treats you right, or I'll knock his block off. They talked about Flaxfield. It was the right decision to postpone selling it, as once Zak finished his GCSEs, he was intent on moving to Norfolk. Without a reason to stay in Epping, Imogen was considering living near her parents. Although Nik had recovered, his illness had shaken her. She generously insisted Gil take a half share of Flaxfield's total worth and would transfer the hefty sum to his account.

They agreed to be available for Zak, as much as he insisted he was coping. His newly awakened lifestyle had impacted them significantly. Imogen was now installed in the UK office, situated in Green Park, which meant less travelling. Malika Lionnet's vision was already challenging traditional business models by promoting mutual cooperation, transparency, and inclusive dialogues, with success as a by-product. For Gil, being more attuned to the landscape had paradoxically turned his focus inward, compelling him to explore the nature of his mind. Olivia Donohue had introduced him to Mary Oliver, Herman Hesse, and other poets whose sensitivity to the natural world resonated. She pointed out that lyrics such as those written by Ian Drury and Paul Weller were also poetic, and why shouldn't Gil try his hand at writing verse. He shared little of this to Imogen, as a lingering self-consciousness prevented it, but now he had seen her again, there was no doubt in Gil's mind he had made the right decision.

It was almost one o'clock. Spencer was arriving with lunch any time soon. They were in the process of working through the details of the takeover. Niall had accompanied them to several meetings with the view to taking on a management role. Every engineer's job was guaranteed for five years, with the option to remain or take redundancy, and Spencer got the consultancy position he wanted. Gil had reduced his working week as a means of releasing himself within eighteen months. Many of their clients were happy to work with the new owners whose philosophy wasn't a million miles away from that of Armstrong Solutions.

Spencer clattered through the door. 'Sorry it took so long. I had to queue. Fancy a gym and steam session this afternoon?' He threw a food bag to Gil.

'Sounds like a plan. How'd it go?'

'Old man Marshall was more concerned about a hike in costs than us stepping back. So much for loyalty. Niall was great. I don't know why we didn't get him involved before. Once he got Marshall talking about his coy carp, that was it.' Spencer unwrapped his *fajita* and chomped down. 'Niall's gone home. He's taking Pearl to the clinic.'

'Good lad. I'm ashamed at how little I actually did for Zak.'

'But look at you now, Gil, proper hands-on. So, any idea where you're going to live if it doesn't work out at Number 5?'

Yes, he did, but first he had to ask the all-important question otherwise his idea was dead in the water. 'How would you feel if I moved into The Tower, well, at least until Zak finishes his GCSEs.'

'Are Nicole and I still invited?'

'Duh! I was thinking about the extended family. Lauren's great, but your brother-in-law does my head in. Will they use the chalet?'

'My sister will sleep anywhere. What about our mothers?'

'No problem, although I'm not sure I fancy sharing the same space while Mum's bonking her new bloke.'

'Ha! The Tower's yours for as long as you want.' Spencer took an envelope out of his pocket. 'I picked up the ticket confirmation.'

'Phew – two weeks in New Zealand. I'll miss you, mate.'

Spencer passed the envelope to his cousin and waited. 'Before you say anything, Gil, hear me out. Once you finish work in Auckland, you'll spend a day or two with the Ridleys in Lake Taupo. From there you can drive to Mercury Bay and tell Marianne how you feel about her. I know you don't like flying, and don't give me the 'carbon footprint' caper as you're hardly a globe-trotter. This is a one-off, life-changing trip. Zak can stay with us if Imogen's away.'

'You've got it all sussed.' Gil studied his name on the ticket. Every day that passed was a day nearer to Marianne's return. He'd thought of nothing else since she left England, but never had he contemplated flying to New Zealand. What was to stop him? He could talk to Marianne, away from everything, and everyone. A shiver of excitement ran down his spine.

'No one has to know, Gil. It's a European swansong for the clients' benefit. By the time Marianne returns, it may be too late.'

Gil walked over to his cousin and embraced his comforting bulk. It was a huge moment, and it was the right thing to do.

A RARE SIGHTING

BEATTIE HOPKINS went in search of a fresh box of tissues. The pilgrimage idea was risky, so to find Marianne down in the dumps was to be expected. Not that she wasn't able to do her bit. In fact, the poor girl had tried to hide it by working even harder. Beattie let out a sigh. She had lived on this earth a long time, and had seen many things, and whatever had happened to Marianne had risen the surface for a good reason. 'Here lovey, take these. Finish your tea, and I'll make a fresh pot. Can I tempt you to a blueberry pastry, a parting gift from *Miro*?'

Marianne blew her nose. 'It was naive to think I wouldn't be upset. I'm so embarrassed for going on about Joel as if he were a saint.'

'Look Marianne, you and Joel loved each other, but there must have been things you didn't tell him.'

'Yes there were but seeing Eli like that felt like a cruel joke.' She pulled another tissue from the box. 'As you say, Beattie, it happened a long time ago. Joel's best friend said the same thing.'

The conversation with Kurt the day before was acutely uncomfortable. Marianne should have guessed, as when she told him of her plan to travel to New Zealand, his reaction had been non-committal at best. Yesterday's exchange was so much worse as Kurt had thrown her pain right back at her.

'I met Joel's son today.'

Long pause. 'Joel would have told you at some point. It wasn't hugely important to him.'

'Really, Kurt? Well it is to me. Why didn't you tell me before I booked my flight? Why would you let me walk blindly into it?'

'It wasn't my news to tell, Marianne. Don't fall into the blame game. And anyway, we've all got a backstory. Would you still have made the journey?'

Another pause. 'Is there anything else I should know?'

'Yes. Joel Midwinter was an exceptional man whose lifestyle choices were motivated by the wish to live as long as possible for the benefit of us all. Joel's selfless actions will continue to have a positive impact of the earth, and I will celebrate my good fortune to have known and loved him. Marianne, you were the first woman he took a chance on, and he'd never been happier. I'm sorry you feel hurt, but if you don't let it go, you'll be consumed by it.'

Marianne watched abstractedly as Beattie poured the golden liquid into the mug. Her unjustified anger at Kurt had quickly evaporated, and she sent an email apologising for her outburst, to which he had immediately replied that he and Anya were there for her, anytime. Pip and Vera were aware she had hit the skids and persuaded her not to cancel the festival. So, she put aside her drawings, packed the weekend bag that Beattie had lent her, and determined to enjoy herself.

Gil pulled up opposite the unassuming apartment block and checked the details: Sundown Apartments, 48 Coast Road. Is this where Marianne was living and working? It was 10.35am. He rested his head on the steering wheel, still grappling with the time zone. Since arriving in Auckland a week ago, he'd been here, there, and everywhere: meetings with engineers, site visits, social dinners, and the beginnings of a short break with Roger and Shirley Ridley at their impressive house overlooking Lake Taupo. They generously organised a car and looked forward to seeing him again when he got back from visiting friends.

The driving was undemanding – not a single car for miles, and despite Gil's lack of mental acuity, it was impossible not to be moved by the panorama. He passed a sign, 'make pizza, not war', and several others protesting against mining, and warnings of forest fires. It was sobering. No country was immune to environmental onslaught. Gil had never in his life seen so much space, and so few people. Adjectives, metaphors, and similes pelted through his mind, to be used later in his fledgling attempts at poetry (most of which was aimed at the bin). Nevertheless, he enjoyed watching his thoughts take shape on the page: from words to phrases to tentative lines. Poetry, nature walks, barefoot running, and a revised marital status brought Gil increasing states of clarity. Even his headaches were less frequent, no doubt helped by reducing caffeine and increasing his water intake.

'Jetsam' was the perfect place to stay. The family run apart-hotel with restaurant and bar was a local Whitianga attraction, and its harbour location suited Gil's needs for a two-night stay. After a dart around the town, he fell into a fitful sleep until the early hours. By the time breakfast arrived, his anxiety was on the rise. Just a three-minute drive separated him from Sundown Apartments – three minutes from Marianne! Now, Gil was sitting outside, feeling truly sick, and wishing he'd passed on the mushroom omelette. What if Marianne wasn't here? What if she didn't want to see him? He should have called her but decided against it. There had been no contact between them since she left England. Oh, well, there was nothing to stop him walking along the beach. It would give him time to settle and check the layout before deciding his next move.

Gil pulled the hire car into Sundown's car park, climbed out, and followed the path around the block to the bay. He shucked off his Birkenstocks, instantly grounded by the reassuring grainy texture under his feet, and wandered to the end of the bay, the warm water coddling his toes, passing the occasional low-rise house, and a clutch of impressive trees with roots like cooked spaghetti. After an about turn, and slightly surer of himself, he walked back towards the apartments. Pausing by the open entrance to the garden, Gil scanned the beach. Nearby, a swimmer walked out of the sea, stepped into a beach dress, towelled her short hair, and made her way towards the garden – no bag, no hat. The morning sun partly obscured his vision, but an outbreak of goosebumps prepared his body for a shock. Was it Marianne? No, it couldn't be. Her shape was different, her hair was short and light, and her manner of walking was Côte d'Azur casual. It definitely wasn't her – Marianne couldn't swim. The stranger approached the entrance and stopped beside him.

'Gil?'

'Marianne?'

Marianne threw her arms around him, and just as quickly stepped back. 'Oh, I'm sorry, I've soaked your shirt. How on earth ..?'

Gil laughed, and was euphoric. It was her, *and* she was pleased to see him! 'I've been in Auckland on business, and since I'm so far from home, I felt compelled to seek the company of an old friend.'

'Quiet right, too. I can't believe it! Come on up, and we'll have tea.' She pinched his arm.

'Ouch!'

'Just checking. I've seen a few ghosts lately.'

'This one is friendly.'

Gil followed her up the single flight of stairs where they paused to rinse and dry their feet in the water tray before entering the light airy apartment. Various items of clothing and drawings were scattered around. He assumed Marianne to be tidy, but then again, his visit was unannounced, and besides, so what?

'Welcome to *Poroporo*, my temporary dwelling.'

'It suits you. That's a view and half.' Gil walked towards the window and there on the desk, was a photo of Freddie, Zak, and Esme, at the garden party. Alongside it were Marianne and Joel, under a canopy of trees. It was Gorse Wood, where Gil had helped Meg and Larry carry out path repairs, another of Norfolk's mysterious and entrancing places he had recently discovered. A tea light burned bright, just like the one in Zak's bedroom. Marianne stood beside him. Her fresh, salty scent triggered his swallow reflex. 'How are you, Marianne?'

'I'm alright, – just. And you, Gil?'

'Changing every day. Even my shirt is different.'

Marianne laughed. Gil had ditched the Fred Perry for a pale pink patterned shirt and cargo pants. 'Why don't you make a pot of tea while I jump in the shower. There's so much I want to ask and talk to you about. It's really good to see you, Gil!'

As Marianne disappeared into the bathroom, Gil wrestled with the vision of this unrecognisable woman whom he had comforted on The Tower's balcony after Joel's funeral, barely a month ago. There had been a major shift in her, distinctly on the upward curve and he couldn't wait to find out more. Gil filled the kettle. A surge of fatigue almost knocked him over, so he walked to the bed and rested on the edge. In less than a minute, he was fast asleep.

Marianne picked up her new sketchpad and a soft graphite pencil and drew his sleeping profile. She hadn't yet mastered the art of expecting the unexpected, as Gil's appearance was incredible, but at least the encounter with Toni, Daryl and Eli felt less of a trauma, and she was calm. The temptation to call the boy 'Joel's son' was resisted with all her might. It was much more palatable to think of him in naturalist terms: that Joel was chosen because his character and manner, an inverted Darwinian 'survival of the kindest'. It was all very well for Toni and Kurt to suggest she drop the urge to judge or condemn for fear of trapping herself in a spiral of anger and blame, but it was easier said than done. They'd had years of practise. Marianne finished the drawing and put it inside her folder before stepping onto the balcony. She flipped open the journal. The last entry was three days ago. Until then, she had written oftentimes up to three or four times a day. *Day Twenty-four: Why, Joel?*

It was a miracle she got back to Sundown in one piece. Her instinct was to write all manner of harsh, spiteful things in the journal, but the vitriolic words wouldn't come, and anyway, it wasn't true, she knew that. Although the anger was short-lived, Marianne nevertheless felt a residue of betrayal, although cheated out of what exactly was unclear. If Joel had told her he was a sperm donor and had no relationship with the child, they would have discussed it, and she would have dropped it. Although she'd talked briefly to Beattie, an in-depth conversation had to wait until she saw Della. There was no one else who would understand.

Just as she was about to check on the welcome intruder, the door slid open, and Gil stepped onto the balcony.

'Sorry about that, Marianne. I'm still adjusting to the wonky clock. Hope I'm not disturbing you.'

'Not at all. Freddie suggested I write everything down in this journal, but it feels so self-absorbing.'

'Try a different perspective. How about 'self-cherishing'? The counsellor suggested I do something similar, so I opted for poetry.'

Marianne hid her astonishment. 'Are you hungry?'

'I'm not sure.'

'Why don't I bring few things out. I'm ready for lunch.'

Gil checked his watch. 'Blimey, lunchtime already. I've been out for the count.'

'You really were knocked out.' Marianne busied herself in the apartment, and soon they were tucking into watermelon salad, drinking shandy, and catching up on family. 'How are Lena and Jean?'

'You remember our neighbour, Mr Goodchild? He's taken a shine to Mum. After all these years, she's finally got herself a fella.'

'How wonderful! What does Jean make of it?'

'She's relieved, I should think. Jean didn't expect to take on my family as well as Spencer and Lauren. After Lionel died, I suspect she was hoping to live on her own. The word that springs to mind is *lumbered*. Mum can be tricky, and that's putting it mildly.'

'I've never really considered Lena and Jean to be anything other than natural companions, but now you mention it, their interests are quite different. Let's drink to blossoming romances and happy outcomes.'

They clinked glasses. 'Nice shandy.'

'My afternoon delight, Gil. I must have drunk more during this holiday than in my entire life.'

'Sorrow or celebration?'

'Both. The co-owner of Sundown, Pippa Hopkins and her friends, have adopted me. Their regular get-togethers usually involve a drink or two. That's how I acquired this haircut. Talking of which, you seem to have done the opposite. You'll have to tie your locks back soon.'

Gil found himself laughing with her. 'It's not just the hair. Metaphorically speaking, my life is loosening up fast. I'd never have flown this far, undertaken therapy, or considered leaving the business a year ago. Spencer was meant to come, but ...'

Marianne was at a loss for words. She had been so consumed by grief and hadn't given a thought to anyone else. Gil's divorce must have caused repercussions, and he was in therapy of all things! 'I never apologised for over-reacting at the beach café that morning. Spencer had a point. Not only did I assume you'd have the money to buy my house, but that you would want to. How arrogant of me.'

'We had a bust up after that. Didn't really talk for months.'

Their eyes met. Neither were sure how much to unravel the threads, but both wanted to be done with the past. Marianne was in the mood for untying. 'Spencer's reaction may have been triggered by a particular incident that happened after Bonnie died. He came over to the house to give me something from Nicole and caught me at a bad time. I naively confessed my grief and loneliness, only to discover that he was unhappy at home, and that he loved me. He said we should move away, begin a new life together. I was stunned and asked him to leave. After that I kept out of his and Nicole's way. I thought she knew, and that was the reason for her hostility towards me. If I hadn't learned my lesson then, I've sure learned it now. Pippa's husband might have got the wrong idea during our sailing trip and tour, so I'm lying low.'

'What does Pippa have to say about it?'

'She's too busy to care, although I was warned, in a roundabout way. Hal's nice – not unlike Spencer, but these things can take on a life of their own. You see, Gil, the land of the little people is much safer.'

'I'll drink to that.'

They drank, and he had to look away, towards the blue stone sky, towards the horizon, and wait for his billowing blood to quieten. There was time.

'How is Imogen?'

'Okay, I think. We've dismantled the marriage without too much of a scuffle, but to be honest, even though I initiated it, it still hurts like crazy. She's hanging on at Flaxfield and is drowning herself in work.'

'Where will Zak live, once its sold?'

'My guess is Norfolk, with me. Imogen is okay with that. The way it's going, Zak won't stay on for A levels. He's just about getting through the workload as it is, and that's without all his other projects.'

'Will you be disappointed?'

'Imogen more so, but she won't stand in his way. She never has. Professor Rose may offer Zak a ranger's apprenticeship. My boy knows what he wants. Joel had a massive influence on him.'

'Joel had a massive influence on everyone.' She paused, as if wanting to say more, but didn't. She was still digesting the fact that Gil was here, talking with her, *and* he wanted the divorce. She assumed it was the other way around. 'I haven't asked where you are staying.'

'Jetsam, for two nights.' Gil shifted awkwardly. 'Are you free to have dinner with me tomorrow, before I head back to Lake Taupo?'

'What a nuisance! We're going to an arts festival in Coleville for the weekend.'

Before the disastrous information had time to register, Marianne threw him a lifeline.

'What about tonight, Gil, if you've no plans?'

'No, that's even better. Any suggestions?'

'I'm told Jetsam has the best steak in Mercury Bay.'

'How about the veggie menu?'

'Don't tell me Zak's brainwashed you too?' They laughed, and his ultramarine eyes dislodged something in her. Marianne swallowed hard. 'The menu is nicely varied. What time?'

'Is seven o'clock too early? I'll pick you up.'

'No need, Gil. It's a five-minute bike ride.'

They walked to the door, and for the second time that day, she hugged him. 'Seven o'clock, in the bar. Thanks for lunch, Marianne.'

Gil tucked the towel firmly around his waist and wiped the steamy mirror with the flannel. He took the bottle of Hugo Boss *Eau de Toilette* out of his wash bag. It was Imogen's favourite fragrance. The routine of a one-squirt for work, two for evenings was engrained. But what if Marianne found it overpowering, or thought he was trying too hard? Zak had switched to an organic brand of body wash and deodorant, and encouraged him to do the same, but Gil's neural networks screamed '*waste not, want not*', so he'd wait until his products were finished. Indecision forced him to put the bottle down and walk into the bedroom where a pair of pale raw denims and a white camp collar cotton shirt lay on the bed – appropriate attire for the venue. Imogen's fingerprints were all over him: manicured nails; table manners; the right wine; the right suit; the right chit chat. But what if Marianne wanted to sit at the bar? Frustrated at the futile waste of energy, Gil sat out on the balcony, and sipped the cool spring water. His mouth was threatening to dry, although talking with Marianne earlier had been so easy, there was no reason for nerves. A thrill of anticipation pricked at his skin. He checked the time: Fifteen minutes and counting.

On his way out of Marianne's apartment earlier that day, Gil had bumped into Hal Hopkins who, during their long chat, subtly quizzed him about his appearance in Mercury Bay. Hal was at pains to point out just how much everyone liked Marianne. His admiration was barely hidden behind the friendly manner, but then, didn't Gil feel the same way? Marianne's festival weekend announcement eclipsed his elation. It had to be tonight. He had to find out if there was any hope of a relationship, however remote, despite having convinced himself it was highly unlikely, in light of her love for Joel. But at least she would know how he felt, and he could move on.

Muffled voices filtered up from below. Several boats were mooring up, while a number of cars were parked for the evening. The bars were open for business, and diners were sitting outside, laughing, talking. Gil dressed methodically, picked up his wallet and room key, and was gone. The *Eau de Toilette* was no longer an issue.

Gil lifted the cold bottle of Jurassic Terrace out of the wine bucket while Marianne finished her second short conversation.

'I'm sorry, Gil. It's impossible to go anywhere without someone stopping for a chat. The locals are so friendly.' She put her hand over her half-empty glass. 'Can you be arrested for being drunk in charge of a bicycle with a basket?'

It was startling to hear himself laugh. Marianne was good company, and genuinely nonplussed to find herself so popular. 'I don't know, but it would make a great holiday story. Would you like dessert?'

'The roasted squash quinoa was deliciously filling. Not sure I've room for anything else.'

'Zak and I have a go, but our dishes are nowhere near as tasty as that. How about a brandy, or a liqueur?'

'Jasmine tea would be great, thanks.'

Gil called the waiter. To his surprise, the restaurant had thinned out. He didn't dare check the time, but it was slipping through his fingers alarming fast. Fortunately, Marianne didn't appear to be in a hurry. In fact, she seemed quite at home. Neither had remarked on the other's outfit, but if asked, Gil thought her loveliness was enhanced by the pale lemon shift dress. Interestingly, she wore no jewellery.

'I haven't asked you about the business, Gil.'

'If it goes to plan, the takeover will happen incrementally, giving us time to adjust. There are other things in the pipeline. My father-in-law and I are setting up a trust: The Midwinter Trust, in fact. It was Zak's idea. Nik and I agree it's a fitting tribute to a fine man and will create new rangers jobs around the country.' Marianne's expression was unreadable. 'What do you think?'

'I've changed my mind, Gil. May I have more wine?'

Gil topped up her glass. She wasn't about to toast the success of the venture, of that he was sure. Out of nowhere, tension pulsed in his gut. Still no mention of Joel, or the places she'd seen. After all, he was the reason she was here. 'Zak – we thought you'd be pleased.'

'Why? Because Joel Midwinter is a 'fine man'? Joel Midwinter is a man of secrets. Until Monday, I had no idea he has a nine-year-old son. How about that for a discovery?' Marianne's eyes flashed. 'Tell me, Gil, if you were about to set up home with your beloved, wouldn't that be an event important enough to share?'

Anger and booze were not a great combination, especially when the drinker was not used to drinking. Gil felt her distress, but there was nothing else for it but to talk it through. At least she wasn't angry at him, and she was finally talking about Joel. 'Everyone has a secret buried somewhere, but yes, it's important enough to share. Did Joel have contact with the boy?'

'No. Toni and Daryl expressly wanted Joel's top-grade sperm, in spite of his heart defect, and Eli is as healthy as can be. Joel was everything they were looking for. He never wanted to be a 'father', but they agreed the terms and conditions after which all connection was severed.'

'Are you angry because he didn't tell you, or because you wanted a child with him?' He scanned her face, trying to work out his next move. She was unlikely to make a scene, however entitled she felt to be angry. Gil let himself relax. He'd been in considerably more dicey situations with Imogen, and his mother. 'Marianne, your life has been dedicated to children, and from the little I know of your background, why wouldn't you seek out their company. But Joel gave a tremendous gift to those women. It was a compliment, after all. If he had told you, what then?'

'Kurt asked me the same thing.' She finished the wine. 'Oh, I don't know what to bloody think, Gil. I miss Joel every day. I couldn't believe I'd actually met a sincere, joyful man who overcame his fears to share his life with me. Our relationship was meant to be honest and loving, unlike those with Warren and my mother.'

'But that hasn't changed, has it? You would have shared everything in time.'

'Maybe.' Her sigh was weary. 'I had high hopes for Warren and me as members of the Armstrong clan – how could it go wrong? After such a lonely childhood, it felt miraculous to live amongst an extended, secure family unit. It didn't take long before it wasn't enough for Warren. His ship was always coming in but never quite dropping anchor. He blamed you and Spencer for not expanding. The people he met at the networking group were his ticket to the big time – no more hard graft climbing ladders in all weathers, no more knocking on doors. It was time for suits, property deals, a bigger house, more children. I'm not blaming Warren. I should have got involved, but he was always so confident.'

Marianne's misty eyes settled on his, and for a while they sat quietly. Gil was sure there was more to say, so he waited.

'Joel had so many friends. Once again, it felt as if I had joined a huge tribe. It was enough, just being with him, loving him. I didn't expect to feel so angry.'

Gil's heart broke for her. Marianne trusted him enough to open up, and he was grateful. Her mother, Warren, Spencer – it was no wonder she had sheltered from the world. There was one thing he was sure of: he couldn't burden her with his feelings tonight. He was about to go to her, to comfort her, when the waiter brought the tea.

'Gil, I can't tell you how good it is to talk. Della's the only other person who understands. She packed this new dress in my case. You can imagine how I felt when I saw it.'

'It's lovely, Marianne.' He wanted to say more, but could sense she was ready to talk, so he dived in. 'What made Joel so special?'

'Where to start? Our conversations were unlike any I've ever had. Joel was never overbearing or patronising with his knowledge. For example, I had no idea lichen was so important and so delicate, but his storytelling made me want to know more. Joel would say things like *I love the way the trees rain after the rain*, so one day after it rained, I stood under a tree and saw what he saw. On Christmas Eve, we took a pre-midnight ride around the coastline, through Burnham Market's twinkling lights, and Baconsthorpe Castle's ghostly atmosphere, and welcomed Christmas Day with hot chocolate at Holkham's sand dunes.' Marianne took the tea from him, her smile evocative. 'Joel's exuberance was such a contrast to my reserved ways. Life looked different though his eyes. The world wasn't separate: he was the bird, the cloud, the tree. Joel was a man-child who never lost his wonder for the world.'

Gil's imagination expanded. He wanted to know more and hoped that Marianne would indulge him for a while longer. 'When did you find out about Joel's heart condition?'

'The second time we met. Joel had steered clear of relationships, as the knowledge made people act and treat him differently. He believed me to be mature enough not to fuss, and I took the attitude that if he wasn't concerned, why should I be? He'd be ashamed of me now.' Marianne finished her tea. 'Perhaps he was a catalyst? We've all changed by knowing him.'

'You're so right about that, but I can't imagine he'd be ashamed of you for expression your emotions.'

'No, he encouraged me in that respect. Joel had a theory about the human species. So much of society is driven by the primitive brain, hence the domination of violence, sex, and greed in our culture. He didn't fancy our chances. Joel's motivation was heart-centred, which may have worn it out. He told me once that a heart gets only so many beats in a lifetime, so far better to make them count. Here's a self-pitying confession for you Gil: My list of 'pilgrimage sights' included a retreat centre near Colville and viewing spot in Lake Taupo. I was so angry, I abandoned my project.'

'I can top that, Marianne. I was jealous of Joel because he understood my son better than me. When I saw him hugging you and Zak at the garden party, it wasn't my proudest moment.' Her smile lit him up, and he felt emboldened. 'I also, inexcusably, assumed you'd stay on your own.'

'So did I, Gil. It's liberating to have our minds changed.'

'It sure is. Now you've seen Eli, will you call Toni?'

'No need. The hurt and anger has faded, just as Kurt said they would, and what more is there to say? Anyway, for what it's worth, I think the Midwinter Trust is a fabulous idea, Gil – the perfect way to honour Joel's memory. I love the symmetry: Joel and Zak, you and Nik Marsalis, all working for the same brilliant end. Now, that's worth a toast.'

Gil was relieved to see Marianne's expression soften. The worst was over. 'I think I'm in love with Joel, too. He's a hard act to follow.'

'Ah, Joel's answer would be not to try. Hasn't Zak talked about the Sparrow Feather Manifesto: *my life is my responsibility*? You know, Gil, Lena told me once that she was afraid you might turn out like Jimmy Knox, but I don't see that at all. We lost much of our childhood through no fault of our own. Joel transformed his experience with compassion and insight, and we've not done too badly, have we?'

Gil blinked rapidly.

'Your counsellor will walk you through the residue of anger and into the clean, pure air. Perhaps you can help me with that sometime.'

Still he couldn't speak.

'It's time to take a fresh look at yourself, Gil Armstrong. Your heart is as generous, and as loving as Joel's.'

She reached across the table, stretching her fingers to wrap around his wrist, and he did the same. It felt so good to touch her. Neither spoke, both so unused to talking, to hearing their own voices, and now craving silence. The tranquilising evening altered their senses, unhitching their moorings, drawing them ever closer. Instinctively they stood. He took her hand, and they walked through the empty restaurant, up the softly carpeted stairs to his apartment.

MARIANNE

MARIANNE CLOSED the sliding doors and slipped on a cardigan. Uplifting splashes of blue were breaking through the chill grey clouds, hinting at a brighter day. The weather during her stay had been temperate, and she was grateful. Two storms had disturbed her deep sleeps, the first of which was shortly after her arrival, and she had revelled under the fire and fury of choppy seas and quaking winds. The second occasion was at dawn, just three days ago, on the balcony of Gil's apartment. They were wrapped up together under a duvet as they watched the storm blow itself out, and Marianne finally felt at peace. She had drunk a little more than usual that night, but her decision to spend the night with him was lucid. Inevitability, attraction, shared history, grief: whatever the factors were, their desire was reciprocal. If actions were words, even with Marianne's limited experience, there was no camouflaging Gil's love. For her part, it was enough to feel wanted. The encounter brought her a page closer to the end of an agonising chapter, and perhaps to the beginning of another, but this time she felt sure of her adult self and was less fearful.

When Marianne invited him to join her at the festival, Gil couldn't have been happier. As the site was close to the retreat centre, he tentatively suggested they might visit, during the weekend. She was thrilled by that, and by Pippa and Vera's warm welcome, as if he were an old friend. Hal had gone sailing after all, but far from being annoyed, Pippa was grateful for Gil's help moving her boxes of artwork. According to Vera, his appearance put paid to Hal's hopes of catching Marianne's eye. While Marianne took her turn on the art stall, Gil had mingled and chatted, and during lunch (which he organised for her), he took over the stall. His natural gift for selling was impressive. She had loved hearing him talk about cutting his teeth on Dino Scuderi's women's clothes stall, as there was no rites of passage like it. The evening entertainment was tremendous fun. Gil watched her dance with the crowd until Vera pulled him up to join the line dancing, which had them all falling about. Then, while they danced to Hotdog's fine rendition of *Erase the Miles*, he told her he couldn't believe she was in his arms, wearing her prairie dress, as the last time she wore it, he thought she was lost to him forever.

It was astonishing how quickly she and Gil had eased into each other's company. Even though they didn't know each other so well, it helped that they shared loved ones and early experiences, which tied them in another way. They had hunkered down in the quirky, eccentrically decorated *bach* and had reviewed the day's festivities before embarking on another sensual night. Marianne was greedy for the physical, the tangible, rather than sinking under the unrelenting anguish. Gil hadn't pressed her about Number 5 but said that Georgia was interested in either renting or buying it, with Spencer and Nicole's help. Marianne was unsure what to do. She needed stability – no more surprises, shocks, or dreams of a hazy, sun-lit future. She was happy enough before Joel and would be so again.

At the retreat centre, it was easy to visualise Joel living in the spectacular meadowed valley and learning the art of meditation in the peaceful shrine room. While she talked to a staff member, Gil went to the gift shop. He bought a number of books and several Nepalese-crafted items, one of which was an antique, seven-metal hammered singing bowl. The assistant explained that its harmonic frequencies were tuned to the note F, the heart chakra. Its new home was to be The Tower, and Gil would ring it every day he was there. They made a joint donation to the centre in Joel's memory, walked around the gardens and the *stupa*, and sat together in silence, soaking up the pristine atmosphere, as it was unlikely they would return to this magical place again. Then, Gil clipped an exquisite silver and jade *Om* pendant around her neck, a reminder of Joel, as he had worn something similar. She had taken to feeling for it, resting her hand there, and breathing quietly, with Joel's image at the forefront of her mind.

With her overnight bag packed, Marianne was ready for the trip to Lake Taupo, another of Gil's gentle nudges. Once they'd been to Joel's viewing point, they would join the Ridleys for a final night together. Then, she'd drive his hire car back to Mercury Bay, to use until the end of her holiday. There was no longer a need to accept Hal's offer to take her to the airport, as she would be truly independent for those final days. Marianne made her way downstairs where Gil was waiting in the car. It was time for another experience, another terrain, another connection to her ranger, and perhaps a step closer to each other.

After a long drive and a single rest stop, they arrived at their destination. Joel had marked the spot on his map, way past the lake, in the direction of Pureora Forest

Park. On the second drive by, Gil spotted a tiny sign. He followed the winding path until they came to the base of a steel constructed tower whose circular steps led to who knew where or what. They climbed out of the car. Several North Island robins hopped in and out of the gorse, their sweet song the only sound in the secluded wooded area. The limitless sky had blistered a blue trail from Mercury Bay to the viewpoint, an unforgettable journey across the incredible land mass and the scene was set. 'Are you coming with me, Gil?'

'Why don't you go up on your own. If you're not back in fifteen minutes, I'll rescue you.'

Joel had once said he'd come to rescue her from The Tower, and here she was with Gil, and yet, nothing about it felt wrong. 'Okay. See you in a while.'

Marianne climbed the steps, finally arriving at a platform which was secured by panelling and a handrail. As she scanned the horizon, her breath all but stopped, and for a moment Marianne was convinced her chest was going to collapse. *I felt my entire self atomise.* Joel had attempted to describe the indescribable but finding the right words as she trembled under this boundless view, was impossible. Thoughts dropped away, and the demarcation line which separated her from the world dissolved. A second later, (or was it an eternity?) her brain kicked back in, desperately trying to frame a reference around the unknown experience. As much as Marianne longed to remain in that luminous space, the moment had gone, but it was enough to afford a glimpse at that which Joel had intimated. It was impossible to stay on the tower without her knees giving way, so she took slow tentative steps back to the ground, clutching the cold rail all the way down, and there Gil stood, waiting. Without a word, he went up while she waited by the car, and there he stayed for a good long while.

Soon, they were back on the road to Lake Taupo. Marianne was still reeling from the profound experience, and without realising it, they had arrived at the residential area near Hot Water Beach, in silence. Gil pulled the car on to the drive of an impressive brick and cladded house with a huge deck, and uninterrupted views across the lake. He turned to face her. 'I'm beginning to get a handle on Joel's incredible sensitivity. Being on this island, in the middle of the Pacific Ocean, is as close as we'll to get to seeing what he saw. Thank you for these last few days, Marianne. They have changed me forever.'

'Me too. Do you think our hosts will mind if we go for a walk before dinner? I need time to settle.'

'Sure. I'll pop my head around the door and tell Roger we'll be back in a couple of hours.'

Hand in hand they walked down to the lake, towards the ice cream and coffee stall. Pausing for a while – his waffle cone filled with strawberry, hers with salted caramel – they talked of inconsequential things. Later, they sat with the Ridleys on the terrace, drinking gin and lime from long glasses, admiring the view. Marianne was happy to sit quietly and be entertained by her hosts as they reminisced the East End days. Roger and Shirley didn't miss London. Their daughter wanted them to join her and the children, and there were no regrets. After an early dinner, they left their guests to their early night. Compared to the cosy *bach* at Coleville, the guest bedroom was huge. Marianne luxuriated in the bath, after which they lay naked together, and Gil gently touched her scars, as Joel had done. She would never again be afraid of them. Later, they talked softly, intimately, his long, sinewy limbs enclosing her.

'Can I pick you up from the airport? Freddie, Zak, and Esme want to come.'

'How do you know?'

'Zak and I went to see West Ham play Liverpool at Anfield. We spent the day with Freddie and Rachel.'

'How lovely! So, they know you're here.'

'Sworn to secrecy.' Gil leaned on his elbow and tenderly moved a strand of hair away from her face. 'Marianne, do you remember when we met in Charlie Chan's night club, and Warren introduced me as Gilbert, and you said ...'

'Gilbert's a fine name. You're in exalted company: Gilbert White; Gilbert and Sullivan; and the brilliant Gilbert Scott-Heron.'

'You remember!'

'For a moment I thought there was something between us, but quickly dismissed it as stupid. You were far too good-looking and self-assured for an unsophisticated country girl like me. I don't regret Warren, though. He gave me Freddie.'

'Would you like to see him again?'

'No, and not because I bear a grudge, as that's not my way. I drew a line a long time ago.'

'Have you ever wondered what might have happened if we'd have got together?'

'I don't think we were ready for each other, Gil, but you've always been close by.'

Gil drew her to him. 'I have loved you ever since that night, Marianne – it's been the one constant, but no one

351

else is responsible for my happiness, regardless of what happens between us. This is the most content, the most at peace I've ever been.'

Marianne rested her head on his chest, and when it was time to sleep, he curled around her back, and there they stayed, her hand resting on his wrist, until the gulls announced the morning. After breakfast, she thanked the Ridleys for their hospitality, and walked into the cool fresh air to the car. Gil held her and they breathed each other in before she drove back to Mercury Bay.

A cacophony of noise filled the Hopkin's house. The flock of chattering guests had spilled into the tea-lit garden to celebrate Marianne's final evening. She smiled at the scene. Gil's arrival had reminded her of home. It was time to reunite with her loved ones.

Beattie called her into the kitchen. 'I'm no good at goodbyes, lovey, but here's a small token of my friendship.' She passed Marianne a package. 'We'll write to each other, and I'll have another go with the email. Hal does his best to encourage me. I've never been further than the South Island, so as much as you'd like to show me the sights, don't wait by the door, eh?'

Marianne opened the parcel – a native floral silk satin scarf. 'It's lovely. Thank you, Beattie. I can tell you how good it's been to work with you. I'll treasure our coffee and cake moments.'

'We had a lot of laughs, eh? I'll miss your hard graft, Marianne. You've made these last five weeks easy for me. So there, that's all I want to say, or the waterworks will start. I'll leave you to your party.'

Beattie gave her a fierce hug and was gone. Marianne put the scarf alongside her other gifts: a peacock-patterned beach sarong, and a painting of a dotterel, a reminder of her morning on Opito Bay, where these endangered waders nest. Pippa came in, holding a glass of red wine.

'Here, Marianne – last chance to swill our finest grog. Archie, Hal, and the boys have arrived, so get it down you quick.'

'I just said goodbye to Beattie, and nearly lost it. This is the worst part, and probably the reason why I've never gone anywhere.' Marianne swigged the sob safely down her throat.

'We're only ever a thought away, Marianne.'

The door swung open. It was Vera, clutching an envelope. 'Hey, there you are! Archie's asking after you. Said he's ready for a twirl with his sailor girl.' The women grinned. They were in for a raucous night. 'Your inspired suggestion to use gold leaf on those native fruit paintings worked a treat, Marianne. I sold the last of them this week.' She passed over the envelope. 'I've already started on the next series.'

'Three hundred dollars! Can this be right, Vera?'

'Sure is. Promise you'll keep at the artwork. Now, let's get on with this business of partying.'

Pippa and Marianne stood together. The older woman was suddenly serious. 'I'm sorry if Hal's been a nuisance, but he doesn't mean anything by it. We keep threatening to let each other go, but another season goes by ...'

'It's alright, Pippa, no need to explain. I'll settle up with Hal tomorrow morning.'

'It's done.'

It took Marianne a nano second to work out who was responsible. 'Pippa, will you give this money back to Vera after I've gone. She works so hard, and I know what it's like to be strapped for cash.'

Pippa tucked the envelope into a drawer. 'That's so generous of you, darling. I'll make sure she takes it. You all set for the drive?'

'Yes. I'll never forget your kindness. Thank you so much for everything, Pip. You'll keep in touch?'

'You bet. As soon as the divorce comes through, I'll pack the gumboots and paint pots and be on my merry way!'

Day Forty: My last day. I'm leaving in two hours' from now, happy I came, and happy to go home. Life is so strange, Joel. To think, neither Gil nor I have travelled any distance, and yet, if I hadn't met you, none of this would have happened. Or would it? Thank you my love, for everything we shared, and for everything to come. You are my mirror, and in your reflection I've discovered a path back to me. Somehow I get the feeling that our story has only just started.

❀ ZAK ❀

EVERYTHING WAS ready. Zak checked his list: homework done; garden done; Marianne's house – done. He and Esme were mad keen to help Freddie give Number 5 a freshen up. They opened every window, changed the bed linen, cleaned the kitchen, and stacked the boxes on one side of the living room. Esme put vases of fresh flowers on every windowsill and brought with her a hand-stitched 'Welcome Home' banner made by Nicole, which was now hanging from the curtain rail. Shane had prepped the garden: the daffodils, crocus, and hyacinth were blooming, and the frog spawn had long since taken the leap to tadpole. Gil had brought over a box of farm shop groceries. Marianne wouldn't want a fuss, but it was important to show how her how much they had missed her, and how much she meant to them.

Forty-nine days had come and gone since Joel's passing, but Zak continued to light a candle for his friend. He was less tearful, probably because he was busier than ever trying to keep up with it all. Joel used to warn against moving through life too fast, and to never be afraid of asking for help if it all got too much, so Zak talked to Larry who offered to co-edit the book material, only too happy to help out. Nina was the only one who knew how much he was still grieving as when his family asked, there were no words to describe the immense heart pounding. But far from knocking him off course, Zak was more determined than ever to follow Joel's guiding light and become a ranger. It was his destiny, just as Nina intended to study wildlife conservation, and Esme zoology. His dad stayed at The Tower more often than not. Zak was baffled at the speed with which his parents had moved on with their personal lives. Gil's trip to New Zealand was a bit of a shocker as he hated flying, but a need to see Marianne had overridden his fear. Why it couldn't have waited until she got home was disappointing, but Zak had kept it zipped, remembering what Joel used to say about environmental soap boxes. Imogen had been to dinner with some fella in Singapore, but it was just a date, and nothing serious. Nina said his mother was too beautiful to be alone for long. He was hopeful that whoever she ended up with, he wasn't a *dik dik* or worse, tried to tell him what to do.

Zak chewed his bottom lip, a habit he was desperate to break as Nina said it put his face out of shape. The whole family was loved up! Even Mr Goodchild and Grandma Lena were an item. She stayed at his house quite a lot now, and popped in for tea with his mum, which was totally weird as they never got on before. The other night, Imogen said *I'll always love Gil, and not simply because he is your father.* Marianne loved Joel, and his dad loved Marianne. Zak pulled Rudy onto his lap. He loved his dog as much as his family, and he loved Nina, but not in the same way he loved Rudy, or Esme, or his grans, so maybe there were different sorts of love. Joel used to say that it made the world go round. Freddie predicted that Marianne and Gil would get together, and they'd be stepbrothers – epic!

GIL

'DRIVE CAREFULLY, Gil. You've got the crown jewels in that car, and I want them back in one piece.'

Gil wiped the lipstick from his cheek. ''Course I'll drive carefully, Mum. They're my loved ones too. By the way, that lipstick's the wrong shade. Rose pink suits you better.' He jumped back to dodge her swipe. Had his mother ever been playful? Ever since Oscar Goodchild began his courting, she was a different woman – almost. Jean was also reaping the benefits. They played an entire game of chess without having to listen to his mother heckling at the telly.

'Give Marianne our love, Gil. Hopefully we'll see her tomorrow, but quite understand if not.'

'Marianne will be wiped out from jet lag, Jean. My guess is she'll want a few quiet days.'

'Did I tell you Oscar has booked a table at the King and Queen for tonight?' said Lena, twinkly eyed.

'So that's why you're dolled up. Maybe he's going to pop the question. Poor sod doesn't know what he's letting himself in for. Right, I'd better pick up the kids or we'll be late. Zak and I are staying at Spencer's tonight. We'll see you tomorrow, with or without Marianne.'

Gil left his mother and aunt outside the front gate and drove to Sycamore Crescent. It had been an adrenaline-charged morning. Even Niall and the residents had pitched in. Gil hadn't realised just how much a beloved member of the community Marianne was, although having seen her in

357

Mercury Bay, this was no longer a surprise. Thankfully, his mother hadn't worked out where he'd been. Jean had her suspicions and was overjoyed when he told her. Gil hadn't anticipated how many waves his divorce would make. Nicole had cried, and he had comforted her. Annette had called to reassure him that their long-standing friendship would continue, although they both knew it was unlikely, however kindly meant. Nik Marsalis' sadness was mitigated by their joint Trust project, but Cilla had been genuinely upset, all the more so since Nik's illness, and she made him promise not to disappear.

Still, he had a handful of new friends to prop him up during this unsettling time. And Marianne? There was so much they hadn't said, but somehow it hadn't mattered. Every moment in her company was a revelation. Before she left him at Lake Taupo, she gave him a drawing on what looked like vellum and was framed in lime white with traces of gold leaf. Underneath it, the title read, *In sleep do angels wake*. Gil was no expert, but he'd seen enough art with Imogen to liken it to a Renaissance style drawing and was impressed. The angelic sleeping profile, thick dark lashes, and tousled hair was the image of Zak. When he thanked Marianne for the fine depiction of his son, she had smiled and said nothing further, but when he showed it to Jean, she said, *Marianne has captured the real you, Gil. Her sensitivity has brought yours to light.* Marianne must have drawn him that first morning at Mercury Bay, and he would be forever deeply moved by it.

Whilst staying at the Coleville Festival *bach*, Marianne told him about Claire's letter. He didn't even know she had a sister. Claire had been spoilt by her mother and was jealous of her father's relationship with Marianne. Evelyn and Claire blamed Marianne's so-called attention seeking behaviour on the 'accident', but Mike was convinced that ten-year-old Claire knew exactly what she was doing when she scalded her little sister. He threatened to call in social services unless she underwent a psychiatric assessment, but it seemed to Gil that Evelyn needed it more. During Marianne's long and painful convalescence, the Blys divorced, and Claire was sent to boarding school. Later, she moved to Brussels to work as a translator – no partner, no children – just her mother, who lived with her until she died. Mike's over-protectiveness left no opportunity for healing or forgiveness, although he accepted help from Evelyn's sister, Sadie. Marianne's inability to speak was attributed to trauma and as predicted, her speech returned, but sparingly, each word too precious to be wasted.

When Gil reflected back to the Strong-Arm Security days, it was always Warren who hogged the limelight, while Marianne looked on quietly, affectionately, and if he expected Marianne's tragic history to have in some way closed her down, he was wrong. Their lovemaking, twenty-five years in the waiting, was incredibly moving. Far from being timid or nervous, she sensed his inner turmoil, and absorbed him so completely that his habitual holding patterns had to let go, and he never wanted to leave that safe space. Marianne's profound generosity of spirit came with no strings or requirements, and in a world where everyone wanted something, it was a rare quality. While there was no rush, Gil didn't want to waste a second. He flew home with a renewed sense of purpose. The North Island's energy, the retreat centre, the viewing point: taken together, a collective essence and energy of immense power had seeped into his consciousness and had altered it. If Joel had brought Marianne and all this to him, there was no one happier than Gil.

'Dad, will we recognise her? You said Marianne had cut and coloured her hair and was ...'

"Zak, here she comes!' Esme called out to Marianne, and waved her arms.

Gil and Freddie smiled. Throughout the journey, Zak and Esme's chatter was sprinkled with a kind of nervous hysteria, as if the results of a talent show were about to be announced, and despite trying to keep calm, Gil had been infected by it. 'Okay you two, remember to give Marianne time to catch her breath. Don't crowd her.'

'Too late, Gil' said Freddie, equally nervous about the homecoming, and glad to have such light-hearted company.

Esme and Zak sprinted towards Marianne. She put her bags down and laughingly embraced them. When Freddie recovered from the shock of seeing his mother transformed, he too was entangled in the love-in. When everyone calmed down, Gil stepped forward and she walked into his arms. Yes, it was still there, and he'd have given anything to stay enfolded, but the kids had picked up her bags and they chirped all the way back to the car. Freddie sat in the front, while in the back, Marianne asked Esme and Zak all manner of questions, giving them the chance to offload, and herself time to adjust. Gil had caught her eye in the rear-view mirror, and her smile told him all he needed to know.

When they arrived at Sycamore Crescent, Marianne was overwhelmed by the welcome – flowers, tea, Esme's cake – and everyone loved their gifts. Various neighbours popped in, and Ashely brought baby Pearl for a cuddle. After the second hour, Marianne nodded to Gil. They were already reading the other's signals. 'We'll leave you to it, Marianne. Give me a shout if you change your mind about lunch tomorrow.' She walked him to the door, her hand resting lightly on his shoulder. His relief to have her back home was immeasurable.

'Isn't it strange to be back, Gil? Everything seems so small. Lovely to see the daffodils and the tulips coming through, and Shane's even planted this year's tomato seeds.'

'Yeah – he's a diamond geezer, as we say in the trade.' They laughed. 'If you can't sleep, call me. Chances are I'll be counting sheep.'

'I've so much to thank you for, Gil. That was the best homecoming I could have wished for.'

She kissed his mouth, and a jolt of lightning whizzed along his spine. 'Me too, Marianne.'

MARIANNE

'You look terrific, Mum. New Zealand agrees with you. Was it hard to come back to Blighty?'

Marianne sat on her old sofa and breathed out, long and slow. Six weeks away, and it was as if she'd never been outside of Hazelwood. 'No it wasn't, as I had you to come back to. Shall I make tea?'

'Rest-up for a while. I'll bring the post in.'

'No, leave it. Tell me what's been going on in your life.'

Freddie knew what she was asking, and he was embarrassed to tell her that he had accepted his grandmother's legacy after all. Rachel had told him not to be so blinkered. Owning a home was a practical decision, and pretty much echoed what his mother had said weeks before. In fact, they had already found somewhere and were excited with the prospect of making a home together. 'Rachel and I have ... well, what I mean to say is, I've decided to accept your mother's money. You and Rachel were right. We've seen a house ...'

Suddenly Freddie was laughing with her.

'Seventy grand from my guilty grandmother. Aren't you angry, Mum, or at least a teeny bit peeved she left nothing to you?'

'Actually, I'm a teeny bit more disposed to like her. Not all parents are up to the job, Fred.'

'Funnily enough, Rachel and I have been talking about that very thing, and why I hate Warren so much.

We retraced the steps to see what my life might have looked like if he had stayed. I'd have gone to Noke House, holidayed with the Armstrongs, worked in the City, or for them, but then I'd never have met Rachel, or worked in mental health. She's helping me to see the consequences of blame. My anger has faded from red to salmon.' They laughed. 'She reminds me of you, Mum.'

Freddie's hug was so warm, it was hard to let him go.

'Rachel wanted to be here to witness my U turn, but I promised to be contrite. She was prepared to use all her savings to put towards a deposit. You can imagine how I felt about that.'

'Think of the joy you'll have when you move in, Freddie. You might even get yourself a shed.'

'And a few chickens. So, Mum, how are you – really?'

'Let's just say the holiday wasn't what I expected, and yet, it was so much more. The work was a doddle, and my boss, Beattie Hopkins, was so wonderful, I wanted to bring her back in my suitcase. Mercury Bay is full of talented artists, some of whom took me under their wing, and I visited several of Joel's special places. The south-western Pacific Ocean colours do something magical to the soul.'

'After just two weeks away, Gil was unrecognisable, so I can only imagine how you feel.'

'Gil came twelve thousand miles to tell me he loves me.'

'It was brave of him. What will you do?'

'Keep breathing. I may stay here, work with Della, find my feet.'

'Mum, I know it's none of my business, but if Gil asks you to live together, you should seriously consider it. If you need my blessing, I'm giving it unreservedly. I've seriously misjudged Gil. He's a good man. In the unlikely event of it going pear-shaped, you can always come to Liverpool. It won't be too long before we'll need a grannie.' Freddie got up, elated to see his mother's grin. 'You must be famished. I'll get dinner started. How about a glass of wine to celebrate?'

'Perfect.' She smiled. 'It's good to be home.'

'It's good to have you back.'

When Freddie returned with the wine, his mother was curled on the sofa, fast asleep.

Della put the laptop on the table and picked up her tea. 'Fab photos, Marianne. Must feel like a lifetime ago, although it's only been a week. How's the jet lag?'

'Almost gone, but I still wake up wondering what hemisphere I'm in. Every morning, I used to open the patio doors to listen to the sea roll. It was heavenly.'

'At least now you've nice neighbours to listen to. Have you thought any more about your future? We could do with you at Chickadees, Marianne. There's a waiting list as long as my long arm.'

'Thank you, Della. I really appreciate it. Gil came over last night. First time since we've been back. I've got the feeling he doesn't want to pressure me.'

'Now that I'm over the shock of him pulling *An Officer and a Gentleman* stunt on you, may I enquire as to your new status?'

'Gil and I just sort of slipped into being together. The weirdest thing is, it doesn't feel as if I'm betraying Joel.'

'You're sure it's not revenge? After all, the shock of meeting Eli and his parents made me want to kick a few beer cans, so it must have been agony for you.'

'I was angry, but it passed. Joel didn't deceive me, Della. How could he? It happened a long time ago, and he would have told me in his own time.' Marianne sighed. She hadn't intended to bring it up again, but Della's detective nose had winkled it out of her. 'We've known Gil for twenty-five years, but I didn't begin to know him until he came to Mercury Bay. Last night, he asked me to live with him at The Tower.'

'So you'll be moving to Norfolk after all.'

'I miss the space, and I need time to readjust. It'll be a fresh start. Am I rushing it, Della?'

'After a quarter of a century?' They laughed. 'I may as well tell you Gil came to see me, to ask my opinion: should he go to New Zealand; would you be angry; was he barking up the wrong tree, that sort of thing. I nearly hit the floor! Your man is sincere. I used to think he was buttoned up, and there he was, saying he didn't want to leave this life without telling you he loved you. It was a miracle I stopped myself from blubbing.'

'So I've you to blame for this predicament, Della.'

'Only if it is a predicament.'

'Georgia wants Number 5.'

'The family will be happy, and it will make things easier all round. Is she still a political journalist?'

'Georgia told Freddie that 'Craftivism' is a kinder way to protest than violent conflict,' replied Marianne.

'I don't disagree. The residents will cheer. Georgia's middle name is community or is it communism – I can never remember.' Della grinned. 'Thank you for the gorgeous bracelet, Marianne. Your Mercury Bay friends are as talented as you. When you go to Norfolk, think of all the hours you can spend at your easel. No more house sitting, poo picking, or plumb lines. Gil will keep you in the lap of luxury, except that you wouldn't know luxury if it banged you on the nut. I'll bet you didn't even notice he upgraded your flight.'

Marianne laughed. She had made sure she enjoyed every minute of it on the way home.

The last box was labelled and taped. This really was it. Gil had arranged to pick her up at midday, so there was time to sit in the garden, and soak up the splendour before the neighbours picked up their plants. Marianne sat back on the bench and sighed. Della was right about Gil. He was unrecognisable. It was hard to believe that the controlling, tight-jawed man at last summer's barbeque had cried in her arms when he talked about his father, and his divorce. Gil was vulnerable, fragile, as if he were in the process of being reborn and needed to be handled with great care, and yet he had made new friends, and like her, was embracing the unknown. They both missed the wide-open spaces, the rolling seas, the high-definition colour palette, so Norfolk was the next best thing.

He had driven her to The Tower, as she wanted to see Irene and Dudley, and to revisit what was to be her new home. Without needing an explanation, Irene had hugged her tight, and said she was happy to have her and Gil as neighbours.

Marianne called Meg Swayne to tell her about the Syderstone cottage. Andie Lawton had decided to sell, and soon the purchase was agreed between them. Meg had been effusive in her gratitude and wished her and Gil well.

Marianne had encountered so much goodwill – would Anya and Kurt be as kind?

Gil had offered her his worldly goods. He had redecorated the bedrooms and bought new bed linen, giving her the choice of where to sleep. The courtyard garden could be greened-up, and it was a project they might do together, with Shane's help. The galleried area was perfect for her studio, as he could work anywhere from his laptop. As for entertaining the family, it was her decision how much or how little. At no point had Gil asked her if she loved him. Her feelings for him were different than for Joel, how could they not be, but it felt right. Whatever the outcome, Marianne had no intention of returning to Sycamore Crescent, and it was comforting to know her exits were unblocked.

As of a week ago, however, the world once again had tipped on its axis. Marianne rested her hand on her belly. The test confirmed that their baby, conceived during those five days somewhere in the North Island, was due in December, a winter birth: midwinter. They had told no one, and besides, it was far too early to share. Gil wanted them to revel in the miraculous for as long as was possible, and Marianne was delighted with his delight. Joel had opened her heart: Gil had walked into it and had settled there.

The garden door clattered. A walking stick appeared first – it was her neighbour, stopping by to pick up a tray of cuttings.

'Marianne?'

Somewhere in the back of her mind, the register of his voice was so familiar, but when added to the image of the shuffling figure, it made not one ounce of sense. The bald, sun-scorched man drowning in a pale linen suit, took step by agonising step towards her. Marianne fell back on the bench as the figure placed a posy of multi-coloured snapdragons, her favourite early summer flowers, on the table.

'Happy Birthday, sweetheart.'

Blood drained from her. The formerly vibrant, handsome human had shed his vitality and all that remained was a shell, a ghost, the last flickers of life clinging from behind his yellow, rheumy eyes.

'Not as handsome as I used to be, eh, Marianne. Any chance of a glass of water?' Warren sat slowly, heavily, on the garden chair although he carried no weight. 'Looks as if I caught you just in time.'

Marianne went into the kitchen and filled the glass, her mind spinning, legs trembling. As she passed the glass to him, Warren's quivering fingers ripped at her heart.

'I've often wondered when you'd move on.' He took a sip. 'So, Gil finally got what he always wanted. I can't say I'm surprised, only that it took him so long. You're as lovely as ever, Marianne.'

'How do you know so much about me?'

'Facebook is a great way of keeping up to date if you know how to keep your head down. Don't be hard on Nicole. She's a good sort. It was the only way to find out about Freddie, not that there was much. You were never one for sharing the family album, eh girl?' Warren finished his water and pulled his frail body upright, as if gathering strength. 'I've moved back from Alicante. It's no fun being sick so far from home.'

Marianne moved to the edge of the bench, struggling to comprehend what she was hearing.

'I'd like to see Freddie. He's refused to acknowledge me, and I don't blame him. You never influenced him in that way, and I'm grateful. Always kind, always trusting, weren't you. I never apologised for leaving you in the lurch like that. Some businessman, I turned out to be, eh, Marianne?' Warren's cackle was more of a wheeze.

'That's all in the past Warren. What makes you think Freddie will change his mind?'

'If my son won't come to his dying father's bedside, I fear for his soul. Freddie's not the type to hold a grudge. Always was a softie. This is his chance to see off his anger. He'll feel better for it, even if he can't bring himself to forgive me.'

Her throat tightened. Their eyes rested for a moment, long enough to remind the other of a distant deep affection. 'What is it?'

'Pain started last year, in my back. D'you remember how I used to suffer, and you'd run me a hot bath? I carried on taking painkillers and ignored it, which is easy to do, living above a bar, drinks on tap. It got so bad, my mate called the doctor. They tried to cart me off to hospital, but I wasn't having it. The cancer's too far gone.'

Neither spoke for a while. Marianne wanted to go to him, but her body had shut down. 'Where are you staying?'

'The Travelodge. Clive offered to put me up, but without a car, I'm stuffed.' He took a business card from his jacket pocket. 'I'd appreciate it if you'd let me know either way.'

Warren struggled to his feet, leaning into his stick for reassurance. He waved away her attempt to help.

'Please don't leave, Warren. Stay for a cup of tea. We'll talk ...'

'Ah, that's what I've missed, a good old cuppa. No one has ever made tea the way you did, Marianne. The perfect homemaker, that was you. Thanks all the same sweetheart, but the taxi's waiting.'

'Do you need money?'

'It's good of you to offer, but I've got enough to tide me over. You'll call Freddie?'

She nodded.

He got himself to the gate and looked at her a final time. 'It's good to see you again, Marianne. I'm so sorry for ...'

A fit of coughing cut him off. Then, as suddenly as he appeared, Warren was gone.

GIL

'WARREN'S HERE? In Epping?'

Gil sat open mouthed at his mother's kitchen table with Jean and Spencer, equally as shocked. It was meant to be a quick cup of tea before picking Marianne up as she wanted time to say goodbye to the house and her neighbours. Finally, they were leaving for Norfolk. He couldn't quite believe it was happening. She had agreed to live with him at The Tower as casually as if he'd asked her to go to the cinema. Marianne possessed a unique ability to adapt to whatever was in front of her without fretting or fussing. Eminently practical, she had asked a series of questions about their financial and household arrangements, insisting she pay half of their expenses. With just the occasional visit to the office required, Gil would stay in Norfolk and focus on building the Midwinter Trust, alongside his voluntary work for the Rose Rangers. Marianne's suggestion to host a bare-foot beach break for his friends was inspired – a joint project, the first of many. Dorothea Rose's part-time housekeeping job meant she could prioritise her artwork, but most importantly, they'd get to know each other under the huge Norfolk skies.

That was before the seams of their new relationship were stretched, but not to breaking point. Just a few days ago, they sat at her kitchen table drinking tea, and Marianne put her cup down, and looked at him, and his heart skipped a beat. Before she even said the words, *How would you like to be a father again?* he knew. She'd long since given up hoping for another child, so this was an unexpectedly glorious gift. Gil had buried his wet face in her loving arms and after a while, they laughed at the miracle of it. They were older, hopefully wiser, and would raise their child surrounded by sensitive, engaged people with a gentler outlook. He couldn't wait to be in The Tower, celebrating her birthday, toasting their future, but now Warren was back, and the sands shifted precariously beneath his feet.

Spencer, uncharacteristically serious, said, 'Clive called. Warren declined his invitation to stay. He's booked a hotel somewhere and has important business to sort out.'

'When was this?'

'An hour ago. I tried to call but kept getting your answerphone.'

'I left my phone at Marianne's. Does Warren know where to find her? Surely Clive wouldn't have told him.'

'I'm betting on Nicole. Who else spreads muck like her?'

'Now, Lena, don't be like that. Nicole's been good to this family, you said it yourself,' said Jean.

'Lena is right, Mum. Nicole was in a state. She's so sorry for causing trouble.'

'Look, Spencer, none of that matters. Nicole wasn't being malicious. She and Warren used to get on well. I'd better get over to Marianne's. I want to tell her in person about Warren before anyone else, and he may want to see her. I'll let you know what's happening as soon as I can.'

Gil flew through the garden gate and into the kitchen to find Marianne at the kitchen table, her head in her arms. There was a posy of flowers beside her. He pulled up a chair and gently lifted her face. 'Are you alright, Marianne? Are you hurt?'

'No, Gil, I'm not hurt, not in the way you mean.'

There it was – an all too familiar contraction in his gut. Her swollen eyes tore at him, and fear dried his throat.

'Warren was here. I didn't recognise him ...'

A sob took her words away. Gil passed her his handkerchief before filling a glass of water.

'He wants to see Freddie.' Marianne wiped her sodden face and breathed deeply. 'Warren is dying. The cancer is everywhere. He left it too late, too afraid to seek help. I've no idea how he managed to get to England. There is no way he'll live two months. Warren's spirit has almost left his poor, broken body – even I could see it. It was just like looking at my dad, all over again.'

Relief and sorrow swept over him. Warren hadn't come back for Marianne, but he must be desperate, and would need help. As soon as she was calm, Gil took charge. He went back to his family and once they recovered from the distressing news, practicalities kicked in. Lena insisted Warren stay at the bungalow where he would be loved and cared for, until the end. He had been as good as a son, and hadn't Mrs Silk taken Gil under her wing, all those years ago. Jean wholeheartedly agreed, and immediately telephoned the Macmillan organisation. Gil and Spencer sped off for the Travelodge. It was an emotional reunion. Warren admitted to being much nearer death than Marianne supposed. Years of ill-judged business deals and drowning his misery at his mate's bar hadn't helped. It was his own, stupid fault. He didn't want to go into a hospice, and accepted Lena and Jean's invitation, if it was no trouble. When Warren asked for forgiveness, Gil went to pieces, and held his best friend's fragile body, afraid to break it. Spencer promised him they would do their best to persuade Freddie to see him, and he wasn't to worry about a thing. Warren could say goodbye to his old friends and any family members they could contact.

Two days later, Warren had settled into his last resting place. The little-used dining room, with its double doors leading into the garden, was the perfect setting in which to release the past and make peace with his loved ones. Jean instigated a rota. It was incredible how many people wanted to see their old East End mucker. Clive Osgood moved in for the duration. The Three Wise Men, along with old school friends, relieved their former happy days with so much laughter, singing, and reminiscing, it was a challenge to get Warren to rest during that first week. He had revelled in the attention. The entire Armstrong clan came to see him, including Esme and Zak. Spencer arranged for Dino Bartoli, and Warren's first boss, Bill Brett, to visit, yet another touching reunion of old friends under sad circumstances. Nicole was there throughout, from morning till night. She and Jean cooked Warren's favourite food, even though he couldn't eat much. Lena and Mr Goodchild kept the kettle boiling and beer glasses filled. Breakfast, lunch, and dinner was provided for every visitor, and there were many.

By the tenth day, it was clear there wasn't much time left, but everything was in order. Warren fell into morphine-induced sleeps more often, but had been pleased to see his cousins, and their rabbi. By now, everyone had said their goodbyes – everyone except Freddie. Gil was concerned for

Marianne, as the death of two loved ones so close together might have shattered her, and had a detrimental effect on the baby, but somehow she had kept it together, and had stayed nearby in case Warren should ask for her, which he did. At no time in the history of the Armstrongs had the family been so close, and so supportive, and Marianne thanked them for it. During a rare quiet moment, she told Gil that not so long ago, when there were problems with the car, the roof and the washing machine, she asked Della if good things ever came in threes. *Now I know they do: Warren, Joel, and you Gil, and there will be so many more.*

Marianne had spoken with Freddie several times, and reassured him that whatever decision he made, no one would judge him for it. After their last phone call, Rachel arrived the following morning with Freddie, who sat in the car, unable to take the next step. Gil went out to talk to the distraught man, and soon after, Freddie went with Marianne into Warren's room. Whatever was shared between the family that day behind closed doors was unknown, but a great fracture was healed. The following morning at dawn, Warren passed peacefully away.

JEAN

THE GARDEN was the best it had ever been. Shane had finally persuaded Lena that pollinator plants were as beautiful as her annual sea-side style bedding varieties, and they gave so much more besides. Not that it mattered, as Jean could now choose exactly what she wanted without a tussle. Those two weeks caring for Warren were dreamlike, a time for family reunions and healing, and was marked by a photograph of him and Freddie, lovingly polished, and standing alongside the others on Lionel's bureau. This important job, along with the garden and the housework, was hers alone. To no one's surprise and Jean's secret delight, Lena had moved in with Mr Goodchild (Jean still struggled to call him Oscar, as did the rest of the family) without her beloved photo frames, 'just in case'. Of course Lena would be welcomed back, but that was unlikely. Oscar adored her. He was of sound mind and body and would in all likelihood see them all out.

Jean took her 'tea for one' and small square of *baklava* into the garden and sat on the lounger, under the umbrella. Oh, the joy of space, time, peace! No more 'day-time television', keep fit with Nigel, (she had joined a local Tai Chi class), and Thursday night egg and chips with white bread and butter. Lena couldn't stand anything spicy, and it had been easier to fall in with her rather than make two meals. Jean bit into the pistachio *baklava*, barely stopping herself from cheering as the taste exploded in her mouth. The jasmine tea, like the stir-fries, and rice dishes, still felt illicit. Similar tasty treats had been served at Esme and Zak's end of term presentation at Noke House. They fully deserved their respective 'student of the year' awards, and Zak's garden film had brought the house down. Joel Midwinter's spirit must have been swollen with affectionate pride at the sight of his protégées who sold three hundred copies of his book that afternoon! Marianne had sat several rows back with Freddie and Rachel, despite Lena and Nicole's attempts to change her mind. It was typical of Marianne's good heart, and though the pregnancy was disguisable, she was sensitive to Imogen's feelings.

During the ensuing celebrations, Imogen had sought Marianne out. It was impossible to know what was said, but their embrace boded well. Zak had insisted that he alone should break the news about the baby to his mother. Imogen's reply was stoic. *Armstrong Island is a fine place to raise our chicks. Marianne and I will have that in common.* Lena was even more inclined to look favourably on her ex-daughter-in-law, especially since Imogen had helped Mr Goodchild to select a suitably intimate London hotel in which to celebrate his marriage to his sweetheart this autumn.

The rapidly changing family landscape was invigorating. Georgia had settled into Number 5 and was welcomed by almost all of Sycamore Crescent's residents. Nicole and Spencer had joined Salsa Sizzle, their first ever hobby as a couple. Jean had missed her chats with Gil. He had softened, expanded, even more so after reuniting with dear Warren. It was fascinating to watch him with Marianne. They were such a quiet couple, hardly a candle flicker between them, as if they could read each other's minds. Their love would endure, just as hers and Lionel's had. Jean had visited them at The Tower. It already felt more like a home than a show house, with Marianne's plants in every room, and her desk and easel in the gallery. If Zak's research were correct, Joel's consciousness may have incarnated into the embryo of their baby girl. Zak thought it was marvellous. He couldn't wait to study his as yet, un-named sister (fingers crossed for Joni), for evidence of Joel's character. Jean wondered if it was too late to know the nature of her mind. Perhaps she'd try a U3A or an Open University course. Spencer and Lauren were all for it, and why shouldn't she fulfil a lifetime ambition to study.

It was time to take a last admiring look at the garden before heading over to Grove Road. Lena and Mr Goodchild had invited her to dinner, the second time this week. Thankfully he could cook, or else they'd be living on Lena's steak puddings until the cows came home. Lionel would have something to say about his wild sister settling for a gentle man like Oscar Goodchild, that's for sure.

ACKNOWLEDGEMENTS

In 1976, Boston's epic rock song *More Than a Feeling* hit the UK charts, and lodged in the subconscious of a music-mad London teenager. Fast forward to 2020, and *Marianne Bly* was born. Thank you, Tom Scholz, for the inspiration. Infinite gratitude is sent to rock balladeers and earth healers Tina Turner and Bryan Adams. To the FPMT, whose loving kindness keeps the earth turning. Thanks to Linda Storey for your fine designs and typesetting. I'm indebted to Kirstie Richardson, Lesley Pye, Stacey Hammond, Susie Keen, and to Glenn Stephenson, for generously sharing his insights into the security business. *Norfolk Wildlife* by Adrian M. Riley has provided an invaluable resource, as has the Shropshire, Norfolk, and Essex Wildlife Trusts. To Jane Gregory, soul sister: thank you so much for the music, and for permission to use the lyrics to *Back To The Stars*. Finally, to John Rowland, whose limitless energy and support make it possible.

ABOUT THE AUTHOR

Marianne Bly is Deborah Rowland's fifth novel. In addition, she has published several health and well-being books. Deborah lives in Shropshire with her husband.

Fiction
The Hertfordshire Chronicles:
The Smallest of Dreams, 2019
The Roundhouse, 2020
The Sandglass, 2020
Hawkweed Cove, 2020

Non-fiction
Take the Long Way Home, 2018
Deborah Coote, *The Art of Meeting Yourself: Learning to Live Mindfully in a Busy World*, 2015
Deborah Coote, *Ingredients of a Happy Life: Tea, Cake, Meditation,* 2012

For further information:
email: infodeborahrowland@btinternet.com
www.deborahrowlandauthor.com